Backcountry

A Novel

—◆—

James W. Clarke

The retrospective on Lee Marvin's career in Chapter 2 is drawn from, Manohla Dargis, "A Loving Look at a Cinematic Tough Guy: Gangster, Hit Man, Gunslinger," *New York Times*, May 11, 2007.

The funeral prayer in Chapter 14 is Crowfoot's last words as quoted in C. Carodozo (editor), *Sacred Legacy: Edward S. Curtis and the North American Indian* (New York: Simon & Schuster, 2000).

A short story, "Chief Mountain," adapted from the novel, appeared in the *Whitefish Review*, Volume 4, Issue I (2010).

Cover photo: Lardeau River Grizzly 2003

Author photograph by Jeanne Clarke

Books by James W. Clarke

American Assassins: The Darker Side of Politics

Last Rampage: The Escape of Gary Tison

On Being Mad or Merely Angry: John W. Hinckley Jr. and Other
Dangerous People

The Lineaments of Wrath: Race, Violent Crime, and American Culture

Defining Danger: American Assassins and the New Domestic Terrorists

Backcountry: A Novel.

For
Vine Deloria and Gordon Pouliot
in memory

I shall tell you a great secret, my friend. Do not wait for the last judgment. It takes place every day.

Albert Camus, *The Fall* (1956)

At the canyon's mouth, I'm singing. Soon the path ends. People don't go any higher. I scramble up cliffs into impossible valleys, and follow the creek back toward its source. Up where newborn clouds rise over open rock, a guest come into wildflower confusions, I'm still lingering on, my climb unfinished, as the sun sinks away west of peaks galore.

Li Po, an eighth century Taoist poet

1

―――■◆■―――

Sunday evening, May 14. It was the second week of May and this was his second summer working as a wrangler at Glacier National Park. An all-day rain and the gloom didn't brighten from dawn to dusk. He lay on his bunk bed, staring out through the droplets of rain trickling down the window of his tiny one-room cabin by the Quarter Circle stables. The walls were closing in. He needed to get out. The Trapline Saloon seemed like a good idea.

He thought of his mother's voice on the pay phone the night before. The phone rang eight times. He was ready to hang up when she answered, slurring her words. Boone's Farm Strawberry Hill. Nothing changes. A familiar I'm-sick-this-cough-is-getting-worse-and-I'm-broke-please-call-Love-Mom postcard, addressed General Delivery, had made him dial her number. Eyes closed and jaw set, he listened to the whining, self-pitying bullshit he had heard for as long as he could remember. Tomorrow's Mother's Day, she said. Did you forget? He sighed and lied, saying that's why he'd called, and he'd be sending her twenty bucks, and reminded her that the time left on his phone card had to last the rest of the month if she expected him to call again because he wasn't exactly rolling in cash either. When he hung up, he leaned his head against the phone and swore.

Two or three times a year, when he was between jobs, he visited her at the mobile home park outside of Portland where she had lived since his grandmother died. He always wondered why he went. He never stayed long and left when he became afraid of what he might do when the bad dreams, childhood memories, and the stale odor of her cigarette smoke, cheap wine, and flowery perfume that went with it, started closing in, and he had finished what he felt compelled to do in Portland.

As usual, the Trapline's parking lot held a mix of motorcycles and beat-up pickups parked at odd angles. But it was still early and the lot hadn't filled up yet. He went in, sat at the bar, and ordered two slices of pizza and a draft of Coors Light from the bartender, a bleached blonde with large breasts in a tight pink tank top, chewing gum. A sign above the bar read *Liquor in Front Poker Behind*. He'd smirked the first time he saw it. Now it was like wallpaper.

Here ya' are, hon, she said as she set the microwaved pizza slices down in front of him on a paper plate. He mumbled and barely looked up as he pushed back the Stetson resting low on his brow. She didn't seem to care. Surly patrons in that bar were as unremarkable as bad breath. She moved down the bar to a couple sitting in a cloud of cigarette smoke. The woman, with frizzy hair that was way too dark for the face beneath it, was sucking on a cigarette. An off-the shoulder lavender top revealed some dry, wrinkled cleavage and a freckled slab of fat across her shoulders. Her companion had mutton-chop sideburns and bright pink ears that flared out beneath a Harley-D cap. A powder-blue, *Almost Alive Taxidermy* T-shirt fit him like a salami skin, his hairy mudslide of a belly spilling out beneath it half way to his knees. Freckles was yapping away at Mudslide about something in a two-pack-a-day voice that reminded him of his mother. Mudslide just grunted back as he leaned into a basket of Buffalo wings, sucking and licking stubby fingers one by one, grease gleaming on an untrimmed mustache that seemed to grow out of his nostrils and covered his upper lip like moss on a rock.

Merle Haggard sang behind the bar from a CD player that had its exposed wires looped to speakers resting at either end of the liquor display. A muted basketball game was on a grainy big screen television at the far end of the room. NBA playoffs, someone said. All right.

Who gives a shit? Nigger sport. Great for stupid fucks whose cousins swing on vines.

At nine o'clock, it got worse. A local country rock band began to play. *Where are these losers from?* He rubbed the back of his neck. His head ached. *Yeah, live music, great, but it's killing me.*

He was about to leave when he noticed an Indian woman at a table near the pool table, or maybe she was Asian, it was hard to tell in the dim light. She was sitting across from a big man in a black leather vest and dark T-shirt, with thinning gray hair pulled back tight above his ears into a pony tail. Judging by the crude tattoos on huge biceps, Pony Tail had done time somewhere where you could still lift. The tattoos looked like Aryan Brotherhood, not that he had anything against the Aryan Brotherhood, but swastikas were so obvious.

The woman was slim, with high cheekbones, and thick, straight shiny black hair, parted in the middle, that fell loosely to her shoulders. He guessed late twenties, thirties, thinking she would do. Anyone could see she was drunker than hell.

He watched them out of the corner of his eye. They weren't getting along. The band stopped playing. Pony Tail raised his head and the light caught a jagged scar across a nose that looked like it had been broken more than once. Bitch, Pony Tail said, and something else he couldn't make out. The woman lurched up from the table, spilling a half-full pitcher of beer. The beer sloshed on Pony Tail's jeans. He stood up from the table. It looked like he was going to go after her.

Fuck you, she said, looking him right in the eye. She pulled a parka off the back of a chair, knocking it over. He watched as she staggered toward the door, tripping over another chair.

Fuck you, she said again over her shoulder before she stepped out into the night. Pony Tail took a step toward the door, then sneered, mumbled something, and walked back to the men's room. Patrons looked up for a moment, then went back to the basketball game, pool, or whatever they were doing. Skirmishes like this, like the meth and coke dealing in the parking lot, were not worthy of much attention at the Trapline,

He wanted to follow her out before someone else picked her up. But he didn't want Pony Tail changing his mind and going out after her. Pony Tail could be trouble. He waited at the bar nursing his beer until Pony Tail returned and joined the two guys shooting pool. It was as if nothing had happened. He drained his beer and put a couple of quarters by his glass for the blonde with big tits. He looked around to be sure he wasn't being watched as he eased off the bar stool. He hesitated as a crowd of bikers, in gleaming, wet black leather came in, drawing everyone's attention, then walked out behind their backs.

A wedge of light receded into darkness as the door closed behind him and he walked into the rain that was speckling the surface of a big puddle he stepped over to get to his pickup. Pulling on to the two-lane highway, he saw her in the headlights right where he'd hoped she'd be, standing on the shoulder with her thumb out. He pulled over, stopped, and opened the passenger door.

Where ya headed? he said smiling as he pushed open the pickup door. Her face was wet and strands of dark hair stuck to her forehead below the hood of a red parka. Up close he noticed the faint acne scars on her cheeks, the full lips, and the alcohol on her breath.

As far away from that lyin', no-good sonofabitch as I can get, she said, slurring the words.

Okay, jump in, I'm headed that way. He smiled again.

She hesitated, looking hard at him, still standing with the rain running off her parka and down her cheeks.

What way? Browning? I have to get back to Browning. Can you take me to Browning? She didn't wait for an answer. I got two kids home and I been gone a couple of hours. She really wanted to go to Heart Butte, but she wasn't too drunk to realize there wasn't much chance of getting that ride.

He slapped the top of the steering wheel. Well, damn, you sure hit it lucky, I'm headed to Cut Bank, so I can drop you off in Browning. Come on, climb in. The seat's gettin' wet. What's your name?

Dinah, she said as she got in, not looking at him.

Pretty name. Dinah what?

Doesn't matter.

Blackfeet, I bet. He smiled again. Right?

She turned and looked directly at him. You think I'd be goin' to fuckin' Browning in the middle of the night if I wasn't? Jesus Christ, man, give me a break!

He felt his face flush. But he kept the smile and said nothing.

A few miles later he flicked on his left turn signal and turned off Highway 2 onto a gravel road that disappeared around a curve into a thick, doghair forest of lodgepole pine.

Hey, where you goin'?

It's okay. I live down here. I have to pick up some tools to take to the construction job I'm workin' in Cut Bank. It won't take long.

Hey listen, cowboy, don't try to pull some shit on me, okay? I don't need any more fuckin' games. I have to get back to Browning tonight, or I'm gonna be in trouble. I got two kids. My mother's gonna kill me. I got to get home. That lyin' bastard was supposed to take me back hours ago and he didn't. I was supposed to be back by five. What time is it now? Jesus Christ, why did I ever believe that bastard?

Jaw set, he ignored the question, staring straight ahead, the smile gone as he steered the truck down the curving road through the trees toward the Blankenship Bridge. The bridge was a popular take-out spot for rafters finishing floats on the North and Middle Forks where they converged just above the bridge. Now it was black and deserted, the only sounds wiper blades slapping back and forth, and rushing water running high with snowmelt and rain. A picnic area below the bridge was secluded from the headlights of anyone that might drive across it by a hedgerow of alder and willow bushes and a tall stand of cottonwoods. Except for a few isolated cabins tucked back into the trees here and there farther down, there was not much reason to be driving the road at night. Especially in May, with a cold, steady rain coming down.

She didn't speak again until he drove across the bridge, abruptly down shifted, and turned right onto a rutted road that led into the picnic area. By this time, adrenaline and fear were draining away the effects of the alcohol.

She turned to face him, one hand on the dashboard, the other on the back of the seat. Hey cowboy, where you going? There's no house here. You don't live here. You're lyin' about tools. Take me back to the highway, goddammit.

He pulled into the bushes and turned off the ignition.

No way, cowboy, I'm not what you think I am. I have a family and kids and … Please don't …

Except for the rain pounding on the roof and streaming down the windows, it was quiet and pitch black. He took off the Stetson and set it on the dashboard. Then he looked over at her, a tight smile beneath expressionless eyes she couldn't see.

———————

2

———◆◆◆———

*S*unday *evening, May 14.* Beth Blanchard turned her red Honda Accord left off Going to the Sun Road on to the access road that led into Lake McDonald Lodge. The cold weather and the mist that hugged the long glacial lake and the mountains bordering it reminded her of a boat tour she had taken on Loch Ness during a trip to speak at a legal conference in Inverness, Scotland.

This was her first time in the Northern Rockies, however, and a big change from the balmy, dry weather and urban sprawl she'd left a week before in Tucson, Arizona. Even a little intimidating and ominous. Was there a monster lurking in this lake? She smiled at the thought as she pulled into one of the striped parking slots close to the lodge.

The lodge, a rustic three-story structure built of native timber and stone, sat at the edge of the lake it was named for, surrounded by a thick, dark forest of old growth cedar. Impressive, but almost sinister looking in this weather, she thought. Transylvania and werewolves went through her mind and made her smile as she opened an umbrella and, pulling her parka close around her neck, stepped out into a cold drizzle. Head down, she followed a lighted walkway, barely noticing an Alaskan totem pole, to the main entrance.

She strained against the door before it swung open into the lobby with a rush of warm pine-scented air. As she stepped inside, she gazed up at the massive timbers of Western cedar with bark still intact that rose vertically from a flagstone floor past two balconies and crossbeams of peeled cedar logs, to a rough plank cathedral ceiling three stories above. Six lantern-shaped, parchment chandeliers with hand-painted Indian pictograph designs hung down on long chains from the ceiling, filling the room with soft amber light. Beautiful. She hadn't seen anything like this since a weekend at El Tovar Hotel with her now ex-husband on the south rim of the Grand Canyon.

She turned back to look at the fireplace between the two entryways where a log fire sparked and crackled. The hearth, framed with scored and painted Indian designs, was large enough to walk into. My God, she thought, as she looked above its mantle at the head of the largest moose she had ever seen. The moose, with antlers that she guessed flared at least three feet from either side of its head, was flanked on one side by a trophy elk, almost as large, and, on the other, by an equally impressive caribou.

As Beth turned around, she could see the heads of antelope, deer, big horn sheep, and Rocky Mountain goats adorning the log columns and hanging from the balconies. Creepy, in a way, almost like being in a mausoleum, but still beautiful. She wasn't drawn to such displays, but she had to admit that this worked. Hanging from russet walls, high above the second-floor balcony were two huge oil paintings, one of a lakeside Indian encampment, the other of waterfalls cascading off high cliffs above a lake

A long way from Tucson, she thought. Alone and in unfamiliar surroundings, she felt self-conscious, as if she were the only stranger, and imagined everyone in the crowded lobby could see that. Everyone else seemed to be with someone—men with women, women with women, men with men. But that was what she thought she wanted, anonymity, to be a stranger for a change, no longer recognizable from newspaper photos, the evening news—away from Tucson, a failed marriage, a career that she was burnt out on, and even, at least for a while, old friends who thought she was making a big mistake. She was relieved when two uniformed park rangers set up a slide projector and screen. Good, the program would be starting soon.

Across the lobby, she spotted a chrome coffee urn that sat on a small table beside stacks of Styrofoam cups and napkins near the guest registration counter. She took off her parka and folded it over her arm and walked over and waited as a man and woman filled their cups, nodded, and smiled at her. When they stepped back, she reached for a cup and the parka brushed a stack of cups, upsetting one stack, then another. In what seemed like an interminable cascade, the cups tumbled to the floor, bouncing and rolling in all directions. Goddammit, she whispered to herself, blushing with embarrassment, convinced that all eyes in the room were on her. When she stooped to begin picking up the cups, the parka slipped from her arm and dropped to the floor. She swore again, silently this time. *What's wrong with you?*

Here, let me help you with that. She looked up to see a tall, silver-haired man stoop down beside her and start picking up cups. He smiled at her, a kind smile that seemed to say, I've done that. I know how you feel.

Oh thank you, she said. She realized she was smiling and blushed red all over again. They finished picking up the cups and arranged them in stacks on the table.

Thanks, so much, she said. I'm so embarrassed. I'm glad I didn't knock the urn off the table.

Slim, except for the ruddy complexion, almost gaunt looking, he was dressed in pressed, faded Levis, flannel shirt, and western boots. It looked like what he wore every day, and not a costume he put on for special occasions like a lot of men did on Rodeo Day in Tucson. She noticed the way he moved, balanced, smooth, like a big cat or wolf. He wasn't wearing a wedding band, but there was a barely discernible pale circle on the ring finger of his tanned left hand. Uh oh, she thought, he's probably just gotten a divorce, but the direct, open way he looked at her made her put the thought on hold.

Her first impressions usually proved reliable. And after more than twenty years as a criminal prosecutor, she felt pretty good about her ability to size people up and get a handle on their character. As her friends had often pointed out, the mistakes in her personal life had always come from not trusting her first impressions.

Besides, this guy looked like Lee Marvin, the tall, rangy physique with shoulders an axe-handle wide, the close cropped silver hair over a generous mouth, and that deep, gravelly voice that made everyone pay attention in *Seven Men From Now*, *The Commancheros*, and *The Man Who Shot Liberty Valance*, where he stole scenes from John Wayne and Jimmy Stewart, and *The Wild Ones*, where he did the same thing to Marlon Brando. Because of Lee Marvin, she would even watch *The Dirty Dozen* on late night TV.

In his last years, Lee Marvin lived near a girlfriend's home in the Catalina foothills north of Tucson. As a teenager, she was thrilled when she first saw him at the Safeway. There he was pushing a cart, pulling things off the shelves, polite, unassuming, not at all like the boozing, hell-raising skirt chaser she had read about in the tabloids as she waited in supermarket checkout lines. She wanted to say something to him, how much she enjoyed his films, ask for his autograph, but she was too embarrassed. Instead, she just nodded and smiled. But the way he nodded and smiled back, she thought he probably knew what she was thinking, and it made her a little weak in the knees.

Would you like to try again? the tall, silver-haired man said, startling her out of her reminiscence. He was smiling and offering her a cup.

She blushed again when she returned his smile. Okay, but you better stand back just in case. This doesn't seem to be my night.

He held the handle down while she filled her cup. Pretty place, isn't it? he said, nodding toward their surroundings.

Thank you, she said, lifting her cup to her lips. Yes, it's lovely. My first time here.

Really? On vacation?

Well, kind of. What about you?

No, I live near here. Well, not far from here. Sorry about the cold weather. You should have waited until the Fourth of July. That's when summer starts in Montana.

She smiled. Oh, I don't mind the weather. It's a nice change for some-one from Arizona, and I love wood fires like this one. She turned toward the fireplace. That smell of fresh pine reminds me of vacations when I was a little girl. Isn't that fireplace magnificent?

Yeah, and it feels pretty good tonight. Where in Arizona?

Tucson.

Okay, been there a couple of times, years ago. Nice place. That's the Sonoran Desert there, right? She nodded that it was. Yeah, I guess cold, damp weather like this would be a big change, he said, nodding toward the glass doors on the north side of the lobby that looked out across a wide veranda with wicker rocking chairs to the lake, now hidden by darkness and fog. A steady downpour had replaced the drizzle on the glistening, lighted walkway and steps that led down to the boat dock. They turned to see a young woman in a National Park Service uniform as she walked to a podium that had been placed near the fireplace.

Okay, folks. It's seven o'clock and I guess we can get started. My name is Sue Somers, and I want to welcome you all to Glacier National Park and the first of a series of programs about the Park that we'll be doing this summer. Although it doesn't feel very much like summer tonight, does it?

Chuckles rippled across the audience. Someone said, This is Montana.

Anyway, thank goodness for that fireplace. Tonight's speaker is Roger Sherman. Roger is our park naturalist. This is his sixth year at Glacier. He's an expert on the flora and fauna of the park, aren't you, Roger? The audience smiled with her and the speaker. His talk tonight is drawn from his research over the past several years. The topic: The Grizzly Bears of Glacier National Park and Their Importance to the Ecology of the Region. Roger.

There was polite applause as the young man in uniform at her side nodded and smiled as he stepped behind the podium.

Thanks, Sue. Could we dim the lights? Thank you. Good evening, folks, and welcome to Glacier National Park, the Crown Jewel of the Continent, he said as the room darkened and he turned on a slide projector.

As Beth and the tall stranger turned to look for a place to sit, shadows from the fireplace played across the ceiling of the darkened room, creating a surreal scene of animals slain decades ago staring down on them. At the far ends of the lobby, only the lights of the registration desk, a gift shop, and the dimly lit bar broke the spell.

Here's a couple of chairs, he said, motioning toward two log and wicker chairs placed at either end of a small writing table at the edge of the room. The soft seats are gone. Mind if I sit next to you?

Of course not, she smiled. But for a moment, she wasn't sure. She was wary of male strangers, but what the hell, there was something about this man. He didn't seem like he was on the make at all. Not that she was looking for male companionship anyway. But there wasn't any harm, on a lonely evening far from home, in having a pleasant conversation with a fellow who happened to look like Lee Marvin.

The speaker cleared his throat and began. Glacier National Park is a natural paradise, a special place. It's the only place left in the lower forty-eight that remains much the same as it was when Lewis and Clark passed through this region nearly two hundred years ago. That's probably what brought a lot of you here. A series of slides appeared on the screen, snow-capped mountain peaks, herds of elk grazing in alpine meadows covered with wildflowers, big horn sheep posing on high ledges, soaring eagles, and glaciers glistening above waterfalls.

Yes, it's a paradise, for sure, but nature can be heartless, indifferent, and unforgiving. He paused for effect as a slide flashed on the screen of a large grizzly dragging the limp body of a deer across a stream. Another followed of a grizzly sow and her cubs consuming an elk calf on a blood-stained snow bank.

This is wilderness and grizzlies and other predators like cougars and wolves kill not for pleasure, but out of joyless necessity to live. It seems cruel to us, but predators are important and necessary to maintain a healthy ecological balance in prey populations. It isn't pretty, but grizzlies and other predators are just doing what nature intended. Until wolves were reintroduced in Yellowstone, for example, the elk herds were becoming so large they were destroying the habitat of other animals, threatening those animals and themselves with starvation. Now that's changing as a more natural ecological balance is being restored. But watching a wolf pack take down an elk stranded in a snowdrift, as I did a couple of months ago, is not a pretty sight.

The ranger noted that grizzly bears had been a major topic of conversation in Glacier National Park since a stormy August night in 1967 when two young women were killed by grizzlies in separate incidents, miles apart, by different bears. The ranger went on to describe how one of the victims was attacked and dragged off by a sow grizzly with two cubs from a campsite near Granite Park Chalet, a popular hiking destination. She was found alive the next morning, but was so badly ravaged she died before she could be evacuated. The other victim was killed by a single male grizzly at a remote campsite nearly ten miles west of Granite Park, on the shore of Trout Lake. Since then, the ranger said, bear attacks had occurred more frequently in Glacier National Park than anywhere else in the lower forty-eight states, some of them fatal, all with abundant publicity.

At the end of the talk, there was applause as the lights went up. Thank you. Now you must have some questions, the ranger said, turning off the slide projector.

Hands flew up.

Yes sir, the fellow in the blue sweater, the ranger said, pointing.

I read somewhere that human odors and activity attract grizzlies and that may have been the reason those two girls were attacked. And wasn't one or both of them eaten? Is there anything to that?

The ranger cleared his throat, looked down uncomfortably at his feet before he spoke. Let me answer that this way. Grizzlies have an incredible sense of smell that enables them to pick up scents miles away. They're also omnivorous eating machines. They'll eat almost anything from plants to animals, carrion, or their own kills, and that includes humans. Blood of any kind will attract grizzlies. He paused. And, yes, there was menstrual blood in both those incidents.

A murmur from the audience and more questions.

Five minutes and more questions later, the ranger said, Okay, folks. Time for one more question. How about that lady over there with the flash camera.

Thank you for an interesting talk. I've learned a lot about bears this evening. Some of it pretty scary. What advice can you give us to avoid being attacked? She looked over at the woman sitting next to her. We plan to do some hiking if the weather clears and we sure don't want to run into a bear.

The ranger nodded. As I've said, most of the time grizzlies will try to avoid human contact. But they are unpredictable. You must be very careful about odors, especially food that might attract them if you're backpacking or cooking outdoors. Also, grizzlies are fierce protectors of their own food sources. Steer clear of any carcasses or carrion of any kind in the wild because there's a good chance it has been claimed by a bear and that bear is not going to let anything near it. Kind of like a dog protecting its food bowl. Bears are no different. Also, never get near a sow with cubs. She'll attack anything she perceives as a threat to her cubs. Another thing. Grizzlies don't like surprises. Make plenty of noise when you're hiking so they'll know you're around. You never want to surprise a grizzly. Finally, it's a good idea to carry a canister of pepper spray with you when you're hiking. It's been shown to deter attacking and aggressive bears.

But what if that doesn't work, then what? the woman asked with a half-smile.

The ranger hesitated, then shook his head before he spoke. Yeah, well if worse comes to worst, the only thing to do is drop down into a fetal position, draw your knees up to protect your vital organs, and clasp your hands behind your head to protect your head and neck. If a bear thinks you're no longer a threat, it may back off, but well, you never know with grizzlies. Always remember, folks, in the Glacier backcountry, we're no longer at the top of the food chain. Predators rule. So enjoy your visit, but stay alert and be careful.

More hands went up. The ranger smiled and raised his hand. Thanks, folks, but that's all the time I have this evening. Be safe and enjoy your stay in Glacier.

Another round of applause and the sound of chairs scraping on the stone floor as people rose from their seats. A cluster of people gathered around the ranger with more questions.

Well, what did you think? the silver-haired man asked Beth as he stood up and stretched long arms over his head.

It was fascinating, Beth said as she looked up from a note pad she had been writing on during the talk and turned to look at him. Wow, I've learned a lot about grizzly bears this evening. On the drive up from Tucson, my motel reading was a book a friend gave me about a grizzly bear attack here in the park, the ranger talked about it tonight, you know, the two girls being killed the same night. Needless to say, my friend couldn't understand why I would want to leave warm, sunny Tucson. I think the book was her attempt to get me to change my mind.

Must've been *Night of the Grizzlies* by Jack Olsen.

Yes. Scary. Got me interested in grizzly bears. That's why I decided to attend the talk this evening. She held up a small yellow legal pad. See I've even been taking notes.

He smiled at the notes. Yeah, I read that some time ago. It's a good book. Amazing that until grizzlies killed those two girls in 1967, the Park Service was feeding grizzlies at Granite Park so the tourists could photograph them. The book changed that policy in a hurry.

What about you? she asked. Did you think it was interesting? Maybe it was old hat for someone who lives here, thinking so why is he here if he already knows this stuff?

People were milling around and pulling on their coats to leave. Others made their way back to their rooms, or to the bar behind the lobby for a nightcap.

Well, yeah, I grew up here, and I've hunted and hiked a fair amount, so I was familiar with the stories and most of what he had to say about grizzlies, but it still was interesting. I thought he did a good job. He hesitated, thinking what would she think if he told her the truth, that he was here on doctor's orders. And it was nice meeting you. I'm glad you didn't get the wrong idea when an old geezer like me asked to sit next to you.

He wasn't sure why he said that, except that he didn't want the conversation to end.

Not at all, she said smiling and reached out to touch his elbow. Don't be silly. I'm new here and you made me feel welcome.

Her touch startled them both, and they stood looking at each other for a long moment.

It was nice to meet you, too, she said finally to break the silence. *Find something to do. Don't just stand there.* She began to pull on her rain parka and he stepped closer to lift it over her shoulders. Thank you. She smiled again and extended her hand.

He smiled, nervous, feeling like a teenager on his first date, and gently took her hand. Nice meeting you, he said before he realized he had already said that. Ah, how long you here for?

Oh, I'm here for the summer and maybe longer. I've leased a little place in West Glacier.

Then maybe I'll see you again. I think you'll enjoy your stay. West Glacier is nice, friendly, but people mind their own business, so it can be a little quiet if you're used to the big city life. The big cities up here—Kalispell, Whitefish—fancy restaurants, and movies are thirty, thirty-five miles away. Not like Tucson. But in Montana, that's not much of a drive.

Well, I'm looking forward to a little peace and quiet. I moved in last week and I'm still settling in, but so far so good. I just opened a post office box, so I guess that sort of makes me a resident, doesn't it? She started to extend her hand again before she caught herself. She felt herself blushing. The attraction was real.

No, that makes you a seasonal. Not quite a resident, but more than a tourist, he laughed. West Glacier has a fair number of seasonals, people who come up here in the summer, then head south before the snow starts pilin' up. You'll fit right in. Oh by the way, I'm Harry Dawkins.

Nice to meet you, Harry. I'm Beth Blanchard. She hesitated, as if undecided what to do next, smiled again, and turned toward the door.

I'll probably see you at the post office, he said through a wide grin, That's where most of the socializin' in West Glacier goes on. There and Freda's Bar. Should I offer to walk her to her car? he asked himself.

It's dark. Is he going to offer to walk with me to the car like I hope? she wondered. She was usually cautious about men, even those who appeared nice. Why a local was here for a nature talk was still on her mind. But there was something about Harry Dawkins.

Hey, Beth. Hold on. I'll walk you to your car. It's dark and you never know, there might be a grizzly prowlin' around.

She laughed and waited until he pushed open the door and they walked out together. The wind was gusting, blowing the cold rain in sheets across the parking lot.

Lousy night to be out, he said.

That's my car over there, the red one, she said pointing to the red Honda as they approached the parking lot.

Well, how about that? he said. That pickup across from it's mine.

He held her umbrella over her as she opened the car door. Thank you, Harry. Maybe I'll see you at the post office, she said as she slid behind the wheel.

I hope so, he said as he closed the umbrella and handed it to her. He was trying to think of something else to say, but couldn't. Well, goodnight, Beth. Watch out for those grizzlies. She returned his smile.

As she drove off into the night, Beth felt excited, even elated. She had enjoyed the evening more than she thought she would, and it had everything to do with meeting Harry Dawkins. Dating? She didn't think so. She had been down that road after her divorce two years before. Unsatisfying to say the least. All the men her age were either married, divorced and screwed up over it, or gay. And she wasn't about to start climbing into the sack with young construction workers you meet in cowboy bars like some of the divorced women she knew. But it would be nice to have a friend, someone to just do things with, without the complications of sex, commitment, jealousy, and all that bullshit.

I'm in the mood for change, she said to herself as she steered her Honda along the two-lane blacktop as it followed the lakeshore back to West Glacier. This guy Harry seems nice, attractive, older, kind eyes. But she could tell they didn't miss much. Yeah, but he's probably got issues, she said to herself, like most of the men she'd met in the last couple of years. Probably even Lee Marvin. She sighed. *We'll see.*

Visibility was poor. Rain now mixed with sleet was turning to slush on the road. She drove carefully, leaning into the windshield with the wipers thumping at full speed. She knew that just a few feet beyond the guardrail on the right was a steep drop into a dark, deep, frigid lake. That was on her mind when a large animal leaped over the guardrail on the lake side of the road and bounded into the rays of her headlights. She hit the brakes as it crossed the road in three leaps and disappeared in the thick timber on the other side. My God, she said aloud. That was a mountain lion. That ranger's right, this is wilderness.

Headlights approaching in the rearview mirror caught her attention. A pickup. That's got to be Harry, she said to herself. She smiled.

3

Saturday evening, May 27. The most important thing on Keno Spotted Wolf's mind was the daughter who had been missing for nearly two weeks. He was not a man given to worry, or much reflection on the vagaries of life, but this was different, like no other crisis he had ever faced. *Foul play?* He let go of the thought. He was sitting in Kip's Beer Garden in St. Mary staring at a bottle of beer. He glanced around the dingy bar. A couple of cowboys shooting pool, and an Indian woman nursing a drink and talking to the bartender at the end of the bar. Drunk, he could tell from her slurred speech.

He was depressed, disgusted with himself. All he could think about was all the mistakes he had made that got him to this point. He looked up at his reflection in a cracked mirror behind the bar. The face staring back at him had only remnants of the angular handsomeness of his youth, the looks that got him bit parts in a couple of Westerns filmed west of Choteau. The high cheek bones remained, but his nose showed some wear, broken a couple of times, once by a rearing horse he was breaking, another time in a bar fight he couldn't remember. Now the long braided hair was turning gray at the temples, the athletic build beginning to sag. Still tall, but he was beginning to stoop into middle age. Once he had been proud of his Blackfeet warrior heritage, especially after a few shots of whiskey, fearless after a few more. Now he wasn't sure. Time and whiskey were working him over pretty good and he knew it.

He thought about how many times he had awakened to find himself, hung-over, in the Browning jail. Never anything too serious and usually on weekends—drunk and disorderly, the occasional bar fight, and drunk driving. Nothing dishonest. He was proud of that. When he appeared in court on Monday mornings, there were almost always ranchers willing to pay his, and other Indians' fines in return for their labor, usually mending fences, which no one liked to do. Some deal, but there was no choice if you were broke like he was most of the time. He guessed that he had strung more barbed wire across the prairie than anyone east of the Divide. No one who noticed the scars and callouses on his hands would doubt it.

On the surface, he sometimes seemed like a happy-go-lucky person with a ready sense of humor, and not a care in the world. When he first signed up for unemployment at the agency in Browning, he listed his occupation as pool player. He smiled when he did it and recalling it now, he almost did again in the mirror. The clerk had smiled with him and suggested ranch hand was a better idea.

He looked over again at the woman at the end of the bar. *That could be Dinah* went through his mind. A single mother, his once beautiful, intelligent daughter, full of promise, was now a sad case of alcoholism. Like me, he whispered to the reflection in the mirror. All the mistakes he had made when she was growing up had become a dark tide of guilt and remorse that lapped relentlessly at the edge of his thoughts. So pretty and bright. Then she got pregnant. An honor student, she dropped out of Browning High School. She and the baby lived at home for a while. Then she moved in with the baby's father in a public housing apartment about the size of a motel room, hoping they would marry. Instead, he beat her up. Keno remembered the threat he made to kill him, and not long after that, the boyfriend disappeared. No one knew where he went. She blamed *him* for the breakup. He didn't understand why. Another child was born two years later, to another man, no better than the first, who also drifted off. Not long after that, he and his wife, Emma, split up and Emma moved to Heart Butte to live with her mother and sister. Their son, Vine, joined the Marines.

It made his stomach knot up when he thought about Dinah's eighth-grade graduation. A straight-A student and a gifted athlete who lettered in basketball and track, she was selected for the Student Athlete of the Year Award by her teachers. She was so happy when she told him. He closed his eyes, remembering her broad smile and those dark eyes sparkling with excitement. He promised he would be there for the ceremony. He even bought an expensive silver and turquoise necklace for her and had an inscription engraved on it behind the setting. He looked down at his beer and shook his head. Yeah, I was there—late and drunk, after losing track of the time *right here* at Kip's on the way to the ceremony. She was so embarrassed. With tears in her eyes, she had turned away when he gave her the necklace and tried to apologize. He could never forget the expression of one of her teachers who just looked at him and shook her head in disgust.

Dinah kept the necklace and wore it all the time, so he believed she still loved him, but could she ever forgive him? He knew he would never forgive himself for that and all his many failures as a father. All he hoped for now was her safe return and one more chance to make things right. He even went to Mass to pray at the Little Flower Catholic Church in Browning. It was something he hadn't done in years. Anything for one more chance.

He pushed back from his beer and walked to the men's room, passing the woman at the end of the bar. She looked up, bleary eyed, nodded and smiled at him again through the cigarette smoke. He thought he had seen her somewhere before. Who knows? As he stood at the stained urinal, he sighed and looked up at the cracked plaster and paint peeling on the ceiling. Nothing seemed to work for Dinah, not religion, not Alcoholics Anonymous, and certainly not men who were, he had to admit, pretty much like himself—irresponsible. There was no doubt she loved her two little boys, like he loved her. But it didn't matter. She would seem to be getting her life together, attending Mass or AA meetings, finishing her GED, enrolling in courses at the Tribal College—then she would disappear, often for days, one time for a week, swept under by the tides of alcoholism. Later, there would be a call from the tribal police in Browning, or the police in Cut Bank, or sheriff's deputies who picked her up at bars in between. How long's she been gone? he remembered asking his wife many times when he would call from the pay phone at the IGA in Browning. What can I do? Nothing. It's your fault, Emma would say and hang up. Keno tried to put all that out of his mind, and alcohol, the reason for it all, was the way he did it.

This time was different. No one thought too much about it when she didn't come home that Saturday in May. She'll be back in a few days, or we'll get a call from the jail, he kept telling himself. It was a familiar pattern of behavior. But now she had been missing for over two weeks. She had never stayed away this long before. Not a phone call from her or anyone who knew her. Police had checked her usual haunts and there were no leads. After she was officially listed as a missing person, he was hopeful that photo and background information distributed to local, state, and federal law enforcement agencies would provide some leads. Photos with Have you seen this woman? and an 800 number to call were distributed and posted in public places in the region. But remaining hopeful was becoming more difficult with each passing day. Don't worry, she'll be showin' up soon. She always does, he remembered telling Emma and Dinah's little boys when they drove out to his place. Now he wasn't sure. He was at a loss trying to imagine where she might be and now darker thoughts were crowding in.

For the better part of a week, he had stopped at every bar he could think of within a fifty-mile radius of Browning, showing her photo to bartenders and anyone else who happened to be around. He figured someone must have seen her, or known something about her. Then someone told him they had heard a stranger say that he might have seen her at the Stanton Creek Bar, so he drove west fifty miles on Highway 2, all the way to Stanton Creek, but the man and woman who ran the place said they had no memory of seeing the woman in the photo. On the way back, he stopped and inquired at every bar—the Snow Slip, the Summit, the Firebrand. No one had seen her.

He rinsed his hands in cold water at the stained, single-spigot sink and dried his hands on his Wranglers. The paper towel dispenser had been empty for months.

When he returned to the bar, he nodded when the woman smiled again. He set his empty bottle on three dollars he pulled from a money clip, nodded to the bartender, and walked out in the gathering dusk to his pickup.

As the old Ford roared to life, he decided to check out the Stampede on the road to Cut Bank. It was a long shot. As far as he knew, that wasn't one of her usual hangouts, but who knows? He was desperate. The sun had slipped behind the peaks to the west when he pulled into the parking lot of a low-slung building with a rough plank porch that stretched across the front. The place looked the same as when he'd last been there, ages ago, only worse. It still needed paint. A weather-bleached skull of a longhorn steer hung above a hand-painted *Stampede Saloon* sign. Cowboy bar, no place for Indians. A green-neon Rainer Beer sign still glowed in one of two front windows, a blue Pabst Blue Ribbon sign flickered on and off in the other. He parked his pickup at the end of the building and walked across a gravel parking lot past four other pickups, stepping over mud ruts dried as hard as cement.

Heads turned and conversation stopped when he walked in, a stranger and a braided Indian. He'd gotten into a scuffle when he'd been there before, and he didn't want another one now. It took a minute for his eyes to adjust to the dim lighting before he walked to the bar and ordered a beer from a bartender who didn't speak. He scraped a barstool back and sat down near the end of the bar. Johnny Cash was singing from a 1950s-style jukebox in the far corner at the edge of a small sawdust-covered dance floor about twice the size of the bed of a pickup. He glanced at four men and a woman who were sitting toward the other end of the bar. Except for the woman, it was Stetsons, a farm equipment cap, and all, including the woman with a big ass in skintight jeans, in boots. A younger couple sat at a table near the jukebox. He could tell from the conversations, which resumed after he sat down, that he was the only stranger.

When the bartender set the Bud longneck in front of him, Keno laid a five-dollar bill on the bar and took out the photocopied photo of Dinah from his shirt pocket and asked if he had seen her. The bartender took the photo, squinting in the dim light, turned, and held it up to the light over the cash register. Keno took a swallow of beer and wiped his lips on his sleeve.

Nope, can't say that I have, the bartender replied.

What about the others? Keno asked, nodding toward the patrons whispering and staring at him at the other end of the bar.

The bartender gave him a resigned look then held up the photo and passed it on to the others sitting at the bar. Anyone seen this gal? This fellah here's lookin' for her. Right?

Yes, Keno said.

One of the men at the bar, a large man in a Western-style plaid shirt that sagged button-popping tight over a big belly and silver-and-turquoise belt buckle, took the photo and made a big show of looking at it. Then he took the toothpick he'd been chewing out of his mouth, drained the whiskey in his glass, and looked over at Keno with a drunken, looking-for-trouble sneer. I can see why you're lookin' for this little squaw, chief. Looks like a real hot piece of tail to me. He snickered along with the others at the bar, looking again at the photo, as Keno rose from the barstool. Yes siree, I'll keep an eye out for her.

The words had barely left his lips when Keno slammed both hands into the cowboy's shoulders, knocking him over backward as the barstool skidded out from beneath him. He hit the floor with a surprised look on his face that melded into a snarl. As he rolled to his knees and stumbled to his feet, Keno helped him, grabbing his shirt beneath the chin with his left hand before smashing his nose with a right that began high above his head. The fury. The repeated blows to the man's face sounded like someone chopping wood. Then Keno released his grip and picked up the barstool as the cowboy lay sprawled out on the floor, his face covered with blood streaming from his nose and mouth.

Whoa, whoa, hold on, no more, no more, he didn't mean nothin', the bartender shouted, but didn't move from behind the bar. The others sat stunned, eyes wide, shifting from the man on the floor to the tall Indian standing over him. The cowboy raised his head slightly, groaned, eyes glazed, and dropped back to the floor, blood draining from a nose at an odd angle into one of his ears. Keno looked up at the bartender, nodded, and put the barstool down. He stepped back, reached for his beer, and took a long pull, his eyes scanning the others at the bar.

No one moved or spoke in a moment of silence as the music changed and Waylon and Willie, *Mamas Don't Let Your Babies Grow Up To Be Cowboys*, replaced *Ring of Fire* on the jukebox. Then he set the empty bottle down and turned toward the others at the bar. As they recoiled, he reached down, picked up the photocopy that had fallen to the floor, folded it, and put it back in his pocket. He turned back to the bartender, as if to say something, then turned back, looking down at the cowboy, who was still lying on his back, holding his face in both hands, groaning and whimpering softly. Keno picked up his change, stepped over him, and walked out.

—◆◆◆—

4

Friday, June 1. Two weeks and no one had found the body. He guessed with the Middle Fork still running gray and high with recent rains and snowmelt, it might never be found. Not that it mattered much. He liked reading about his kills in the newspapers, and enjoyed listening to people talk about them, but the upside was he could relax, take it easy, until a body was found or the urge returned like it always did.

The tourist season at Glacier National Park didn't get under way until the middle of June when schools let out, and the big rush started on the Fourth of July, so he spent his days getting ready. He stacked hay, mended saddles and bridles, fed and groomed horses and mules, and helped move both animals and gear to the different stables located in the park on big stock trucks. Just like his first summer on the job the year before, he'd been assigned to manage the weekly pack string that took supplies six miles up a steep mountain trail to Sperry Chalet, a rustic vacation lodge for tourists. With animals, everything was plain and simple. They acted the way you treated them. You couldn't rely on that with people; that was for damn sure.

The outfitter who had the concession at Glacier hadn't put him in the same housing this year. That was a plus. Instead of sharing a crowded bunkhouse above the stable with other wranglers, he had a one-room cabin next to the stables on the Quarter Circle Road just inside the west entrance to the park. It wasn't much, fairly primitive—a small electric hot plate, a table and three chairs, one of them an old, faded upholstered easy chair, a metal bunk bed, and a small shower. But he had his privacy and didn't have to put up with all the bunkhouse bullshit, the Texas-cowboy posturing of younger twenty-something assholes, incessant country music, the odor of farts, sweat, and after-shave that made his head ache and annoyed the hell out of him.

Living in West Glacier had another big advantage. He owned two horses that traveled with him in a trailer he pulled behind his pickup. His first summer there, he had worked out an arrangement with his employer, Sundown Outfitters. The foreman agreed to let him pasture his horses, at no charge, with the company stock. Sundown used the pasture to rest and rotate the couple hundred horses and mules they worked in the park. It was a sweet deal for him. The stables and corral were located next to a lush green pasture that spread out a half-mile all the way from the stable to Lower McDonald Creek, a crystal clear stream that flowed around the base of Apgar Mountain. In the evening, it was common to see elk and deer grazing with the horses and mules.

He liked the change of scenery that came with working for concessionaires in national parks. He had been doing it for more than ten years. Winters at Big Bend or Death Valley, summers at Grand Canyon, Yosemite, or Glacier, he moved with the seasons and the tourists. There were two types of people who worked the parks. Some lived a lot like he did, drifters, moving from park to park with the seasons, most of them working as waiters, clerks and cooks. The anonymity of this rootless, vagabond way of life had great appeal. No last names, and inquiries about anyone's past were unwelcome with this contingent. That worked for him. He kept to himself, didn't ask questions, and didn't welcome any.

Then there were the college students on summer vacations. They were different—very social, buddy-buddy, chattering, partying, and fucking one another all summer long. The two groups usually didn't mix after working hours, except when drugs were involved, pot mostly, but the last few years he saw more coke, and noticed meth had become popular with the locals because it was so cheap.

He stayed away from drugs and didn't much like the college students either. Rich, pampered, and privileged, they worked summers for fun, to hike, bike, raft, or whatever. Money wasn't a worry, as it had been for him all his life. The meager wages they made were of little consequence to them. If they ran out of money, they called home and got more. It was a completely different story for people like him who had to earn their own way.

It was still cool and wet most of the time, just like the year before. If you don't like the spring weather in Montana, he was sick of hearing, wait a minute, it'll change. The mornings and evenings were usually cold and dreary. Rain and sleet broken by periods of sunshine described most of the afternoons as successive storms rolled in and out over the mountains. Blue skies, sunshine and a sixty-degree afternoon brought out the locals, recovering from the long winter, in shorts and T-shirts. The days were lengthening; the columbine, lupine, and arnica were blooming in splashes of color below the fresh green of aspens and cottonwoods leafing out. Serviceberry bushes were in full bloom, the white blossoms looking like dogwood he remembered in Arkansas, but the evenings were still long with no television and lousy radio reception in the cabin. He had a CD player there and one in his truck, which he rarely played. Lately he had lost interest in music. Country was all the same.

Sometimes in the evenings after work, he got in his pickup and drove a couple of miles to the Amtrak station in West Glacier. He liked to watch the trains. And there were lots of them, usually long freights, requiring two or three pusher engines, in addition to the two engines pulling at the front, to get up the long climb to Marias Pass. He also liked to watch the passengers get off the Amtrak when it pulled in on its east-west run around nine in the evening, if it was on time, which it rarely was. He never spoke to anyone, just watched, especially if there were young female passengers, backpacks slung over their shoulders, pulling fleece tops tight across their breasts, headed for adventure in the park. After that, he might drive to one of the several saloons scattered down the highway in Coram, Martin City, or Hungry Horse, in what locals called the canyon.

According to the locals the towns hadn't changed much since the Hungry Horse Dam was completed in the 1950s and jobs went south, then logging tanked. Now it was food stamps, junk cars, old pickups with cracked windshields, prefab houses, 1950s style, singlewides tucked back in the trees, and a lot of domestic violence. But no one asked questions. He liked that.

This cold morning he needed a break from the instant coffee and snack food he usually ate at the cabin. He decided to treat himself to breakfast in Coram, a wide spot in the road seven miles west on Highway 2 from West Glacier. As he drove into town, he noticed the flakeboard addition on the Pastime Saloon remained unpainted like it was the year before, sitting there next to an auto repair shop in a two bay cement block garage. It looked like the same old cars and pickups were still waiting to be fixed or sold, in a weed-filled dirt lot between it and a boarded-up restaurant with a weathered, hand-painted pizza sign. He put on his right turn signal at an Exxon station that also sold milk, beer, candy, and bread, made the turn, and parked next to the Spruce Park Café which shared a roof with the gas station. An okay place with him. Good food, plenty of it, and you could get out of there for six or seven bucks.

He parked beside a flatbed logging truck, eased out, and locked the door of his faded blue 1984 Dodge pickup. After gently easing the crotch of his Wranglers away from sore testicles, he turned up the collar of his flannel-lined denim jacket, adjusted the angle of the Stetson he wore, and walked across the parking lot to the restaurant. A couple of ravens bickering over food someone had dropped squawked at him and flew off as he approached. It was overcast and a cold spring rain was falling. He stepped over a puddle with a skim of ice and pushed open the door.

A welcome rush of warm air and the smell of frying bacon and coffee and the sound of people talking. There was always a lot of talk there in the mornings when the locals congregated for breakfast. But today the conversations were louder than usual, ricocheting back and forth from the lunch counter to the tables between it and the door. It seemed like everybody in the place was getting their two cents worth in about park rangers finding the remains of a hiker who had been missing in

Glacier National Park. He'd heard about it on the radio on the drive to Coram and didn't think too much about it. Big deal. Someone got whacked by a bear. Pass the Tabasco. The victim, a young man, had been killed by a grizzly bear or bears on the Scenic Point trail, a popular hike that climbed steeply out of the Two Medicine Valley and crossed a high barren ridge to a rock outcropping with spectacular views of the Rocky Mountain Front and the Great Plains. The victim never made it to the ridge, someone said.

Even worse, the bear ate him, a tall man with close-cropped silver hair said to the waitress. He was sitting at the end of the counter half-way through an order of scrambled eggs and bacon with the newspaper he was reading lying next to his plate. He wore western boots, neatly pressed jeans, and a dark green, military-style turtleneck sweater with shoulder patches.

I know, I saw that. It's horrible, Harry, the waitress, a big-boned woman, said as she refilled his white porcelain mug.

About to sit at a table near the window, he hesitated, turned, and walked outside to a vending machine and bought a newspaper. He read the headline: REMAINS OF MISSING HIKER FOUND—RANGERS LOOKING FOR GRIZZLY WITH CUBS. The front page was all about bear attacks. A chronological history of past attacks appeared in a sidebar. Stories about marauding grizzlies sold papers in western Montana and were always front page. When he returned, he went back to the same table and sat down. When the waitress came over and poured his coffee, he said, Eggs over easy, bacon, hash browns, and toast, without looking up at her.

He folded the paper double and read how the young male victim, a seasonal park employee, was hiking alone and probably surprised a sow and her cubs on a high switchback where the subalpine trees and brush were thick and tangled and visibility poor. Rangers speculated that the bear and her cubs might have been feeding on ground squirrels or marmots in the area when he surprised them. Park investigators at the scene said his backpack, a parka, and other gear were found scattered down a steep scree slope some distance above what little remained of the body. The evidence wasn't clear about whether the victim tried to run from the bears, or whether they had dragged him down off the trail. Three other hikers far below on the trail told park rangers that they thought they heard a scream or shout about the time the attack probably occurred. The story went on to describe how, a year before, another young man simply disappeared on a hike in the same area. The chief suspects then and now were a sow grizzly and two yearling cubs that had been observed in the area.

When his order arrived, he folded up the newspaper and laid it on the floor at his feet. As he forked in his eggs and hash browns, he listened to the conversation that involved everyone sitting at the counter and a few others scattered around at the tables. A burly man with a full white beard and a face baggy and creased with age and hard work was sitting at the counter near the tall, silver-haired man. He wore logger boots and his big belly pushed against soiled canvas overalls held up by wide maroon suspenders. He spoke through a mouth full of biscuits and gravy.

I heard from a guy works for the park that was over there, that they didn't find much there to haul down the mountain. Biscuits and Gravy hesitated to swallow, an effort that made his eyes bulge and water, before he continued. They found what was left of him down near Appistoki Falls. All that was left was a skull licked clean and one foot inside a boot with a chewed-off shinbone stickin' out.

Oh my God, that's sickening, Andy, the waitress said, grimacing as she handed change to four loggers standing at the cash register. One of them blew his nose with a loud ripping sound into a large, soiled handkerchief. You won't catch me hikin' in that park as long as there's grizzlies runnin' around.

Aw, that's crazy, Alice, the pony-tailed cook said leaning into the opening from the kitchen where he had just placed an order of pancakes. You're in more danger drivin' home from work than you are havin' a grizzly attack you. More people are killed in the park fallin' off cliffs and drownin'.

Yeah, maybe so, Biscuits and Gravy said, but when the Feds started regulatin' everything and decided no more huntin', you know, Endangered Species Act and all that environmentalist bullshit, that's when we had to start worryin' about grizzlies. Those goddamn bears—sorry, Alice, he nodded to the waitress—are predators. It's their nature. And without a gun to defend hisself, a man's no different than a deer or ground squirrel to them, a little kid's no different than an adult. Why, hell, a couple weeks ago a griz with cubs went after three skiers near Swiftcurrent Pass. Lucky they got away. There's no knowin' right from wrong with animals. We're food. Fear's the only thing they understand, and thanks to the enviros and the Feds, they've lost their fear of humans. They need fear put back in 'em, and the only way to do it is start killin' a few. Then they'll get the message.

Biscuits and Gravy took a deep breath. Just like the death penalty, Alice. No death penalty, no fear, more murders. Same deal. Grizzlies weren't attackin' nobody in the Bob Marshall and the Jewel Basin when you could hunt 'em down there. Hell no, them bears knew they could get shot. Park bears don't have no fear, so they'll kill ya' if they get a chance.

Gary looked at his watch. It was time to get back to the stables. He forked in the last of his hash browns and eggs, took a final swallow of coffee, and wiped his mouth with his napkin. He arranged his soiled napkin and silverware on his plate and pushed the salt and pepper shakers and Tabasco sauce back against the napkin container before he scraped his chair back from the table and stood up.

You got a point there, he said, looking over at Biscuits and Gravy but not making eye contact. It was unusual for him to talk with strangers if he didn't have too. But this was something he had strong opinions about. Killin's normal behavior, and fear's the only thing that controls behavior.

Wait a minute, the waitress said. We're not wild animals. People have consciences, we're taught right from wrong as children, and we know it's wrong to kill other people.

What about people who ain't worth nothin'? he shot back. All I'm sayin' is we're all animals, and there's predators and prey. That's nature. Predators are necessary to maintain balance in nature. Darwin's rules. Right and wrong ain't got nothin' to do with it.

How could a bear killing that poor young man have anything to do with keeping nature in balance?

Who knows? he shrugged with a half-smile as he picked up the check she had put by his coffee mug.

That's crazy, she said, thinking there was something funny about that man's smile and his eyes. What was it? She wasn't sure except it made her feel uneasy.

Harry Dawkins watched the man check the addition on his bill and then pull a money clip out of his pocket, lay down a five, a one, and some change by the cash register and walk out. Something strange about that guy, Harry thought.

Biscuits and Gravy took a big swallow of coffee and wiped his mouth with the back of his hand. Who the hell's Darwin? he said, a quizzical look on his face. He the guy got the place on the river, owns Glacier Raft?

Oh, my God, no, no, no, not that Darwin, Alice said, looking up and rolling her eyes as she wiped the table where the loggers had been sitting. He's a famous … Oh, never mind, Andy.

Harry Dawkins smiled though the last sip of his coffee. He stood up, put a ten-dollar bill under his water glass and pulled on his coat. See you next time, Alice, he said, still smiling, nodded to Biscuits and Gravy, and walked outside. The stranger who'd talked about Darwin had pulled an old Dodge pickup with Oregon plates up to the gas pumps.

5

———— ◆◆◆ ————

Saturday, June 2. The last thing I want to do, he was thinking as he walked to the corral to greet a group of pudgy clubwomen he would lead on a trail ride along Upper McDonald Creek. He reached down and gently touched his testicles. *Prairie nigger bitch.* It had been a couple of weeks and they were still sore.

Hello ladies, he called out. How y'all doin'? My name's Gary and you're goin' with me today. How's that sound?

Sounds great to me, a gray-haired matron said and her friends laughed and someone said, That Arlene's such a flirt.

He knew he wasn't bad looking, five eleven, slim, with a prominent Adam's apple and the squint marks of time spent outdoors. Even with a mouthful of crooked teeth below the dark sunglasses, a woman, whose photo he kept in an album, had told him once that he looked like a cowboy on a Coors Beer poster, the one sitting on a corral fence with sandy-colored hair hanging down to his collar beneath a weathered Stetson. He liked that. The All-American cowboy, he said to himself. How about that? He didn't smile much because of his crooked teeth, but he'd learned that acting courteous in an old-fashioned yes-ma'am-no-sir way, dropping his *g*'s and affecting a folksy, cowboy twang, triggered good feelings in the kind of women, older women mostly, who tended to show up for trail rides.

Like the fat lady all decked out in brand new western boots and riding outfit who gave him a big smile and nudged a similarly dressed woman next to her. He's kinda cute, don't you think? he heard her whisper to her friend. They both giggled.

That's a lot of pork on the hoof, he thought as he returned the fat lady's smile. Poor horse. You ladies on vacation?

Oh no, we're up from Kalispell, schoolteachers there. We have the day off and thought a horseback ride in the park and a nice lunch afterward would be a fun way to spend the day. My name's Arlene. Nice to meet you, Gary, she said, thinking no Steve McQueen, but he would do.

Yeah, with an ass the size of yours, Arlene, sure looks like you need a nice big lunch. You sure picked a pretty day after all that rain last night. Air's nice and fresh. Whad'ya teach?

I teach junior-high biology, she said. Marian here teaches history.

Cool, biology and history, my favorite subjects, he said as he adjusted bridles and stirrups. I think Darwin was one of the greatest minds of all time. No way was he going to mention that he felt the same about Hitler.

I'm impressed, she said. Have you read *The Origin of Species*?

Cover to cover, he lied. Have my own copy. That was true, and he had read parts of it.

Interesting, she said smiling. What impressed you most?

A twinge of anxiety. *What is this, a fucking quiz? This fucking Jew bitch is zeroing in on me.* He took off his sunglasses and wiped them, casting a hard look at his questioner.

Memories of grade school. He hated it. It wasn't lack of ability. He knew he had plenty of that, an IQ in the high-normal range, he learned, when he sneaked a look in his file when he was in the principal's office for punching someone. And he hated the teachers who picked on him because of the way he smelled and dressed and put him on the spot with their fucking questions, like this fat bitch, and that hatchet-faced one in second grade who gave him low marks for cleanliness because he smelled bad. He hated those sweeter smelling, better-dressed little bastards in his classes. What do you expect? he felt like screaming. I can't help it I smell like stale piss, the fucking bedwetting I can't control and living in that goddamned dump of a trailer with no washing machine and a shower without hot water half the fucking time.

Well, you know, survival of the fittest, he finally stammered. That idea.

She could see the anger. Those eyes. Her smile turned glassy, thinking there's something strange about this fellow; I shouldn't have asked the question. Oh, she said, and dropped the subject.

Except for the sound of McDonald Creek in the distance, some murmured conversation, and the snorts and soft clomp of hooves on a wet, pine-needle-covered trail, it was quiet as the ride began. Arlene and Marian were in the middle of the string of riders when he reined in his horse and motioned to a squirrel bouncing across the trail ahead. Then, lifting a finger to his lips for silence, he pointed with the other to a large hawk perched in a tall tree. Suddenly the hawk swooped down on the squirrel. Flapping wings, scattering leaves, and squeals as the squirrel struggled against the sharp talons. Most of the women turned their heads as the hawk ripped loose and swallowed strips of flesh from the still struggling squirrel.

He watched for a minute then turned to face the group behind him, a look of satisfaction on his face. Pretty cool, don't ya think? The way that hawk took out that squirrel. Quick, efficient, and a tasty breakfast is the payoff. At the sound of his voice, the hawk flew off with what remained of its prize. He was smiling, savoring the discomfort of the women.

Pretty cool? Tasty breakfast? Did you hear that? Arlene whispered over her shoulder. That poor little squirrel and he *enjoyed* that.

Sure did, Marian replied. Your kinda cute guy seems very weird to me. Did you notice his eyes when he took his sunglasses off? Empty, no feeling at all above that smile.

Arlene grimaced and nodded.

Gary was aware that those expressionless eyes could produce an almost visceral unease, even fear, bringing conversations to an abrupt, awkward ending. That's why he often wore dark aviator sunglasses and wore that Stetson low, keeping those eyes hidden in the shadow of its brim. He knew he was good in other ways at concealing his dark secret. In a short statement he kept in a photo album of his victims, he wrote:

I never abducted any of these bitches. I _seduced_ *them. Every last one of them went with me willingly. None of them had a clue they were going to die until it was too late because I am an expert at what I do. I, Gary Ray Kemp, am a master predator and all these photos are living (no pun intended) proof of that.*

—◆—

6

———◆———

Saturday evening, June 9. It was warm. Gary had showered and was on his way to the Trapline when he noticed a crowd spilling out of the West Glacier Bar, better known to locals as Freda's. Young women, lots of them. He decided to stop and have a look. He parked his pickup in the trees next to the gas station and walked across the road to the bar. He knew it was a college crowd and that's why he chose the bars in the canyon where he felt more at home. *But maybe she'd be there tonight.*

At least a dozen people were standing on the wood-plank porch, sitting on the steps and on a bench in the soft blue glow of a Kokanee Beer sign that hung in the window above it. Others were sitting on the porch, some cross-legged, some with their backs against the porch posts or the side of the wood-frame building.

He sidestepped his way around them and went inside. Bar stools were filled, but he found a space standing next to the long, polished mahogany bar that stretched twenty feet from the entrance almost to the back wall and the door to the restrooms. He looked around at the Charley Russell prints of cowboys and Indians hanging on the knotty-pine-paneled walls, often at odd angles, opposite the bar. He was nervous, feeling out of place surrounded by this college crowd. He turned toward the back of the room where people were playing pool, the light hanging above the table showing the dark stains of years of spilt beer on the worn green felt. The space between the pool table and a dartboard on the far wall was crowded with people sitting at a clutch of small, round tables and chairs. A darkened television hung from brackets in the corner. Another TV with a baseball game no one was watching rested on a shelf above the bar next to the door. He guessed it was muted because all he could hear was noisy conversation and blue-grass music coming from two speakers hanging above the liquor display behind the bar.

How's it goin', dude? I like the Stetson, a short, wiry young man sitting on the barstool next to him looked up and said. You just arrive for the season?

Wise-ass college fuck, he thought, but he played it cool.

Yeah, I guess you could say that. What about you? Gary could see from the glittering eyes and loopy grin that this asshole was way ahead on beer.

Yeah, got in earlier in the week, or was it the week before, right after exams … anyway this is my second summer here. Love Glacier, and Freda's is the place to be, right?

Gary ordered a Coors Light. So what's so special about Freda's? Looks like any other bar to me.

Look around, man. Decent people, good lookin' women, not like those bars down the canyon like the Trapline and what's the other one, can't remember, you know … Oh yeah, the Pastime. Losers hang out there, we call 'em canyon critters, actin' tough, pickin' fights, hittin' on your women, that shit. He took another swallow of beer from a longneck bottle.

Gettin' after it is what the Freda's crowd is all about, not winnin' the fuckin' lottery, gettin' your elk, or bitchin' about environmentalists, the Endangered Species Act and the federal government's restrictions on loggin', snowmobiles, and ATVs, like those assholes who hang out at the Trapline and the Pastime. Look around, man, the photos on the wall, he said swinging his arm around and nearly knocking over the beer the bartender had just set down in front of Gary.

Gary looked up at the photos hanging above the liquor display and around to those tacked to the pine beams that ran across the ceiling—rafts and kayaks dipping and cresting in roiling white water, climbers edging across narrow ledges, clinging to sheer rock walls, skiers in plumes of powder cascading down almost vertical slopes. That's when he noticed *her* walk into the bar.

* * * * *

Gary licked his lips, a flush excitement as he looked at Vicki Hathaway's tanned cheeks, bee-stung lips, and thick auburn hair pulled back and tied in a ponytail. He watched the men's heads turn and their admiring looks. He'd first seen her early one evening three weeks back. She was riding a bicycle along Going to the Sun Road as he was returning from work at the Lake McDonald stables. He followed behind for nearly a quarter of a mile, pretending that he couldn't pass, fixated on the lean, smoothly curved hips enclosing the bicycle seat, and the rhythmic motion of long, tanned, athletic legs. She nodded and smiled when he finally passed. It took his breath away. She was the most beautiful, appealing woman he had ever seen.

Figuring she was the type to frequent Freda's, Gary found her there a couple of nights later. That evening he'd overheard her name, that she worked as a waitress in the restaurant at Lake McDonald Lodge, and she was boarding at the employee dormitory located in a stand of old-growth cedars near the lodge. A surreptitious check of the list of employees rooming there revealed the location of her room and that she shared it with another female employee. He also wrote down her days and hours of work which were posted weekly on a work schedule in the entryway. He began to track her activities when their days off coincided and in the evenings after she got off work.

Only a few days before, he'd photographed her as she played volleyball in a blue string bikini on the grass behind the employee housing. He added it to several photographs of her he put in an album with his collection of others zippered in a waterproof vinyl bag he kept in the cabin under his bunk. He brought them out to masturbate. The frontal shot of her squatting with legs wide apart to return a volley, immediately became his favorite turn-on. He imagined he could see a fringe of pubic hair. But merely looking at her was not enough. He needed more. Two nights ago he'd lifted a pair of her panties from a clothesline. And last night, he'd run his tongue over her bicycle seat. Her scent was intoxicating; he couldn't get her out of his mind.

He was thinking about that as he watched her wave a greeting to friends. Then he saw the smile as her eyes locked on to a particular young man. Gary could see he was a popular guy, athletic, with a tanned face, Paul Newman eyes, and a mop of sandy hair above an easy grin.

Gary watched them embrace as she kissed him on the cheek. He took her hand and led her toward a crowded table of smiling friends. Hey Vicki, one of them called out. You're late. Where you been?

When the short, annoying guy moved away from the bar to join a group on the porch, Gary slid onto the vacant barstool and cocked his ear to listen to the conversation at their table. They were talking about climbing mountains, something he had never done. In the course of their conversation, he learned that the young man's name was Matt Margolis, that he worked as a guide at one of the raft companies, and that he had bagged the summits of most of the park's most challenging peaks. He could see that Vicki was all ears. He couldn't miss her admiring smile when Matt admitted that the one he was most proud of was Mount St. Nicholas, a dangerous climb up thousands of feet of sheer cliffs, across narrow ledges, crumbling rock, and breathtaking exposure. Gary could tell this sonofabitch and Vicki Hathaway had something going and it made him angry.

* * * * *

Shortly before closing time, Gary followed Vicki and Matt back to her dormitory. He parked his truck in the public parking lot and watched them enter the dormitory. He made sure no one was around and then he crept over to the building and hid behind bushes below her first-floor window. The sounds of their lovemaking stirred his sexual desire, while at the same time, it elevated the rage he felt toward the young man she was with. He had to have her and vowed to kill the boyfriend if he remained part of her life. She was going to be his alone. But he knew that would be complicated and he had to do it right. Tonight was not the time.

In the days that followed, his stalk continued as he pondered some way to accomplish that objective. All his other crimes had been crimes of opportunity, spotting someone at a bar, or hitchhiking, or soliciting at a truck stop. There was never much time required for a successful abduction. This one would have to be different. Vicki Hathaway was a keeper.

* * * * *

A few nights later at Freda's, as he sat on the same stool at the end of the bar near the door, he heard Matt Margolis describing a plan to go swimming the next afternoon at a tiny, secluded, unnamed lake off what locals called the inside North Fork Road. Gary was familiar with this muddy, rutted road, where fallen trees were always a risk. It ran along the western edge of the park from Lake McDonald in the south to Kintla Lake near the Canadian border and attracted little traffic. Apart from the trailheads it connected, it was best known as a route to take if you had time to spare and wanted to see wildlife, especially wolves. The unnamed lake's shallow and the water's warm, Gary heard Matt tell Vicki. He knew exactly where it was. He had ridden his horse back there the previous summer.

This time he drove his pickup, arriving in mid-morning to get there before them. The lake was not visible from the road, but he had no trouble spotting the unmarked trail into it. Continuing on another quarter-mile, he parked his truck at a pullout and walked back to the narrow, overgrown trail. It ended among some huge glacial boulders at the water's edge. Just beyond the boulders, there was a tiny open area of gravel and grass. He guessed that would be their destination. Making his way through thick trees and brush and open areas where bear grass bloomed white above dark green stalks, he circled around to the opposite shore of the lake and climbed a rocky alder covered escarpment. The boulders blocked the view of anyone approaching from the road, but they were no hindrance to Gary's view from no more than a hundred yards across the lake. He took cover in a thicket of alder bushes, adjusted his binoculars, and waited.

It was a bright, warm sunny day. Several hours passed. *Where are they?* He was about to leave when he heard voices and saw Vicki and Matt emerge from the trees and walk the shoreline to the tiny beach of gravel and grass. He watched as they spread out a blanket on the grass and set down a picnic basket. Vicki kicked off her sandals and undressed down to her blue string bikini and waded into the clear water. Matt followed behind her. Nude. When she turned around and saw him, Gary heard her make a squealing sound of surprise and watched as she began splashing him and telling him to get away. He saw him reach for her as she bolted for shore. She was in his arms at water's edge. Gary caught his breath as he watched him lift her up, squirming in his arms, and carry her to the blanket. He could see her resisting, pushing and shoving, but he could also hear the sound of her laughter. Then the sonofabitch was on top of her and Gary, realizing that he had been holding his breath, sucked in a mouthful of air.

His heart was beating fast with excitement and anger, as their laughter subsided and he watched as she spread her legs and the sonofabitch moved between them, easing himself slowly down the length of her body, kissing her breasts and stomach until her thighs rested on his shoulders. Gary saw him pull the bottom of her bikini loose and throw it to one side as he slipped his other hand beneath her and tilted her hips upward. Gary watched as she drew up her knees, thighs pressed against her lover's head. He caught his breath as her head began rocking slowly from side to side, then faster and faster. Gary was breathing hard and masturbating moments later when she stiffened, back arching upward, legs trembling as she held it. Gary ejaculated. Desire and rage. That combination always set him off.

Sometime later, when they'd finished making love, Gary watched as, now completely nude, she rolled over and lifted a lavender bandanna from her fanny pack and wiped between her thighs. Then she waded back into the water and rinsed off. In the soft golden light of late after-noon, she was radiant, a scene an artist might have imagined.

For the rest of the afternoon, Gary watched as the couple ate their picnic lunch, swam, and frolicked in the water, and made love again, this time with him beneath her. It was early evening and the temperature was dropping when he saw them gather their things together and leave. He waited until he was confident they wouldn't return, and then made his way back around the shoreline to the tiny beach. He stopped and rolled over a rock and retrieved the lavender bandanna, damp with their pas-sion, he had watched her place beneath it. He stooped down to rinse it out in the lake and noticed that her name, Vicki, appeared in black in the design along its edges. When he got back to the road, Matt's car, the green Subaru with the ski rack, was gone.

In the days and weeks after that, his anger and desire became a deepen-ing obsession. He had always prided himself on his self-control. He figured it was why he was so successful at what he did. He wasn't some stupid, impulsive street killer with low self-control like he had read about in crimi-nology books back when he was still trying to understand himself. He was different—smart, calculating, and *in control*. But the weeks of listening to their laughter, straining to hear the reasons for it, and watching as they smiled and kidded and winked at one another were becoming intolerable. The anger welled up inside as he watched them. He hated it when Vicki playfully bumped her hip into Matt as he tried to line up a shot playing pool at Freda's. *Why him?* was something he couldn't get out of his mind.

He concentrated on learning their habits and routines, all the while looking for an opportunity to make his move. She wasn't like the others. She was too special to waste quickly. He wanted to spend what remained of an empty, unhappy life with her. When he reached the end, then he would decide what to do about her. At this point he wasn't sure. He would figure that out later. The problem now was how to get to that point, mak-ing the capture, the beginning of the end, the end of the beginning. Who said that? he said to himself. Someone famous, maybe Hitler.

7

---◆◆◆---

Wednesday morning, June 13. Meeting Beth Blanchard at Lake McDonald Lodge was the best thing that had happened to Harry Dawkins in a long time. Thinking about it made him smile as he parked his gunmetal-gray Chevy Silverado pickup outside the post office. Attractive, intelligent, and pleasant, easy to talk with, and slim. He liked her looks, especially the high cheek bones and squint marks showing beneath the edges of those bookish wire-rimmed glasses she put on to read. Her thick, dark hair was turning gray and he liked that, too, the way she wasn't trying to hide it, or the faint age lines above her lips. He found that kind of honesty appealing.

These were welcome, almost forgotten, thoughts and feelings. He was socializing the night he met Beth because of doctor's orders and the urging of his two children. He thought about the darkness of the past year, the struggle with depression after his wife of nearly forty years died. For months he saw no one, talked to no one except for brief greetings at the post office and grocery store. A worried daughter, who lived in California, called on the weekends, but even those conversations were brief. And his son, serving with Special Forces somewhere in the Middle East, was out of contact except for an occasional letter or phone call. He closed his eyes and shook his head as he thought about the loneliness of those long, dark winter evenings, and how close he had come, on one of them, to reaching for the long-barrel Colt 44 six-shooter he kept in a stand by the fireplace. The despair, looking into the black hole of that pistol barrel. Then his golden retriever, Ginger, climbed up on the couch beside him and fell asleep with her head pressed against his leg. Without that dear old dog … he put the thought out of his mind. He gave Ginger a pat and went into the post office.

He'd been hoping to run into Beth there, but nearly a month had passed with no sign of her. Then his luck changed. He was standing at the bank of post office boxes shuffling through his mail when he saw her pull in and park. When she walked inside, he said with a big smile, Hello there, nice to see you again. How you been?

She looked up. Still the tall, thin, rail of a man, and as distinguished looking in boots and Levis as she remembered him that night at the lodge. Well hello, Harry. Good to see you, too, she said returning the smile. I was wondering when I would, thinking, *hoping.*

That made him feel good, that she'd been thinking of him as he certainly had of her, more than he thought he would. Things were still quiet in West Glacier, but the aspen and birch were bright green, almost in full leaf, and the seasonal residents were starting to trickle in from down south, most of them from Arizona and California, and the post office and restaurant were busier than either had been since the summer before. It looked and felt like summer was just around the corner. They talked about the weather and the townhouse she was renting on the golf course. When she closed and locked her mailbox, Harry suggested they walk over to the restaurant and have coffee.

Ginger had her head out the window of his pickup. Her tail began wagging as they approached, one paw swiping the air to shake hands.

Oh, what a sweet old dog, Beth said as she reached in and rubbed the dog's ears, her eyes filmy and a muzzle turning white with age. Bet you don't make him, or is it her, ride in the back of your pickup.

No way, Harry said, as he gently tugged the old dog's right ear. Beth, meet Ginger. Ginger, meet Beth. Ginger rides up front, doncha, girl? He smiled as he watched Beth lean in and let Ginger lick her cheek. Another plus, he thought, she likes dogs.

Yeah, she's a sweet old girl, likes everyone, sometimes too much. You watch, if I let her, she goes over to greet everyone who pulls in. Beth felt her heart tug as Harry opened the door and gently lifted the old dog and put her on the ground.

They both looked up when a blue pickup truck pulled in and parked a space away from Harry's truck. Standing a little behind Beth, Harry recognized the truck and the male driver from the Spruce Park Café. Like then, the driver was wearing a Stetson pulled low over aviator sunglasses, and he didn't speak or nod a greeting as most people did at the post office. Stepping out of his truck, he saw Ginger and hesitated. Beth noticed the scowl on his face when Ginger began to walk over to him, tail wagging.

Keep your dog away from me, the man said, looking angrily at Beth as he slammed the door of the pickup.

Oh, she's friendly. Just wants to say hello, Beth said, but she could tell being friendly didn't matter to this scowling individual, and what's behind those glasses?

Look, lady, if you don't mind, I'm not in the mood to deal with your dog today, okay. So keep it on a leash like you're supposed to.

As the old dog ambled closer, he stopped and pulled back a booted foot. Harry stepped around Beth, leaned down, and laid his hand on Ginger's back. Still wagging her tail, Ginger stopped and looked up at Harry as he straightened to his full height.

That's my dog, punk. You kick her and you'll be dealin' with me, he said evenly.

Beth watched as the stranger blanched, surprise and fear evident in his uncertain posture. She almost smiled. *Just what that mean sonofabitch deserved.*

Gary Ray Kemp, fixed in Harry's unblinking stare, hesitated, then turned away and walked quickly into the post office.

Can you believe that guy? Harry said, not taking his eyes off Gary until the door closed behind him. He reached down and rubbed the old dog's ears with one hand as she licked the palm of the other.

You really nailed him, Harry. What a creep. A broad smile. Maybe I should call you Dirty Harry.

He looked up and shook his head, still thinking about the punk. She could tell he didn't get it.

You know the tough cop, Dirty Harry, Harry Callahan, in the Clint Eastwood movies, the guy who has his pistol drawn and dares the thug to make his move. Remember that line, 'Go ahead, make my day?'

Harry, still distracted, smiled and nodded, Oh yeah, sure.

Cool, soft-spoken, and fearless. God help the person who messes with this guy, was running through her mind as she said, What an incredible bully! I've seen plenty, and most of them are behind bars. Who would want to hurt this friendly old dog? There's something very strange about people who don't like dogs.

Harry liked her toughness, her cool. No Pollyanna. Yeah, I agree. What's that old Tom T. Hall song? Remember, somethin'about old dogs, children, and watermelon wine?

Beth nodded with a smile, stooping to put her arm around the dog, leaning close enough for her to lick her cheek.

People like that are hard to understand, Harry said. I've seen him around, a couple of times at the Spruce Park Café. Always alone. You can see why. Someone said he works in the park for the trail rides concessionaire. He shook his head. Yeah, I think he's trouble. Something weird about him that I can't quite … Anyway, let's get that coffee, he said, flashing a smile. And, hey, what was that about seeing lots of bullies behind bars?

Oh, I'll tell you about my sordid past over coffee. Some of it anyway, she said, but her thoughts were on Harry and his past as she rubbed Ginger's head. He was different from anyone she had known. *Dirty Harry, I love it.*

* * * * *

It was to be the first of almost daily coffees they shared together over the next two weeks. Beth looked forward to everyone. A retired lieutenant colonel in the Marines who served in Vietnam, an experience he didn't say much about, Harry had done so many interesting, different things, and he was a fascinating storyteller. As an amateur historian and self-taught archeologist, he'd tramped the banks of Montana's rivers and streams, locating and identifying little-known campsites of the Lewis and Clark expedition. With a metal detector, he'd explored the ruins of old whiskey forts in Alberta where he found graves, bullets, shell casings and buttons from the jackets of the Royal Canadian Mounties who struggled to control the whiskey runners. He had countless stories about adventures in the mountain ranges and on the prairies of Montana. Meeting Harry Dawkins at the post office, she realized, had become the most important part of her day. He deserves a biography, she decided, maybe one I could write. Harry Dawkins was the most attractive man she had met in a long time. Maybe ever.

She was thinking about Harry, instead of the words on the laptop screen, early one evening as she sat in the living room of her townhouse, sipping a glass of wine, trying without much success, to write a chapter of a book on vengeance and justice, drawn from her experiences as a prosecutor. It was no use. This was not a day for writing. When Rimsky-Korsakov's *Scheherazade* finished on the CD player, she looked at her watch, then printed out what she had written that day, all of it uninspired, and logged off the laptop. It was five thirty in the afternoon, a little too quiet, and outside a light drizzle was dripping off the eaves and puddling on the deck. She switched on the radio for *All Things Considered*, thinking West Glacier's a beautiful place, but there's not a lot going on for a person like me, accustomed to city life and a demanding career. She poured another glass of *pinot grigio* and thought about her going-away dinner with some old friends at *El Mezon del Cobre* a few days before she headed north. The *enchiladas de camaron* that evening, so delicious with an icy margarita; the *Mariachis Azteca* so cheerful, and Monica, with that voice to die for, singing *Sabor a Mi* with Charlie, that handsome devil, at their table. She looked out at low hanging gray clouds over snowcapped peaks in the distance. Gloomy. Admit it, she said to herself, you're bored and lonely. Maybe this was a big mistake.

In Tucson, at this time of day she'd still be working, always until six thirty or seven. She would tune into the later edition of the *All Things*

Considered on the drive home, maybe with a stop at Miguel's for a drink, then a microwave dinner while she read over legal briefs and trial depositions for the next day until she got sleepy. Too busy to be lonely.

That was history now. The past. Her career as an attorney was over; even the adjunct professorship at the law school was in doubt. She had some regrets about retiring early but, in some ways, it was a relief. She knew she had compromised herself ethically and legally as an attorney, but deep down she felt she had done the right thing.

Those were her thoughts when the phone rang. She was startled. The phone that drove her to distraction in Tucson was dormant in West Glacier. And she was beginning to miss it. She nearly spilled her wine reaching for the phone. It was Harry. The first time he had called.

I have an idea I wanted to try out on you, he said after the pleasantries. How 'bout takin' in a movie tomorrow? *Fargo's* playin' in Whitefish, supposed to be funny. Maybe the late afternoon matinee and get a bite to eat afterward at Tupelo Grill. Before she could answer, he continued, Now I know it's short notice, so I understand if you have other plans.

Other plans, are you kidding? Harry, that's a wonderful idea. I'd love to. What time?

———•◆•———

8

---◆---

Friday, June 29. A warm evening and Freda's was packed. Gary Ray Kemp sat at the end of the bar near the door, pretending to watch a baseball game on the television above him. He was surrounded by a boisterous crowd and the beer was flowing. Matt Margolis was the center of attention, smiling, suntanned, and hard-muscled. And Vicki was sitting beside him. Their body language said she was his, and Gary hated him for it.

Hey, barkeep, Matt yelled above the chatter and music to his friend behind the bar. You in the dirty apron, start trotting, my friends here are thirsty. Lay down that smelly rag you're holding and draw that pitcher of Moose Drool I ordered five minutes ago.

Five minutes ago, Henry? I have no memory of that order, the bartender called back.

Everyone in the place knew the bartender, a skinny young man about Matt's age, with a ponytail and a goatee that didn't quite make it, was part of the routine. It was a familiar one with the regulars who guffawed as he and Matt mimicked scenes from the film, *Barfly,* the 1980s cult classic about alcoholics that's so bad it becomes satire.

I distinctly remember ordering that pitcher, Tully, Matt said. What are you out of brew, or has that lobotomy finally taken hold?

Oh, so you really need a drink?

Yeah, Tully, like a spider needs a fly.

Smiles and ripples of laughter spread through the crowd as conversations stopped and heads turned to enjoy the routine with its ongoing adaptations. Nightly entertainment was another reason Freda's was a popular place to hang out.

Why don't you stop drinking, Henry? Anybody can be a drunk.

No, no, you got it wrong, Tully. Anybody can be a non-drunk. It takes a special talent like mine to be a drunk. It takes endurance, and endurance is more important than truth. You might say, my friend, that I am unacquainted with the torments of ambivalence on that subject.

Is that so, Henry? the bartender said, tilting his head back with an aristocratic sniff. When you're drinking, let me say that there is a lava flow of moral dinginess that curdles about you, symbolizing everything that disgusts me—obviousness, unoriginal macho concupiscence, the pretentious inelegance of a posturing lady's man.

Lava flow? Concupiscence? Lady's man? The plethora of metaphors is, indeed, dazzling and, I might add, not very perceptive, don't you think, Wanda? he said, putting his arm around Vicki's shoulder, drawing her close with a lascivious leer.

No, you're wrong about the lady's man, barkeep, Vicki said. A smile as she reached up and squeezed the back of Matt's neck. He's all mine now. There was laughter and applause as the crowd roared its approval.

Everyone, except Gary. He took a sip of beer, eyes fixed on the television screen.

After the laughter died down and people returned to their own conversations, Matt and Vicki resumed theirs with the three couples who shared the two small tables they had pulled together near the bar. Gary kept his eyes on the television, but turned his head toward them to listen.

Yeah, Matt said, still smiling, Vicki and me are gonna go backpacking after Labor Day when the tourists are gone and things quiet down. Into the real backcountry, right, Vicki?

Vicki smiled and nodded, then tilted her head back and drained a glass.

Where you going? asked a plain-looking young woman in khaki hiking shorts with Teva tan lines on her feet.

Morning Star Lake, Vicki said. Matt said it's beautiful. It's like way over on the eastside. I've never been there. Have you?

Oh yeah, it's a cool hike and the lake's beautiful. Great place to camp.

Well, that's just the first day and night, Matt said. Beautiful spot, good fishin'. Vicki smiled and kissed his cheek as he put his arm around her and squeezed her shoulder. I'm going to teach California girl here how to catch and fry tasty, wild cutthroat trout in butter and fresh chives we'll pick on the slopes above the lake.

Gary's jaw muscles tightened, his eyes still fixed on the television he wasn't watching.

Day two, Matt continued, we're gonna take the trail past Pitamakin Lake and up over Pitamakin Pass and down the other side to Old Man Lake.

That's at the upper end of the Dry Fork, right, down below Flinsch Peak? one of the other guys at the table said.

Yeah, man. We'll spend the second night right there, right there, man, in the shadows of Flinsch Peak and Rising Wolf, Matt said, referring to the imposing peak and massive, red-hued mountain that dominate the skyline between the Dry Fork and Two Medicine valleys.

Too cool, Vicki said, smiling and clapping her hands quietly. Can't wait. I love that Two Medicine area. When Karen and Sue and I hiked to Cobalt Lake last week, like it was so beautiful.

Excuse me. Barkeep, barkeep, *cerveza por favor, senor.* We're ready for another pitcher, Matt called out. I can't keep up with the lushes at this table.

Isn't that the trail, Cobalt Lake, where they think a grizzly killed a guy they never found a while back? one of their male friends asked.

Yeah, it's the same trail, a young man at the bar who was listening to their conversation said, but that guy who disappeared was gonna climb Sinopah, so they think he was bushwhackin', looking for that route up through the cliffs on the back side—you know, it's way off the trail to Cobalt Lake and Two Medicine Pass—and probably stumbled into a bear. At least, that's what the park rangers suppose happened, because they've never found any trace of him.

Yeah, I know, but I heard that guy might've lied about climbin' Sinopah, and left his car there in the parking lot at Two Med to make it look like he had, someone at the end of the bar said. You know, like I heard that it was a setup. He just took off to avoid bad debts and a lot of issues he had with his parents back in Minnesota, or someplace.

Yeah, I heard that, too, the bartender said. Could be, but I don't think so. I bet a bear got him. Speaking of which, you guys better watch out for Melvin over there. Everyone says he likes to hang out on those big avalanche chutes on the north slope of Rising Wolf.

Who's Melvin? Vicki asked.

Who's Melvin? the bartender asked, an incredulous look on his face as he looked up from filling pint glasses of Full Sail Ale. You mean you've never heard of Melvin and you're gonna hike to Morning Star? Whoa, daddy! Melvin is probably the biggest goddamn grizzly anyone has seen in years. People say he goes at least—repeat, at least—eight hundred pounds and stands about eight feet tall on his hind legs. He is one monster bear but, as far as anyone knows, he's stayed out of trouble, you know, not killin' any cattle or sheep on the reservation, or botherin' hikers. Yet. Even so, I sure as hell would not want to run into him.

The topic continued to generate interest far beyond the table. Even the couple shooting pool stopped to listen. Gary was one of only a few in the bar who wasn't turned around looking at the table where Matt, Vicki, and their friends were sitting.

Doesn't bother hikers? What about all the hikers who just disappeared in the park? Maybe he's the reason, someone at the bar chimed in. Maybe that's the bear that got the guy you're talking about, the one who disappeared climbing Sinopah.

Who knows? And how about that poor guy who bought it in early May over there on the Scenic Point trail, the bartender said. Amazing that it happened on that trail. Open, good visibility, except for a couple of stretches right before you break out of the krummholz near the ridge.

Krummholz? What the hell is krummholz? someone asked.

That's that thick tangled subalpine scrub that grows in patches right up at the edge of the tree line, the bartender replied. It's really old trees, matted together, that never grow more than a few feet high because of the harsh climate and short growing season.

Krummholz. Is that spelled as it sounds? k-r-u-m-m-h-o-l-z? said a young man with wire-rim glasses who looked up from the paperback he was reading at a table near the dart board. Sounds German so I assume its spelled with a k rather than a c.

Correct. It is with a k, the bartender replied.

Thank you. Well, how about that? I've finally learned something in here for a change.

Krummholz, that's what they called me in graduate school, a tiny, young Asian woman in an orange safari shirt, khaki hiking shorts, and boots said laughing as she pulled a chair up to join the others at Matt and Vicki's table.

Krummholz? That's funny. Why? Where was that? Teva Tan asked.

Because I'm short. Missoula, U of M Forestry School.

That figures, Matt said as he put his arm around her and gave her a hug. Only a bunch of chauvinistic loggers with academic pretensions would call a beautiful young thing like you, krummholz, Mia. Then he returned to the previous topic. Yeah, Scenic Point. That's a popular hike. Lots of people do it. Families, kids. Weird. Very strange that it happened there, but you never can tell about grizzlies.

And not only was that guy killed, the bear and her cubs ate the poor bastard, the bartender said.

Oh, my God, said a tanned young woman with sunglasses pushed back on a thick mop of brown, sun-streaked hair. A college friend of Vicki's, she had just flown in from San Diego the day before. Vicki, are you sure you guys want to hike over in that place? Like bears and all? Like sleeping in a tent? Not me. Too scary.

As the bartender slid the pitcher of beer they ordered toward the edge of the bar, Matt walked over and reached across between Gary and the person sitting next to him to pick it up. When he did, the pitcher tilted and beer splashed down on the bar and spilled over on Gary's leg.

Hey, man, Gary said angrily, wiping the beer from his Wranglers, watch what the fuck you're doin'.

Easy, fellah, easy. Lighten up. It was an accident. I'm sorry, I'm sorry, Matt said, as he laid a ten-dollar bill on the bar. Here let me buy you a beer. Barkeep, barkeep, he called, trying to defuse the situation, bring this gentleman a draft of his choice with my apologies. And please, sir, give him a clean glass this time.

Nervous laughter rippled through the crowd.

Aren't you just too fuckin' funny, Gary said, as he looked up into Matt's face. I don't want your fuckin' beer, asshole. He pushed back from the bar and stood up. The laughter subsided quickly as all eyes turned toward the two men facing one another at the bar. But Gary didn't swing.

You're just a laugh a minute, aren't you? he said as he picked up his change, turned, and walked out. All eyes were on Matt.

Whoa, did you see that? Where's that comin' from? Matt said as he turned to set the pitcher down at the table.

Yeah, weird dude, the bartender said as he wiped the spilled beer from the bar. Been coming in pretty regular lately. Doesn't say much. Dresses cowboy, the belt buckle, boots, and all. I think he works at the stables. You notice his eyes?

No, man, I was watchin' his hands, waitin' for a sucker punch. I thought sure he was gonna swing. What about his eyes?

Dead. Empty, no expression, sorta like that kid Damien in…what was that horror flick? Anyway, I'd give that guy plenty of room.

Hmmm, plenty of room you say? Matt said, feigning seriousness as he slipped back into the *Barfly* dialogue. He was all about having a good time and didn't want to lose a minute of it for any reason. I give everyone plenty of room, Tully. You see, it's not that I don't like people. It's just that I feel better when they're not around.

That might be the best line in the whole movie, a muscular young man in a purple *Wilderness Guides* T-shirt said, as he set his empty glass down. I gotta go. See you guys later. By the way, Matt, he said, patting Matt on the back. He's right. I would give that guy plenty of room, if I were you. He looks like a serial killer to me. Then he laughed.

Okay, okay, he's probably just having a bad day, Matt said. Back to bears and beer, or beers and bears.

For sure. Bears are more interesting than that jerk, Vicki's friend Kim said. What an asshole.

You have a point, Kim, you know about bears bein' dangerous. Everybody knows grizzlies are always a risk you take in the Glacier back-country, Matt said. But let me ask you this. You got sharks swimmin' around where you guys surf off La Jolla, right? A Great White nailed a guy off Solana Beach, right? So are you and your surfin' friends gonna stop surfin'? Not likely. Life is full of risks. Avoid risk and you'll live a boring life.

Hey, you got that right, bro, the boy with the wire-rimmed glasses and paperback called out. I had a professor at Berkeley who said the same thing—the greatest risk is no risk at all.

You went to Berkeley, Knapweed? someone at the bar said over his shoulder. Wow, I'm impressed.

So okay, Matt, where are you guys goin' after Old Man? You hikin' out the Dry Fork back to Two Med? one of their friends asked.

No, man, on day three we're gonna retrace our steps and hike back up the switchbacks to Pitamakin Pass and follow that ridgeline trail about three miles south across the Divide to Dawson Pass. Then maybe, if we have time and Vicki feels up to it, he squeezed her shoulder again, maybe we'll climb Flinsch Peak.

Come on, man, a young man sitting across the table said. You guys are gonna to be pretty tired to be climbin' Flinsch Peak. Especially since you'll still have that knee-bustin' four-mile descent from Dawson Pass to the boat dock at Two Med.

Yeah, maybe you're right, Matt said. Anyway, we'll see how we feel. But, I don't know. When Flinsch Peak's right there, and it's not that hard to do, seems like we oughta do it. But that'll be Vicki's call. Whadda you think, love?

Watch it, Vicki, someone called out. The guy's an animal on climbs.

I think I'll see how tired I am when we get there. How's that? she said, as she looked into his eyes with a soft I-want-you glint and gave his shoulder a gentle squeeze. There was no doubt in anyone's mind that Vicki Hathaway had fallen for Matt Margolis.

Anyway, Matt said, either way we'll be sure to meet you guys that afternoon at the other end of the lake when we take the tour boat back. Have to check the times. They cut back the schedule after Labor Day. Probably around five, I think. Don't want to miss that dinner and cold beer at Serrano's. We'll be ready for that, right, Vicki? He smiled and kissed her on the cheek.

* * * * *

Driving back to his cabin on the Quarter Circle Road that night, Gary's anger was consuming. That wise-ass, cunt-lickin' sonofabitch is gonna get his, he said aloud to himself as he smacked the top of the steering wheel with his fist. When he got inside, he took a shower and went to bed, but couldn't sleep. He turned on the overhead light, got out his map of the park, and spread it out on the Formica table. With a yellow felt marker, he traced the trails they planned to take. He thought for a minute, drumming his fingers on the table. The best opportunity to kill him and capture her would be at Morning Star Lake. It was remote and, in September, it was unlikely there would be any other hikers camping there, especially in mid-week. He circled the spot on the map and almost smiled. Now all he needed was the date. He got back in bed, turned out the light, and was soon asleep.

———◆◆◆———

9

---◆---

Sunday morning, July 8. Gary had the day off. He had worked a long day on the Fourth and, the next day, Monday was going to be another long one, but one he didn't mind, taking a pack string up to Sperry Chalet. He arose at dawn. After a candy bar and a cup of instant coffee, he went out to the corral next to the cabin, saddled and bridled his buckskin gelding, and led him over to the trailer hitched behind his pickup. The horse was excited and anxious to go, like a thoroughbred at the starting gate. Easy, Buck, he said as he led him into the trailer. Gary held his long dark tail away as he closed the trailer door and bolted it. Then he checked the hitch to be sure it was secure, and climbed into his pickup.

He followed US Highway 2 nearly sixty miles around the southern boundary of the park over Marias Pass to the community of East Glacier. There he flipped on his turn signal and turned left onto Route 49 as it cut between the East Glacier Lodge on the left and the Amtrak station on the right, and meandered through a tiny village of Mom-and-Pop rental cabins, gift shops, and cafes with hand-painted signs, then into open country. He followed the narrow, winding blacktop north twelve miles through wind-scorched aspen forest and open range of the Blackfeet Reservation to Kiowa Junction where he turned north on US 89. Fifteen minutes later, he turned left on a gravel road marked by a small metal-staked sign, CUT BANK RANGER STATION, and followed it four miles to the park boundary.

On the way in on the curving, lightly traveled road—dusty when its dry, puddled and rutted when its wet—he noticed a forsaken-looking ranch on the left with a hand-painted TRAIL RIDES sign nailed to a log gate that opened to a rutted road that ran down to Cut Bank Creek then disappeared in the trees. Fucking loser Indians, he thought. But he wondered if it might be a place to board his horses. He decided to check it out on the way back. A couple of miles farther, after he had braked for cattle wandering across the road, he slowed as he drove by the park entrance sign and the ranger station, a small log cabin set back in a grove of aspen. It looked deserted. No fees collected at this remote entrance. He drove another quarter-mile and parked next to the trailhead sign near an empty campground. He unloaded his horse, checked the saddlebags to be sure he had what he needed, cinched up the latigo, and swung up into the saddle.

The trail followed the creek west through rolling meadows with scattered groves of aspen before giving out to a thick forest of jack pine, spruce, and Douglas fir. To the south he looked up beyond the tree line to the talus slopes and cliffs of massive Bad Marriage Mountain. Four miles and an hour and a half later, he dismounted and watered his horse at Atlantic Creek, a desolate-looking backcountry campsite partially visible through the trees. An orange warning sign, GRIZZLY FREQUENTING THIS AREA—BE ALERT, was posted on a tree, but the trail was still open. He looked around before walking his horse to a hitching rail and checking out the empty campground, muddy and puddled from recent rain. The fire pit was black and muddy. It was obvious no one had camped here lately. A good sign, he thought. There was no one around now, and there would probably be no one after Labor Day either.

He walked back to his horse and pulled out the map he carried tucked in his belt behind his back and spread it out across the saddle. The trail forked at right angles south to Morning Star Lake and west to Medicine Grizzly Lake. With his index finger, he traced the trail to Morning Star Lake. It was easy to get turned around in unfamiliar territory and he wanted to be sure he took the right route. Confident of his direction, he mounted up and turned the buckskin south past the waterfalls at Atlantic Creek and followed the trail as it wandered through the timber in patches of shadow and sunlight until it began a gentle ascent through a broad open valley. Except for the squeak of the saddle and the clump of hooves on soft ground, it was quiet. To the east he could see the maroon argillite cliffs and ridges of Eagle Plume and Red Mountains. The gray eminence of Medicine Grizzly Peak dominated the view west.

Wild, lonely backcountry, he thought, feeling a twinge of anxiety brought on by the scale and immensity of his surroundings as the trail wound along the western edge of the valley through thick alder and cow parsnip bushes that reached to his saddle and limited his visibility. Bear country. That was on his mind when he noticed a large dark form ahead in a meadow near a small stand of aspen. The warning sign and big grizzly flashed through his mind and ramped up his heart rate. The stories at Freda's a week before and in the newspapers since the Scenic Point mauling had gotten him thinking. He wasn't worried about black bears, but given the open country and its size, this had to be a grizzly. He watched and waited, at first sensing movement and then not being sure. He reached back and took his binoculars out of the saddlebag, then urged his horse forward a short distance to get a better look. He'd left his rifle in the truck, knowing he couldn't chance an arrest if he happened to encounter a ranger. Now he was regretting it. He waited and watched. There was no movement. Just a big rock, he decided, and breathed a sigh of relief, for the first time noticing the four waterfalls that fell from high cliffs behind him, but missing a huge grizzly standing motionless on its hind legs in a stream below one of them, its eyes fixed on him.

After climbing a forested ridge, the trees opened up and he got his first glimpse of Morning Star Lake, a turquoise-blue gem surrounded by subalpine meadows and forest with a backdrop of high cliffs and ridges in every direction. He rode slowly, pausing to take in the terrain, as the trail traced its eastern shoreline. A flotilla of mergansers bobbing on the surface fluttered away as he approached. When he reached the campground on the far end of the lake, he swung his right leg over the buckskin's neck and slid out of the saddle and checked the time. It had taken him just about three hours, walking the horse the whole way. He guessed it would take *them* about the same time on foot. He tied the buckskin to the hitching rail and took a drink from his canteen.

The campground was empty. He walked around, surveying the area, making mental notes about the layout of the campground set in thick forest that opened up at the edge of the lake. To the west sheer cliffs rose from talus slopes streaked with gullies of crimson, lavender, and yellow wildflowers to the rimrock of the Continental Divide etched against a blue sky thousands of feet above. There was a lot for him to consider. They had to think they were alone. He took off his Stetson and ran his fingers back through his hair, looking toward the pass, again wondering about other campers approaching from that direction. *Not likely, mid-week after Labor Day.* If there were, he decided his fallback plan would be an ambush the next day at their campsite at Old Man Lake. He looked at his watch. No time to check that out today.

He walked to a bare stretch of ground near a fire pit, knelt down, and spread out his map. With a finger, he traced the trail as it continued south climbing a steep, forested ridge another two miles to Pitamakin Lake. He folded the map and got back on his horse to look for a concealed campsite where he could spend the night before the couple arrived. A quarter mile down the trail he found the spot, a small clearing not far off the trail, but concealed by the scrub pine and alpine fir trees that surrounded it on three sides and blocked the view from the lake. It could only be seen by someone descending north from Pitamakin Lake, an unlikely event after Labor Day.

A short distance away, as he returned along the trail back to the lake, he found the other site he was looking for. After returning to the campground, he looked over the four campsites. He was sure they would choose the one that fronted on a pebbled beach. Across a shallow inlet from the campsite, he noticed a thicket of willow bushes reached the shoreline at the mouth of a small stream. Perfect for an ambush. He could wait there unseen and have a direct line of fire to the beach area and the presumed campsite.

There were still a few hours of daylight left when he got back to the Cut Bank Creek trailhead and the still empty campground. He fed his horse a ration of oats before loading him back into the trailer, checked the hitch again, and took a long pull of water draining his canteen before climbing into the pickup. A lot on his mind. First a place nearby to board the horses.

* * * * *

Trail Rides hung at an angle from one of the posts of a crude gate built of logs. A rack of bleached-white elk antlers was nailed to the cross beam above. He shifted into first-gear as he turned and steered down the rutted, rocky road that turned and twisted through a meadow of buffalo grass, rocks, mudholes, and scattered stands of cottonwood and aspen, bent and twisted southward by the relentless north wind. It was slow going down the half-mile slope to the creek. When he crossed the creek, water flowing at hubcap depth, the old Dodge groaned, wheels churning on the loose rock, as he slammed it into four-wheel drive. A loud scraping sound. The trailer hitch dragging on hard ground. He heard his horse stumbling as the trailer rocked from side to side and let off the accelerator. Then he eased the truck forward, water, mud, and gravel splashing and spraying as it bumped and fishtailed up the steep embankment on the other side. When he reached level ground above the creek, he stopped and got out to check his horse. Hey, Buck, you okay? Sure you are, he said, patting its rear.

The road smoothed out into two rounded tracks through prairie grass that brushed against the chassis of the pickup before entering a small patch of forest. When he reached the clearing at the other end, he could see two dilapidated, singlewide trailers, leaning with the wind, old tires scattered across their frayed aluminum roofs to hold them down. A rawhide-colored teepee stood at the far edge of the clearing, a dark profile of a wolf howling at a crescent moon painted above the entrance. A pack of dogs, barking and growling with hackles raised, rushed out to meet him. The uproar continued as he pulled to a stop beside an old wringer washing machine lying on its side next to a large white propane tank that sat on an angle near the front door of one the trailers.

Gary sat with the engine idling, looking things over. The two trailers were joined together by a lean-to constructed of rough-cut boards below a roof of corrugated sheet metal that rattled and hummed like an off-balance fan when the wind blew. At one end of the trailers, a large satellite dish lay bent and twisted on the ground, another casualty of the relentless wind. A corral and loading ramp of wired-together lodgepole logs stood off to the side at the edge of the clearing right where the ground started to rise steeply through layers of exposed rock toward a high ridge. A shed, scoured gray by the elements, leaned to one side not far from the corral, its double doors propped open with two rocks. The hulks of four old vehicles completed the scene, a car and three pickups— rusted, hoods up, doors open or missing, scavenged parts scattered on the ground around them. Another, an old faded green Ford F100 pickup, he guessed about 1980, looked like it might run.

As yelping dogs circled his truck, Gary broke into a sweat, his mind flashing back to his childhood. Eight years old, lying on his back, screaming, a large dog tearing flesh from his forearms as he tried to protect his face and neck. Pit Bulls and Rottweilers. It seemed like everyone in that fucking trailer park had one chained or fenced by their trailers. This one got loose and would have killed him, had an old man not beaten it off with a rake. He'd feared and hated dogs ever since. Never saw one on a highway that he didn't swerve to hit. Those were his thoughts when the door to the trailer swung open and a tall Indian stepped out, his long hair in braids.

Hey, Bo, Kip, Suzy, Tonto, get over here, goddammit, the Indian in a soiled white T-shirt called to the dogs. Crazy. Got Blue Heeler in three of 'em, he called over the ruckus, looking briefly at his visitor. You lost? The barking began to subside and stopped as the dogs circled him, panting, tails wagging.

Is it safe to get outta my truck? You got 'em under control? Gary said, nodding toward the dogs through a window partly rolled down.

Yeah, it's okay. When they know I'm okay with whoever it is, they don't bother no one.

Gary turned off the ignition, opened the door, and stepped down cautiously from his truck, eyes fixed on the dogs.

Noticing his fear, the Indian said, Ornery. Gotta watch 'em around strangers. Usually just go for your heels, nippin', but you can't never be sure about Heelers. They'll try to herd dinosaurs. But not old Tonto here, he said, as he scratched behind the ears of an old black Labrador that pressed against his leg, wagging its tail.

I saw your sign on the road and was wonderin' whether you boarded horses.

The Indian ignored the question, looking down at the dog as he pulled on a worn flannel shirt that was hanging on the doorknob and rolled the frayed cuffs to his elbows. He likes everybody, doncha, old boy? He swatted a mosquito on his arm before he looked over at Gary. Can you believe some sonofabitch dumped this poor old guy out on the highway? Watched 'em drive off. Coyotes or a cougar would've had him the first night. He shook his head as he stroked the old dog's head. Special place in hell for people like that. He could tell the stranger didn't like dogs, wasn't interested in what he was saying, and that's why he stayed with it.

Gary interrupted, Yeah, that's too bad about the dog, thinking fucking prairie niggers talk in circles about nothing, never get to the point. With an eye ever on the dogs, he glanced at four horses as they moved close, curious about the commotion, standing shoulder to shoulder against the plank gate that opened into a pasture that stretched back a quarter mile to the edge of the trees. He could see it was good pasture, probably at least fifty acres, with water and plenty of grass, fenced with barbed wire. The location near the park and seclusion were perfect. Just what he had in mind.

Yeah, I can board here, the Indian said. I'm pretty much outta the trail ride business. Season's too short, people fall off horses, try to sue you, not worth it. But I can board. Got plenty of good grass and clear water in the creek. How many? Just the one? What kinda time you lookin' at? Week? Month?

I got two, the one in the trailer and another. It'd only be for about a week, late August, the week before Labor Day. I'd be pickin' 'em up that weekend, Labor Day weekend. What would you be askin' a week?

Usually get fifty bucks a week a horse, he lied. He hadn't boarded a horse in a long time.

How about seventy-five for two and I let you use my trailer if you need it? Gary had noticed an old horse trailer sitting at an odd angle near the loading ramp of the corral. One wheel was missing and it looked like the axle was broken.

Seventy-five a week for both horses?

Yeah, and you can use the trailer while I'm gone if you need it.

The Indian rubbed his chin, looking down at the stone he was rolling back and forth with the toe of his boot, and didn't say anything. Gary was about ready to agree to the original offer when the Indian sighed, I, well … I … Okay, I guess … I guess I can live with that. Week's cash, right? Up front. If it's more than a week, the rest when you come back to pick 'em up. He chuckled. Yeah, straight cash. I don't take credit cards or checks.

Gary forced a glassy smile, thinking *really?*

Cash. Sure. No problem. Oh, another thing, he said. When I pick 'em up, I'll be goin' back into the park on some research I'm doin'. I'm gonna need some place to park my truck while I'm gone. Could I leave it here with the trailer? Park it out of your way some place, like over in those trees, he said motioning to the trees at the far end of the pasture. I can pay you extra when I get back if you want, thinking *I'm never coming back to pick up that fucking truck*.

The Indian knew he was lying. Why wouldn't he just leave the truck and trailer in the parking area at the trailhead, or at the ranger station? Especially if he's working for the Park Service. He told Gary that it was a deal on both the horses and parking the truck and trailer.

But like I said, I'm gonna need the cash up front. That gonna be a problem? By the way, what's your name? the Indian said, looking directly at Gary. People call me Keno.

Up front. Sure. No problem. Oh yeah, Gary replied, looking away. My name's Gary.

They didn't shake hands. Keno could tell this stranger was hiding something behind those aviator sunglasses. But, what the hell, he was used to dealing with people he didn't trust. Besides, he had more important things on his mind.

* * * * *

When Gary Ray Kemp drove back to West Glacier that evening, he was excited. The sun reflecting off the crack in the windshield made him squint, but he didn't mind. The day had gone well. It wouldn't be long now. Things were beginning to fall into place.

10

———◆———

Sunday evening, July 8. It was early evening when Gary Ray Kemp made the turn under the railroad overpass into West Glacier on his return from the scouting trip to Morning Star Lake. Just across the highway, Harry Dawkins and Beth Blanchard were pulling into the parking lot of the Belton Chalet where they were going to have dinner. Coffees after picking up their mail in the mornings had expanded to a movie and dinner in Whitefish, and a hike the day before on the Highline Trail to the Granite Park Chalet. No real romance yet, just nice times together, Beth noted in her diary, but it couldn't be far off.

She was all smiles on the short ride from her townhouse on the golf course to the Belton in Harry's pickup. Somehow she never imagined dating a man who drove a truck with a gun rack in the rear window and a Marine Corps decal on the rear bumper. What a kick, she thought.

Harry was dressed in his customary pressed Levis and Western boots with a tan shirt under a soft, dark leather vest. She wore dark slacks and a silk maroon top with a Navajo squash-blossom necklace that matched her Hopi inlaid silver-and-turquoise earrings. She poked him in the ribs when he looked over with a smile and told her she'd be the best-looking lady at the restaurant.

Harry parked and came around to open the door for her. Pretty old place isn't it? he said nodding toward the four rustic wood-frame and native-stone buildings.

Yes, it sure is. I've been wanting to come here, she said.

Yeah, a few years ago the place was a wreck. Then someone bought it and did a complete restoration. Now it looks pretty much just like it did when it was first built by the Great Northern Railway nearly a hundred years ago.

Yes, charming. The stonework is beautiful, and I love that veranda that stretches across the front.

How about the two cabins there between the restaurant and the hotel? See the names carved on those wooden signs above the porches?

Oh, that's clever. Lewis and Clark, she said smiling.

They walked up the plank steps and paused on the broad veranda where diners sat at café tables in the fading rays of evening sunshine. A sculpted wood railing extended across the front and around one side of the restaurant. Beth was admiring the hanging flowerpots and weathered antlers spaced across the front of the building when they heard the whistle of an approaching train. Moments later a Burlington Northern Santa Fe freight rumbled into view and rolled past, stopping conversation as it headed west to Seattle, the end of the line. In the distance to the northwest, they could see the dark hulk of Apgar Mountain backlit by the sun sinking behind patches of high clouds streaked with watercolor hues of lavender and peach. Harry pointed out the fire lookout, barely visible on its forested peak. Maybe we could take a hike up there sometime, he said. It's only a few miles and it's probably the best view in the park of Lake MacDonald and the Livingston Range. Across the valley, east of the lookout, the Belton Hills defined the rest of the horizon, the ridgeline etched in the clear air as if by an artist with a fine-point pen.

As they entered the restaurant, the old wooden floors creaked with each step. A smiling hostess escorted them to the window table Harry had requested. Through the entrance to the bar, they could see an old river-rock fireplace and a couple playing checkers at a low table in front of it. As Beth arranged the napkin on her lap, a rainbow spectrum of refracted sunlight shone through antique glass windowpanes and played across the white tablecloth. Harry pointed out the colorful display of hand-painted serving plates and the Winold Reiss prints of Blackfeet Indians, painted nearly a hundred years before, that adorned the white plaster and dark wainscot paneled walls.

So what do you think? he smiled. Do you like it? Is this okay?

Oh, Harry, it's lovely. I'm so glad you thought of this, she said as she reached over and patted his arm. He noticed the way her fingers lingered with the smile. It felt almost electric.

While Harry was looking at the wine list, Beth watched as one by one, tables were being filled by an assortment of people. She tried to imagine where they were from. She guessed that the two forty-something couples attired in current L.L. Bean fashion and unscuffed outdoor footwear were probably big city guests of the Chalet who took the Amtrak in from Seattle, Minneapolis, Chicago, or someplace like that. Since Montana had been discovered in the Escapes supplement of the *New York Times*, the Belton Chalet had regained its status as a destination resort.

I guess Montana's changing with all the new growth and development, she said.

Yeah, sure is, he said as he put the wine list down and arranged the napkin on his lap. I guess it was inevitable, once it was discovered by the celebrities. But I'm not sure it's for the better. Hard to say. When I was growin' up here, the timber companies ran things. Those guys looked at old growth forests and all they saw was plywood and two-by-fours. Now it's the big developers rearranging the landscape to build eight-thousand-square-foot trophy homes for these corporate fat cats, with more money than they know what to do with, to spend two weeks a year here to play golf at some goddamn country club. That's as close to nature as a lot of them get, ridin' around in a golf cart, talkin' on their cell phones. Yeah, in a way, you can see what set off people like Ted Kaczynski and these Earth First types.

Ted Kaczynski, the Unabomber?

Yeah, lived like a hermit in a shack he built down near Lincoln. He might have been a troubled guy, a little crazy maybe, like they tried to make him out to be in the press, but what really set him off was when they started clear-cuttin' the forests around his cabin. He just wanted to be left alone. A lot of people in this part of the country can relate to that. He stopped to smile. Like me.

And me, the waitress, who had just come to take their order, said with a smile. After clearing it with Beth, Harry ordered a thirty-five-dollar bottle of Napa Valley *pinot noir*. Beth ordered the trout and crabmeat soufflé and Harry the buffalo meatloaf wrapped in bacon with Chipotle sauce. They both ordered the French onion soup appetizer.

While waiting for the wine, the conversation was easy. Strangers from completely different backgrounds, neither was sure what they really had in common beyond an interest in the outdoors, and a mutual and, as yet, an unexpressed, physical attraction. But there was obviously something else. They enjoyed one another's company.

The Napa Valley *pinot noir* the waitress poured into their glasses set off the white tablecloth. Beth said it looked like a photo in a gourmet magazine. Take your time, Harry said to the waitress as she set the bottle down. We're not in any hurry.

By the time they finished the French onion soup and drained their second glasses of wine, the waitress returned with the main entrees. Harry took a bite of the buffalo meatloaf, nodding with pleasure, and offered Beth a taste.

Umm, that's delicious, she said after he placed a slice on her plate. Would you like to taste my trout?' she asked, lifting her fork toward him.

Harry leaned over and, enclosing her fingers in his, guided the fork to his lips. That's good, too, he said and motioned to the waitress. Shall we stay with the *pinot noir*? A nice *chardonnay* or *sauvignon blanc* might be better with the soufflé, Beth thought, but it didn't matter. The food was delicious and she was enjoying herself. With a mouthful of food, she smiled and nodded yes.

Throughout the dinner they talked about Montana, Glacier Park, Blackfeet Indians, weather, tourists, and real estate values. But little about themselves. They both were private people who didn't open up easily. It was after dinner and well into the second bottle of wine that the conversation deepened. Recently Harry had told her about his depression following his wife's death and Beth had told him about her divorce. She had also told him about feeling burned out after more than twenty years as a prosecutor and deciding to retire. She hesitated, staring at the wine she was swirling in her glass, considering whether to reveal the complete reason she'd quit. She decided she wasn't, looked up, and said, I realized it was time to do something else, so I decided to leave prosecuting behind and write a book.

The great American novel, or about your experiences in the courtroom?

No, certainly not a novel, and not exactly about my career, although that experience does have some bearing on what I'm trying to do. I want to write about the psychology of killers, about their lives and fates, especially repetitive violent offenders like serial killers, about how they become what they are. I think child neglect and abuse are major causes. Then I want to get into how we deal with them, you know, how justice is administered, the death penalty, and all that. That gets into how questions of justice and vengeance are reconciled. That's something I've wondered about for a long time, thinking about the reason for her resignation. She stopped and smiled at him as she took another sip of wine. *Should I tell him the truth?* But I don't want to talk about that now. Some other time. That's what I think about all day, she lied. *It's you I think about all day, Harry. You're the reason I can't write.* Let's talk about you. Tell me, what's it like being a Marine officer, you know, a leader of the few, the proud, or whatever, all that gung ho stuff? Is it true, once a Marine, always a Marine?

He shrugged and allowed that there was something to it. He told her that he had joined the Marines out of high school after he read Leon Uris's book, *Battle Cry,* about marines in World War II. He retired thirty years later as a lieutenant colonel. Along the way, he had picked up a college degree, an officer's commission, and served two tours in Vietnam. He didn't mention his Silver Star.

When she asked about Vietnam, he shook his head, stared out the window for a moment, and took a sip of wine before he answered. Then he sighed and said softly that the war was a tragedy of lives lost and bodies maimed for no purpose. He said he hoped she would understand, but it was something that was difficult for him to talk about.

There was an awkward silence, then she said, I understand. She paused. Harry, I want to tell *you* something I've never confided to anyone else.

His expression changed. He took a sip of wine and set his glass down. Oh, oh, this sounds serious.

Yes, kind of, at least for me. Are you ready for this?

He nodded.

You see the real reason I ended my legal career was because I did something that could have led to my disbarment. Do you want to hear my confession? She smiled, but he could see she was uncomfortable.

Of course. What happened?

She waited as people left the table nearest them.

She took a deep breath and let it out, Well about five years ago, I tried a case involving a serial killer. He had killed two, probably three, teenage girls. The body of the probable third victim was never found. It was a huge case in Tucson, even attracted national attention. He was a brutal killer who raped his victims then bludgeoned and strangled them. But he was intelligent, good-looking, curly dark hair, blue eyes the color of gas jets—and very manipulative. You could see why he would appeal to his teenage victims. A textbook sociopath. Absolutely no conscience, but after his arrest he pretended to be remorseful, weeping during a television interview that his attorneys hadn't approved, and apologizing for what he had done.

I asked for the death penalty, but the judge, a real jerk in my opinion, sentenced him to natural life because of his age. He was just eighteen when the crimes were committed. I was very disappointed. The victims' families were outraged.

Anyway, a few years later, this guy, his name was Charles Gowan, was brutally murdered in prison in a manner that mimicked the way he killed his victims. The chief suspects were two fellow lifers, but there were no witnesses and no one was talking, not even prison guards who must have recognized this was a contract killing. Case closed. She paused. Not quite. Are you sure you want to hear all this, not going to ruin our evening?

No way. I'm hooked. Please continue. She could see he meant it.

So it was maybe a year afterward that police got a tip from inside the prison that a substantial cash payment had been placed in a safety deposit box recently opened by the wife of one of the suspects. The source of the money was allegedly the father of one of the victims, a wealthy car dealer in Tucson. My chief investigator, a guy I've known and worked with since law school, followed up on it and the evidence was pretty solid that $50,000 had been withdrawn from a blind account in Chicago set up by a close associate of the one victim's father, the car dealer.

She stopped and took a sip of wine, then looked directly at Harry. Ready for the punch line?

He nodded. Can't wait.

We withheld the evidence. Concealed would be a more accurate description. We didn't indict the guy. His attorney, of course, knew about it and was very grateful, needless to say. Others who might have known looked the other way because of sympathy for the father. She looked down at her hands and shook her head before looking up. So you're probably wondering why I did it, right?

No, I think I know, Harry said. But go ahead.

Because this young girl's father and these families had suffered enough, and I believed—and still believe—that Gowan got what he deserved. You see, when I was fourteen, my older sister was raped and murdered. Her killer was never found. It wrecked my family. My mother became deeply depressed and I'm sure my father's stroke and death soon afterward was a direct result of his grief. That's why I decided to become an attorney and a prosecutor. And I was *tough*, especially on violent sexual offenders. I headed up the sex crimes division. I saw each one as maybe being my sister's killer. Victims' rights groups loved me.

I believe it, he said, nodding with a smile. My kind of woman.

But, Harry, I stepped over the line. It was *wrong* to do what I did. I violated my oath as an attorney to uphold the law. I realized afterward that I had to let go of the vendetta that had ruled my life since my sister's murder. Our system of justice depends on attorneys *not* doing what I did.

She took a deep breath and tried to smile. So here I am in Montana trying to write a book about vengeance and justice to clear my conscience.

Harry cleared his throat. At first, Wow was all he could think to say. Then he said, I would've done the same thing.

* * * * *

When they pulled into the driveway of her townhouse, she was feeling the wine and thinking about what she had told him. Maybe she shouldn't have spilled her guts, but she felt better for having done so. She was feeling a lot of things she hadn't felt in a long time, and wondering how this evening was going to end.

How about a cup of coffee before you drive home? I don't know about you, but I'm feeling all that wine we drank. I don't want you to have an accident.

He smiled. Or worse yet, get stopped for a DUI. He had told her about being ticketed twice for DUIs when he was struggling with depression. A third would mean a loss of his driver's license. You know, that's probably a good idea, he said.

Okay, but there's one condition and that is we don't talk anymore about my ethical problems that I probably said too much about already. Enough is enough of that.

Come on, Beth. I'm flattered that you would share something like that with me. Where it will remain.

As they entered the small townhouse Beth rented, Harry took in the rustic mission style furniture and *faux* Navajo rugs spaced out on the synthetic hardwood floor. Glacier Park posters and colorful prints of mountain vistas and wildlife hung on the walls. Hey, this is a nice little place, he said. A sliding glass door opened onto a deck and the first fairway of the Glacier View golf course. When he commented on the convenience, she laughed and pointed to the protective net at one end of the deck to ward off errant drives. As she was in the kitchen preparing to grind coffee beans, he walked around the main room, a combination dining and living area separated by a wood paneled bar. Stairs along the wall led up to a loft. He stood for a moment in front of the sliding glass door to take in the view. The reflection of a bright full moon glistened on a small pond and cast shadows from clusters of aspens and pines along the fairway.

This is a nice little place, he said again. I watched them being built and wondered what they looked like on the inside.

Yeah, it's okay, she called over her shoulder. I just wish it had a fireplace or a woodstove for when it cools off in the evenings like tonight, you know, something to take the chill off. I love the feel and smell of wood burning, don't you? Electric heat just doesn't do it.

That's true. There's something about a wood fire.

After a moment, he turned back to look at the books and papers he had noticed scattered around a laptop on her dining table. Plastic file crates and more papers were stacked on the floor beneath it. So this is what's going into the book you're writing?

Yeah, that's it, the case files and stuff I've brought up from Tucson with me, she said, turning to look at him as the water began to boil in the coffee maker. But a lot of this is just in my head, so I'm trying to sort things out and get it all down in note form on the computer before I begin to try to put it all together. This is a new experience for me, so we'll see whether I can pull it off.

I bet you can. From all you've told me, not just what you said over dinner, it should be an interesting book, one I'd like to read. So don't give up. He walked back toward the kitchen and paused to look at one of the prints on the wall.

I'll do my best. It's a bigger challenge than I realized. Some days, I sit for hours and can't write anything worthwhile. Other times I write and rewrite, and at the end of the day, I read it over and realize it's just terrible. The transition from thought to paper, and voice to print, is a lot more difficult than I thought, even after twenty years of writing briefs and closing arguments. This is completely different. Then when I come across something really good that someone has written, I get discouraged and think I'll never be able to write like that, and I'm ready to give up and then what? Sell real estate or something? No, not really. But that happens about once a week.

He sat down on the couch and watched her in the kitchen as she poured the coffee, thinking about the strong attraction he felt for her as she walked toward him with a serving tray and two mugs of steaming coffee.

Here let me read you this quote. It's brilliant, she said, as she set the tray down on the coffee table in front of him and picked up a notepad from the table. Listen to this. If I could put insights like this on paper:

A need to devour, punish, humiliate, or surrender seems to be a primal part of human nature and it's certainly a big part of sex. To discover what normal means, you have to surf a tide of weirdness.

Hmm, that's interesting, he said with a puzzled look on his face, not being sure whether it was or not. Who wrote that?

Charlotte Rampling, the English actress. She didn't actually write it. She was quoted in an interview. Brilliant. Isn't it perceptive? I mean the way she pulled together all these elements I'm struggling to explain about killers, and she did it in just two sentences. When I read it, I thought, Gee, that describes exactly how I've felt when I was trying some of these cases, especially that Gowan trial, you know, like I was surfing a tide of weirdness.

How about that? Charlotte Rampling. Charlotte Rampling is maybe my favorite actress. I think I've seen most of her pictures. Intelligent, beautiful older *gal*, he said deliberately, with a big smile. She reminds me of you, Beth. Looks, intelligence. He decided not to mention sexy, which was also what he was thinking. Could be your sister. No kiddin'.

Oh, don't I wish, Harry, she said as she put the notepad down and walked over to a bookcase with a Bose player and a stack of CDs on the top shelf. How about a little music? I just got this Rod Stewart CD. I love Rod Stewart. Reminds me of twenty years ago when I was young and he was one of my favorite rockers. You like him?

Yeah, he's pretty good I guess, if you like rock. I'm more of an old standards, big band, guy.

Wait till you hear this. I think you will. I saw him in concert once in Phoenix. Remember, Do You Think I'm Sexy? So funny. He's such a great performer. Then he came out with this CD here where he sings these old standards from another era, you know, songs that Sinatra and Tony Bennett recorded. But with that gravelly voice of his, it's different, very cool, I really like it.

She inserted the CD and walked over and sat down next to Harry, kicking off her shoes and drawing her legs up beneath her. Stewart's raspy, but somehow smooth, strains of You Go to My Head filled the room. She smiled at him, thinking how much she wanted to take this interesting, different, older guy to bed.

They sat without talking for a long time. Beth closed her eyes, humming to the music until Harry said, That's nice, as Stewart finished It Had to Be You, and eased into That Old Feeling. He set down his coffee mug and reached for her hand. Wanna dance?

She tilted her head back and smiled at him. Then she leaned close and kissed him softly on the lips. For the first time. I'd love to, Harry, she said as she set her mug down and stretched, rolling her shoulders back. When she did, her silk top pulled tight over her breasts. They held one another close and didn't speak as they danced.

When the CD finished, she kissed him softly again and walked over and pressed the replay. Then she turned back, holding out her hand. Come with me, she said with a sly smile, nodding toward the stairs to the loft.

* * * * *

The next morning she was awakened by ravens squawking in the tall pines that grew on the hillside above the townhouse complex. Those damn ravens, she thought as she opened her eyes briefly then closed them again. Thin rays of gray morning light leaked through the venetian blinds and across the bed. She sighed and reached over to touch him.

The bed was empty. Rubbing her eyes in disbelief, she turned on her side and lifted herself up on one elbow. He was gone.

Devastating disappointment, then anger, swept over her as she threw her head back into the pillow and stared at the ceiling. In and out. And I thought he was different, that this was different. I bare my soul to him, then this. Fucking men, she whispered to herself as hot tears welled up in her eyes.

Then she smelled coffee and heard footsteps coming up the stairs. Room service, he said smiling, as he reached the top. He walked over to the bed and set a mug of fresh coffee down on the nightstand. The joy she felt was as overwhelming as the despair it had replaced. She couldn't help it; she started to cry.

What's wrong? he asked, a puzzled look replacing the smile.

She swallowed and wiped away the tears with the backs of her hands before she spoke. I thought you were gone, she whispered.

After last night? Are you kidding? he said, a shy smile on his face, as he put his mug down next to hers and sat down on the edge of the bed. He took her hand in his and kissed it gently. Then he embraced her. She buried her head in his chest and held him tight. She wanted to say, Harry please don't ever leave me. But she didn't.

⸻ ✦ ⸻

11

───◆───

Thursday, July 12. Worry and depression were weighing heavily on Keno Spotted Wolf as he moved his horses to the lower pasture by the creek for fresh grass. Two months had passed and not a trace of Dinah. When he returned, he kicked the mud from his boots and went into the trailer to make himself a cup of instant coffee. He had just poured the hot water into his cup and was about to sit down on the steps outside his door when he heard a car approaching and the dogs started raising hell. Moments later, he saw the unlit dome lights and the familiar logo of the Blackfeet Tribal Police as a patrol car emerged from the forest and, bouncing over the ruts, stopped in front of the trailer. Two uniformed officers got out of the car and walked toward him. Keno was acquainted with them both.

What's goin' on? What brings you guys out here today? he asked, trying to act unconcerned, thinking this can't be about that guy I roughed up weeks ago. Then, like a bolt of electricity surging through him— *Dinah?* Heart pounding, he called off the dogs.

The two policemen didn't answer until they got close. I'm afraid we got some bad news, Keno, one of them said. Then he hesitated and Keno's heart sank. I hate to tell you, pardner, but they found a body in the Middle Fork ... He paused. Keno knew what was coming and took a deep breath. Mouth dry, he could feel himself begin to tremble.

We're pretty sure it's Dinah from the identification you and Emma gave us when you first reported her missin'. We're hopin' you can help us locate her dental records, the dentist, and all. We're really sorry, Keno.

Grief washed over his face as he looked away, catching his breath, his worst fears confirmed.

Are you sure it's her? Can I see her? he said finally.

The officers looked at each other, but said nothing.

Well can I? She's my… But the words caught in his throat.

I don't think that's a good idea, Keno, one of them said finally. It's been a couple of months and … He didn't finish.

Keno held the officer's gaze for a moment then sat down, nearly collapsing, on the steps. Leaning over, he grasped his legs around the shins and bent his head forward until it almost reached his knees. It was as if he was trying to squeeze out the clouds of nausea that had floated up from deep inside and caught in his throat. He remained in that position for minutes, not moving, not making a sound. Finally he raised his head and looked up directly at the sky, clasping his hands behind his neck. The two officers saw the tears in his eyes and looked away. Still he didn't speak. When he finally lowered his head, he stared ahead, his eyes fixed somewhere in the middle distance, seeing nothing, as images of Dinah swirled in his mind, his little girl, the young woman, the sadness of her adult life. Now the horror.

One of the officers walked over to him and placed a hand on his shoulder. When he did, Keno looked up. What happened to her? he said softly, looking up into the officer's face in an oddly childlike way. Why was she in the river? Was she in a wreck? Did she drown? Jesus, tell me, what the hell happened to her?

We're not sure at this point, Keno, but it looks like there might have been foul play. We'll know more when we get the official report from the Flathead County Medical Examiner.

Keno's jaw dropped. He was speechless, perspiring, hands trembling, eyes moving quickly from one officer to the other, hoping someone would say that maybe it wasn't true, that maybe it wasn't Dinah, that …

Who did it? Where was she? Where did they find her? he finally stammered, having difficulty matching words with the thoughts that were churning through his mind.

The two officers could see he was losing it and one stepped forward and put a hand gently on his forearm. It was the stretch of river between West Glacier and Hungry Horse, some rafters found her. We're not sure who might've done it, if it turns out … But they're workin' on it big time.

Keno said nothing, eyes fixed, the thousand-yard stare.

Keno, is there anything we can do for you? Can we take you anywhere, get you anything? We're really sorry, man.

He blinked and shook his head. Does her mother know?

She'll know by now. A couple of officers from Heart Butte were going to see her when we left to come out here. They also notified the priest at St. Anne's and he's probably with her.

Why would anyone hurt Dinah? he said softly. She never hurt anyone but herself. Never.

12

---

*F*riday, July 13th. It was a beautiful bright morning. Gary had the day off. The gift shops, restaurants, bars, gas stations, rafting companies, everyone was gearing up for the last month of the summer season. The Glacier Highland Restaurant was packed. He had to sit at the counter rather than at a favorite table by the window. That meant he couldn't see the passing trains. Fucking tourists, he said under his breath.

While he was waiting for his order of hot cakes and sausage, he walked outside to pick up a newspaper at the vending machine on the porch. He was fumbling in his pocket for change when the headline of the display paper caught his attention: Body Found in Middle Fork. He felt a rush and the quarters he was about to slip into the slot dropped from trembling fingers.

He had been checking the Kalispell and Hungry Horse newspapers all summer to see if the body had been discovered. Things had quieted down since they had found his first victim, the Indian woman whose body he had dumped near Bigfork. Exciting. He liked the publicity and the anxieties it stirred in communities when the bodies of his victims were found. With perspiration gleaming on his brow, he took a deep breath and read,

A badly decomposed body, believed to be that of a woman, was discovered by rafters Wednesday on the Middle Fork below the Blankenship Bridge. The body was lodged in the limbs of a fallen tree and had been concealed by high water. Flathead County Coroner Lars Johnsrud ruled the death of the unidentified victim a homicide. Flathead County Sheriff Pete Jorgenson said an investigation is under way and asked anyone with information to contact the Flathead County Sheriff's Office.

There was a photo of Search and Rescue people standing on the riverbank next to a Zodiac raft, but no more information. In a sidebar to the story, Gary read that the Flathead County Sheriff's Department was still investigating the death of his other victim, one Beverly Nicholson, whose body was found in early May in a marshy area south of Bigfork. Other evidence had raised the possibility of a hate crime directed against Native American women, a representative of the Sheriff's Department said. The Confederated Salish-Kootenai Tribe had posted a $5000 reward for information leading to the arrest and conviction of the person or persons responsible.

It was the kind of excitement he enjoyed, the cat and mouse game with investigators that he had been winning for years. The authorities had to have his DNA from his more recent victims in Oregon, California, and Arizona. He wondered if they would ever discover the match with the woman he killed in Bigfork, thinking it was doubtful they'd ever match him with the one they just found. The time under water should make that impossible.

A man sitting alone at a table near the window made fleeting eye contact with him. It made Gary nervous, like maybe this stranger knew what he was thinking. He took a sip of coffee, paid the cashier, and left, leaving the hot cakes and sausage barely eaten on his plate.

* * * * *

A few miles away, at her townhouse on the golf course, Beth Blanchard put down the newspaper after reading the same story as she sat at her kitchen table sipping a second cup of breakfast coffee. She remembered that, shortly after arriving in West Glacier, she had read about an Indian woman's body being found south of Bigfork. She wondered if the victim whose body had just been found was also an Indian. If so, maybe there was a connection, maybe the same MO, especially if other evidence fit. A serial killer preying on minority women would not be unheard of by any means.

She had cut out several articles on the Bigfork murder, she wasn't sure why, maybe intuition. She set her coffee mug down and walked into the living room where she kept her files in plastic filing crates, and found the clippings in a manila folder. The article on top, BODY FOUND NEAR BIGFORK, was dated May 16, just days after she arrived in West Glacier. She took the folder back to the kitchen, retrieved her coffee, and began to read:

The body of a Pablo woman, missing since early May was found by a jogger Saturday in a marsh south of Bigfork. Flathead County Coroner Lars Johnsrud ruled the death a homicide. According to a press release issued by the Salish-Kootenai Tribal Police, the victim, Beverly Nicholson, was reported missing on May 5. Her car was found later parked on Electric Avenue in Bigfork. The cause of death was strangulation, Johnsrud said.

A second article reported that Salish-Kootenai Tribal Police and the Flathead County Sheriff's Office were investigating the possibility of a hate crime because of a note found attached to the victim and other physical evidence which was not disclosed.

Undisclosed physical evidence. Based on her years as a county attorney, she knew that probably meant torture and mutilation. But hate crime? That was misleading. All serial violence was inspired by hatred. Serial killers and rapists were usually selective, choosing victims with the same characteristics like gender, race, age, appearance, or occupation, because they hated what or who their victims *represented*, and derived sadistic satisfaction out of harming them. John Wayne Gacy and

Jeffrey Dahmer killed only young gay men. Ted Bundy preyed on young women, especially young women with long dark hair parted in the middle. Henry Lee Lucas killed prostitutes, or women who looked like prostitutes and reminded him of his mother. Westley Dodd killed little boys. Hatred—the need to devour, punish, and humiliate, that Charlotte Rampling described—motivated them all. She tapped her fingers on the top of her coffee mug and asked herself, is this a killer whose preferred victims are *Indian* women?

At the edge of her thinking were two possibly related and, as yet, unsolved murders of Indian women in Coconino County, Arizona. That must have been at least three or four years ago, she decided, as she returned to the kitchen, turned off the coffee maker and rinsed out her mug. Back in the living room, she began rummaging through her files, looking for the information she had collected at the time. She removed a single manila folder labeled Flagstaff Cases, and began to leaf through the newspaper clippings and police reports. There wasn't too much in the Flagstaff newspaper, basically that the bodies of two Indian women were found near Flagstaff, over a five- month period three years ago. Another Indian woman was reported missing during the same period, but never found. The first victim was killed in May, and the body of the last victim was found in September, but the coroner's report estimated the death had occurred at least six weeks before. For the next half hour, she read through the police reports, making mental notes. She thought she could discern a pattern.

All the victims had a history of alcoholism, drug abuse, and, probably, prostitution. DNA evidence confirmed what markings on the bodies suggested, that one person, who had sliced an *X* above the victims' left breasts, was responsible for both murders. But what was the significance of the *X*? A western states alert was issued that a serial killer was probably responsible. Tribal police on every reservation were notified. Then the killings stopped and remain unsolved.

She walked to the sliding glass door, slid it open, and stepped outside to take in the morning sunshine that was warming the deck. Chickadees and pine siskins were flying back and forth between a large birch tree and her deck, carrying off the sunflower seeds she'd scattered across the railing. Ideas and questions cascaded through her mind as the feeling that she might be on to something began to resonate. Indian women. Could it be the same killer? And what if the killer was leaving some sort of signature mutilation of the bodies? Was it the same signature on both the Arizona and Montana victims? Why would the killer select victims in northern Arizona and others more than a thousand miles away in Montana? What did those areas have in common?

She was pacing back and forth, her mind doubling back on itself, when, she stopped and snapped her fingers. That's it, she said aloud. Big Indian reservations in both states. That means a large population to choose from. Makes sense. Easy pickings. That's got to be it.

She pressed her palms against her eyes and tilted her head back. What else? Flagstaff and Kalispell. What did they have in common? Both were small gateway cities to two large national parks—Grand Canyon and Glacier. The two Arizona murders and the disappearance were spaced over the peak tourist season at Grand Canyon. Now the two Montana murders were following the same pattern with the advent of the tourist season at Glacier. Okay, she asked herself, but what does that suggest?

She put the manila folder down and walked over to the deck railing as a chickadee cocked its tiny head, did its *tic tic* sound, and fluttered off. A threesome was about to tee off. She watched absentmindedly as the first golfer off the tee sliced his drive into the pond, sending a pair of mallards into the air, but it didn't register. Grand Canyon and Glacier National Parks, was there some connection?

She was pacing the deck, too excited and nervous to stand still when she decided to take a walk down to the river to calm down and try to sort through it all. She walked along the edge of the road to a path that led to the river. Someone driving by honked a greeting, and she waved back without it registering in her mind who it was—one of her neighbors presumably. She cut through a stand of tall cottonwoods and made her way around large rocks and tangles of driftwood that cluttered the river's banks. Stumbling and scraping her knee, she stopped and sat down on the trunk of a large fallen tree, its bark stripped off in its turbulent journey downstream. Her mind was racing as she looked briefly out on the river where a couple of bright blue commercial rafts, loaded with tourists, floated toward her, lingering snow in the ravines of Strawberry Mountain providing the backdrop for what would have been a pretty photo. She returned their waves absentmindedly, thinking that the Indian woman's body might have floated right past where she was sitting. She guessed the Blankenship Bridge couldn't be much more than a few miles downstream.

She stood up, excited, clasping her hands together, talking aloud to herself. That's it, that's got to be it. National parks. Tourist season. Sure, that's got to be it. The killer must have some connection to national parks. A ranger? Probably not. Too much at stake. A seasonal worker's a better bet. A lot of marginal people were employed as seasonal workers at national parks, basically drifters, like the people who work carnivals and amusement parks. Yes, yes, of course, she repeated, shaking her fist, that would make sense, perfect sense.

She decided to call the Flathead County Sheriff's Office. If the coroner's report revealed the MO and signatures of the Bigfork and Blankenship murders were the same, she would call the Coconino County Sheriff in Flagstaff to double check and confirm the same information on the Arizona murders.

She decided to call Harry first. Across the river, she noticed an osprey gliding to a landing atop a tall dead lodgepole pine before she turned and walked rapidly back to the townhouse.

At his house in the Nyack flats, eight miles upstream, Harry Dawkins had just come in from his own walk along the river with Ginger, when the phone rang. He thought it was his daughter calling back. She and his granddaughter were planning to visit and he needed dates so he could get tickets to the Bigfork Summer Theatre.

Harry, Beth said immediately. Did you read the paper this morning about them finding a woman's body in the river? Before he could answer, she said, Well, I think I might be on to something, but I'd like to run it by you first.

Sure, your place or mine?

It's a nice day. I'll drive out to your place if that's okay with you.

He laughed. You know you're always welcome here, Beth.

Great, I'll see you in about twenty minutes. What's that milepost, again, where I make the turn to your place?

* * * * *

Harry was standing on the porch of his log home when she pulled up and parked her Honda in the driveway. Sunlight streamed through the branches of tall spruce and fir trees that shaded the house, highlighting the bright colors of the petunias and pansies that bloomed in beds beneath them. Hummingbird feeders dangled above the porch where an old-fashioned wood porch swing and wicker rockers looked out on pink and purple columbines that lined the gravel pathway she was following to it. Behind the house and a rail fence horses grazed along a stream that flowed to the Middle Fork through a daisy-filled pasture.

Hey, this is a nice little surprise, Harry said as Ginger rose and stretched, then walked toward the car wagging her tail. Beth bent down and rubbed the dog's muzzle with one hand. She had a legal pad and a manila folder in the other.

See there, look at that tail waggin', you've made old Ginger's day. Mine, too.

Beth smiled and gave him a quick kiss. They sat on wicker rockers on the porch and as hummingbirds buzzed back and forth between the tall trees and the feeders Harry had put out, Beth laid out her thoughts on the connection between the Arizona and Montana murders.

When she finished, he said, So you think it might be a seasonal worker in the park. Hmm, interesting. Sounds plausible to me. Go for it, Beth. Call the sheriff's tip line. See what they say.

No, I'm thinking this is bigger than the tip line. I'm going to call and see if I can get in to talk with the chief investigator.

———•◦•———

13

⸺◆⸺

*M*onday, *July 16th.* Detective Moore stood when Beth entered his office.

Hello, my name's Elizabeth Blanchard. I'm the person who called about the murders of the two Indian women, she said as she extended her hand.

Yes, it's nice to meet you. I'm Louie Moore. Have a seat, he said, motioning to an upholstered gray, metal chair that faced his desk.

She smiled. Thank you. Tall, fiftyish, not bad looking, but he reeked of tobacco. She noticed a package of Nicorette on the desk.

He returned the smile, looking resigned, expecting an inconsequential conversation. Now you said you're a prosecutor from Tucson, Arizona, right?

Well, former prosecutor. As I said on the phone, I retired this spring and moved up to West Glacier in May. Familiar indifferent expression, she thought sizing him up. He's thinking is this woman serious, worth my time. She assumed that he had already checked her out in Tucson.

Big change, I bet. How do you like Montana? he said, covering a yawn with finger tips.

So far, so good. Beautiful country. She paused, enough small talk, and got right to the point. About these two murders. I wanted to run some ideas by you because three years ago in Arizona, two Navajo women were murdered and another's still missing, as far as I know, in the Flagstaff/ Grand Canyon area. Authorities in Coconino County, where the bodies were found, said DNA evidence and the killer's MO confirmed both homicides were committed by the same person. Both victims were street people with histories of probable prostitution, alcoholism, drugs, and, of course, they were Indian. And, most importantly, both had *X*'s cut above their left breasts and had paper stuffed in their mouths with the words 'prairie nigger.' I'm wondering whether that bears any similarity to the two murders you're investigating here. The newspaper mentioned a note found on the first victim's body and other physical evidence.

Moore leaned forward in his chair, looking surprised, his chair squeaking as he rocked back. He didn't say anything at first, his eyes fixed on Beth, making up his mind about her, uneasy with opinionated women. Finally, rocking forward, he said, Yeah, that's interesting. Very interesting. The Pablo woman had that kind of wound above her left breast and a 'prairie nigger' note was stuffed in her mouth. We also got DNA. Semen. There was no note found with the body found in the Middle Fork, and no DNA, obviously, under water all that time, but there was a wound above the left breast which the medical examiner decided could have been an *X*. So we're pretty sure both women were killed by the same person.

And the same person almost certainly killed the women in Arizona, Beth said, excitement in her voice.

Nodding, eyes widened under raised eyebrows, Moore said, Yeah, looks like you're definitely on to something. He opened a file drawer and took out the case folders.

Looking satisfied, Beth cleared her throat. Okay are you ready for this? I've got a suspect in mind, a category of suspects, actually.

Okay, let's hear it, he said, looking up at her over reading glasses he had put on.

What about seasonal workers in the national parks? Think about it.

As she explained her thinking, Moore began scribbling notes on a yellow legal pad. When she finished, he looked up, put down the ballpoint pen, and began drumming his fingers on the desk. Yeah, this just might be the break we've been hoping for. He rubbed his hands together, thinking. Then he said, We'll get right on it, checking out the employee rosters for all the park concessionaires, seasonal employees, and businesses in the park vicinity that employ seasonal workers. We might be able to identify previous employment and pull out anyone who worked at the Grand Canyon when those murders occurred down there. Depends on what kind of personnel records these employers keep. Probably uneven. We'll see, but it's going to take time. We're shorthanded and a lot's going on, but I'll put as many people on it as I can. Right now that's lookin' like myself and one other detective.

What about the FBI? she asked. Serial killing across state lines is part of their jurisdiction, thinking, surely he knows that. If this theory holds up, there's a good chance he's killed in other states with Indian populations near national parks.

Yeah, probably so, we'll check that out, but let's hold off a bit before we get the Bureau involved. I don't know about your experience with those people, but they're kind of frustrating to work with, the way they throw their weight around. Let's see how far we can go with this before bringing them in.

Are you sure? They could be important with the DNA evidence and...

He rubbed his chin, thinking. Then he sighed, Yeah, you got a point. Our chief suspect up till now has been an ex-boyfriend of the Pablo woman who can't be found, but now this second victim...yeah, those Arizona murders...your theory kind of raises questions about that. Yeah, we'll check out this possible park connection. And, yeah, on second thought, yeah, maybe we better get the Bureau involved.

Good. Thanks for your time, she said, standing up and extending her hand, wondering about this guy's competence, thinking about how inter-agency rivalries often compromise investigations. Here's my card. Can I use one of your pens? Let me put my West Glacier number on the back. Please give me a call if anything comes up. You can call me Beth. I'm interested and would like to help in any way I can.

14

———◆———

Wednesday, July 18th. Keno Spotted Wolf drove into Browning on the main drag, Route 89, passing the gas and convenience store, an assortment of run-down businesses in buildings in need of repair, among those already boarded up. He turned left on a side street just beyond the dry goods store and an IGA supermarket where drunken Indians often loiter in the parking lot, hands out for change to buy the drink they're dying for. A short block north, he parked his pickup on the street next to the Little Flower Catholic Church.

For as long as he could remember, the church had been a bastion of hope in a reservation town well acquainted with despair. As he walked slowly to the front entrance, he looked at its walls of smooth river rock in shades of gray, pink, and amber accented with stained glass windows that Blackfeet artist King Kuka created, depicting the stations of the Cross blended with religious beliefs and figures of Blackfeet significance. At the entryway, Keno hesitated at a statue of the Madonna in buckskin, her arms crossed over her heart, a crucifix in her right hand, rosary beads hanging from the left.

Memories flooded back as Keno walked slowly up the steps to enter the church. He remembered Dinah's confirmation there one Easter, a pretty little girl in a white dress, holding a bouquet of prairie wild-flowers. He remembered the clean smell and feel of the soft black hair, shining in the sunshine, that fell to her shoulders. He almost smiled as he remembered her looking at the Madonna and asking if Jesus's mother had really dressed in buckskin. He'd said that he was pretty sure she did sometimes. Then she'd asked about Jesus.

Did he wear buckskin too, Daddy?

Buckskins on his days off, he'd told her, but robes when he was working, like the ones he wears in the pictures in your catechism book.

But wouldn't he do it the other way, Daddy? Wouldn't he wear buckskin when he was working and robes on his days off? He almost smiled at the thought as he did then.

Maybe you're right, that does make more sense. I guess that's why the sisters say you're so smart.

She'd cocked her head and given him that funny little smile of hers, the one when she thought he might be kidding.

He sat down in the pew directly in front of the casket next to Emma. Dinah's two little boys sat between her and their son, Vine, home on leave and dressed in Marine summer tropicals. The family had requested a brief service. The priest, a young man with an Irish brogue, went through the timeless ritual of the Church as Dinah's soul was committed to the angels in the hope of eternal life. Then her brother and five other young Blackfeet men carried the casket to a hearse that waited outside on the street. Keno, Emma, and their two little grandsons walked behind them. The undertaker, a white man in a necktie and dark suit that seemed out of place, stood at the curb until the mourners had left the church and gotten into their vehicles, all pickup trucks. Emma and the two boys rode together with Emma's sister in her truck. Keno and Vine climbed into Keno's old Ford. Then the undertaker got into the hearse with his driver to lead the grim caravan on the drive to Heart Butte.

Keno and Vine, lost in thought, didn't speak as they began the twenty-five-mile drive south across open range where buffalo once grazed in the shadow of high, irregularly shaped escarpments. The sadness was overwhelming. There was nothing to say. Except for the peaks and ridges of the Rocky Mountain Front to the west, the horizon seemed endless and empty under the big sky. There wasn't a power line or billboard the whole way.

Keno was staring straight ahead as the procession moved slowly on two-lane blacktop that curved and dipped across rolling prairie before it descended into a deep gorge and crossed the bridge over the Two Medicine River. He glanced briefly at a ranch house and outbuildings clustered in a grove of cottonwoods along the river where cattle and horses grazed along its banks. He'd once bought a horse there. A few miles later, the procession crossed Badger Creek and stopped for cattle crossing the road.

That's when Vine turned to his dad. I think it was Joe Sanders did it. If I ever find that half-breed sonofabitch, I'll kill him with my bare hands.

Keno looked over at him and nodded. I was thinkin' the same thing. They drove on in silence.

Keno downshifted to get up a rise, and the town of Heart Butte appeared, a tiny community of mobile homes, government housing, pickup trucks, and collarless dogs. To the west, he could see the high dark butte that gave the town its name. He used to joke that its heart-shaped formation brought to mind images of Jesus on Catholic calendars holding his raiment apart to expose his crimson, anatomically correct Heart of Love.

Keno pointed to the tops of cottonwoods that marked the course of a distant coulee on the eastern horizon. Remember she was with us when we got that nice buck in that coulee?

Vine looked at him briefly and nodded. Yeah, she cried, said it was too pretty to shoot.

Keno saw tears in his son's eyes and felt the sting in his own.

The funeral caravan drove slowly into town, passing the Trading Post, and across the road from it, the US post office, the only modern brick building in town. It looked out of place, too substantial, too white. The town seemed abandoned, its streets empty.

Where is everybody? Vine said. The place looks deserted.

Keno nodded and pointed ahead to a small crowd of people in the parking area of the Catholic cemetery located between the town's two churches, the Whitetail Baptist and St. Anne's Catholic. How ordinary they looked compared to the Little Flower.

The doors of pickup trucks closed softly in the parking area as mourners got out and walked slowly in clusters through a metal archway with three crosses toward the gravesite where people from town stood waiting. Keno joined Emma, her sister, and the two boys and they walked together as Vine joined the other pallbearers at the hearse.

To the west, on the slope of pine-studded hill, a weathered Madonna looked out over the graves from a concrete enclosure. They walked past faded bouquets of plastic flowers and tiny American flags that provided the only contrast to the dry summer weeds and bare rocky ground that separated the graves. Most of the graves were outlined with stones and marked with simple white wooden crosses. Here and there engraved granite gravestones were scattered among them.

Keno thought about the surnames and flags as one of Dinah's little boys reached down and touched one. He had forgotten what a special place this was. Names like Day Rider, Many Horses, Two Guns, Heavy Runner, Calf Robe, the many flags marking the graves of fallen soldiers and marines. The Blackfeet warrior tradition. He looked over at his son, head bowed, but standing ramrod straight after setting the casket next to the grave, then down at his grandsons.

A storm front was moving in from Canada. Keno looked up at the heavy slate-colored clouds, broken by occasional shafts of sunlight that fell on a prairie that looked gray and desolate. Far to the north, he could see flashes of lightning and hear the distant rumble of thunder. The mountains to the west, partially obscured by dark storm clouds, looked gray and forlorn except for occasional glimpses of snow visible on the highest peaks.

Family and friends waited in silence for the service to begin. Keno looked over the gathering, nodding to old friends he hadn't seen in a long time. The older women stood with heads bowed, their hair in traditional braids, some in long buckskin dresses decorated with turquoise and coral beads. The younger women were dressed in jeans and tops, many with designer logos, the way Dinah dressed. In the chill wind that blew from the north, most of the women pulled on jackets or draped them over their shoulders. A few of the older men were dressed in traditional buckskin with beaded headbands but most, like Keno, wore flannel shirts, Wranglers, and Western boots. His son's tan uniform was conspicuous as the mourners formed a semi-circle around the casket of Dinah Spotted Wolf.

An old medicine man, white hair parted in the middle and plaited in two long braids, stood by the casket, one hand on a bouquet of flowers that lay on top, holding it against the gusting wind. Keno had known him for years and respected him as a mystic whose powers could not be explained.

The medicine man was dressed in traditional buckskin decorated with coral and shiny black beads woven with porcupine quills in a geometric design across his chest. There was only the sound of the wind, as he began to speak in Blackfeet. Two other elders kneeling on either side of him began to beat rawhide drums, joining the rising and falling cadence of his speech. When he reached to pick up bunches of sweetgrass that lay at his feet, the bouquet of flowers blew across the top of the casket and fell to the ground. A little girl moved forward to pick it up and place it back on the casket. She gave Keno a sad smile when he reached out and touched her arm as she walked back past him.

After several minutes, the medicine man stopped speaking and the drums fell silent. He held bunches of sweetgrass tied in sheaths and, with his back to the wind, lit them with the flickering flame of a small oil lamp. Keno watched as the smoke began to rise and thicken, thinking about the stories he had heard the elders tell since he was a little boy—how the smoke was the Great Spirit's breath drawing Dinah's spirit and their prayers to the Ones Above. The medicine man nodded to him to take his place at the head of a line of mourners with Emma, their son, and grandsons. They were joined by other family members and friends, men, women and children, forming a single line in front of the casket. Then as the medicine man silently held the smoking sweetgrass out to them, they immersed themselves in the smoke, raising their arms and with open palms, pulling the spirit of Dinah Spotted Wolf toward their faces, and letting it flow over their bodies in a gesture of cleansing, love, and final communion.

Keno wiped the tears that welled in his eyes with the palm of his hand. He couldn't bear to look at Emma who wept quietly beside him. He put his arm around her, as did their son who stood on her other side. Dinah's little boys looked perplexed, tears in their eyes, clinging to their grandmother's long skirt.

When everyone had passed, the medicine man lay the smoldering ashes on top of the casket and spoke in Blackfeet. Then he repeated the words in English. What is Life? he said. It is the flash of a firefly in the night. It is the breath of the buffalo in the wintertime. It is the little shadow which runs across the grass and loses itself in the sunset.

Keno lowered his head, hot tears rolling down his cheeks. *The little shadow that runs across the grass and loses itself in the sunset. My little girl. Dinah, my little girl, I'm so sorry, so sorry.*

———•••———

15

Thursday, July 19th. Gary's plan to kill Matt Margolis and kidnap Vicki Hathaway was almost in place. But he still didn't know exactly when, only that it would be sometime after Labor Day weekend. It was unlike anything he had ever done and he was feeling anxious about pulling it off in unfamiliar, unforgiving backcountry. Most of his experience was taking tourists out for a half- day or day on well-traveled trails. He'd gained a lot of knowledge of horses, wildlife, and the outdoors over his years working as a wrangler, but he'd never been one to set off by himself on backcountry expeditions.

For starters, he had to find a hideout, a place to take Vicki, after he got rid of the boyfriend. Lying on the bed in his one-room cabin, he ran through the list of places in his mind that he'd already rejected, and realized once again that none of them was far enough off the beaten path. Dejected, he turned on his side and stared at the map of the park hanging on the wall. It must have been there for decades, he thought, because none of the newer park buildings was on it. He got up and traced a finger along the trail Matt Margolis had described that night at Freda's. Morning Star Lake. He drew a circle with his finger around it, thinking there had to be someplace in the area no one would ever find where he could take Vicki.

He was about to lie down again when he noticed a cabin indicated on the map. He didn't remember seeing it on the newer map he'd used to scout the trail to Morning Star Lake. Gary feverishly got the newer map out: *no cabin.* The date on the map was 1995, and the map on the wall was dated 1960. The old map showed the cabin was in the remote Nyack Creek Valley.

The Nyack Creek Valley. Serious backcountry. He pulled a worn copy of Erik Molvar's *The Trail Guide to Glacier National Park,* from the shelf next to the shower and turned to the description of the area. Interesting, this could be the place, he thought as he read about the Nyack Creek Valley having the most primitive hiking conditions found in the park...*hazardous stream and river crossings...not recommended for inexperienced hikers.* If the derelict cabin indicated on the old map was still there, it might be the perfect place, the spot he was looking for, to spend what remained of the rest of his life with the woman of his dreams, their paradise in the center of this wild, remote wilderness. After consulting his map and the guidebook, he used a yellow felt marker to trace the route he could take from Morning Star Lake up and across the high ridge at Pitamakin Pass and then follow the cut-off trail that slabbed around Mt. Morgan to Cut Bank Pass. From there, it looked like he could pick up a steep trail that descended down to the headwaters of Nyack Creek and then follow the creek west to the cabin. He figured it would be a long day's ride, but something that could be done if he got an early start.

The next morning was his day off. He rose early, gulped down the usual candy bar and cup of instant coffee, and packed a quick lunch of two peanut butter and jelly sandwiches and an apple for the day ahead. As he walked to the corral in the thin early morning light, he hesitated to watch a coyote across the road, creeping low, belly to the ground at the edge of a patch of tall grass at the end of the pasture. Then he spotted the snowshoe rabbit it was stalking, its summer coat brown with a just a hint of winter white returning on its rump. Sensing the danger, the rabbit bolted into the pasture, zigzagging, as the coyote raced to one side, causing the rabbit to dart back toward the trees along the road. Gary smiled when he saw another coyote waiting in the trees. It ended with a squeal and a puff of fur and dust.

The buckskin saw him coming, saddle in his arms, and trotted over to the gate, whickering a greeting. Gary saddled and bridled the horse and walked him into the trailer and bolted the door. He pumped the accelerator and after a couple of chugs the old Dodge started, destination Red Eagle and the Nyack Creek trailhead.

Some thirteen miles south on Highway 2 from West Glacier, he flicked on his turn signal and turned left at Red Eagle, a small settlement hidden in the timber, down shifting into second on a gravel road that dead ended at the Burlington Northern Santa Fe tracks. He parked his truck in a muddy pullout near the trailhead next to a stock loading platform. After backing the horse out of the trailer, he locked the pickup and led the horse on foot across the railroad tracks. As they edged down a steep embankment on the other side, he held the horse back to keep it from stumbling. On sure footing, he swung up into the saddle and followed a faint trail through thick knapweed, willow and cottonwood scrub of the flood plain until the vegetation gave out on smooth river rock and gravel near the river's edge.

He dismounted to look things over. The sight and sound of rushing, swirling water brought back memories of a close call, a near drowning a few years before at a high-water crossing of the Rio Grande at Big Bend. He reached under the horse's belly and cinched up the latigo and tightened the straps holding the saddlebags. After one last tug on the pommel to be sure, he put a foot in the stirrup and swung back up on the horse.

An old packer who helped out sometimes at the stables had told him that the river was usually manageable at Red Eagle by the end of July, but cautioned that the deceptively swift current and slippery rocks could still be treacherous. Crossing on foot was like walking on marbles, he said, even when the water was low. Horseback was better, but not much. Had to be careful. Four legs were better than two, but the current was strong and the water deep enough to roll a man and horse a long way downstream before you could regain your footing. That's if you're lucky and didn't get pinned under a snag. Downstream on the far bank, Gary could see a small wooden cross wedged in a pile of rocks, a faded blue ribbon fluttering in the breeze, he guessed, for someone who didn't make it.

He cautiously nudged the buckskin into the water. The horse was tentative and edgy on the smooth, slippery rock. They moved slowly out into the main channel where the swirling water reached the gelding's belly. That's when he slipped and reared. Gary struggled to keep him under control, speaking in soft tones as he sidestepped him into what he thought was shallower water. But the horse slipped again and stumbled backward into a deep pool. He thought they were going over, and was about to kick out of the stirrups, when the struggling horse regained its footing and lunged forward—Gary clinging with both hands to the saddle horn—and up the steep embankment on the other side. He was soaked to the waist, but felt lucky to be on dry ground.

A rock cairn on top of the bank marked the trail. He could see another cairn not far away as the trail meandered through a jumble of downed timber and piles of driftwood washed up in the spring runoff. Tall cottonwoods marked the edge of the seasonal high water flows. Pushing through a thick understory of alder and willow, he followed the trail north for nearly a mile to the banks of Nyack Creek. The footbridge he'd expected to find there had been washed out. A few planks attached to loose cable and remnants of its stone and log foundation were all that remained. But he was relieved to see the creek was wide and shallow at that point and easy to cross.

A trail marker on top of the opposite bank pointed left to the fire lookout on Lone Man Mountain six and a half miles to the north. A directional arrow and mileage marker pointed to the Lower Nyack campground, 5.4 miles to the east. The derelict ranger cabin he hoped to locate was supposed to be in that vicinity, he guessed no more than a couple of miles beyond the campground.

After nearly three hours of stop-and-go on a scarcely traveled trail choked with brush and downed trees, he came to a small, grassy clearing. At its far edge, he could see the shadowy profile of the derelict cabin in the trees, its faded brown and gray hues blending in with the forest. It would be easy to miss unless you were looking for it. A rickety moss-covered outhouse without a door was barely visible in the bushes behind the cabin. A doe and her fawn, feeding on serviceberry bushes near the cabin, stood motionless, staring at him, then bounded off into the timber as he dismounted and tied his horse to a weathered hitching rail. He took a small crowbar from the saddlebag and pried the latch off the door.

The odor of mildew filled his nostrils when he pushed open the door, the draft stirring dust motes that floated through narrow shafts of sunlight that angled down from windows coated and streaked with dust. Above him, cobwebs draped from the rafters and clung like ghosts to the corners of the log walls. A layer of dust and pine pollen covered the floor and spare furnishings, a couple of metal bunk beds, a table and two chairs, a bench, and a woodstove. It reminded him of a trailer his mother had rented on a rainy afternoon some place he couldn't remember when he was a little boy. He remembered thinking then that that's what a tomb must be like. He walked back outside and checked out the small spring-fed stream that flowed nearby. Plenty of fresh water. Then he removed his lunch from the saddlebag and sat cross-legged against a tree to eat his peanut butter and jelly sandwiches. With a little preparation, this would do, this would do just fine, he thought as he took a bite of the apple and tossed the rest to his horse.

Gary began to make weekly trips into the cabin on his days off to clean, repair, and stock it with the food, supplies, and cut plenty of firewood that he and Vicki Hathaway would need to survive. For how long, he wasn't sure.

— ◆ —

16

─◆─

Sunday evening, August 26th. A big week coming up, Gary was thinking as he sat on the stoop at his cabin on the Quarter Circle. Events were accelerating as the Labor Day weekend approached. An overheard conversation earlier at Freda's between two of the couple's friends had confirmed their plan to hike into Morning Star Lake the Tuesday after Labor Day. See you then, he was thinking, as he pushed back from his spot at the bar and walked out, relieved that he could now move ahead with his own plans.

He had been having trouble sleeping in the weeks since he'd learned that Dinah Spotted Wolf's body had been found. Excitement, anxiety, fitful nights of sleep made him edgy, wary, alert like a cat. Not long now. He turned on the radio for the hourly local news. No new developments in that case and the cabin was stocked and ready for a new adventure, the biggest of his life. On his last trip, he'd installed an aluminum swivel—the kind used for dogs—in the cabin floor with a large wing nut anchoring it beneath the floor in the crawl space beneath the cabin. At the end of the chain, he'd attached a thick, adjustable steel-and-leather collar that could be locked around a person's ankle or wrist. He'd fashioned it from a dog collar and hardware he'd lifted from the stable. Pretty ingenious, he was thinking now. Just in case she didn't like it there. He stood up, stretched, and looked at his watch. Still early evening and nothing else to do. He decided to stop at Freda's for a beer. Maybe *she* would be there.

* * * * *

Beth and Harry were sitting at a table in Freda's sipping icy drafts of Full Sail after a walk along the river to the Old Bridge, when Gary walked in. Beth turned to Harry and whispered, Harry, look. It's that guy we had the run-in with at the post office.

Harry nodded as he looked over at Gary seating himself at the bar. Maybe we should go over and say hello, he said without smiling.

A short time later, when Harry walked up to the bar to order a second round, Gary ignored him. When he returned with the drafts, Harry said, I don't think he's in the mood for any more trouble.

I'm not so sure about that, Beth said. That guy is weird. I've seen guys like him before and they're trouble.

It was past eight o'clock and the place was beginning to fill up with the usual young crowd when Matt and Vicki walked in and joined two other couples at the table next to Harry and Beth's.

Harry looked over at Beth and smiled. Hey Beth, I think it's time for us dinosaurs to leave the place to the next generation. We're takin' up space.

Matt heard him. Hey now, come on, there. Don't feel that way. They need some class in this place, people with a little seasoning like you guys. A brief, pleasant, no-names conversation followed as the two couples talked about where they were from and what they were doing in West Glacier.

Well, you guys enjoy that backpacking trip next week, Harry said as he and Beth got up to leave. You'll be hiking through some beautiful backcountry, Morning Star, Pitamakin, a lot of history in that Cut Bank Valley.

When they got outside, Beth said, Harry, did you see that weirdo at the bar looking at that couple? Every time he saw me looking at him, he looked away, acting like he was watching the ball game on TV, but he had his eye on that girl.

＊ ＊ ＊ ＊ ＊

The next day, Gary called in sick at the stables and made a quick trip to Keno's ranch to pay him, board the horses, and drop off the trailer. August 31, the Friday before Labor Day, he quit his job. Quitting abruptly like that was tricky, especially before a holiday weekend. He didn't want to arouse suspicions. He hated to put them in a bind for the Labor Day weekend, he lied with all the sincerity he could muster, said he was sure sorry, but he had to return to Oregon to see his mother who had been diagnosed with terminal lung cancer and did not have long to live. He said he had to leave for Portland as soon as he could get packed up.

It worked. Everyone believed him. His boss, a skinny, middle-aged, born-again Texan, who liked Gary's hard work and reliability, offered his sympathy. The sympathy expressed by the other wranglers he worked with, who didn't like him and were glad to see him go, was obviously forced, but satisfying. What assholes. When his boss said he would send his final paycheck to his mother's address, Gary didn't know what to say. No, no, he said finally. I'm not sure what the situation is there. I'll get back to you on that. Can you give me, say, a hundred bucks out of the till to tide me over?

Sure, Gary, his boss said as he opened the cash drawer and instead counted out eight twenties. Here's a little extra. God bless, Gary. Just let me know where you want us to mail the check for the rest we owe you. And, Gary, your job's here next summer if you want it.

He thanked his boss as he pocketed the money and told him that he thought he would return. As he drove the ten miles back to his cabin on the Quarter Circle, the whole scene made him smile. What a bunch of dumb fucks, he said to himself.

———◆◆◆———

17

Saturday, September 1. This was the moment he had been waiting for, planning for, all summer. The morning was misty and cool as he loaded the two saddles and well-packed saddlebags into the bed of the truck. The rifle he laid on the floor of the cab. Summer was fading fast and he could feel the stillness and smell of fall in the air. He went back into the cabin to be sure he hadn't forgotten anything and left the key on the table for his boss to pick up later. He'd planned to remove his Oregon license plates and replace them with an expired Montana plate he had taken from an array of license plates and horseshoes nailed on the wall of the Lake McDonald stable. But he decided to do that right before he got to the Indian's ranch just to be sure he wasn't stopped by the highway patrol.

He pumped the gas pedal and let the ignition grind until the old pickup coughed and chugged to life. He sat for a minute letting it warm up and watched the wipers clear the morning dew. Without the trailer, he could take the shortest route across the park, Going to the Sun Road, but decided not to. Better take the long way again on Highway 2, he reminded himself, to avoid the chance of being seen going the wrong way by his fellow employees at the stables.

He was thinking about the lie he told about his mother. Would he care if she died? The thought reminded him of a novel he had to read years before when he was in juvenile detention, working on his GED. He loved the opening line, never forgot it: *Mother died today. Or was it yesterday maybe, I don't know.* Or care, he said aloud and smiled. What the hell was his name? French guy.

As he drove out the Quarter Circle road for the last time, the leaves on the sarsaparilla bushes had already turned gold and were dropping, the first sign of summer's end and the approaching autumn. A thought occurred to him as he approached the post office. He pulled in and parked. Inside, he purchased a stamped envelope and walked to the writing stand in the far corner of the room, away from the others who were trickling in to check their mail. He took the ballpoint pen attached to the counter and addressed the envelope to Loretta Jean Kemp at a Portland, Oregon, post office box. He reached into his pocket, counted out four twenties, hesitated, then added a fifth. What the hell, I'm not going to need all this where I'm goin', he said to himself. After scratching a brief note, he folded the note over the money and placed it in the envelope. He knew it was the end of one season and the beginning of another, the most important of his life. The end of the beginning, the beginning of the end, his recurring thought.

When he turned east on the highway, he slapped the steering wheel, thinking damn, it was exciting. A few miles down the highway, on the straight stretch through the Nyack Flats, he braked for a couple of deer. That's when he remembered—Camus, *The Stranger*. Yeah, he really nailed it with that line.

The sun was now an hour higher in the sky as he crossed Marias Pass, but the air seeping through the vent he'd closed was colder. The prairie that rolled out in front of him was drenched in sunlight. He stopped for breakfast at the Two Medicine Grill in East Glacier, a windswept little community of low-slung buildings where the prairie meets the foothills. Instead of parking along the highway, he drove around to the back of the building and parked on one of the dirt side streets. When he entered, he nodded to the cook behind the counter where three customers were sitting, then made his way back to a table in the rear.

He sat down at the end table behind an Indian couple and their small baby who were sitting beneath a window where the sunlight made the moisture on their recently wiped table glisten. They hardly looked him when he sat down. Two old men and a younger man sat in a booth across from him talking about how big rainbows were biting on spinners at Duck Lake. The small dining area was paneled in knotty pine adorned with paintings, price tags attached, of snowcapped mountains and rolling prairie. Through the window, he could see rays of bright sunlight shining down through a canopy of tall cottonwoods on a shed with bridles and halters hanging from nails on the inside of its open door.

When the waiter, a short, spidery, rock-climber type with a butterfly tattoo on the side of his neck, brought him the menu and coffee, he ordered ham and eggs over easy with a side of pancakes. He was nervous, self-conscious, worried that people were looking at him, and trying hard not to show it.

He took a sip of coffee, then got up and walked back through the café to the newspaper vending machine outside the front door. When he returned, he scanned the *Great Falls Tribune*, but all he could think about was the next forty-eight hours. The waiter returned and set down his order of ham, eggs and hotcakes, which he shoveled in like he was starving, washing it all down with coffee. When he finished he wiped his mouth and arranged the salt and pepper shakers and Tabasco neatly beside the napkin dispenser. He looked at his watch. No need to get there too soon, he thought, and motioned to the waiter and tapped his mug for another refill. He'd noticed the empty vodka bottles in the bed of one of the derelict pickups when he dropped the horses off and guessed this Keno character wasn't an early riser, just another drunken fucking Indian.

A short time later, after the Indian couple and the fishermen left, he was beginning to feel conspicuous in the back room by himself with a counter-full of men, he guessed all locals, sitting in the other section near the door. Time to go. He laid a five and three ones on the table with the bill, used the restroom, and left. It was after nine when he drove through the railroad underpass, past the flower gardens and manicured grounds of East Glacier Lodge, and headed north on Route 49 through the Two Medicine Valley. A billboard caught his eye:

LET'S GET TOGETHER THIS WEEKEND.
GOD

He almost smiled. *Sorry, God, I've made other plans.* Ten miles farther down the road, he stopped briefly at a scenic pullout to change his license plates.

* * * * *

When he pulled up to Keno's trailer, the dogs were waiting, barking and running beside the truck until it stopped. Keno was already outside, standing on the stoop yelling at them. It was turning into a bright, warm Indian summer day.

Can you call off the dogs? Gary called, waiting to get out of the truck. He could feel his heart pounding and sweat prickling under his arms. Fucking dogs, he was thinking. The pickup door creaked open a crack, but he didn't get out.

Gary's two horses, the buckskin and the sorrel, trotted to the side of the corral to greet him as soon as they recognized the truck. With the dogs under control, he eased out of the truck and walked over to the corral to stroke their muzzles and necks. How'd they do? he asked, as they snorted and whickered softly at his touch. Any problems?

No problems. Good grass, fresh water, and me, Keno said, forcing a smile through the grief that was weighing heavily on him. He was determined not to show it, especially to a white stranger he didn't trust or like. Nodding toward the horses, he said, You wanna sell that little filly? She likes it here.

Ha Ha, that's funny, Gary thinking how much he disliked Indians. He ignored the question and walked back to the truck to get the tack out of the back. Without speaking, he walked back to the corral, bridled the buckskin, put a halter on the sorrel, led them out of the corral, and tied them to the tailgate of the pickup.

Oh yeah, nearly forgot, Keno said, breaking the silence, that little filly's got a loose shoe on her right rear hoof. Not too bad yet, but she's probably gonna throw it on rough ground. I didn't notice it till yesterday.

Goddammit, Gary said as he gave Keno a quick angry look, were Keno's fault. Wish I'd known before this. He reached down, eased the horse's hoof off the ground, heaving a big sigh. Yeah, shit, loose all right. Goddammit to motherfuckin' hell. He stood up, hands o hips, and stared straight up, mumbling, considering what to do. Ah, fuck it, he said finally. No time to do anything about it now.

Keno was going to ask when was the last time he had his horses shod, but decided the hell with it. Instead, he said, I know a guy on the road to Browning, shoes my horses. If he's around, he could take care of it. You got time to haul her over there? Not too far, about ten miles. But, then again, he might not be there. You never know about him.

Gary looked over at Keno, a brief angry stare, but didn't say what was on his mind, which was that he didn't have time to fuck around with any more dumb fucking prairie niggers.

Fuck it. Gets worse, I'll just pry it off, he mumbled as he kicked a stone across the ground and swore again, thinking how in the hell could he have missed the loose shoe earlier. Too much on my mind, he said to himself.

Someone goin' with you? Keno asked as if nothing was wrong. He was still shirtless, exposing muscles starting to sag on a hairless chest. He sat down on the trailer steps and pulled on socks and Western boots, trying to figure out why he'd had an immediate visceral-deep-gut dislike of this stranger on first sight, a feeling that was coming back strongly now.

No, why'd you …? Gary started to answer, then he saw Keno looking at the two saddles in the bed of the pickup. Oh yeah, the two saddles. Well, ahh, he stammered, I'm gonna meet up with another guy workin' on the project. He's already in the backcountry and he's … we're gonna need another horse. I mean, you know, a packhorse, you know, an extra for research equipment and … He was stammering as he ran out of words and lies.

Bullshit. Pack horse? So why the saddle? Keno knew he was lying, but he didn't say anything as Gary repeated his earlier story about doing wildlife research.

Keno let it go. So how long you gonna be gone?

ot sure. Could be a week, maybe two. Depends on how the research .

What kind of wildlife, you studyin'?

Gary was ready for that question. Grizzly bears. Part of a big DNA study on bears.

Keno stood up, rubbed the back of his neck, and yawned as he stretched then pulled on a denim shirt he lifted from the inside doorknob.

Oh, yeah, I heard about that, he said. Well there's grizzlies back in those Atlantic and Cut Bank Creek drainages. There's a reason they call that high peak out there and the lake below it Medicine Grizzly. Seems like the park is always closin' that trail into Morning Star and Pitamakin because of the grizzlies. They come right by here sometimes, movin' up and down the drainages. They go way out on the prairie, like that big sonofabitch they darted and tagged down in Dupuyer, especially in the fall and spring, right before and right after they hibernate. Occasionally they'll kill a calf or a steer, or some sheep. He looked up on the high slopes at the aspens beginning to turn. Yeah, we're gettin' near that time of year.

Keno reached down, picked up a stick, called to the dogs, and threw it, smiling as he watched them race after it. Then he turned back to Gary. Yeah, they're lookin' for food, especially this time of year. Sow griz took down a heifer couple miles from here, not far from the main road, about this time a couple years ago. Tribe gave some guy permission to shoot her after that when she killed some sheep. Got her stuffed in a display case down at the restaurant in Saint Mary. You ever see it there? I always know when one's around, dogs go crazy. Heelers hate bears, it's in their blood.

Keno could tell Gary wasn't listening and he didn't care. He didn't believe anything Gary said. *Working for the government, with an expired Montana plate on his truck and an Oregon plate on the horse trailer? No way. He think I didn't notice he had Oregon plates when he first came by?*

Keno watched but didn't offer to help as Gary draped saddle blankets over two saddles and lifted them out of the bed of his pickup. After saddling the horses, he fastened and adjusted the latigos and strapped saddlebags behind the saddles. When he finished, he strung a lead rope from the filly's halter and attached it to a metal ring on the cantle of the buckskin's saddle.

Don't see that much anymore, Keno said in an easy-going way as he watched Gary attach a scabbard to the saddle and slide a lever action Marlin 30/30 he had taken from the front seat of the pickup into it. I mean a man carryin' a rifle in a scabbard into the park. You know, unless you're duded out in a Park Service uniform. A half-smile as he paused to swat a mosquito on his arm. But I guess scientists like you, doin' research and all, can carry weapons and don't have to wear those silly damn Boy Scout uniforms the Park Service wears, right?

It was an aggressive remark intended to provoke a man he didn't like, the kind of comment Keno had used before, usually after a few drinks, to stir things up in a saloon, like he had last fall, when a big, noisy hunting party from Kalispell made an unwelcome stop at Kip's for late afternoon drinks during elk season. Today he was sober but hung over.

Gary hesitated, then let it pass. He knew he was being set up. Yeah, we're all carryin' rifles on this project. He didn't look at Keno when he answered.

As Gary mounted up, Keno didn't pursue it as he felt like doing, and surely would have, if he had been drunk. *What's the point? The guy's a liar.* He knew rangers in the backcountry carried large caliber pistols, .44s, .357s, or 10-gauge shotguns, not old-fashioned lever action Marlin 30/30s.

Where 'bouts you headed today? Keno asked, shifting back into a friendly, disinterested tone that caught Gary off guard.

Ahh, Medicine Grizzly Lake, meetin' my partner there. He's camped back in there. Then we're headed up toward Triple Divide. That area. We'll be workin', takin specimens, all that, out that way into those drainages. Direction's gonna depend on what we find.

Bull-fucking-shit, Keno thought, but he just nodded. Well you're better off takin' the road to the ranger station. That trail you're looking at leadin' off in the timber winds back in toward Morning Star and Pitamakin, not Triple Divide. Yeah, and it's pretty rough, deadfall, washed out in places, not maintained anymore. Old Indian trail when they ran cattle back in there till the park raised hell about it and made 'em stop.

Yeah, I been in there. It's okay. I got some time today, so … but Gary didn't finish the lie. He planned to follow the trail to just beyond the park boundary in case there were rangers around he might encounter on the road. Once past the park boundary, he was going to cut back to the north, cross Cut Bank Creek, and pick up the main trail.

Keno nodded and rubbed his chin, affecting a thoughtful manner. The thought was, what a crock of shit.

Oh yeah, nearly forgot, Gary said, stepping back from the horses. I'll park the pickup back there in the trees outta your way. That okay with you?

Keno just shrugged. Since the funeral, he had lost interest in everything, and the empty vodka bottles were the evidence. Why am I letting this bastard rile me? he said to himself as he watched Gary drive the pickup into the trees and park it. If he don't show up in a couple of weeks, hot-wiring that pickup won't be a problem. He had a single set of Montana plates that he could use on it, switching plates like he did with his other trucks, depending on which one he needed to use, or had running.

When Gary returned and mounted his horse, Keno watched him ride off and disappear into the trees. He wondered if he'd return. Not that it mattered. But for some reason, he doubted it.

A few days later, Keno was sitting on the front steps of his trailer in bright mid-morning sunshine. It was Tuesday, the day after Labor Day and another beautiful Indian summer day. But good weather didn't matter. He was hung over and his mood was dark. A cool, dry breeze blew up through the cottonwoods in the creek bottom, carrying with it the melancholy smell of leaves about to fall and the approaching autumn. Deeply depressed, he hadn't slept well, bad dreams and all the vodka he drank didn't help. In the distance he noticed dust rising from a car headed in the road toward the ranger station.

18

Tuesday, September 4. The first day out was perfect. Beautiful blue skies, just enough breeze to keep the mosquitoes away, and temperatures creeping toward seventy. It was early afternoon when Gary saw Matt Margolis and Vicki Hathaway arrive at their campsite and set up their tent. The day after Labor Day, not a soul in sight. He had set up camp two days before, scouted the trail of his planned route to Cut Bank Pass as far as Pitamakin Lake and, now, awaited the opportunity to strike.

They'd chosen the pebble beach campsite just as he'd guessed they would. Hidden by trees and brush across a shallow inlet from their campsite, Gary watched them with binoculars as they spent the next couple of hours, setting up their tent, gathering firewood, and picking huckleberries from the bushes that grew in open areas among the trees. Then he looked on as they bathed, both naked, in the lake's chilly, clear waters and then warmed themselves, sitting on top of their sleeping bags in the late summer sunshine. It was pleasant in the sun, but the fleece vest he pulled on felt good in the shadows and dampness where he sat in a thicket of willows. Except for an occasional cool breeze that blew down from Pitamakin Pass, it was still.

After making love beneath two sleeping bags they had opened out and covered themselves with, he could see they had fallen asleep, curled up against one another. He was trying to decide when to make his move—that afternoon, later at night after they were asleep, or wait until the next morning. Either way, surprise was essential. Watching them as they slept, fantasizing about how good her body would feel, he decided to hold off until it was dark.

Sometime later, when they awakened, he could see them shading their eyes and pointing, he guessed, to take in the views. A crystalline blue sky with billowy white clouds was mirrored on the calm surface of the lake. Patches of lavender colored asters and golden rod grew among huckleberry bushes in open areas near the shoreline. To the east Eagle Plume's and Red Mountain's barren slopes rose above the tree line in shades of red argillite. A pretty place, he thought, a perfect place for that wisecracking fuck to make his exit. Get out the violins, Vicki.

It would be risky. He had to get close without them detecting him, closer than when he'd crouched beneath her dorm window at the beginning of the summer. Surprise was important. Wait until they're asleep, slash through the tent, then across his throat. Should be over quick. The Buck knife was razor sharp, and he knew how to use it.

* * * * *

Wow, Matt, you think you've seen all the beautiful scenery there is to see and then you come here. It's breathtaking, like the Bierstadt and Thomas Moran paintings we looked at in art history. I thought the Alps were something, but this park is incredible, isn't it?

He yawned, gave her a broad, sleepy smile as he reached over and squeezed her shoulder. Yeah, I told you this is God's country, Vicki. Glacier backcountry, the last best place. And this is the time to be here. It's never crowded, but now there's no one but us.

I know. It's great, Matt. Just you and me. She sighed and stretched back, raising her arms over her head, tan marks visible on her bare breasts. I feel so happy, so content. I'm so glad we did this, you know, to have this time together in this special place.

Yeah, and this is just the beginning. Wait till you see the view from up there on the pass, he said, pointing behind them to the high forested shelf that blocked their view of Pitamakin Pass. Once we get past the trees, it'll feel like we're on top of the world.

Top of the world. I already feel that way, she said. You know right now I feel like I could stay here forever ... I don't know what to say ... It's magical.

She sighed again and sat up, hugging knees drawn up under her chin. You know what? I'm getting cold. I'm going to put some clothes on. Are you getting hungry?

Yeah, we better do that before it gets dark. You notice how the days are gettin' shorter? When that sun starts tiltin' west, drops behind that ridgeline, the temperature'll drop real fast. Thirty-forty degree swings this time of year. I'll gather some wood in a minute and build a fire.

As Vicki got to her feet, Matt watched, thinking about how good those long legs felt wrapped around him, those perfect calves, narrow hips and waist, the way the nipples on those firm little boobs stiffened and tipped up when he kissed them. She stretched her arms above her head, then wrapping the sleeping bag around her shoulders, walked carefully on tiptoes among the stones back to the tent. Wow, am I lucky or what, he said to himself as he clasped his hands behind his head.

What did you say? she called from inside the tent.

He chuckled. I said I'm ready to eat. He thought about saying *you,* but didn't. But first I brought a little surprise.

You did? I love surprises.

Matt rolled over and picked up his hiking shorts that were draped over a log near him.

He pulled them on, zipped his fly, and slipped a fleece top over his head. Then he walked back to his backpack propped against a large rock next to the tent and lifted the flap.

Are you ready for this, Vicki Hathaway? Drum roll please.

Okay, wait just a minute, she called from inside the tent. A moment later, Okay, got my clothes on, but I don't know how to imitate a drum roll. She poked her head out of the tent and then stepped out.

Ta da, he said as he pulled a bottle of wine from his backpack with a flourish. A bottle of Rosemount Estates *shiraz.* A fine Australian red on sale at the West Glacier Merc for a mere $9.99. Bought it instead of my usual half-gallon of Carlo Rossi burgundy. And it's just for you, beautiful lady, because you are so special.

Sweet boy, she said smiling as she walked over and kissed him lightly on the cheek. Then her face turned into an exaggerated frown. Matt, what am I going to do next week when you're gone and I'm back in Davis in a hot, stuffy dorm room getting ready for classes?

Well, you're just gonna have to stay here with me. We could hang out in Whitefish at Larry and Emily's place for a while, get jobs on Big Mountain, or at one of the restaurants, get ready for the ski season, and stay warm and cozy together through the long Montana winter. How's that sound?

Wonderful. But no way that's going to happen. My folks would kill me if I dropped out of school.

They sipped wine from tin cups, watched the shadows lengthen and felt the temperature drop as the mountains to the east took on the golden glow of the setting sun.

The golden hour, Vicki. Is this livin' or what? The backcountry of Glacier National Park. Where would you rather be?

Nowhere. She hesitated, thinking about it, then whispered, No, nowhere else. This is perfect.

Yeah. This spot, this fine wine, and a beautiful woman to share it with. This time will not be subtracted from the sum of our lives, Vicki.

Matt that's so beautiful. You're a poet.

I wish. John Muir said that. He called this care-killing scenery.

She smiled and leaned her head against his shoulder. He sure got that right.

They sat side by side without speaking for a long time. Then Matt said, You know it makes me think about something my grandma said one time that the world is so beautiful, that it made her sad to think we all have to die. I was little and it kinda scared me, because I'd never thought about dying, but now sometimes like in a beautiful place like this . . . He let the thought hang before he stood up, stretched his arms over his head, shook his head and smiled. Whoa, enough of that. I better get that fire started before we drink any more wine. Maybe you could get the steaks and wrap those two potatoes in foil. We'll bake 'em in the coals.

Yeah, this is so beautiful and relaxing that I almost forgot about the food, but I'm starving, she said, as she stumbled and giggled getting to her feet. She stretched and yawned, then made her way to his backpack for the food. Must have been the hike and the sunshine, 'cause I'm feeling that wine and it's a very nice feeling.

Well enjoy dinner tonight, 'cause it's freeze-dried food from now on, he said as he slipped on his hiking boots. Well, maybe not, if I catch a couple of cutthroat for dinner tomorrow with my trusty little telescopic fiberglass rod over at Old Man Lake. Wait till you see that lake, Vicki. Beautiful. And tasty wild chives grow on the slopes above it. Perfect with trout fried in fresh butter, which I also remembered to bring, strangely enough, the butter that is.

He walked back to the edge of the camping area and returned with an armload of twigs and sticks which he stacked in the fire pit and lighted with the help of a small container of lighter fluid. Vicki walked along the shoreline a short distance and returned with a couple of pieces of dry driftwood. The fresh wood brightened the fire.

Perfect. Now that it's goin' good, we'll let it burn down slow, he said as he stood over the fire, then we can cook over the hot coals. But first, nature calls, he said over his shoulder as he turned and walked to a tree at the edge of the campsite.

The light was fading from dusk to darkness when they finished their dinner and half a second bottle of wine. The campfire had burned down to smoldering coals and a fine mist was settling over the lake. I'm gonna get my parka, she said. I'm getting cold.

Yeah, me too, he said. Would you please toss mine over. It's right there by my sleeping bag. Unseen, far out on the lake, they heard the lonely call of a loon.

Hear that? he said. That's backcountry.

I know, so haunting, she said as she handed the parka to him. He lifted her hand to his lips and kissed it. I have another little surprise, he said as he took a plastic baggie from his shirt pocket and pulled out a neatly rolled joint. How about finishing off a lovely evening with a little Merry Wanna?

She smiled as he lit it, inhaled, and handed it to her as she sat down next to him. She took a drag, and neither of them spoke as they held it in and waited for the effect. When they exhaled, each took another deep pull and let it settle.

This is good stuff, she said as she exhaled after another hit, the high, dreamy sound of her voice already revealing its effects. Where'd you get it?

Some little guy in Hungry Horse grows it in an old barn he rigged up with those lights, what the hell you call 'em, you know, the ones that make plants *glow* in the dark … and his voice trailed off.

She started to giggle. You mean makes plants *grow* in the dark, don't you? Wow, that's a revolutionary idea, Matt. You mean like photosynthesis with artificial light? That guy must be brilliant. She was laughing harder.

What the hell is photosynthesis? he said, slurring his words, a blank look on his face as he stirred the coals with a stick. I forget.

Because you're so fucking stoned, she said, choking with laughter. That little guy in, you know, the genius … where was it, that town you … She couldn't finish the thought. Matt was doubled over with laughter, rolling back and forth, holding his sides. Vicki was laughing so hard tears ran down her cheeks. They couldn't speak. When their laughter died down to chuckles, he pulled her close and nibbled her ear. What's that Jimmy Buffett song? 'Let's get drunk and screw?'

Why am I not surprised by that suggestion? she laughed. Did I tell you I went to a Jimmy Buffet concert last year in San Francisco? I went with my dad, my stepmother, and her daughter. There was a pause as she struggled to collect her thoughts. My dad and people his age love him. And I can see why. What an experience. He's so cool. It's like he puts thousands of people in a good mood when he sings, makes people forget their problems, makes the boomers like my dad feel young again. And when he sang that one, you know the one about screwing, they really roared.

Yeah, he's a cool dude. I remember my dad and mom liked him when they were still together, Matt said slowly, staring at another joint he had just lighted glowing between his fingers. Sells out all his concerts, just like the Grateful Dead. He looked off in the distance and shook his head. Yeah, love the Dead. Now, poor Jerry's gone. Very sad. Never be the same. Well, anyway, I think he had a great idea, you know … that steep trail … Pitamakin Pass tomorrow, he said, motioning behind him to a high ridgeline of trees silhouetted against the darkening sky.

Who? What? You are making absolutely no sense at all, she giggled. How did we get from Jimmy Buffett to Jerry Garcia to Pita … what? How do you say it?

Pitamakin. That's spelled capital P-i-t-a-m-a-k-i-n. You know what Pitamakin means in Blackfeet? His speech was slurred, the tone serious.

No, but I bet you do.

It means Running Eagle

Gee, I'm impressed. How do you know?

They grew quiet, just staring out at the darkening lake. Matt offered her another hit and when she shook her head, he smoked what remained until it singed his fingers, then flipped the butt into the campfire coals.

Hate to do that. There mighta' been one more hit there, but forgot a roach clip … don't need blistered lips … He hesitated, trying to remember what he'd been talking about.

What was I sayin'? Oh yeah, this old guy in West Glacier who knows all about native American languages wrote a book about the names of places in the park. Good guy, I heard. I see him at the post office sometimes. Crippled, walks on crutches. Lives alone, doesn't say much except hello. Eccentric I guess. He has a wolf hybrid that rides around in the back of this little station wagon he drives. You ever see it? Fucking fierce. I would not want to be around if that animal got loose.

Oh, yeah, I've seen it in that station wagon, but I didn't know it was a wolf. Really scary. Never got close enough to look. So he's the person who wrote the book?

Yeah, that's him. That damn wolf goes berserk if anyone gets near. Big. Must weigh at least a hundred and fifty pounds. And Katie bar the door if a dog comes near. Has the back upholstery ripped all to hell, tryin' to get at other dogs. I think he's, you know … what's his name's, the guy who owns it … he's the only one who can get near it.

He reached over and put his arm around her shoulders, drawing her close. Shades of a pink and peach sky were fading fast into lavender and gray on high cirrus clouds when the sun disappeared behind the ridge behind them. It's getting pretty damn cold, wanna get in the tent? I'll clean up this stuff in the morning.

She smiled and kissed him on the cheek, then on the lips. Not yet, she said, as she rose and placed a log on the fire. I love this campfire. Let's watch the stars come out while this last log burns down. They didn't speak as they stared into the flickering flames of the campfire.

* * * * *

When their conversation stopped, so did Gary. He had crept to bushes on the embankment above their campsite beyond the circle of light radiating from the campfire. The night was an astronomer's dream, clear with no moon, and the stars were spectacular. Their campfire was almost out, but he could see their silhouettes in the last fluttering shadows cast by fire. Holding his breath, he listened and waited, the Buck knife clutched tightly in his right hand. Then he eased down the embankment and circled around behind them in the darkness. He hesitated, crouched behind low bushes and a fallen tree at the edge of the faint glow of the fire behind their tent. A dry branch cracked under his foot.

Vicki sat up straight and turned toward the sound. Matt, what was that?

Ah, probably nothin', some critter sneakin' around, lookin' for scraps. Raccoon probably. Nocturnal. Real campsite bandits. Gary could hear Matt chuckle as he poked a burning log with a stick making sparks fly.

Yeah, I got your raccoon right here in my hand, motherfucker, Gary said to himself, pulling his foot back, holding his breath, as Vicki hesitated, her eyes fixed on the darkness behind the tent.

Matt, it sounds like something moving.

Yeah, it's probably a damn raccoon, maybe a porcupine, but let's see if this works. Matt picked up a rock and, without looking, tossed it over his shoulder into the darkness behind them.

Gary ducked and caught his breath as the rock landed a few feet away and bounced past him. He waited tense, ready to spring, until they turned their attention back to the fire. I'm cold, Matt, he heard her say and then she got to her feet. Let's get in the tent. But first I have to pee, but no way am I going to walk back to that privy in the dark. Do raccoons attack?

Only beavers, he laughed, so be careful.

She rolled her eyes then turned to look into the fluttering shadows and darkness behind the campsite. I'm going right there, so don't look, she said over her shoulder as she walked toward a small bush close to the tent. She giggled. Maybe I'll see that raccoon.

Gary remained motionless, holding his breath as he watched her approach. She was no more than ten feet away when she stopped and turned, her back toward him. He watched her slip down her hiking shorts and panties, and squat down. Anxiety and lust made his heart pound, imagining he could smell her scent. *What if she sees me?* But she didn't. When she returned to the campfire he watched her place her hand on Matt's shoulder and heard her say, Let's go inside, Matt. I want to make love.

A short while later, he edged closer, crouching in the darkness next to the tent. He could hear the sounds of their lovemaking, her murmurings, moans, and whispered cries had him aroused, breathing fast, worried that they might hear him, wanting her so badly he could feel the pressure between his legs. Finally the torment ended and after a while, he could hear the soft sounds of Matt's snoring. *Only inches away, slash the tent open, then his throat.* He touched the edge of the blade with his thumb. Razor sharp. Then he shook his head and quietly got to his feet. *No, too messy. She could get hurt. A bullet in the morning's better.*

19

———◆———

Wednesday morning, September 5. Gary was awake at first light and moved to his vantage point in the willow thicket where he had a clear view of the blue nylon tent where the couple slept. Movement on the far shore of the lake caught his attention, a dark shape in the gray early morning mist. He lifted and adjusted his binoculars. As the view came into focus, he could see a bear browsing on sedge grass that grew in a meadow that stretched back from the lake. It was a massive animal with a broad bronze-colored head and back and dark chocolate legs. Was it the monster grizzly he'd heard them talking about at Freda's, the one that roamed the Two Medicine, Cut Bank, and Nyack Creek valleys? He guessed it had to be.

The cold breeze that drifted down from Pitamakin Pass made him shiver as it rustled through the willows and over his shoulders, stirring thin wisps of smoke from embers still smoldering in the fire pit at the campsite, then rippling across the glassy surface of the lake. Gary watched as the grizzly lurched upright on his hind legs, thrusting his nose high, turning his head from side to side as the breeze washed over it, *catching the scent.* Oh shit, he whispered, as he watched the great bear drop down on all fours and begin making its way south along the shoreline toward him and the couple's campsite.

* * * * *

Vicki Hathaway woke up shivering as the sun's first rays shone through the blue nylon tent. Matt was snoring softly beside her. She looked at the tousled hair and suntanned face beneath the two-day stubble and knew she was in love. She could see her breath. The temperature had dipped during the night and her teeth were chattering. Except for the silk, long-sleeve T-shirt she wore, they were both nude, and the sleeping bag was cold and damp from the previous night's passion. Then much to her dismay, she saw the menstrual blood.

Matt, she said, shaking him gently, Wake up, Matt. We have a problem.

He groaned and then mumbled, Oh, baby, what's the matter? as he rolled over and looked at her with sleep-hooded eyes.

I hate to tell you, I'm so disgusted, but I started my period during the night and this sleeping bag is a mess. Wouldn't you know this would … Now what are we going to do on the rest of the trip? I've ruined everything. She had tears in her eyes.

He rose up on his elbows, coughed, and cleared his throat. Now, now, relax. After last night, nothin' matters, he said with a sleepy smile. We'll take care of it. No problem.

Oh, Matt, just look at this, she said as she lifted the top of the sleeping back to look inside. Last night was wonderful, but now look at this mess, so disgusting.

No, no, not disgusting. You were more than wonderful. Such a woman. The passion … God, just thinking about it …

Don't talk about it, she whispered. You'll ruin it. It must have been all that wine and pot.

Or *us*, maybe? You were so …

Matt, come on, please don't. I mean it. Now we've got a real mess on our hands. How are we going to clean this up? I feel like screaming.

Let me see, he said as he looked inside the sleeping bag. Whoa daddy! Yeah, I would say that *is* a mess, or as an Englishman might say, a bloody mess. Looks like the floor of a slaughterhouse.

Matt, stop it. It's not funny.

Now, now, don't lose your sense of humor, he chuckled. That'll wash out in the lake. These Polartec bags clean up nice, and dry quickly. We'll let them dry out in the sun for a while. Then we can drape them over our backpacks when we leave. They'll be dry before we get up to the pass.

You sure?

Absolutely, unless it rains, and that wasn't in the forecast. He leaned back and clasped his hands behind his neck and smiled. Ah yes, what was that Al Pacino flick? *The Scent of a Woman.* Love it, myself, he said taking a deep breath. Come here, Vicki, I can't get enough of you.

Come on, Matt, stop it. I'm dirty and smelly and I don't like being made fun of. I hate having you see me like this. It's embarrassing, a real turn-off.

Now, now, Vicki, don't be like that, don't be embarrassed. It's a natural thing, no big deal. Did I ever tell you that joke about the couple drivin' home late one winter night and they see a small animal in a snowdrift beside the road?

She sighed and closed her eyes, saying through clenched teeth, No, but I'm really not in the mood for jokes.

Anyway, she tells him to stop, so he backs up and she gets out and picks up this baby skunk. She goes on about how cute it is and how they can't leave it there along the road to freeze to death. And he says, 'Okay, okay, get in.' So she gets in the truck and says, 'It's so cold, how can we get it warm?' He thinks for a minute and says, 'Put it between your legs, it's nice and warm there.' She says, 'But what about the odor?' And he says, 'Hold its nose.'

Oh, that's terrible, she said, throwing her head back in laughter. Matt Margolis, you are a filthy, rotten, sexist pig.

Through the laughter, he said, But you're beautiful, and I just have to do something with this, he said, exposing the erection between his legs, or I won't be able to get my pants on.

Oh, no you don't, her laughter ending. No way, Matt. Get over it. I'm a mess.

No, you're a dream, he said as he gently pushed her legs apart and eased between them.

Matt, don't. Stop it. I mean it, she said, as she pushed against his shoulders. I'm not ... Oh no, oh ... oh baby, her voice dropping to a whisper, as she lifted her knees and drew him inside. You feel so good … so warm, oh, yes … don't stop, so good, wait, wait, oh yes, yes …oh, I'm going to …

Me too, he whispered, as he pressed his tongue into her ear.

Later, they held one another close, her head on his chest as he stroked her thick auburn hair. She lifted her head and kissed him softly on the lips.

Matt, I hate to admit it, because you can be such a jerk, but I think I'm in love with you. She smiled, squinting in the bright morning sunlight that now illuminated the walls of the tent and brought out the blonde highlights in her hair. The only thing you could do to make this morning better is to make me a nice hot cup of coffee before we clean up this mess.

You're beautiful and wonderful, and … and what can I say? I love you and you're the best thing that ever happened to me, and I want to spend the rest of my life with you, Vicki Hathaway. But, first things first. Before I do anything, I gotta pee. Be back in a minute. He kissed her on the forehead and rolled out of the sleeping bag. Then he squeezed her hand before he lifted the tent flap and crawled out into the sparkling light of a new day.

⸻ ❖ ⸻

20

—◆—

As Matt stood naked relieving himself, he was still thinking about
the sex and how good it was, and how to convince Vicki to remain
in Montana with him instead of going back to college. Falling in love was
something he hadn't planned on. He was looking up toward the high
ragged ridgeline of the Continental Divide, the morning sun lighting up
talus fields that sloped down from a fortress of rimrock, when he heard
a snorting sound behind him. He had barely turned toward the sound
when the big grizzly came through the underbrush behind him, knocking him to the ground, hurtling past toward the tent and the blood scent
it had been tracking.

Gary lowered the 30/30 Marlin he'd had trained on the young man's
back and watched, fascinated but fearful for his own safety. Vicki, Vicki,
look out, a bear, he heard Matt call out and watched as he struggled to
his feet and reached toward a partially burned piece of driftwood on the
ground near the fire pit. Gary saw the bear hesitate at the tent, rooting
at its base, smelling, but not seeing its quarry. That's when Matt raised
the driftwood above his head and brought it down with such force on
the bear's shoulders that it snapped in two. The bear snarled and whirled
back on him. Gary was awed by the force of the animal. With one swipe
of its huge paw, it knocked Matt, twisting and somersaulting him into
the fire pit. Then it was on top of him in a cloud of embers and gray ash,

tearing fist-size chucks of flesh out of his bare shoulders, chest, and neck. Seconds later, all Gary could see was its broad, bronze-colored back and Matt's bare legs extending out beneath it, kicking uselessly. Then the bear lunged into the tent, crumbling it to the ground.

He heard Vicki's screams and watched as she somehow scrambled free of the twisted nylon that had collapsed over the bear's head and shoulders. She ran behind the bear to a tree at the edge of the campsite. But he could see the tree offered no escape as she tried to pull herself up through its sagging and breaking branches. She was no more than ten feet from the ground and without branches that would hold her weight, within easy reach of the bear. Tearing loose from the tangled tent, the bear rose on its hind legs to its full height, towering over the motionless body in the fire pit. Then it hesitated, as if deciding its next move. Gary caught his breath. Oh shit, he breathed as he saw the bear turn toward the girl and begin a slow, deliberate pigeon-toed walk toward her, head low, swaying from side, ears flattened against its skull. *He's going to get her.* Vicki was screaming.

He raised the rifle to his shoulder and steadied the barrel on the trunk of the large fallen tree he had been hiding behind. He took a deep breath, held it, took careful aim, then squeezed off the shot he'd intended for Matt Margolis. It was an easy shot, less than fifty yards, at a large, slow-moving target. Gary aimed for the grizzly's head, but saw a puff of dust and hair as the copper-jacketed bullet slammed into its humped right shoulder. The big bear roared, staggered, then shook itself before bounding up the embankment. Gary stood up, levering in a second bullet, aiming, and firing a second time, then a third. Both shots missed as the bear disappeared into thick brush and trees. He stood up and reached into his jacket pocket and replaced the three rounds he'd fired. Then he waded in knee-deep water across the narrow inlet, approaching cautiously, eyes fixed on the spot where he had last seen the bear. Vicki was hysterical.

Oh, my God, oh, my God, please, please help us. Matt, oh no, no, oh God he's bleeding, Matt's bleeding, she cried as she looked at the motionless form lying near the tattered wreckage of the tent. Oh, dear God. Please help him.

Stay where you are. Don't move, Gary shouted. That bear could come back.

Holding the 30/30 at the ready, he continued his approach, turning from side to side and completely around every few steps, as he watched for any sign of the bear's return. He was confident he'd hit it, but was unsure how much damage had been inflicted. He knew a single 30-caliber shoulder wound was not a kill on an animal this size, not with all the muscle and bone protecting its heart and lungs. And a wounded grizzly was an extremely dangerous animal.

Please, please … please do something, Vicki called out sobbing. Matt's not moving. Oh, my God. Oh, my God. Matt, Matt, are you okay? Please be okay. Do something, do something. Please help him, see if he's okay.

Gary walked slowly to the bloody, motionless figure on the ground. He hesitated, looked around again for the bear, ignoring her calls as he bent down over the body. Matt was lying on his back, an expanding pool of blood around his head and shoulders. The top of his scalp had been ripped loose and hung down, covering his eyes, almost to his nose. Gary could see blood pulsing from a gaping neck wound. Carotid artery, he said to himself, thinking the bastard's done. Only ribbons of bleeding flesh remained on one shoulder and upper arm, exposing the bone. He squatted down for a closer look, removing the Buck knife from the scabbard on his belt and opening the blade. Carefully he used the blade to lift the scalp flap.

Anyone home? he asked, a lilt in his voice, not expecting an answer. Only a pool of blood remained in one empty eye socket. But the other eye blinked through blood clotting in the gray ash that covered the side of Matt's face. I'll be damned, Gary whispered.

Matt coughed, blood leaking out of the corner of his mouth, and whispered, Help me … please, stop the bleedin', gettin' dark … can't see … can't see … don't let me die.

Gary just looked at him, then cocked his head to one side at a jaunty angle. Why not? he whispered with a smirk on his face.

Is he okay, can you …? Vicki called out and started to climb down from the tree. Oh, please do something, please, please do something. Oh, Matt, darling Matt…

Darling Matt made him angry. Stay where you are, goddammit, he called over his shoulder. I'll take care of it.

Gary remained squatting beside Matt's body, his back blocking Vicki's view, watching and waiting as the blood pulsating from the neck wound slowed with each heartbeat. His eyes shifted from the dying man on the ground to the surrounding brush as he continued to look for any sign of the bear. When Matt made a soft choking sound and his remaining eye glazed, Gary slowly rose to his feet and turned toward Vicki, shaking his head. He's dead. I'm sorry. There was nothin' I could do. He turned and reached for the rain fly that was tangled in the nylon cord and bent fiberglass poles of what remained of the tent. He jerked several times and finally pulled it loose and draped it over the body.

No, no, no, no ... What are you doing? He's not dead. Please no, he can't be ... No, no, please no ... Matt, Matt, don't die. Dear God, please, please don't let Matt die.

Her grief angered Gary, but he tried to conceal it as he walked toward her. He laid his rifle on the ground and reached up to help her down from the tree. Do what I say and you'll be all right. Her crotch and thighs were stained with blood and he could see her nipples through the silk T-shirt. When he lifted her down from the tree, her breasts brushed against his face and stirred a quickening between his legs. Sobbing hysterically, she tried to push away to approach the body on the ground.

No, you can't go there. He's gone, dead, I told you. There's nothin' you can do, he said as he held her back. The blood, he said, pointing to the blood on her thighs. How? The bear?

No, no, no...I'm all right. Help Matt. Oh please don't let him die, she said as she tried again to push away from Gary's grip.

It's too late for him. What's all the blood? You hurt?

No, no. It's nothing, nothing ,doesn't matter. Please help him.

Look, I told you, he's dead, he said, raising his voice as he restrained her. Dead. Get it. Dead, D-E-A-D, he repeated, spitting out each letter. It's just me and you now. We gotta get out of here fast. Sure as hell, that grizzly's comin' back. So get dressed. Where's your clothes?

I don't know … don't know … I don't care. Matt, Matt, oh Matt … she said as she sank to the ground on her knees weeping. After a while, her sobs stopped and she looked up at Gary with a pleading expression on her face. We can't just leave him here. He needs me … I know he can't be …, her voice drifting off in a whisper.

Gary looked at her, but said nothing. It was so still he could hear his heart beating.

Oh my God, she whispered, staring up into the bright blue September sky. She began to wail. It sounded like a wild animal in distress, as her shoulders and back heaved with sobs. Noooo … Nooo … He can't be dead … He can't be …

Gary reached down and lifted her chin. Get hold of yourself. Listen to me, goddammit. Which of these is yours? he said, walking around the body, pointing to the backpacks, clothing, and sleeping bags scattered on the ground.

With hands covering her face, she whispered, I don't know, I don't know …

As he lifted one of the two sleeping bags, an opened package of sanitary pads dropped out. *The blood. So that's it.* He dropped the sleeping bag and reached for the opened backpack and dumped it on the ground. He could tell from the contents that it was hers. He tossed socks, bra, hiking pants, shirt, a couple of fleece tops, parka, and windbreaker in her direction.

Okay, get hold of yourself. He was breathing hard, his patience running thin. Get hold of yourself, Vicki. Get your clothes on. Now. We gotta get movin', get to the horses in case that bear comes back. When she hesitated, he held her shoulders in both hands and shook her gently.

Eyes wide, she blinked. What horses? Where? What are you talking about? How do you know my name? A strange feeling swept over her, thinking that his being here could not be a coincidence. *He must have been watching us.*

Never mind, goddammit. The horses we're gonna fuckin' ride out of here.

As he watched, she sat on the ground and began to pull her clothes on.

Then she stopped, dropping a sock to the ground, and looked up at him. No, no, we can't just leave Matt here, she said and choked back a sob, still thinking *who* is this, *why* is he here? Fear now blended with shock and grief, not only about the bear's likely return, but the sudden appearance of this mysterious man who had saved her life.

Look, I'm sorry, he's dead, D-E-A-D, he said spitting out the letters again. How many times do I gotta fuckin' say that? The bear, he said, his voice breaking with the elevated pitch, remember the fuckin' bear? Now get your fuckin' shoes on. NOW. Before that goddamn grizzly comes back and kills us both.

When she finished tying her boots, he extended his hand and helped her to her feet. He was sweating and breathing hard from excitement and stress when he pulled her sleeping bag from under the tent. He could see the large, damp, dark stains on it.

Blood? he said, pointing and certain of the answer.

She nodded and looked down at her feet.

That stays here. Bears go for it, they can smell fresh blood for miles, he said, realizing that had to be the reason for the big grizzly's unprovoked attack. I got some extra clothes for you here, he said stuffing a few items in her backpack. Leave the rest of your shit here. We gotta travel light.

As Gary was stuffing things into the saddlebags, Vicki moved behind him and walked toward Matt's body. Only his shins and bare feet were visible. She knelt down and lifted a corner of the rain fly. Oh, my God, she gasped, reeling backwards, dropping sideways to the ground.

When she regained consciousness, Gary was wiping her face with a lavender bandanna and cold water he poured from a canteen. I told you not to look, he said, when she opened her eyes. Are you all right? Can you stand up? his voice soft, almost kind, as he took her hand and pulled her to her to a sitting position. Eyes vacant, she didn't answer.

You walk with me. The horses are back there, he said as helped her to her feet, motioning toward the trail that led to the thicket of subalpine fir where he had hidden the night before. He picked up the rifle and her backpack. Stick close to me and watch for that bear, he could be anywhere. A blank look. She didn't respond.

When they reached his hideout, the two horses, tied to trees, were nervous, whinnying and snorting, prancing, tossing their heads back against the restraining ropes. Each was saddled with saddlebags strapped behind. Somehow they had not pulled loose in the noise and chaos of the bear attack, as he feared they might have. Gary quickly removed her clothing from the backpack and stuffed everything into the saddlebags on the sorrel. Then he threw the backpack into the brush.

She was expressionless, silent, in shock, as he packed up his belongings. When he finished, he held her hand and walked with her to the sorrel filly, then boosted her up into the saddle.

* * * * *

Two miles away from the campsite on Morning Star Lake, on the banks of Katoya Lake, vultures circled above a sow grizzly and her two yearling cubs as they lingered on the remains of a moose calf she had killed a day before. Only hooves and skull and remnants of its hide were left when she reared and lifted her nose high as the wind shifted, blowing from the north across the bloody campsite toward them. She turned and, with the two cubs following, headed north into the wind toward Morning Star Lake, following the compelling promise of a fresh kill.

21

———◆◆◆———

By the time the sow grizzly and her cubs arrived at the bloody camp-site at Morning Star Lake, the killer bear was more than a mile to the east, bedded down and nursing its wound in thick timber on the lower slopes of Red Mountain. Gary and his captive had ridden two miles south, climbing the high-forested shelf, to the shores of Pitamakin Lake.

Gary squinted into the morning sunshine at the azure lake at the base of a broad cirque of steep slopes of jagged scree and rock ledges the color of sand that rose steeply to the rimrock of Pitamakin and Cut Bank Passes. After watering their horses, Gary let the buckskin set its own pace up a series of switchbacks that snaked through loose rock and scree toward the ridgeline that he had to lean back to see. The little sorrel filly Vicki was riding followed ten feet behind on a nylon lead rope. The trail was rough and both horses stumbled often and stepped sideways to regain solid footing. As they neared the crest of the ridge, Gary looked back and noticed the filly was limping. Suspecting the worst, he cursed and pounded the saddle horn with his fist.

Where the trail leveled off before another steep rise, he dismounted, muttering under his breath. The wind was blowing in gusts around huge slabs and chunks of shattered rock that surrounded them. Holding the lead rope for balance, he made his way carefully back along the narrow trail. Steady, girl, steady. Don't step sideways, he whispered, as he edged past a rock outcropping and around the sorrel, gripping the saddle to move around Vicki's foot in the stirrup. It would be a painful slide if he slipped, down through talus that would cut through flesh like broken glass. Vicki sat gripping the saddle horn with both hands, still in shock, only occasional flashes of *who is this* surfacing in the black hole of her grief.

Goddammit to motherfuckin' hell, Gary said as he lifted the filly's right rear hoof and saw the bent nails and one side of the shoe pulling loose. He set the hoof back down and threw his head back, looking up at the clear, sunny sky. He was furious. That fuckin' loose shoe, goddammit to hell. Fuckin' trail. Fuckin' rocks and scree. Of all the rotten motherfuckin' luck.

He was behind Vicki when he spoke. When she didn't look back, he reached up, grabbed her arm, and pulled her around. She nearly fell from the saddle, eyes fixed and vacant.

Look at me. Can't you say anything? he asked, releasing another torrent of profanity, the earlier hints of compassion gone. Is anyone home? Say something, Vicki Hathaway. He's gone. Dead. It's just me and you now.

At the mention of her name, she turned toward him and blinked, pale and expressionless, but said nothing. The memory of the lavender bandanna flashed through her mind, stirring memories she couldn't quite recall.

He turned back and looked down at the loose horseshoe, thinking that he should have taken that fucking Indian's advice. That fueled his anger. He made his way back to the buckskin and looked through the saddlebags. He swore again. He'd left the pliers in the truck. He considered trying to twist it off, but was afraid he might split the hoof. He knew few would risk the trail ahead on horseback, let alone on a horse with a loose shoe. He remembered the trail guide—*not recommended for horses or the faint-hearted*. But there was no choice. Turning back was not an option on this trip. Maybe it would be all right. They had to keep going.

When they reached Cut Bank Pass, the view west down into the depths of the Nyack Creek Valley was as daunting as he had read. He got off his horse, lifted a canteen of water that hung from his saddle, and took a long pull as he surveyed the situation. Narrow and steep. A mistake would mean a long slide over a staircase of cliffs and certain death.

You want a drink? he said finally as he walked back to Vicki, offering the canteen, his anger chastened by the reality of what lay ahead. She blinked and looked down at him, but still didn't speak, numb with grief and what was unfolding with this mysterious man. Her hands remained in the same position, gripping the saddle horn, as she had throughout the ride. Gary grabbed his Stetson and held tight as a strong chill blast of wind blew down from McClintock Peak and across the pass, sweeping her loose auburn hair back from a face drained of color and expression.

Here, drink some water. You'll get dehydrated, he said as he held the canteen up to her. She looked at it for a moment, then blinking several times, reached down and took it from his hands and lifted it to her lips.

Don't drink it all, for Chrissakes, he said as she kept swallowing. There's no more until we get down to the creek, and it's gonna be a long slow ride to get there.

She lowered the canteen, resting it on the saddle, staring off into space. He reached up and took the canteen from her hands.

Want to get off and stretch your legs? Might not be any place to get off after we start down.

When she didn't respond, he said, Okay, have it your way. Hang on to that saddle and just do what I say. Understand? It's a long way down.

Gary remounted and urged the buckskin forward as the trail began its descent from the pass, weaving across and around a series of cliffs, loose shale, and steep avalanche chutes. Narrow, barely wide enough for a single horse and rider in many places, Gary found himself holding his breath as the trail dropped at a dangerously uncomfortable angle, with few switchbacks to ease the descent. The exposure reminded him of sections of the trail down from the North Rim of the Grand Canyon. He let the buckskin have its way as it stepped cautiously through talus that covered its hooves, making footing unsure and fraught with peril. Rocks that dwarfed the two riders, loosened by wind and runoff, had fallen from cliffs above, blocking and ripping loose sections of the trail.

Gary kept his eyes focused on the trail ahead, the next step, oblivious to the views north and south to the snowcapped peaks of Razoredge and Tinkham Mountains. As they approached a switchback with a precipitous drop-off, he reined in his horse, hesitating, thinking about what the hiker's guide said about the risks. It was no exaggeration. Only a fool would remain on a horse at this juncture. Even a sure-footed mule would be dangerous. After a moment, he took a deep breath and let it out. There was no choice or time to spare. He had to keep going.

He nudged his buckskin forward slowly and carefully, letting the horse find solid footing while he kept an eye ahead and to the rear where the sorrel and its dazed rider followed on the lead rope. Is she really that out of it crossed his mind. He couldn't comprehend how anyone could care that much about someone else. As his horse stepped out on a smooth dangerously sloping slab of rock, it slipped and stepped sideways to regain its balance. Gary grabbed the saddle horn with one hand and reined the horse back sharply to avoid falling. A steady seep of water trickled down from a crevice in the rock above, spreading as it drained across the slick surface. He hesitated, considered dismounting and leading both horses across, especially the less surefooted little filly with the loose shoe. No time. Had to keep going.

The buckskin had just made it across when he heard a shrill whinny from behind and the clatter of hooves against rock. He turned to see the filly slipping back on her haunches, the loose shoe on her right rear hoof snagged on the edge of the rock, her left rear hoof slipping on the wet surface, throwing her backwards. Gary caught his breath and grimaced as he watched the little horse land hard on her side then slide sideways across the slick rock and off the edge, skidding down a bank of jagged scree until the lead rope snapped tight, twisting the filly's neck at a sickening angle. It stopped the fall on a narrow rock outcropping that sloped off into space, but the horse lay motionless, eyes set, her neck broken. Vicki was still clinging to the saddle, one leg pinned beneath the fallen horse. Below her a small avalanche of rocks and shale triggered by the fall, rattled over ledges and cliffs and down deep ravines below.

Gary was all motion, swinging quickly off the buckskin, pulling and pushing it back away from the edge of trail, sidestepping it against the face of the cliff. The impact and tension on the lead rope pulled his saddle to one side. *Would it hold?* Only the smaller size and lighter weight of the filly enabled his horse to maintain its footing. For now. He could see Vicki's eyes wide with fear as the dead horse's hindquarters, its head held stationary by the rope, pivoted and began to slide slowly toward the edge. If it slipped over the edge, he knew there was no way the buckskin could hold the dead weight.

Grab the lead rope. Grab the lead rope, he shouted to Vicki. Grab the lead rope, goddammit. Now. Listen to me. Now. Now. Grab it. Frozen with fear, she finally released her grip on the saddle and gripped the lead rope with one hand then quickly with the other. There was a pause in the slow, lethal slide of the dead horse as her weight shifted away from it.

Okay, okay, hold on 'til I get down there, Gary called against the wind which was gusting with greater force, blowing the words back into his face, snapping his Stetson wildly against the chin strap, and back off his head. Then he looked down. The exposure made him dizzy, the sweet-sour taste of fear rising in his throat. He hesitated. *Should I? Is she worth it?* He looked down at Vicki, saw the terror, the pleading look in her eyes, and then she mouthed, *Please.*

Gary swallowed hard and then, heart pounding, he eased over the edge of the trail and, holding tightly to the lead rope, made his way carefully down through the loose scree toward her, hoping that the rope would hold and the buckskin wouldn't spook or lose its footing. Still holding the lead rope with his left hand, he pulled the Buck knife from the scabbard he wore on his belt with his right, and opened the blade with his teeth.

Okay, listen to me. Look at me, goddammit. Look at me, he screamed, the wind whipping the words from his mouth. I'm going to cut this lead rope below you and let the horse fall. You have to hold tight to the rope. Understand? Hold on to the rope. I'll grab hold of you as soon as I cut the horse loose. Got it? Look at me. Got it? Pale, eyes wide, mouth open, she didn't speak. Yes or no. Help me goddammit, he screamed, the wind

stronger now, pushing against him. Nod your fuckin' head. She finally
nodded.

Gary tried to dig the heels of his boots into the scree for solid footing,
but there was none, as loose rock gave way beneath him with every movement he made. It all depended on the buckskin and the lead rope holding.

Here goes, he yelled into the wind as he drew the knife across the
taut rope a few inches from the dead horse's halter. There was a snap and
recoil as it separated and the clatter of falling rock. Gary let the knife
fall as he quickly reached for Vicki and slid his arm under her armpit
and around her chest. He watched as the horse slid sideways and somer-
saulted out into space, bouncing from one ledge to another as it fell, the
saddle breaking, leather splitting and tearing, the contents of the saddlebags tumbling out like confetti, blowing in the wind, marking the path of
the fall. Finally it came to rest, a small dark spot at the base of a narrow
ravine more than a thousand feet below. He shook his head and swore.

Breathing hard and weak from exertion, Gary was afraid to move
for fear of joining the doomed horse at the base of the cliffs. Finally, he
looked at Vicki and shouted through the wind, Okay, Vicki. Here's what
we have to do. Can you move your leg?

Her eyes seemed more focused when she looked at him. Her lips
moved slightly, but she seemed unable to speak.

Look goddammit, snap out of it. I can't do this all myself. You wanna
die here? Answer me! he screamed. Can you move your fuckin' leg?

Vicki's eyelids fluttered. Then she lifted her knee and moved her
ankle.

Okay, now listen to me. Real close. I'm gonna hold this end of the
rope to keep it tight so it doesn't sway back and forth. Very slowly now I
want you to go hand-over-hand up to the ledge. I'll be right behind you
in case you slip. Can't take a chance on that horse bein' able to hold the
weight of both of us pullin' on it. Now take your time. Get the best footing you can. You understand?

She nodded that she did.

When you get to the ledge, be calm. Don't spook the horse or I'm
fuckin' gone. I'm gone, you're gone. Understand, Vicki? The blank

expression. Vicki, goddammit, he shouted her name again. Look at me. Do you understand? No sudden moves. Don't do anything that would scare the horse and make him bolt.

She looked startled, then nodded.

Okay, get goin'. Easy does it.

When Vicki turned on her stomach and tried to dig her toes into the scree, Gary tucked his head into his shoulders as a shower of loose rock cascaded down over his back.

Easy, easy, for Chrissakes, he shouted. Take your time. Don't get us killed.

With each move, Gary hunched his shoulders and flinched as more rocks slid and tumbled over and around him and bounced out into space. He looked up again and could see that she had one knee on the ledge and was trying to raise the injured leg, holding the rope with one hand and pushing down on the ledge with the other, when her knee slipped. Gary couldn't see the look of terror on her face, but he knew it was there. Jesus, he muttered, she's gone. But somehow she was able to hold tight with one hand before grabbing the rope with the other. He held his breath as he watched her slowly pull herself up over the ledge and take hold of the buckskin's leg.

No, no, not his leg Gary whispered to himself, afraid to divert her attention. He's gonna pull away and we're all goners was running through his mind. But the horse held steady as she made a final push and rolled beneath it.

Gary took a deep breath and blew it out with relief. Okay, my turn. Hold steady, Buck. Don't wanna die on this fuckin' mountain, he said under his breath as he turned on his stomach and began to inch his way up the rope, the muscles in his arms aching knots. When he reached the ledge, he pulled himself over the edge and rolled to a sitting position. We made it, he said. He blinked, shook his head, and waited to catch his breath.

After a few minutes, he licked the sweat from his upper lip and spoke softly. I don't believe it. I thought we were goners. He stood up slowly, still shaken, unsure of his balance, and embraced the neck of his horse, pressing against the smooth flesh of its withers and gently rubbing its soft nose, thinking the hiker's guide was right—the trail was too treacherous for horseback. But there was no choice now with her injured leg. He looked over at her and said, You climb up on the horse. I'll lead him down the rest of the way.

She shook her head. It was the first time she had responded so quickly to anything he'd said. I can't. I'm afraid, she whispered.

There's no choice, you gotta do it, he said as he took her by the hand and helped her to her feet. She stumbled as she put weight on the injured leg. He caught her and eased her to the ground. Pulling her pant leg up, he examined the injury. Ugly abrasion, but not broken, he guessed. He helped her to her feet. She shook her head as he boosted her into the saddle anyway. Look, you can't walk on that leg. Even if you try, it'll take too long. We have to get off this mountain before dark. Won't be able to see the trail as bad as it is if we don't.

With Gary leading the horse and Vicki clinging to the saddle horn, they reached the headwaters of Nyack Creek on the valley floor at dusk. They had descended nearly four thousand feet of elevation in five perilous miles. The temperature was dropping fast as the sun in a clear sky dropped behind the high peaks, and shadows began to lengthen and darken the valley. After glacial rock and high wind, the smell of damp earth, the sound of running water, and the serenity of the valley floor was a relief. Gary believed the worst was behind them.

But he knew he had miscalculated, thinking they could travel the distance from Morning Star Lake to the cabin on Nyack Creek in one long day's ride. Possible, if everything had gone right. But it hadn't. Now what, he said to himself, thinking it's almost dark and we're stranded here for the night deep in a goddamn wilderness with only a few provisions, the rest lost with the sorrel. He looked over at Vicki, still on horseback. Except for what she wore, her belongings were lost when the horse fell. They had only his sleeping bag and a small tarpaulin he had wrapped around it.

This is as far as we go, he said, as he helped her down from the horse. Have to make camp here tonight,

Vicki looked around, but didn't speak before sitting down on a large flat rock. Then she said in a whisper, I have to pee really bad. She looked like a little girl when she said it. He almost smiled. Over there, he said, pointing to some bushes.

When she returned, he held out the canteen to her. Here, drink some water. You're probably dehydrated. I'll build a fire, plenty of firewood, and there's grass, and water in the creek for us and Buck. He reached for the reins and walked the buckskin through tall grass to the edge of the creek. So this is where Nyack Creek begins, he thought, recalling the many trips he had made coming the other way along it to prepare the cabin.

He paused and turned to look at her standing alone—frail and vulnerable in this immense wilderness—trying to understand the strangeness he felt about her, like no other woman he had known. Something more than desire. Was it pity? Affection? Alien emotions for Gary Ray Kemp. His vocabulary for feelings was limited. He couldn't figure it out.

After he removed the bridle, saddle and saddlebags and hobbled the horse in the grass near the creek, he walked back to her. Here, you can use this sleeping bag; it'll keep you warm with the tarp beneath it. He pulled a hooded parka for himself from the saddlebag. I got this, the saddle blanket, and the fire.

He moved closer to where she sat and reached down to her. He had taken off his sunglasses. Here's a couple of candy bars. It'll be okay. I'm gonna build a fire. We're almost there.

She looked up at him and whispered, Thank you. For the first time she held his eyes with hers, still wondering about this strange man who had appeared out of nowhere and risked his own life twice to save hers. For a moment there on the ledge, when he hesitated, she didn't think he would. She could see the uncertainty. But then at great risk to himself, he'd crawled down to save her. Still, there was something ominous about him, something not right, something that made her fearful. But why? His eyes? So strange. She let go of the thought. Without him, she knew she couldn't survive.

Gary couldn't believe what he was *feeling*. Saving a life instead of taking one. A very different feeling. It reminded him of the way he'd felt when, as a little boy, he had given his grandmother a box of candy for her birthday. She was so surprised and pleased. The hug and kiss on top of his head brought tears to his eyes.

He watched as Vicki crawled into the sleeping bag and pulled it up over her head, then built a small fire and sat down by it, staring into the flames, thinking about all that had happened in the last twenty-four hours. It was hard to imagine how it had played out. He removed the rifle from the scabbard that was lying next to the saddle. As the fire began to die down, he threw a pine branch onto the smoldering embers and watched it flare. Then he zipped the parka up tight around his head and covered himself, as best he could, with the saddle blanket. He leaned back into the saddle and stared up at the stars, thinking the end of the beginning, the beginning of the end.

22

---◆---

Thursday, September 6. The next morning Gary was awake to see the sun just rising above the high eastern ridgeline of the pass they had traversed in such peril the day before. The Nyack Creek Valley was enclosed in a ground-hugging fog and beneath it, frost sparkled on the marsh grass and bushes along the creek. Between the cold and the need to keep the fire going, he hadn't slept much as he tried to stay warm huddled by the fire in the hooded parka with the saddle blanket wrapped around his legs, his back resting against the saddle. They had survived a difficult day and he felt energized as he relieved himself then walked over to the buckskin hobbled in the grass near the creek. Kneeling down at the edge of the creek, he broke a thin film of ice, cupped his hands, and rinsed his face in the icy water. He stood up, wiping the cold water and sleep from his face with the lavender bandanna, inhaling deeply the crisp pine-scented air. He turned and walked back to where Vicki was lying, looking small, knotted up in his dark sleeping bag with only the top of her head showing. He reached down and touched her head. Time to get up, he said softly when she stirred. You wanna candy bar? That's all I got.

Vicki pushed back the sleeping bag and looked up, rubbed her eyes, and then jerked upright, clutching the sleeping bag against her chest. What? She shook her head, then looked at him as if this was the first time she had seen him. What happened? Where am I? Then she remembered.

Don't you remember? The bear? Then your horse fell. I saved your life. You don't remember that?

She hesitated, looking at him, then nodded, confusion and consternation etched in her face, thinking *who is he?*

You remember comin' down off that high ridge up there yesterday when your horse fell? he said, pointing up toward the pass.

Yes, she said softly. What about Matt?

You don't remember?

Is he okay? Where did he go? her voice rising with anxiety.

Gary didn't know what to say. Total denial. He wanted her to realize that Matt was dead, but he didn't want to risk having to deal with a hysterical woman.

What's the last thing you remember? he asked.

She shook her head and tears filled her eyes, the memory of Matt's death too painful to recall. I don't know … can't think … so confused … don't understand what's going on.

What's the last thing you remember? he asked again.

She thought for minute, wringing her hands, and then looked up at him. The horse falling … that ledge … in a tree … I can't … so confused.

He smiled. That's true. I saved your life on that ledge. But is that all? Don't you remember me shootin' that bear and liftin' you down outta that tree?

She didn't say anything for a long moment. Yes, she said softly, nodding, the horror edging past the denial into her consciousness. Then she lifted her hands to her face to hide the tears.

He put his hand on her shoulder. Okay, okay. Forget it. You'll be all right. I'll take care of you. Don't worry. Right now we have to get goin'. It's cold. Wrap that sleepin' bag around you. You'll feel better if you start movin' around. Eat that candy bar. You're gonna need energy. We still have a ways to go.

Go where?

To a safe place, he said as he stooped and picked up the saddle and saddle blanket and walked over to the horse. You gotta piss, there's bushes over there, he motioned with his head.

As she stood up, he could see she was favoring the injured leg. Let me check your leg, he said. Does it hurt?

She looked at him as if she didn't understand, but then whispered, Not bad.

When he lifted her pant leg to the knee, he could see the abrasion and dark bruising along her calf, but knew it wasn't serious. You're lucky, he said. It'll be sore for a while, but it'll heal. I got some aspirin and bandages at the cabin. He watched as she limped toward the bushes. When she returned a few minutes later, he had the horse saddled. He rolled up the sleeping bag and slung the saddlebags over one shoulder. We're gonna ride double on the horse as long as we can, unless he starts givin' out. Then I'll walk. But for now you can ride behind me. Just hold on to the saddle. I'll hang the saddlebags and blanket roll over my lap.

Vicki sat staring at him, blinking occasionally, still in a fog, the horror of Matt's death just below the surface of her consciousness.

Cabin? What cabin? My mind … I'm … I'm so confused … you … The lavender bandanna flashed through her thoughts again.

Look, I'll explain later. Right now you have to get on that horse unless you want to stay here by yourself. You'll be all right. I know what I'm doin'. You just have to do exactly what I say. Now, come on, finish that candy bar, and let's get goin'.

Vicki finished the candy bar and got to her feet slowly, pressing her fingers against her temples, stumbling as she walked to the horse. Gary put his left foot into the stirrup and swung up on the saddle. Then he reached down to her. Here, give me your left hand and reach up and grab the back of the saddle with your right. When I say three, you jump and I'll pull you up behind me.

Out of sight, not far away, two grizzlies browsed on huckleberry bushes turned bright crimson by recent frosts on an avalanche chute that stretched down the side of Razoredge Mountain. The bears, giving one another plenty of room, raised their heads when they picked up the scent of the couple on horseback below them, then returned to the berries, preparing for the long winter's sleep.

* * * * *

It was early evening when Gary and Vicki came to a break in the trees and saw the derelict ranger cabin. Above the forest canopy, they could see the rays of a sinking sun illuminating the cliffs high on the north face of Mount Stimson rising out of the dark forest. A doe and her fawn looked up briefly from where they were browsing on serviceberries at the edge of the clearing, then ambled off into the trees. They had ridden more than ten miles, detouring around deadfalls and washouts, fording the creek twice. It had been slow going on a horse that was worn down. Gary had walked the last several miles, worried that the buckskin might go lame.

Except to ask for water and respond with halting answers to Gary's infrequent questions, Vicki had not spoken throughout the long ride. When they stopped to water and rest the horse, she relieved herself and rinsed her face in the creek. Otherwise, when Gary spoke to her, she only looked at him and did what he told her, her expression vacant.

There was a flash of lightening and a thunderclap from gathering storm clouds that had blotted out the sunset. We made it, and just in time, he said as he led the buckskin to the hitching rail.

Okay, he said over his shoulder as the rain began to fall. Here, take my hand; I'll hold you while you just kinda roll off. Easy does it, now, so you don't hurt that sore leg of yours. He put his arm around her waist and eased her to the ground. This is where we'll be stayin' for a while, he said, nodding toward the cabin. She stood staring at the cabin as he removed the bridle and replaced it with a halter and rope that was hanging from the hitching rail. After he secured the buckskin, he removed the saddle, saddlebags and saddle blanket, and the blanket roll. There, that feels better don't it, Buck, he said as he ran his hand over the horse's withers. I'll explain everything to you later, he said without looking at Vicki as he slung the saddlebags over his shoulder and cradled the saddle and blanket roll in his arms, and nodding again toward the cabin, Just do what I say and you'll be fine.

You mean we're going to stay here tonight? I need to call my folks. Her words surprised him. It was the first hint that her long-term memory remained.

Well, that's not possible. No way to do that. We're a long way from a phone, he said as he set the saddle on the ground and unlocked the padlock he had put on the cabin door.

When Gary opened the door to the cabin, a streak of fading light traveled back to a woodstove in the center of a dark, colorless interior. Vicki hesitated on the stoop in rain dripping from the eaves. Her apprehension crested when she stepped inside. Dust motes stirred by the draft from the open door floated in the sunlight and disappeared in the gloom. The damp, musty odor filled her with dread. Thoughts of isolation, confinement, and death made it hard for her to get her breath. She could see two metal bunk beds set against the far wall. A crudely made table of rough-cut pine boards, with two chrome and Formica chairs at either end, stood near the center of the room. She watched without speaking as Gary set all he was carrying in a corner and lifted an old kerosene lamp from the table and struck a match to light it. Its fluttering glow revealed a shelf stacked with canned goods. On the floor beneath it were sacks of sugar, pinto beans, onions and potatoes. He walked across the small room to where another kerosene lamp sat on a wood bench against the wall opposite the bunk beds and lit it. Instead of warmth and cheer, the shadowy room took on an ominous amber glow like the funeral parlor that frightened her as a little girl when her grandfather died.

Not far from the table and chairs, rust was streaking down the sides of the stovepipe that stretched through the rafters to the roof. Gary ran his hand over the cold metal stovetop, as she stood motionless, still near the door. Without looking at her, he said, I'll get a fire goin' and soon it'll be real nice 'n' cozy in here.

When he opened the woodstove, she could see that it was half filled with torn and crumbled paper and kindling wood. More kindling wood, old newspapers, and magazines were stacked beside the stove next to an ash pail and scoop. Gary flipped through the stack and smiled. Lookit here, he said. Lookit these—*Readers Digest, Field and Stream, Outdoor Life, Montana Wildlife*—all 1970s. She glanced at the magazines and then around the room, saying nothing.

A dark blue enameled tin coffee pot with just a hint of rust rimming its base sat on the stovetop. Two aluminum pots and a cast-iron frying pan hung from nails on one wall next to a Charlie Russell calendar, 1973, from a Kalispell feed store. The other walls were bare. A broom stood in one corner next to an old-fashioned, metal washtub that was large enough to bath and wash clothes in. Gary pointed to a white metal chamber pot with floral design and a lid that sat in the corner away from the door. You know what that's for, right? he said to her. No way would you want to walk out into the trees to that outhouse to take a piss at night. She stared at him, not moving from the doorway, thinking she wanted to run away, but couldn't.

Come on now, he said, smiling a smile that suggested he was thinking about something else. We made it. We're here safe and sound. Enjoy. Make yourself comfortable. I'm gonna build a nice fire. Need to warm this place up. He tried to affect a folksy air that didn't work. I'll heat some water. There's that big ole washtub over there. I'll slide it over closer to the stove where it'll be nice and warm. Then you can take a nice warm bath, get yourself cleaned up.

She watched as Gary struck a match and lit the fire. When the flames blazed up, he closed the stove door and poured water from a large plastic container that sat against the wall into a metal bucket and set it on the stovetop. He looked over at her and smiled. There's water in the tub and a hot bucket full will warm it up real nice. Then he walked over to a rough plank shelf that was bracketed to the wall and looked at an assortment of canned goods he had stocked. You hungry? he said over his shoulder. You gotta be. I sure as hell am. He selected two cans. Corned beef hash or chili? Your choice. Which do you want?

She nodded yes, then clutched her head with both hands and looked up at the ceiling.

Yes? What the hell does that mean? I said which one do you want?

I don't know. I ... I don't care ... anything. She began to wring her hands, tears welling in her eyes. What's this all about? Why did you bring me here?

He ignored the questions, pressing on, still affecting a pleasant mood and folksy air as if all that was happening was normal as he opened the cans, placing a metal spoon in each, and walked over to the woodstove where he set them on top next to the pot of water to heat.

I'm takin' the corned beef hash. You can have the chili. I got some crackers to go with it. Christ, I'm starvin'. Then he hesitated and smiled. On second thought, maybe you better get washed up before we eat.

As she sat on the edge of bunk bed, fear and adrenaline were beginning to clear her mind. She realized now that she was the captive of a very strange and unsettling man. She could sense from the way he was looking at her that it wasn't just food that Gary had on his mind.

Any lingering doubts she might have had about his intentions disappeared when Gary lifted a chain attached to the floor and showed it to her. He had a strange smile on his face when he spoke, a mixture of satisfaction and maybe embarrassment, as if he was ashamed for what he was about to say and do. This is for when I'm gone, he said as he reached down and gently placed the leather-padded, metal collar around one of Vicki's ankles and locked its two metal rings with a small padlock. The other end of the chain was attached to a steel swivel he had bolted to the floor. The chain was about the size used to restrain large dogs. It didn't quite reach to three sides of the room and the door.

This is just for when I'm not around, until you get used to bein' here. I don't want you to be gettin' any ideas about runnin' off. That would be dangerous out here in the backcountry. He patted her ankle gently and smiled, as if he was fitting her with new shoes. That feel okay, not too tight? She stared at him, fear trumping disbelief, and didn't answer. I keep the key when I'm gone. When I'm here, it'll be hangin' over there on that nail, he said, walking to the far wall and, reaching high, he pointed to a nail. Then he returned and unlocked the collar. He looked up from where he was kneeling and smiled at her. But there's no need for it when we're here together.

She put her head in her hands and said what she was thinking. I'm scared. What's this all about?

Of what? Me? There was an edge to his tone. Remember I saved your fuckin' life. Twice. You remember? Twice. He began to pace, turning his back to her. Then he whirled around to face her, a big smile, and the folksiness returned. He cleared his throat.

Okay, I understand where you're comin' from, so let me explain how it's gonna be. You're gonna stay here with me for a while. Don't worry; it'll be all right. I'm gonna take good care of you. We have everything we need. I stocked the place with plenty of food, warm sleepin' bags, the works. Plus I'll be huntin' to bring in fresh meat when we need it. You know, kinda like the old days, pioneers, livin' off the land. Should be nice. Just you and me. All you have to do is follow the rules, do what I say and everything will be fine. The main one you need to remember and never forget is that I'm in charge and you do what I say. Follow the rules and there's no problems. When I'm out of the cabin huntin', doin' whatever, you stay here and wear the ankle bracelet. I don't want you gettin' any ideas about runnin' off. It's for your own protection. It's a long way to anywhere. And it's fuckin' dangerous—you know about grizzlies, he half-smiled, but there's also cougars and wolves out there. This is real backcountry. Predators rule.

Vicki could see any challenge to his authority, any questioning of his control over her triggered the anger. The shock of the cabin forced her to think, clear her mind, concentrate. There was no choice. She knew she was in a desperate situation and had to play his game—whatever it was, she wasn't sure—if she wanted to survive.

I'm not going to run away. To where? I don't know where we are, or which way to go ... I'm ... I don't understand why ... please just tell me what this is all about.

It was as if she hadn't spoken. The water's about ready, he said looking at steam rising from the pot. I want you to get yourself undressed while I fill this tub. I'm gonna move these kerosene lamps a little closer so you can see better. That odd smile heightened her anxiety, as he poured a steaming bucket of water into the washtub. You'll look real pretty, smell real nice, after you get cleaned up. He walked back to the shelves and returned with a bar of soap, a washcloth, and a towel with a motel logo on it. Here you go. Now get undressed. I'm gonna have a little drink of whiskey to celebrate our arrival while you get yourself cleaned up, he said as he took a fifth of Jim Beam from the shelf and took the bubbling cans off the stove. We can eat after that. Those cans'll stay warm here next to the stove until we're … he smiled and cleared his throat … I mean *you're* finished.

Her mind, now more focused, was racing. She looked at him leering at her as he lifted the bottle to his lips. Could I please do this alone?

No, no, don't be shy. You're gonna have to get used to me bein' around, he said as he swallowed and then smacked his lips. Damn that whiskey hits the spot after a hard day. Then with an edge to his voice, Now get undressed before that water cools down.

Turning her back toward him, she hesitantly removed her clothes, placing them on one of the chairs. She reached down and felt the water, covering her breasts with her other arm, before stepping into the wash-tub, still facing away from him. Except for the stinging sensation of her injured leg, the warm water felt good rising to her waist as she knelt down.

Okay, have it your way, he said as he stood up, scraping his chair around to the other side of the tub to face her. He repositioned one of the kerosene lamps for a better view before sitting down, one elbow resting on the table, his head cocked to the side at a jaunty angle, as he took another swallow of whiskey.

She kept her eyes averted as she began to bath, feeling his eyes as he watched from the shadows behind the lamp, swinging the bottle back and forth between his knees. Except for the sounds of her bathing, it was still. A moth fluttered soundlessly in the glow above one of the lamps. She was as beautiful as he remembered when he first saw her nude at the lake on the North Fork earlier that summer.

When she finished, she reached for the towel hanging on the chair nearest the tub and stood up, covering herself as best she could. Her wet skin glistened in the flickering lamp light, bikini tan marks visible on her breasts, stomach, and hips. Trembling in the chill of the room, she toweled herself quickly and wrapped the towel around her. She could see him out of the corner of her eye and feel his stare. He set the Jim Beam down, his fingers making a galloping rhythm on the table.

Throat dry, face flushed, he swallowed hard when she dropped one hand from the towel and reached for her clothes. A dry cough. Never mind, he said, the words thickening in his throat. Then he walked over and pulled away the towel she clutched in front of her and draped it over a chair. Now over here, he said, as he took her hand and motioned to one of the bunk beds.

She hesitated and pulled back. Please don't do this to me, she said, meeting his eyes, one arm across her breasts, her other hand covering between her thighs. Please, no, I'm having my period. Please, please don't do this.

Gary breathed in the clean, fresh soap smell of her body before he spoke. Don't do this? Baby, a little warm blood doesn't bother me. I can't not do this. Now kneel down on that bunk and raise up that pretty little ass of yours. I been waitin' all summer for this, ever since I saw you ridin' that bike. He unbuckled his belt and unzipped his fly. An aura of whiskey, horseflesh, and saddle sweat hung around him. She knew better than to resist. Now you're all mine, he whispered, catching his breath as he moved up against her. The tension of her body excited him. He raped her, breathing fast through his nose, Wranglers sagging over his boots.

—————◆◆◆—————

23

---◆---

Saturday, September 8. It was early afternoon on a clear, cool, day with fall in the air. Keno had just given the horses a ration of oats and was feeding his dogs when he heard sirens out on the highway. More than a few. Walking out beyond the trees for a better view, he could see and hear Park Service vehicles, lights flashing, sirens wailing, as they slowed to make the turn from the highway then accelerated on the gravel road, leaving billowing clouds of dust behind. Moments later he heard the thumping sound of a helicopter, then saw it fly over the ridge behind his ranch toward the broad valley leading into Morning Star Lake. What the hell's going on? Must be something big. Someone hurt back in there, he said to himself. He walked over to the corral and put a bridle on the horse closest to him, an old Appaloosa mare, and rode it bareback out to the road to see what he could find out.

At the edge of the road, he waited, watching a patrol car as it turned off the highway and headed toward him. He nudged his horse forward and waved as the car approached and began to brake.

You need help? the ranger said as he slowed to a stop.

No, not me. What's goin' on back there? Keno said, motioning toward the mountains.

Bear mauling. Hikers.

Where at?

Not sure. Either Medicine Grizzly or Morning Star. Gotta get back there to find out.

As he accelerated, the car fishtailed, spraying gravel behind as it sped down the road. Moments later, Keno heard the wail of another siren and saw an ambulance speeding down the road toward him, its dome lights flashing. He reined his horse around and walked it behind the gate to give the ambulance plenty of room as it passed. He waited until the dust cleared. No more cars, only the receding sound of the helicopter as he turned his horse and headed back down the road to his ranch. He could see the peaks of Medicine Grizzly and Triple Divide Mountains on the western horizon. That's where that Gary character said he was going, he thought. Wonder if it's got something to do with him?

24

Sunday, September 9. Harry Dawkins stopped at the Glacier Highland for breakfast and bought the Sunday paper. The headline, COUPLE BELIEVED KILLED BY BEARS got his attention. He read the article and immediately called Beth and told her about the attack. I hate to say it, Beth, but I bet it's that young couple we met a couple weeks ago in Freda's, remember the one's that said they were going on that hike into Morning Star Lake after Labor Day.

* * * * *

A gentle shower was pattering on the cabin roof. Vicki was lying on the bunk bed, watching droplets run down a windowpane, the sound of a leak dripping somewhere in the room. Going out to hunt, he had told her earlier. She wasn't sure how long he had been gone. Maybe she had fallen asleep; she wasn't sure. She had lost track of time and place, waking at night to a dark and silent world, often wondering whether she was awake or dreaming, conscious and subconscious no longer clearly defined her state of mind. She was about to close her eyes when a gunshot shattered the stillness. She rolled off the bunk and walked quickly to the window, the chain around her ankle dragging behind. At the far end of the clearing, she could see him standing over something he'd killed.

Then, cowering in the trees beyond the clearing, she saw it, the spotted fawn. Tears welled up in her eyes and trickled down her cheeks. *He shot the doe.* That morning she had watched the doe and her fawn browsing in the clearing. Unafraid, curious daily visitors, they seemed almost tame the way they would stand and return her stare.

She couldn't restrain the anguish when he dragged the carcass back to the cabin. Why did you shoot her? What's wrong with you? she said softly through tears. Look at that little fawn, now it's going to die, too, without its mother. Did you have to kill …

Now wait just a fuckin' minute, he said evenly through clenched teeth as he turned from the slain deer and walked over to where she stood just inside the cabin door. He took a deep breath, trying to control his anger. Look, I didn't find anything to shoot on the hunt and we need fresh meat, so here it is, a goddamn deer. Big deal. Get out the violins. You want food to eat, or don't ya? So just keep your fuckin' thoughts about what I do or don't do to yourself.

I'm sorry, I just …

Never mind he mumbled, bothered by her response, reflecting on what he'd done, something he didn't often do. She stepped aside as he entered the cabin and walked to the center of the room. Turning to face her, his shoulders back, head held high at a jaunty angle, a sure sign, she had learned, that a lecture was coming.

Look, out in the backcountry there are predators and prey, and both are a necessary part of nature. He paused, looking intently at her, but she had lowered her eyes.

Sit down, I want to explain somethin' to you, he said, pointing to a chair at the table. Go on, sit down. He waited until she did, then, Right and wrong has no more to do with what happens than right and wrong has to do with sunrise and sunset, or if it rains or doesn't rain, or someone, or something like this goddamn deer, lives or dies.

She lifted her hands and rubbed her eyes.

You know what a paradigm is? He asked, hoping to impress with the word.

She looked at him and nodded.

Good. Well nature is a paradigm, a paradigm of life and death. He began to pace back and forth. It was a performance he had longed to do. Now he had an audience. Not only an audience, but a beautiful young woman, someone he desperately wanted to impress and, now, whose attention he commanded.

Look out that window, he said, pointing with a sweep of his arm. That's nature Vicki, and nature's a war where the superior species kill and inferior species die. Everything around us is constantly destroying something else in order to survive and make the world better, not just so-called predators like bears, wolves, and cougars, he hesitated for emphasis, and *me*.

Look at me, goddammit. Don't cover your face when I'm talkin' to you. You understand what I'm sayin' … saying? He repeated, hanging on to his *g*'s, intent on impressing her. He stooped down, unfastened the lock on the chain to free her, then walked over and hung the key on the nail.

Still averting his eyes, she reached down and rubbed the red mark on her ankle.

Her sadness was frustrating, made him angry. He wanted her to be happy. Well do you? Are you listenin' to what I'm fuckin' sayin'? he said, dropping *g*'s as his anger rose. Answer me, goddammit.

I'm listening, she whispered, as she looked up at him. Hoping it would calm him, she added, I think I understand.

Okay, that's better, he said, flashing that odd smile below those empty eyes.

I didn't mean to make you angry, she said softly. I'm sorry I said what I did. I … I just … I'll do whatever you say.

Let's put it this way, he said, pleased by her submissiveness and pronouncing his words carefully, so she would know he wasn't just some stupid hick, there's way too many rich, fucking college boys who don't work regular jobs like other people because they come from families that already have more money than they know what to do with. So they're really parasites, living off trust funds, living just to have fun. Their whole life has been fun. No worries, no cares. I see them all the time in the parks where I work.

He's crazy, she thought. What's this have to do with killing the deer?

Talking about college boys like Matt, he'd rekindled his anger and the g's disappeared again. You know, they're ski bums or hikin' guides or mountain climbers, or rafters, or some fuckin' thing like that. And, yeah, they all have suntans and act real macho, talkin' about 'gettin' after it,' 'baggin' peaks,' 'class five and six pitches,' 'runnin' class five rapids in fuckin' Nepal … I get so fuckin' sick of listenin' to their bullshit, like that guy you and your fuckin' asshole friends were listening to, braggin' in Freda's a while back. Looked like a fuckin' Jew boy to me, talkin' loud on his goddamn cell phone so everybody could hear what a big deal he was. Nepal, for Chrissakes.

Oh my God, the weird guy at the bar flashed through her mind.

Who the fuck his age can afford to go to fuckin' Nepal, except some worthless parasite for Chrissakes? But women like you eat that shit up. He was running out of breath. Why? The scene at the lake flooded his mind. Because someone licks your pussy like some kind of disgustin' dog in heat? Nothin' but a fuckin' dike doin' that shit, a lesbo in a college boy's body.

Vicki watched as he stalked over to the window, paused, and pulled something out of a stuff bag. You remember this? Got you name on it, he said waving the lavender bandanna, then he pounded the wall with his fist.

Her mind was reeling back in time, for the first time making the connection between the spilt beer incident at Freda's and the lavender bandanna she'd left at the lake that early summer afternoon with Matt. The realization that he had been watching them sent a chill through her.

Gary didn't speak for a while. Then he turned around to face her, his dark figure backlit by the afternoon sun that was breaking through gray clouds after the brief shower.

This country's being ruined by people like him—the rich fuckin' privileged class. He shook his finger at her, still clutching the lavender bandanna in his other hand. You should see the kind of shit I put up with most every day. It's the same wherever I work. Everyone thinks they're so fuckin' special just because they have money. He stopped and took a deep breath, thoughts of being taunted in primary school about crooked teeth there was no money to fix rippling through his mind.

Anyway, the way I see it, that big griz did somethin' about it. One less rich boy to deal with. Every time I hear of one of those bastards fallin' off a cliff, drownin' in their kayaks, or gettin' killed by a bear, like your fuckin' boyfriend, I say good. Nature's way. He looked over at her, waiting for a response, but there was none. She willed the memory of Matt's death away.

I can tell you really don't get what I'm talkin' about, he said, walking over to the stove and then back to the window, twisting and rolling the bandanna around his fingers.

No, I'm trying. It's just that ...

No you ain't, he said. You're just sayin' you are because you don't want to hear the truth about what's really wrong—not with *me*, goddammit, but this fuckin' society. So just listen to me. Get it? Listen.

She looked up at him and nodded, aware of how eye contact and her attention pleased him. But the way he looked at her, the intensity of his gaze, sent an unsettling rush through her own body that she didn't understand. Appalled, she wanted to wrench her gaze away, but feared what he might do if she did.

Like I said, everything has a purpose—like what I do sometimes. I'm going to tell you about myself, because I think you're intelligent and you might understand if you clear your mind and listen to reason. That's why I brought you here. Most people wouldn't because they're too fuckin' stupid to understand common sense.

He began to pace back and forth in front of her and she let her gaze drop for a second, lifting her head just in time as he stopped directly in front of her and stared at her for what seemed like a long time. Maintain eye contact, she told herself. But doing that and the strange feeling that accompanied it bothered her. It was quiet except for a breeze stirring outside.

The buckskin whinnied, breaking the spell as he quickly glanced outside and started pacing back and forth again. Her heart was pounding. What now? she wondered.

Then he stopped, standing at a slight angle facing her a few feet away. As he cleared his throat and took a deep breath, folding the bandanna and putting it into his back pocket, Vicki realized how desperate he was for her attention and approval. Agree with whatever he says, she told herself. Your life depends on it. But the look in his eye meant more than that: he sincerely wanted her love. The thought made her shudder and drop her eyes to the floor, looking anywhere but at him.

You know, if you travel around the country like I do, he began. Then he exploded. Look at me when I'm talkin' to you goddammit! He stepped closer and put his hand under her chin, pulling her face up roughly, leaning into it with warm, sour breath.

She flinched, waiting for the slap, whispering, I'm sorry, I …

Shut the fuck up and listen to what I'm sayin'. He let go of her chin and stepped away. With his back to her, he spoke now in a calm voice. If you travel around the country like I do, you see a world that doesn't exist in airports and fuckin' two-hundred-dollar-a-night motels, which is all people like you see when you travel.

She forced herself to hold his gaze, trying to look understanding, sympathetic, interested, anything to keep his anger from exploding.

He stopped, took another deep breath. Everywhere, there's these pigs, these fuckin' whores, he sputtered, roamin' the streets, truck stops, fuckin' guys for money. Dirty, filthy whores, givin' blow jobs to buy drugs, spreadin' diseases like AIDS, herpes, clap, every goddamn thing. You have to be crazy to fuck one of 'em. Everywhere I go, I see 'em. They're outta fuckin' control, so I decided to do somethin' about it. Here let me show you.

She wanted to look away, but forced herself not to. She knew she had to play along.

Gary stood quietly for a minute, not moving except to press his eyes shut with the palms of both hands, collecting his thoughts. Then he opened the door and stepped outside. She could hear him urinating, then, after a while, sounds coming from beneath the cabin floor. A few minutes later, he returned, carrying a blue vinyl bag. Setting it down on the table, he ripped open the Velcro cover and took out a photo album the size of an ordinary book. For every serial killer, there is a story. Gary decided now was the time to tell his.

Lookit these, he said, as he opened it, revealing photographs of nude women displayed beneath clear plastic. He turned the pages slowly so each photo could be viewed. Vicki was appalled. The Polaroid photos were neatly dated with locales, and arranged chronologically. The dates went back nearly ten years. When he got to the final page, he told her there were twenty-three of them. Almost all were young, racial minorities, their faces expressionless. Dead. His victims. In the frontal close-ups, she could see bruise marks on their necks and open wounds above their left breasts.

Whores, he said, looking over at her, then back to the album, filthy, disgusting pigs. Every fuckin' one of them. Every herd has to be culled, and that's what I do.

Oh, my God, she gasped, turning away, feeling the nausea rising up, the sour taste catching in her throat. What's wrong with you? She knew at once that was a mistake.

He exploded. Wrong with me? What's wrong with *me*? Not a goddamn thing, voice rising, arms spread wide in a gesture of disbelief, as he stepped toward her. She lowered her head, raising her hands to protect her face. I know what I'm fuckin' doin'. And it's necessary, very fuckin' necessary. Understand? The wrong is *them* and it's been fuckin' eliminated. By me, by me, he almost shouted, pounding his chest. And here's the proof. He lifted the album and shook it in front of her face, like preachers shake Bibles in tent revivals. Look at me, goddammit! He thumped his chest harder with a clenched fist. Me, goddammit, me.

She cringed, but then that strange smile flashed across his face, the slap she expected replaced by a hand placed gently on her shoulder. Let me explain and you'll see what I mean, he said in a soothing voice.

He began to describe the circumstances that preceded each photo, his interest and enthusiasm varying, but with no more emotion than an ordinary person might express discussing photos of a family vacation. She remembered a professor in an abnormal psychology class say that psychopaths kill their victims with no more guilt or remorse than a normal person would feel swatting a fly. Gary was proving it. Gary's cruelty to his victims knew no limits.

See, except for a few white trash, they're all niggers. Most of the black niggers—oh, excuse me, I mean the *original* niggers, the Afro-fucking-American niggers—were from Portland. Fuckin' streetwalkers, he explained in a mocking tone with a smirk. When I was growin' up, there weren't as many. You hardly ever saw niggers in Portland. Now they're all over, takin' over, he said as he flipped slowly through pages. Mexicans, Orientals, Indians, they're all dark-skinned, all the same, all niggers. I usually pick 'em up at bars, or hitchin' at truck stops.

He rubbed the back of his neck, leaning back, moving his head side to side before turning the page. Unfortunately, I don't have photographs of them all. Here, lookit this one. Wait a minute, he said. The shadows were lengthening. We need better light. He stood up and pulled a pack of matches out of his pocket and lit the kerosene lamp on the table. After turning up the flickering light, he continued. She was kind of interesting, pointing to a young, once-attractive brunette, with large breasts and bruise marks visible on her neck. Mexican. Picked her up at a bar in a little town outside Yosemite. Can't remember the name. Mexican name. Socorro? No, that's New Mexico. Sonora? Yeah, here it is, Sonora, he said running his finger along the bottom of the photo. Anyway, she could tell I was very intelligent, so she tried to act real educated to impress me. Educated fucking Mexican, is that a joke, or what? He was chuckling. You heard why Jesus wasn't born in Mexico, right? God couldn't find three wise men and a virgin. He stopped chuckling and waited. When she pretended to smile, he said, Yeah, pretty funny.

Anyway, he continued, this bitch talked about books she'd read and how she dropped out of community college in Bakersfield to work for a while, how she planned to finish and teach school. It was all bullshit. She was so strung out on drugs it was pathetic. Needle tracks up and down both arms that she tried to keep covered. Must have been, what's the word *ambi* … something. He chuckled, then sighed. All she had going for her were those big brown tits. Funny, that's the last thing I said to her. Last thing in this world she heard.

Vicki glanced over at him as he looked down at the photos, obviously pleased with himself as he turned the pages, pausing briefly on each photo for her to view.

She turned her head and closed her eyes. He smiled, speaking again in a soft, pleading tone, as he reached over and gently turned her head back to the album. Come on now, take a look. They're just niggers, not like us at all. Anyway, I cut all of 'em I can, if there's time. He turned a page and pointed with his index finger. You notice the X on 'em, see there right above their left tit? Vicki turned away, covering her eyes.

Come on now, don't be shy, he said as he reached over and gently pulled her face back. You're probably wondering, why the left tit, right? Guess. She looked up briefly, then lowered her eyes, and didn't answer. The anger flared. Answer me when I ask a question, goddammit.

She started to stammer, but he couldn't wait to tell her. See, that X I slice there right above their hearts? That's me, crossin' 'em off, you know, X'ing 'em out, one less nigger. See, lookit here on this one, he said, pointing to a photo of a tiny, childlike Asian woman. Biting her lip, Vicki closed her eyes and shook her head, thinking this was what he would do to her in the end if she didn't escape. But how? She was trapped, completely trapped.

Lookit those slant eyes and those little doorbell tits. He was smiling as he waited, looking at her and back to the photo, his fingers drumming on the opposite page. Come on, take a look.

I can't, she whispered, pressing her palms against her eyes. Please … He let it go.

Probably Korean, Jap, Thai, or some goddamn thing, all the same, smell like fuckin' fish. Pretty good, huh?

Lookit this, over here, this Indian bitch, he said, turning another page. Now the story on her is pretty cool.

Vicki hung her head down, wanting to hold her ears, wanting to scream. No, she had to keep some hold on herself, couldn't give in to fear, she thought. She had never seen him so happy, so pleased with himself, relaxed, feeling at home in his folksy mood, dropping the g's, adding a twang like a country singer.

Yeah, picked her up in broad daylight when I was workin' at Grand Canyon. Navajos and Hopis all over the fuckin' place down in Flagstaff. See that high peak, snow on it, kinda blurry in the background? That's… what the hell, forget the name, dammit, but that's the highest peak in Arizona, sacred fuckin' mountain of the very fucked up Navajo Nation. Look at her, just another prairie nigger whore, fuckin' scum, layin' around Flagstaff drunk, doin' drugs, throwin' up on the street, beggin' for handouts, sellin' themselves for whatever they can get to pay for the next fix. Right there in the shadow of their big-fuckin'-deal sacred mountain. Then they hitchhike back to the rez. That's where she was headed when I picked her up. What a piece of shit she was. Smelled bad. Said she needed a ride to Bitter Springs. You know, on the road to Page … Oops, forgot you're from California. He laughed. Anyway, she got bitter springs, all right. Mine, right down her throat. He looked over at her, smirking.

She forced herself to look at the photos, at the trophies he was bragging about, thinking *those women are dead,* thinking *that's me unless I can keep this psychopath from freaking out.*

Lookit here, he said, turning to another photo. Here's another. Got one more before I left Arizona. Looks like the first one, don't she? Ever notice how Indian bitches all look alike? Anyway, I got tired of takin' mule strings and Jap tourists up and down Bright fuckin' Angel Trail—desert heat, flies, piles of mule shit, puddles of piss—so I headed north to Glacier where it's a helluva lot cooler and not so crowded. Hardly ever see niggers or Japs up here. Japs all over the South Rim like little camera-totin' ants. He looked for a smile. It wasn't there. Come on, now, where's your sense of humor?

He paused to think, then said, So whad'ya think? The *X*'s, I mean. Pretty cool, right? See that's my personal *signature.* Oh, sorry, you probably don't know what I'm talkin' about so let me explain. She could see that his specialized knowledge was a source of great personal pride, a big part of who he was. He was *the* authority, not merely a student of the subject.

Signature, that's what these so-called FBI experts on serial killers call it. The *g*'s were back again. You know these phony fucking profilers who spout off on cable news every time someone like Ted Bundy, Jeffrey Dahmer, or that BTK—you know that bind, torture, kill guy who taught Sunday School—is arrested. Where was it? Some fucking town in Kansas or some goddamn place? What a bunch of fucking phonies, you know, making up all that shit, craving attention. Funny, never thought about it till I heard them talking so much about it, you know, like on that Greta Van ... something show, what the hell's her name? You know the one. He gave her a big smile. People like me keep Greta in business. Anyway, these so-called experts say serial killers leave a *signature* to identify themselves. Okay, I say to myself, what the hell. You want a signature, Mr. Big Fucking Profiler, I'll start leavin' one. A nicely carved *X* over the left tit.

He was about to close the album, when he stopped and leafed back through its plastic folders. Whoops, nearly forgot, he said. Here's my favorite. He pulled out a photo and handed it to her. Vicki gasped, her heart in her throat. It was a photo of her in her string bikini playing volleyball at the lodge. So whad'ya think? Pretty cool, right? The smirk. I've had my eye on you for a long time, girl, and here's the proof. He took the photo from her fingers and put it back in the album. He grinned at her as he closed the Velcro flap and patted the top.

Heart pounding, throat dry, she realized that he'd been stalking her for months.

Anyway, you can see they come in all shapes and sizes, but I can spot pigs a mile away. Just the way they look. Then when you get close, they all smell the same. Cigarettes and cheap perfume. Sickening. Disgusts me. I'm sure glad you don't smoke. A course, I wouldn't let you if you did. The smile broadened. So whad'ya think of me now? By the way, I forgot, my full name's Gary Ray Kemp. Weird, we been here how many days, and I forgot to tell you my full name. Anyway, maybe someday I'll be famous like Bundy and Dahmer and, just think, you've had the privilege of knowin' me, maybe someone will even write a book about me. Maybe you. You like to write? How 'bout this for a title: *Gary Ray Kemp, My Savior and Serial Killer: A True Story by Someone Who Should Know*? He chuckled, slapped his knee, and stood up. Sounds like a best seller to me.

That's cool, Gary, she said softly, looking at him briefly, a furtive glance toward the key hanging on the wall, then back to the leering smile before she lowered her eyes.

He put the album on the chair and reached down and ran his hand along her thigh. The photos had aroused him, as they always did.

She pulled away. Please, Gary, no, don't … not now. He squeezed tighter. Please, Gary, not now. You saved my life and I'm very grateful. But please let me go. Please take me back to West Glacier. I need to call my folks. I won't mention you. I'll make up a story. Please, Gary, I just want to go home. Gary, please.

Hey, I like that, he said, savoring her fear and the exhilarating sense of his control over her. Don't worry, Miss Hathaway, I'm not gonna to hurt you. You're different, special. That's why I chose you, that's why I brought you here. You're not like the others I coulda picked up a lot easier.

He walked over to the window and looked out across the clearing. The fawn was still there. His mood changed. When he spoke, the tone was restrained, sad, almost as if he was talking to himself. She had to strain to hear him.

You know, didn't seem like Mom thought I was much, you know, like worth spendin' her time with … He paused and took a deep breath and exhaled with, Growin' up was shit. Oh yeah, Mom. Mom, what a fuckin' joke. He fell silent as he pulled up a chair and sat down. He leaned over, hands clasped, elbows resting on his knees, staring at the floor, deep in thought.

It was getting dark. A fresh wind whining against the windowpanes, then a distant rumble of thunder. Vicki held her breath. *Where's he going with this? What's he going to do?* Except for the kerosene lamp's flickering glow and the fading light through the west window, the cabin was almost dark.

I'm sorry, Gary, she said after the silence had gone on too long, every child deserves a mother's love.

His head snapped around toward her, eyes sparkling with rage. Who the fuck are you to say anything about *my* mother?

I … I didn't mean that, she stammered. I thought that's what you were saying, you know, like maybe it wasn't a very happy …

He leaped from his chair, sending it skidding backward. She ducked, but the slap caught the side of her head. As she reeled from the blow, the chair tipped and she fell to the floor, ears ringing. It was the first time he had struck her.

Please don't, Gary. I'm sorry. I didn't mean … He slapped her again. Don't, Gary, please don't hit me, you're acting crazy. I didn't …

Crazy? Crazy? You think I'm crazy? Who the fuck are you to say I'm crazy? I'm not crazy! He turned away and began to pace back and forth, waving his arms. John Hinckley was fuckin' crazy. Shoots Reagan to impress Jodie Foster. Thinks they're going to live in the White House together. Now that's crazy. That's very fuckin' crazy. I ain't like that.

The anger vanished as quickly as it appeared, the odd smile returned, and in a calm voice he said, But, you know, come to think of it, in a way, you're gonna be kinda like *my* very own Jodie Foster. You know, you even kinda look like her. Anyone ever tell you that?

Cowering on the floor, desperate, terrified, she nodded, knowing she must agree with everything he said.

He rolled his eyes, smiling at the thought, and walked to the window and looked out. Across the clearing, he could still see the faint outline of the fawn, confused, afraid, *alone.* He put the thought out of his mind and turned to face her.

Look at me, Vicki. Look at me, he said, the anger back, his voice rising, as he pulled her to her feet and pushed her back into the chair he had righted with his other hand. I'm what a serial killer looks like. Not some dirty old man. Me! Gary Ray Kemp! Aren't you impressed?

She looked up, held his gaze briefly, nodded, and lowered her eyes.

The jaw muscles relaxed, the crazed look on his face slowly faded, and he became silent again. He turned back to the window and again looked out at the fawn. The wind had stopped and it was very still. She watched him, pale, one hand across her chest, the fingers of the other pressed against her lips, waiting for his next move.

When the silence had become almost unbearable, he spoke again in a voice that was soft, almost dreamy, Yeah, that's me all right. I was kinda like that fawn out there you're bawlin' your eyes out about. He coughed a short dry laugh. Funny, and this is where it ends for me, too. The backcountry. Right here. He hesitated, bowing his head, and rubbing the back of his neck. He didn't look up when he spoke again, the words thickening and catching in his throat. No one ever shed any fuckin' tears for me, not a fuckin' one.

———◆◆◆———

25

---◆◆◆---

Thursday, September 27. Vicki wasn't sure what day or month it was. How long had it been? Sometimes Gary tuned into local news broadcasts on the battery-operated radio, but the reports rarely mentioned the day or date, and he kept the radio out of her reach when he was gone. There was only the useless, out-of-date calendar still hanging on the wall, so each day when he left the cabin, she took a paring knife and pressed a mark on the inside of one of the table legs. On this particular day, she counted nineteen marks and she was sure she must have missed some days when they first arrived. At least three weeks in captivity, maybe longer and, except for the underwear she washed out in a bucket, wearing the same soiled clothes.

She couldn't be sure of anything, even oddly enough, her increasingly ambivalent feelings toward Gary. As he often reminded her, he had saved her life twice. In both instances, he had risked his own life to save her's. The fog of memory that followed those traumatic experiences had begun to lift and with it, a strange bond had grown out of a sense of obligation to him for what he had done.

Now she realized she was completely dependent on him for survival, even as she was totally intimidated and dominated by him in his presence and chained to the floor when he was gone. She was terrified when left alone and fearful when he returned. What mood would he be in? The wild mood swings between his delusions of grandeur and understandable feelings of persecution were unpredictable. She tried to please him, but the bitter childhood memories that made him depressed and stirred his anger—especially toward women—were never far beneath the surface. Would he berate her after the oral sex he demanded? Or would he show her affection in his clumsy fashion with pathetic acts of kindness, as when he gave her a bouquet of wilted, end-of-season wildflowers? At those times, she actually felt sorry for him. Poor Gary, she sometimes said to herself, he's never been loved and has no idea how to express it. She couldn't understand her feelings about him. Fear and pity but, also, a compelling need for his approval. She couldn't deny it. She needed him.

She had learned earlier from a crackling, static-filled report on the Grundig that she was still officially listed as missing by the Park Service, but authorities believed she was probably dead. Gary had snickered and mumbled, Dumb shits, when a newscaster reported that park rangers had killed three bears, a sow, and two cubs that were believed responsible for the Morning Star maulings. Gary noticed that mention of Matt's death didn't seem to register with her. He took that as a good sign, unaware that she was concealing her true feelings for fear of displeasing him.

Gary was pleased with these reports, he told her, because it meant that park rangers had scaled back their search and were now looking only for her remains, and probably with limited personnel. Basically, that means they've given up. Besides, I got your remains right here, alive and glad to be keepin' me company, right? he said smiling, unzipping his jeans as he took her by the hand and nodded for her to kneel before him as he sat down on the bunk bed. She closed her eyes and bit her lower lip when he did, but she had become accustomed to the routine—the warm, soapy water, the fondling, and when she finished, his anger. She forced a half-smile and nodded, I'll heat some water. She knew her life depended on it.

Afterward, when Gary left to hunt and gather firewood, she found herself sitting at the table staring at a cup of tea that had gone cold. The sun had burned through the ground fog and she was wondering what the rest of this day would bring when a shot rang out. Moments later there was a second shot. Gunfire no longer surprised her. Because they had no refrigeration to preserve meat, and they were running low on food, Gary was shooting something every two or three days, usually deer or small game. She could tell he enjoyed killing, seeing himself, as he often reminded her, as part of some grand Darwinian scheme. By this time she knew by the popping sound that these were pistol shots. That meant small game like snowshoe rabbits, squirrels, or grouse that he shot with his .38 revolver. Deer he shot with the 30/30, a louder, lingering report. He had yet to kill an elk or moose, but he was confident he would. The elk rut had started and they could hear the bugling bulls, especially in the evenings. Gary said that would make it easier for him to locate them and the cows they were breeding with. He had also told her about a blind he had built near a marsh where he had seen abundant moose sign.

On those hunting expeditions, he would be away from the cabin for two or three hours, sometimes longer. Alone and helpless, tethered to the swivel chain in his absence, she hoped and prayed someone would find her while he was gone. But at other times, she worried that something would happen to him and he *wouldn't* return. What would she do then? Once when it was growing dark and she was still alone, she was near panic. When he finally returned, she even welcomed the sex and let him know it. Afterward she wondered why. She knew he was a violent and remorseless killer of women, but she also knew that without him she would die alone in the wilderness. She was afraid of him but, except for the oral sex which was, at this point, the only sex he wanted, he hadn't harmed her and even tried, in his fashion, to be kind.. The occasional slap and verbal tirades after sex she had come to accept, almost as if she deserved them. Normality had lost its meaning. Gary had become the most important person in her life.

She looked up when he opened the door holding two rabbits by their hind legs, their bloodstained, chocolate-brown fur had begun to turn the color of snow. Lookit here, he said with a big grin, lifting a dead rabbit in each hand to eye level. Snowshoes. See here back along their sides and rump how they're turnin' white. Nice fat ones. Rabbit stew tonight. You'll like it the way I'm gonna cook it, slow outside in the pot on a wood fire with wild chives, pinto beans, and what's left of the potatoes.

She nodded, forced a smile, but looked away from the bloodstained rabbits that reminded her of the stuffed animals she'd kept on her bed as a little girl.

You know rabbits are so fuckin' dumb it's pathetic, he said, holding the rabbits up higher for closer examination, a satisfied look on his face. I'm out lookin' for firewood and see these two out there under a bush eatin' serviceberries. So when I shoot the one, the other jumps back and runs into the bushes. So I wait. Sure enough, pretty soon the little fucker pokes its head out and comes over and sniffs the dead one. So I dropped it too.

She could hardly conceal her revulsion. That's interesting, Gary. You sure are a skillful hunter. *Anything to please him.* She knew he wouldn't get it.

Hey, he said from the doorway as he was walking out, it's almost time for the news. Wonder if they found your remains. He laughed as he laid the rabbits down on a tree stump he used as butcher block.

When he returned, he wiped his hands on a rag and turned on the radio. The Grundig crackled and whined as he adjusted the setting and antennae and turned up the volume. The lead story was about new developments in the case of his latest victim, a Blackfeet woman identified as Dinah Spotted Wolf of Heart Butte. The newscaster went on to say that there was evidence suggesting that the case was possibly related to the homicide of another Indian woman whose body was discovered late last spring south of Bigfork. Based on evidence that was not revealed to the public, the newscaster said police were investigating the possibility that both women were victims of the same killer.

Gary was intent, hunched close to the radio and turning away only when the newscaster moved on to other news. Same person. How about that? That means serial killer, he said smiling. Hmm, my reputation is growing.

You mean you killed those two women?

Well now, what do you think? Sure I did. Thought I told you that. Don't you remember? Only thing is, I don't have any photos like the others. It was just dumb luck on both of 'em. I didn't have the Polaroid with me.

What if they're looking for you?

Doubt it. They'll probably connect these two to the Indian bitches I killed back in Flagstaff now that they have DNA and everything on computers. But all they'll know is that the same person killed 'em all, but not *who*. They got me once for assault in Portland. No DNA though. Bitch was a prostitute. They won't know it's me, unless they find me. Which they ain't gonna do, right?

If you say so, Gary.

Tell me why.

Vicki didn't say anything.

I said tell me why, Vicki, he said, an edge to his voice.

Because no one is going to take you alive, she said softly looking down at her feet, her jaw muscles tightening.

That's right. Just don't forget it.

Can I build a fire and make some coffee? she asked to change the subject. Is there any left?

Yeah, and make me a cup. But go easy on it. Once it's gone …

She struck a match on the side of the stove and was coaxing flickering flames through a handful of twigs when, from outside the cabin, they heard a voice call out, Hello, anyone around?

Vicki dropped the coffee pot as Gary bolted from the chair he was about to sit down on and rushed to the window. Outside he saw a lone figure with a backpack walking across the clearing toward the cabin. He retrieved his pistol from the holster hanging on the far wall. Damn, he said as he spun the cartridge chamber, not loaded. He kept the bullets for both the pistol and the rifle locked up in a metal army surplus cartridge container, a precaution in case Vicki got any ideas. There was a knock on the door.

Just a minute, he called as he unlocked the container and shook out a handful of bullets for the pistol, loaded it, and tucked it under his belt behind his back.

Come here, he whispered, as he lifted the restraining collar at the end of the chain. She extended her foot as he fastened the collar around her ankle and locked it. Now, you just sit over there on that fuckin' bunk and don't move or say anything, he hissed through crooked teeth. You understand? Not a goddamn sound. Eyes wide with anxiety and hope, she nodded. He waited a moment, opened the door just wide enough to fit through, and stepped outside, closing it quickly behind him.

A short, thin young man in soiled hiking clothes stood before him, a big grin on his face. He had taken off his backpack and was about to prop it against a tree.

Hello, he said again, as he pushed the hood of his orange parka back off his head, revealing days of stubble on his face. Man, I didn't expect to see anyone back in here.

Gary didn't return the smile. Yeah, me neither. What're *you* doin' here?

The hiker tried to make the best of it. Well, just hikin', man. Been on the trail more than a week and real anxious to get back to civilization. You're the first person I've seen since I left. I just wanted to check to make sure I'm where I think I am. According to my map, there's no cabin here, but here it is. Confusing. Is this is the lower patrol cabin on the Nyack Creek trail?

Gary hesitated before he answered. Could be, he lied, knowing the derelict cabin wasn't on recent park maps. Where you comin' from? Anyone with you? he asked, fixing the hiker in a hard stare that made him drop his eyes.

No, man. All by my lonesome. He looked up with an uneasy smile. Started at the Nyack Creek trailhead and was gonna do the Coal Creek loop that hooks around up over Surprise Pass to Upper Nyack Creek. But, man, I got turned around back in there. Got lost, fell crossin' the creek. Wasn't sure where to ...

You talk to anyone? Get a backcountry permit before you left?

No, man. This time a year, I figured, no one's around, you know, didn't need one ... He nodded toward the buckskin tied at the hitching rail. You with the park?

Gary saw him glance at the dead rabbits, certain that he would know it was illegal to hunt in the park, and ignored the question, never taking his eyes off the hiker. So how long you say you been gone?

Like I said, gotta be more than a week, but I kinda lost track of the time 'cause I missed a cutoff, got lost. Anyway, it's been a while, longer than I planned. What day is it, anyhow, Thursday, Friday? I'm not sure.

Gary, thinking, *Bullshit. He doesn't know what day it is*, still ignored the questions. So how'd you get to the trailhead? You leave a car there?

No, man. It's a long story. I took the Amtrak back to Minnesota for my brother's wedding. On the way back here, I got off the train at West Glacier, stayed at the Highland that night. Next morning I hitched a ride from there back up to the trailhead at Red Eagle.

You tell anyone at the motel where you were goin'?

No, man, it was late. I just crashed, got up the next morning, ate breakfast, and left.

Seems like a funny time a year to be hikin' back in here.

Yeah, I guess, but I've hiked a good bit in the park and the Coal Creek loop's one I've never done. I'm livin' in Whitefish and got a few weeks to kill before I start work at Big Mountain for the ski season, so I just decided to do it. He smiled and shook his head. More than I bargained for, I'll tell you. He looked at Gary, the malign intensity of whose stare he had been avoiding, and broadened the smile. Man, like I'm ready for a cold beer, a hot shower, and a soft bed.

Gary could tell he was nervous by the way he kept talking and rubbing the back of his neck. That heightened his suspicions.

Anyone know you were gonna do it, you know, the hike?

No, man. Like I just decided when I was back at the wedding. Had some time on my hands, so I shipped some stuff UPS back to my friend's place where I been stayin' in Whitefish, then loaded up my backpack, took the Amtrak, and got off at West Glacier like I said. Anyway, here I am. I'm hopin' to get to Red Eagle before dark. No way I want to ford that river in the dark. I should be able to do it, right? What's it, about six, seven miles?

Yeah, somethin' like that.

Then with a little luck, I'll hitch a ride to Whitefish. If not, I should be able to pick up a hitch to West Glacier and stay over at the Highland.

When's your friends expectin' you back?

Before he could answer, there was a faint scraping sound of metal against wood from inside the cabin. Gary looked briefly toward the cabin, then back at the hiker. He could see from his quick glance toward the cabin and the expression on his face that the hiker had heard the sound, but the sonofabitch was trying to act like he didn't.

So wha' what about you? You workin' for the park? the hiker asked again, the stutter betraying his nervousness.

Gary hesitated, a quick nervous smile, but the eyes remained expressionless. Yeah, I'm involved in this ecological project. We're doing studies of different animals and the ways they adapt to the winter. You know, like those two snowshoes there. Don't like to kill things, but we gotta take tissue samples and such … you know …. He paused. He felt foolish and could tell the hiker didn't believe him.

Wow, the hiker said. That must be interesting. He reached down and lifted his backpack. Hey, man, gettin' late. I gotta keep on truckin' if I'm gonna make it out to the highway before dark. Nice talkin' with you. Good luck with the project.

As he swung the backpack up on his shoulders and fastened the waist buckle, Gary saw him glance again toward the cabin.

These damn things don't get any lighter do they? The hiker smiled. Take care.

Gary thinking, he's too anxious to leave. *He heard it. He knows. I know he fucking knows.*

So you didn't answer my question: You got friends in Whitefish expectin' you?

The hiker had started to walk away and turned back to face Gary. Yeah, if I'm not there by tonight, they'll be wondering where I am. Supposed to call and let 'em know when I get in. Hey, gotta go, take care, man. Nice talkin' with you, he said as he turned and began to walk quickly away.

The stutter, the unease was there, and it showed. Gary stood watching as the hiker crossed the clearing and followed the trail into the timber, then went back into the cabin. You connivin' bitch, he said quietly through clenched teeth as he entered the cabin. It was the first time he'd called her a bitch. He slapped her hard across the face. She stumbled backward, groaning, and falling to the floor, blood trickling from her nostrils. Then he grabbed the 30/30 that was propped against the wall and loaded it. I'll settle with you later, bitch, he said over his shoulder before he stepped outside and quietly closed the cabin door.

Gary moved quickly across the clearing, loading the rifle and levering a bullet into the chamber. When he got into the forest, he moved stealthily, crouched low, moving quickly from tree to tree as he did when he was stalking deer. A few minutes later, he could see the orange parka and the dark backpack rocking from side to side about a hundred yards away. He quickened his pace until he had closed to less than forty yards. He stopped, raised the rifle to his shoulder, and took aim.

Damn, he said under his breath. The backpack was in the way of a clean kill. He took a few more steps off the trail to a tree and took aim, steadying the rifle against the trunk. Hey, Minnesota, he called out. The hiker stopped and turned. It was the last thing he ever did. A copper-jacketed .30 caliber bullet exploded into his chest, knocking him over backward. He was dead before he hit the ground.

Gary waited, watching for movement. There was none. He walked to the body which was lying face up on the backpack, the eyes sightless, staring up at him, blood spreading across the flannel shirt beneath the parka from the fatal chest wound. He watched as the young hiker's ruddy complexion slowly turned gray. Another college boy bites the dust, he thought. Well, *probably* a college boy. He reached down and unbuckled the waist belt on the hiker's backpack. Then he rolled the body over and removed the pack, lifting each limp arm through the shoulder straps. He stood and looked around until he spotted a small gully away from the trail made by a seasonal stream gone dry. That'll work, he breathed aloud. He lifted the hiker's feet and dragged the body over to it and rolled it in. Gary took his time, covering it with branches and brush and pine needles and loose dirt he kicked from the edges of the gully. Satisfied that the body was no longer visible from the trail, he slung the backpack over one shoulder and started back to the cabin, an overwhelming sense of betrayal and rage welling up inside.

26

Vicki heard the shot. There was no doubt in her mind about what Gary had done. She was pale, trembling, biting her lower lip when he reached the cabin and pushed open the door, slamming it back against the wall. He glared at her, rage stenciled across his face, as he stood in the doorway. He removed the hiker's backpack and let it fall to the ground outside. Then he backhanded her across the face. She recoiled from the blow, staggering, clutching her face.

Gary, please I didn't …

Don't lie to me, you lyin' fuckin' bitch. You lyin' fuckin' bitch, he screamed as he drew back to strike her again. Still reeling from the first blow, she flinched, a large red welt swelling above her eye and across her nose, stabbing fingers of pain radiating through her body. But it was just a feint.

Sobbing, she pleaded, Please, Gary. Please don't hit me. Visions of his victims flashed through her mind. She was certain he was going to kill her. I'm sorry. I didn't do anything. I couldn't help it. The chain, it slipped off the bunk when I laid down. I'm sorry, I'm sorry. I didn't mean to make noise. I was trying to be quiet like you said. He didn't know, did he?

Gary was standing over her as she cowered on the floor, fists clenched at his sides. Didn't know, didn't know, he screamed. Oh sure, how could he not fuckin' know? Maybe because you not only rattled that goddamn chain, you fuckin' signaled him, didn't you? He raised his fist, hesitated, then wiped the spit draining down his chin. Didn't you? Don't lie to me, bitch. You did somethin', signaled him or somethin' from the fuckin' window, didn't you? I saw his expression change when you did it. Goddamn you to hell.

He slapped her again twice, back and forth, open palm then back-hand, hard across each side of her face. Blades of light flashed before her eyes as she tumbled back, hitting the edge of the bunk and fell to the floor, the pain and ringing in her ears blotting out the sound of her own sobs.

No, Gary, no. I didn't, honest. I didn't mean to make any noise. It was an accident, honest. Don't hurt me anymore. I'm sorry, I'm sorry.

He stared down at her, considering his next move, then bent down and removed the lock on her ankle, throwing it aside. His backpack's layin' outside. Go out and see if there's anything worth keepin' in it. She looked up through the tears, but didn't respond. Did you hear me, bitch? Get the fuck outside and do what I told you or I'll slap you some more. Fuckin' two-timin' bitch. Saved your life twice. Twice, goddammit. Do you care? Fuck no. He was screaming, the rage choking off his words. Take care of you and what do I get? Fuckin' betrayed. He turned away and leaned his head on his forearm against the wall and pounded it with his other fist.

When she returned, she said almost in a whisper, There was just his clothes, Gary, camping stuff, nothing. She was wringing her hands.

He didn't look up. Just like *her*, he said, voice lowered, now talking to himself, the same shit … never cared … never … whatever I did … nothin' mattered … nothin'.… You only mean somethin' if someone cares about you, and no one ever … Aw fuck it, everything's so fucked up … always … The words thickened and caught in his throat. He turned away and lowered his head, leaning against the wall. He made a cough-ing sound, his shoulders trembling.

It was a long time before he stepped back from the wall and wiped his eyes with his palms. When he turned to face her, he sniffed and wiped his nose with the back of his hand. She could see the expressionless eyes were pink-rimmed, moist from his tears, thinking, *He's going to kill me like the others.*

He took a deep breath. Okay, he said letting it out, I'm gonna take your word that rattlin' that chain was an accident. But if somethin' like that ever happens again ... he hesitated and took another deep breath, the anger returning, his face reddening, fists tightening with the memory, If you ever ...

She held her breath. Then something caught his attention outside.

Lookit, that damn fawn's still hangin' around, he said pointing out the window, the anger fading. Amazing, nothin's killed it yet. He turned to see her looking at it, a sad expression on her bruised and swollen face. The sight bothered him, but only for a moment, as he turned back to watch the fawn wander hesitantly, lost, at the edge of the clearing.

See, that's what I been tellin' you. Killin' isn't about right and wrong. If that fawn's supposed to survive, it'll survive. If not, it won't, like that goddamn hiker nosin' around, and all those fuckin' whores I got rid of. He paused, turning away from the window and looking directly into her eyes. She felt herself cowering, fingering her lips, like the supplicant she had become. The same for me and you, Vicki Hathaway. Our fates are locked together now. Then he smiled that odd smile. Till death do us part. Morality has nothin' to do with what becomes of *us*. Darwin's rules.

* * * * *

In West Glacier, Harry and Beth were playing checkers and sipping wine in front of a crackling fireplace at the Belton Chalet. It was late afternoon and they had just returned from a short hike to Avalanche Lake.

This is so nice, Harry. What a wonderful summer I've had. All the outdoor adventures, seeing and doing things I had only read about. It's just been terrific, thanks to you. She took a sip of wine, then kissed him on the cheek.

Yeah, it has been great. And it's not over yet. Wait till you see that Nyack Creek gorge when we hike there this weekend. Be sure to bring your camera. It's really something. He smiled and patted her hand. You know, you're really something, Beth. Honest. Changed my life. I'm a lucky man.

27

Thursday, September 27. Keno Spotted Wolf leaned against his corral fence and rubbed the nose of his spotted black-and-white paint stallion. The depression that enveloped him after learning of his daughter's death had deepened after her funeral. Earlier that morning, he had bought the *Great Falls Tribune* at a convenience store in Browning and read that authorities in Flathead County believed that a serial killer had killed Dinah and another woman, also an Indian. Why hadn't *he* been informed? He stuffed the torn-out article into his shirt pocket and decided to go to Kalispell.

It was early afternoon when he drove down South Main Street to the Flathead County Courthouse, an imposing, century-old gothic structure, surrounded by tall trees, that dominates downtown Kalispell. He parked his pickup in a public lot just beyond the building and walked back, pausing for a squirrel that bounced across the sidewalk in front of him. A security guard noticed him looking around when he entered the lobby, asked what he wanted, and explained that the county sheriff's office was a block south in the Justice Building.

Keno was already nervous and feeling uncomfortable in this white man's world and the confusion made it worse. When he reached the Justice Building and entered the lobby of the sheriff's office, he felt like he was being watched. He walked over to the information desk.

I'd like to talk to someone about Dinah Spotted Wolf, he said to the officer at the desk, an older man with a pencil-thin mustache and a bristling fringe of white hair circling a bald head. She's my daughter. Someone killed her.

The officer looked startled, cleared his throat, and sat up straighter. I'm sorry, he said. Let me see if I can find someone you can talk to. Please have a seat, I'll be right back.

The officer got up from his gray metal desk and disappeared into a maze of glass-paneled cubicles. Too nervous to sit, Keno walked around the room, looking, not really seeing the framed commendations and photographs of men in uniform and black robes that adorned the pastel-green walls. A few minutes later, the officer returned followed by a tall man, Keno guessed late forties, with sharp features and graying dark hair combed straight back.

Louie Moore, the tall man said in a tobacco-scorched baritone as he extended his hand. Keno, a brief look of surprise at the extended hand, shook it.

Detective Moore can talk with you about the case, the older officer said as he stepped back.

Could I see some identification? the detective said. Sorry, about that, but I'm sure you understand we have to be careful about who we're talkin' to about sensitive matters like this.

I understand, Keno said quietly as he pulled out his wallet and flipped it open to show his driver's license. The detective looked at it and up again at Keno and nodded. This way, Mr. Spotted Wolf. I'm very sorry about your daughter. We're doing everything we can to find the person responsible.

Moore opened the door to an office with drawn Venetian blinds on its windows and motioned Keno toward a cushioned, gray metal chair. The overhead fluorescent lights made everything look colorless and brought out the veins in the detective's cheeks as he slid into a swivel chair behind his cluttered desk, cleared his throat, and began to describe in general terms the evidence they were working.

Keno wanted to ask why he hadn't been informed before the press, but figured there was no point. He knew the answer. Instead, he listened intently, then asked, Why do you think it was a serial killer and not some-body who knew her, like her ex-husband or her last boyfriend? Have you questioned them? Both no good sonsabitches. Beat her up all the time. Maybe one of them did it.

Yeah, we got that from the tribal police. We've talked with one of them. Richard Rides High's the ex, right? Moore said as he looked up over half-glasses from the contents of a manila folder he had just opened.

Keno nodded.

Nothing there at this point, but we have him down as a person of interest, so we're keeping tabs on him. And we're still looking for the other one. What's his name? Wait, here it is, Joe …

Joe Sanders, Keno interrupted, a no-good, half-breed sonofabitch.

Yeah, Sanders. Looks like he left the state more than a year ago and no one has seen or heard of him since. But we intend to do all we can to find and question him. We put out a BOL western states alert—that's a *Be On the Lookout* alert—with info we got from the tribal police in Browning. Says here he's got multiple DUI's, drunk and disorderly, pos-session of stolen property, you know, the usual … He was going to say reservation bullshit, then caught himself, but no domestic violence.

That's because she was afraid to report the no-good bastard.

Yeah, sounds familiar. Moore put the folder back on his desk and leaned back in the squeaking swivel chair, clasped his hands on his lap, and heaved a big sigh, dreading what was coming, the worst part of his job.

The evidence we have now points to one person being responsible for both your daughter's death and the woman from Pablo who was murdered last spring. Both were young Indian women and there's *other* evidence that suggests the killer's focused on that kind of victim. No way was he going to mention pursuing the Arizona attorney's tip that the killer might be a park employee, thinking you never can tell about Indians taking the law into their own hands, especially in a brutal crime like this one. Believe me, we're working this case hard. We want to find this person, real bad, Mr. Spotted Wolf. He paused, took a deep breath, and let it out before he spoke. We're concerned there'll be more killings if he isn't caught.

Keno didn't say anything for a moment. He was looking down at his hands squeezing his knees. Then he looked up. What's the other evidence? he asked, not sure he wanted to know.

The detective cleared his throat. The swivel chair squeaked again as he shifted his position and looked down at the ballpoint pen he began to tap on the side of the desk. Then he looked directly at Keno. This is pretty brutal stuff, Mr. Spotted Wolf. I'm not sure it would be useful to put you through …

Look, Keno interrupted, his voice strained, but even, this is my daughter. I want to know *exactly* what happened. Not knowin's drivin' me crazy. So let's have it.

Okay, okay, sure, of course. Look, I'm very sorry for you, I mean that. I just thought … well, I have a daughter and I … He motioned toward framed photographs on a file cabinet behind him. Well I just don't want to make it any harder on you than it already is.

Keno leaned forward, elbows resting on his knees, hands clasped in front of him. He looked down at the floor then up at the detective before he spoke again. Then, in almost in a whisper, I appreciate that, but I need to know, so …

Moore looked directly at Keno, straightened his shoulders, took a deep breath, and let it out slowly through tight lips, thinking. He knew he was violating procedure, that this was something he should *not* do, but, as a father himself, he empathized, imagining how he would feel, knowing *he* would want to know if the roles were reversed.

Okay, sure, whatever you say, I understand, but you stop me anytime, you know, if it's too … Another deep breath and sigh. Okay, here's what we know for sure. Whoever killed your daughter did it with a sharp instrument, probably something like a screwdriver or ice pick. The medical examiner couldn't be absolutely sure because of the time factor, but it looks like she was stabbed once in the back of the neck and it penetrated her spinal cord. He hesitated and took another deep breath and let it out, So it was probably pretty quick.

Keno, head down, was staring at fists clenched hard, resting on his knees as the detective continued, his mind awash with grief, anger, helplessness.

Because of the time between the murder and the recovery of the body, in the water and all, the medical examiner couldn't determine whether your daughter had been raped, but we don't think so since we know the first victim was not and both victims were clothed from the waist down. But tops and bras were torn in one case and missing in the other. So we believe the killer in both cases was sexually motivated. He stopped and looked over at Keno.

Go on, what else? I wanna know.

Moore hesitated, took a deep breath. Well with the first victim, the one before your daughter, the Pablo woman who was found south of Bigfork ... well an X had been cut into her chest above her left breast. A piece of paper was stuffed in her mouth with the words 'prairie nigger' written on it.

Keno's body began to tremble, perspiration beading on his forehead, as he gripped the metal arms of his chair, grief and rage welling up inside him. The detective paused and cleared his throat. The room was silent except for the muffled sounds of voices and phones ringing beyond the drawn blinds.

Go on, Keno said again in a whisper. Tell me everything. I gotta know.

The detective looked back at Keno, took another deep breath before he spoke. We didn't find any note with your daughter, but ... he hesitated, looking down at his hands.

Go on, tell me.

The detective sighed again, looking directly at Keno for a moment, then dropped his eyes. There was a wound on her chest, probably an X, just like the Bigfork victim.

Keno sat motionless, his knuckles white on the armrests. He stumbled to his feet, the room tilting before his eyes. The detective moved quickly from behind the desk and gripped his shoulders to steady him.

Easy, easy. I know how you ... and then he stopped because he didn't know. He had never lost a child.

Give me a minute. I'll be okay, Keno whispered. The detective stepped back. It was silent, except for the sound of Keno's breathing as he tried to regain his composure. After a while, he said, Is there anything else you can tell me?

No, that's all we have at the moment but, as I said, we're workin' some strong leads on these two cases, but I can't say any more than that right now. Rest assured, we wanna get the person responsible for both these …

I appreciate that. Thanks for all you're doin', Keno said softly and extended his hand. You'll keep me informed, right?

You betcha, we can sure do that, the detective replied, relieved that it was over, as he gripped Keno's hand. What's your phone number?

Keno started to answer but remembered that the phone company had cut off his service for non-payment. He was embarrassed. Look, I don't have a phone right now, but I'll get it reconnected. Until then, would you mind if I called you every now and then, you know, for updates?

Sure, that'll work. Here's my card, the detective said as he pulled one from his shirt pocket. Wait, here let me put down my cell number. He pulled a ballpoint pen from the same pocket and wrote down the number on the back of the card.

Thank you, Keno said as he was handed the card. He was about to say something, then hesitated, as the thought disappeared. He looked at the card, then put it in his shirt pocket. The phone rang. Forgot what I was gonna … Anyway … well I guess that's it, he said finally. Thanks for your time. Keno walked out to the reception area, still feeling light-headed. He stopped at the water cooler and took a long drink.

As the door closed, Louie Moore was thinking, *Did I make a mistake? Maybe I told him too much.* He picked up the phone. Portland? About time. Yeah, of course. Been waitin' for this call.

———◆◆◆———

28

---◆---

*F*riday, *September 28.* The day following his meeting with the detective at the Flathead County Sheriff's Department, Keno rose early, dressed, made coffee, went outside, and sat on the stoop for a long time. Thinking. He hadn't slept much, tormented by images of the way Dinah died. He had to do something, but what? It was a clear, cool morning and the denim jacket he had pulled on felt good. The temperature on the thermometer hanging by the door showed mid-thirties, but as the sun crested the ridge behind him, it was bright and warm as he lifted a crust of ice from the surface of a water bucket and added fresh water from a hose for the dogs gathered around him. Old Tonto, the gray-bearded black lab, pressed close, a big paw resting on Keno's foot, as he reached down and scratched his ears. The dog turned and licked his wrist. After a second cup of coffee, he tossed what was left, set his mug down on the stoop, and walked to the corral to check the horses, the dogs following behind.

As he approached the corral, the four horses trotted over to greet him. His favorite, the paint, pushed the others aside to nuzzle him. The horse looked like one of those turn-of-the century paintings of Blackfeet warriors on horseback by Julius Seyler. He had one of Seyler's prints hanging above his kitchen table.

Hey, Poia, how you doin'? he said as he reached up and patted the smooth neck. Keno was proud of this majestic stallion whose bloodlines went back more than a century to the buffalo runners, horses bred by Plains Indians for the great buffalo hunts of yesteryear. Prized for their speed, endurance, and courage, Keno could see it all as he stepped back to admire the stallion's conformation, the black mane and tail and black-on-white markings, the proud way he held his head and carried himself, the arch of his neck matching the arch in his tail. Presence. Symmetry. Keno was convinced that horses show breeding the way men show character; he could spot both a mile away.

Let's take a ride, Poia. You need it and so do I. He walked over to the shed and lifted a bridle from a nail on the wall, the smell of straw and manure heavy in the still air. He was about to pick up a saddle that rested on a sawhorse, but didn't. No, let's do it the old way, he said.

Keno bridled the horse and led him over to the loading ramp to mount, a concession he reluctantly made to age and stiff joints. The dogs began to bark and whine in anticipation, chasing and snapping at one another, as he swung a leg over and settled on Poia's back. He trotted the horse out the ranch road to the entrance gate, holding him back as he threw his head back, snorting and shaking it side to side, wanting to run, then turned onto the gravel road that led into the park. Relaxing the reins with a nudge of his heels, the paint lunged into a full gallop like a racehorse at the starting gate, the acceleration taking Keno's breath away as they raced down the road. He leaned forward into its flowing mane. The dogs, yelping in the chase, soon gave up and straggled back to wait at the trailer.

I needed this, Keno thought, as windswept tears streamed back into his ears. The sheer excitement as he pressed his knees tight against the stallion's ribs, feeling the surging muscles, hearing the staccato beat of hooves pounding the ground rushing beneath him. Two miles later, as he approached the ranger cabin at the park's entrance, he reined in, slowing the lathered horse to an easy canter, then a trot, letting it cool, a cloud of dust catching up behind. A Park Service pickup was parked beside the cabin. The ranger, a short, stocky Hispanic man he knew, was carrying boxes out of the cabin to it. He looked up as Keno approached.

Keno, how the hell you doin'? Don't think I've seen you all summer. What's goin' on, *amigo*? What's an old guy like you doin' ridin' bareback? he said with just a hint of Texas or Oklahoma in his voice.

Keno smiled. Not that old, he said, as he trotted the horse over to him, lifted a leg over its neck, and slid off. Hey Manny, good to see you. Yeah, I been around. Guess we're on different schedules or somethin'. The two men shook hands. Looks like you're closin' up for the season.

Yeah, we'll be comin' in and out, but basically, we're closin' it down here. That's one beautiful horse you got there, Keno. Yes sir, whad'ya think he's worth?

Million bucks? Doesn't matter. I'd never sell him. Right, Poia? Keno said as he looked at the horse and ran his hand along its sleek neck. What's the park up to these days, besides watchin' the glaciers melt?

What's his name? Poia? That Blackfeet?

Yeah, Poia was the son of Morning Star.

The ranger gave him an inquisitive look and shrugged. You mean like the lake over in Many Glacier?

Well, not quite. It's a Blackfeet legend. Kinda like your Christmas story. He thought about mentioning the Creation story, as well, but decided not to complicate things.

Hmm, son of Morning Star. Okay, you mean sorta like the birth of Jesus and all that?

Keno shrugged, half-smiled, and nodded, Yeah, sort of.

Poia, how 'bout that. Learn somethin' new every day, the ranger said, shaking his head, then changed the subject. Man, I guess you know what a shit storm we had over here with those maulings at Morning Star Lake. What a deal. Like nothin' I've experienced in over twenty years with the park. After Labor Day, things always slow down. Not this year, man. All hell broke loose that weekend with those two kids gettin' killed.

Yeah, bad stuff, young kids and all. I guess they got the sow and cubs that did it, right? That's what I read in the Great Falls paper.

Yeah, we sent some people in and got all three. Hated to do it, but there's not much choice when they eat their victims like those bears did. The bear people think the same sow might've killed and ate that hiker last May on the Scenic Point trail. But there's still a lot of unanswered questions. He lifted one side of a cardboard box and set it back down. Keno, could you give me a hand with this box? Damn back. Not that heavy, I just can't get my arms around it and I don't want to throw my back out again, and it's full of a lot of shit I don't wanna have to pick up if it spills.

Sure, Keno said, as he dropped the reins, stepped closer, and stooped to help.

Thank you, my friend, the ranger said as they slid the box into the bed of the pickup. Yeah, no question that sow and her cubs were on that boy's body and basically ate him. Never found the girl's body so ... But did they kill them? Hard to say. I'm not so sure, myself. But the bear people think they *probably* did. You know how that goes. There's any number of grizzlies roamin' that area between the Cut Bank and Two Med valleys that could have killed them and then left like bears usually do. It's not that common for the attacker bear to eat human victims. But, as you know, grizzlies are unpredictable as hell, and any bear'll eat dead flesh. Just because you find a bear on an elk carcass doesn't mean it actually killed the elk, right? So, who knows?

Keno nodded in agreement as he walked back to his horse and picked up the reins. Keep talkin' I'm listenin'.

The bear guys, you know, the specialists, are aware of all that, but everybody agreed that the sow and her cubs was probably a pretty good guess. You know, grizzlies are eatin' machines, especially with cubs, and this time of year and all, packin' in calories before they hibernate.

Keno nodded. I been kind of out of it lately. What happened exactly? The ranger had his hand on top of a metal file cabinet that was sitting next to the tailgate on a dolly. Here, let me give you a hand with that, Keno said, dropping the reins. Tilt it back so I can get a grip underneath.

Thanks, pardner. Got it? Easy does it, the ranger said as they tilted and slid the cabinet into the bed of the truck. Let's just slide it back against that crate and I'll tie everything down. No, not a trace of the girl. Well, no that's not quite right. They found a lot of her blood, but no body parts, like with the boyfriend. Blood on the sleeping bags. They had 'em zipped together. That blood checked out to be hers. They got the DNA match from her soiled laundry and clothes they found scattered around and stuff from her dorm room at Lake McDonald where she worked. Found her backpack away from the campsite. Possible she had it on when the bears dragged her off, but it was empty, so who knows? Combed the whole area. Nothing. He grimaced and shook his head. We also found a well-chewed and partially digested sanitary pad in the bear scat. Wrap your mind around that.

Keno looked down at his feet, shaking his head. Yeah, terrible, he said, thinking a young woman and his own tragedy.

Yeah, you usually find somethin', the ranger said. You know, a skull, fingers, teeth, rib cage, pieces of chewed bone here and there, like they did with the boy. That's about all that was left of him. But, *nada,* not a trace of her except the blood.

What about those people who were back in there before it happened, you know on that bear DNA study the park was doin'? They have anything to say about it?

DNA study? You mean that Northern Divide Grizzly Bear Project they been talkin' about doin'? the ranger asked as he threw a rope over the load to tie it down.

Keno shrugged. I'm not sure. I guess that's what he, this guy I met who boarded a couple of horses with me, was talkin' about.

No, nobody's doin' that now. Might be in the works, but that's still pretty much in the talkin' stage at this point. Hell, that's at least a couple of years down the road, if they're lucky. All depends on funding, and the Feds are pretty stingy. It's a big project, a lot of money involved, the whole Northern Divide ecosystem, Great Bear, the Bob Marshall, not just Glacier. Fish and Game's in on it. I'm not sure who else's involved. I know they're anxious to do it. Could be a big deal, you know, collectin' hair samples and all, the first of its kind bear census to see how many bears, grizzlies especially, are out there. But, at this point, they're still lookin' for funding, far as I know. Not even close to bein' in the field.

Funny, like I said, I boarded a couple of horses for this guy a while back—in fact, it was only a week or so before that couple was killed. He told me he was working for the park on a DNA study back in the Triple Divide/Medicine Grizzly drainages, or somewhere back in there. Wasn't very clear on details. Name was Gary. Didn't get his last name, and I haven't seen him since. You know any Garys workin' for the park?

The ranger took off his hat and scratched a thinning head of graying hair. Gary? Only one, a USGS guy named Gary used to be there, but he moved down to Yellowstone a couple months ago on a geothermal project. It wouldn've been him. That guy musta been bullshittin' you, Keno. There's no one doin' that now.

Well he came by that weekend, Labor Day, saddled and packed up his two horses and headed into the park, left his pickup and horse trailer at my place. Said he'd be back in, can't remember, a week or two, so he had to be back in there somewhere when all that happened.

Hmm, got me. That is strange. You say you haven't heard from him since?

Nothin'. His truck and trailer's still sittin' there at my place. Wonder why he'd be tellin' me that if it wasn't so?

Got me, the ranger said. Then he looked at his watch. Oh, shit. Gettin' late. Gotta get going. I have to drop this stuff off in St. Mary, then get over to West Glacier by one for a meeting at headquarters. Some big shot from the regional office is supposed to be there. Anyway, good seein' you, Keno, and thanks for the help, the ranger said as he shook Keno's hand and patted him on the shoulder. Probably saved me a trip to the chiropractor. Everything goin' okay?

Keno realized that the ranger didn't know about Dinah. He wasn't even sure whether he knew his last name. Yeah, life goes on, he said. Take it easy, Manny. See you later.

* * * * *

When Keno got back to his place, the dogs had straggled back from the gate and were waiting at the trailer. He brushed down the paint and led him back to the corral, wondering what that guy Gary was up to. Nearly a month and no sign of him. He walked back to the shed and hung the bridle on a nail and looked down toward the pickup and horse trailer parked in the trees at the edge of the pasture. He decided to take a look inside. The dogs followed him over, yapping and running in circles, happy he was back.

The trailer was empty except for some spare tack, a bridle, and reins. Keno opened the unlocked door on the driver's side of the old Dodge pickup and leaned in. It smelled musty, with a faint flowery odor coming off an air freshener hanging beneath the dash. There were some stains on the seat and duct tape on a tear in the vinyl upholstery below the steering wheel. He looked up and ran his fingers over a star-shaped crack in the rear window. Cracked windows were nothing unusual in Montana. He popped the latch to the glove compartment and looked inside at a soiled rag, a long Phillips screwdriver, a pair of pliers, a pair of old leather work gloves, and a stack of road maps held together with a rubber band. The registration and other identification had been removed. He tilted the seat forward toward the dashboard to look behind it. There was a jack lying on top of a tangled set of jumper cables, a tire iron, a loop of yellow nylon rope, and more oily rags.

Then something shiny caught his eye. He lifted the jumper cables for a look and caught his breath. It was a necklace, a silver pendant with a turquoise stone. His heart rolled over in his chest and his throat went dry. The silver chain that held it had been broken. He reached down and lifted it up. The back of the pendant had been engraved:

> *To Dinah,*
> *With love,*
> *Dad*

It was the necklace he had given her at her eighth-grade graduation. His hands were trembling when he pressed it to his lips, tears clouding his vision. A blinding rage welled up inside him as he slammed his fist down on the back of the seat. You sonofabitch, he said aloud, choking on the words as he repeated them. He slumped against the truck and closed his eyes. The old black lab standing at his side nosed his hand

and pressed against his leg. Keno reached down with his eyes still closed and placed his hand on the old dog's head. Neither moved. After a while, he dried his eyes with the back of his hand and stepped away from the truck, slamming its door. I'm gonna get you, sonofabitch . . . whoever, wherever you are, if it takes the rest of my life, he whispered as he looked out toward the mountains.

He walked back to his trailer, speaking softly with the pendant held to his lips. Dinah, Dinah, I'm so sorry, so sorry. I love you, Dinah. He's gonna pay. I'll get him if it's the last thing I do. That sonofabitch's gonna pay with his life for what he did to you.

He felt old and weak when he entered the trailer and threw himself on the bed, burying his face in a pillow, the necklace held tightly in a fist pressed against his chest. The necklace and the memories, her childhood, that smile, the sound of her voice as the happy, smiling little girl who ran out to greet him, *the little shadow that ran across the grass and lost itself in the sunset* was gone. Gone forever.

———◆———

29

Saturday, September 29. When Keno finally gathered the will to open his eyes, it was pitch black inside his trailer. He reached down and picked up the plastic alarm clock on the floor next to his bed. Nearly three in the morning, the luminous hands told him. He got up and walked outside. As he stood relieving himself, he looked up at a sky clear and cold and full of stars. But he didn't notice the stars or feel the frosty air. Deep in his gut, he knew that the man who killed his daughter was involved in some way with the tragedy at Morning Star Lake. He got back in bed, but didn't sleep.

At first light, he got up and showered, pulled on a fresh pair of Wranglers and a clean wool plaid shirt, and put a pot of water on the stove to heat for coffee. He took a bone-handled hunting knife in a leather sheath that was on top of the refrigerator and put it on his belt, thinking about what else he would need for the trip he was about to take. He hadn't been eating much lately and needing groceries hadn't crossed his mind until now. A look in the cupboard revealed there wasn't a lot to choose from—a box of crackers, a couple of packages of buffalo jerky that had been in there for who knows how long. He looked in the fridge, some apples, and part of a wedge of cheddar cheese he cut the mold from, then, after a second look, threw in the garbage. When the water boiled, he poured enough into a mug for instant coffee and placed four eggs he had taken from the refrigerator into the boiling water. After a couple of swallows of coffee, he reached for a gray-and-maroon, felt-covered aluminum canteen that was hanging by its shoulder strap from a hook on the wall and filled it with water. When the eggs were done, he cooled them in tap water and put them and the rest of the food, except for an apple he'd started to eat, in a soft rawhide bag and tied the draw-strings. Then he brushed his teeth and combed out his still damp hair before braiding it in two long braids that fell just below his shoulders.

After folding a red bandanna and tying it around his forehead, he walked into the living room and removed a Model 1873 Winchester 44-40 from a rack on the wall. He had a couple of newer rifles, but this was his great grandfather's rifle and he felt, for some reason he wasn't sure, that it was the weapon he should take. It had a rawhide sling attached at either end of a worn walnut stock that he kept polished with linseed oil. He could remember how, as a little boy sitting at the feet of this frail old man with snow-white hair and wrinkled, coppery skin, he'd listened to stories of times past. In halting English and Blackfeet, the old man told how he'd killed buffalo with that rifle on the great hunts. He said it was strong medicine, that the braves who defeated Custer at Little Bighorn had carried the same kind of rifles. Keno took a box of ammunition from a chest of drawers and shook the loose rounds that he'd specially loaded himself into a beaded rawhide bag that had also belonged to his great grandfather. A dark green military footlocker sat on the floor at the foot of the bed. Stenciled across the lid, it read:

SGT. KENNETH SPOTTED WOLF
1534994 USMC

He opened it and pulled out two Hudson's Bay wool blankets. Moths from another time had gnawed the edges of one. More memories of how his grandmother had told him and his brothers and sisters that his great grandfather had gotten both blankets from traders at Fort Benton years ago, in exchange for buffalo hides. The blankets smelled like moth crys-tals. He shook and spread them out on the bed.

An old buffalo robe was folded in a closet, but he decided it was too bulky for this trip. The blankets would have to do. He folded and rolled the blankets together to a size that would fit behind a saddle. Then he walked into the kitchen and removed an olive-drab nylon poncho and a fleece-lined denim jacket that were hanging from pegs next to the door. After rolling the blankets into the poncho, he pulled on the jacket and, with the rawhide bags in one hand and the rifle and blankets cradled on his arm, walked outside, closing the door behind him. Locking it was something he never bothered with.

The first long rays of morning sunlight broke above the trees and made the frost on the ground glisten and a stand of aspens in the middle of the pasture shimmer silver and gold like Christmas tinsel in a freshening breeze. The smell of autumn and the approaching winter couldn't be missed as he ran fresh water from a leaky hose into a bucket for the dogs gathered around him.

The paint, his breath steaming in the frosty air, was already waiting at the corral gate when he whistled, the sharp, singular sound piercing the morning stillness. A gust of wind lifted the stallion's black mane and tail as Keno bridled and walked him over to the shed, the horse prancing and snorting with anticipation. He dropped the reins and walked inside, lifted a saddle from a sawhorse, and picked up a set of worn leather saddlebags that were lying next to it on a bale of hay. After saddling the horse, he strapped the saddlebags behind the saddle and stuffed the bags of food and extra ammo into one of them and hung his canteen over the saddle horn. He walked back to a grain bin inside the shed and, with a metal scoop, filled a cloth sack with oats that he carried back and put inside the other saddlebag. He secured his blanket roll between the saddlebags and the saddle, then stepped back to look things over as the three other horses stood shoulder to shoulder at the corral fence staring at him. He made sure the shed door was propped open against the wind wide enough for the dogs to get in and out when he spotted a coil of rope hanging on the wall. He hesitated, rubbing his chin, and decided to take it. Before he mounted, he lifted the rifle over his head, sliding the sling across his shoulders and chest. He had a foot in the stirrup when he stopped and turned. Damn, he muttered, remembering the dogs. He returned to the grain bin and lifted a fifty-pound bag of dog food out and dumped half, hesitated, then all its contents into a large feeding trough as the dogs gathered round him, looking up, wagging their tails, expecting a walk. No you guys can't go today. You gotta stay here and watch the place, he said as he stroked heads and backs with both hands. Then he picked up the reins and passed them over the paint's head. He put his foot in the stirrup and stood up into the saddle, thinking that if he didn't find anything to support his gut feeling about Gary by late afternoon, he would return home. If he did, well, the dogs would be okay for at least a few days.

* * * * *

It was mid-morning when Keno rode into the campground at Morning Star Lake. It was empty, unremarkable, nothing to indicate that two people had been savagely killed and eaten by bears there. He dismounted and began to look for some clue as to the exact location of the fatal campsite. He was an experienced tracker, something he'd learned from his father and uncles as a young boy, but after a half-hour of looking, he realized there was little of interest left to see. He guessed the couple had camped by the pebbled beach, but the rangers had cleaned everything up. He picked up a torn piece of yellow crime scene tape someone had missed and dropped it in a fire pit. Looking out to the south toward Pitamakin Pass, he wondered whether there was anything of interest on the trail to the pass. If somebody wanted to leave here unnoticed, he reasoned, that's the way you would go. But to where? His daughter's killer was all he could think about, but he still couldn't imagine how Gary might have been involved in the fatal bear attack. It didn't make sense, but the feeling remained.

He mounted the paint and followed the trail south up a steep forested ridge toward the pass at a slow walk, his eyes searching the ground and adjacent landscape, for what, he wasn't sure. He'd traveled nearly a mile before something caught his eye. The trail had been muddy in a shady spot where a small, now ice-crusted, seasonal stream flowed across it. In what had been a pool, he could see tracks where the mud had frozen. He dismounted and stooped down for a closer look as the paint nosed the remains of a puddle and began browsing on the frost-scorched grass that grew among the rocks.

That's when he saw it. There was no turning back now. There frozen among a season's tread marks and scuffs of hikers' boots were hoof prints. Not unusual on this trail, to be sure, except one print that caught his eye. There were two horses and one of them had a loose shoe. A wave of excitement swept over him. He squatted down on his heels for a closer look. The right rear hoof. He knew at once it was the little sorrel. That meant Gary. And he was heading for the pass. Was someone on the sorrel? He couldn't tell, but he had a hunch there was.

He checked his watch and swung back up into the saddle. A mile later, he stopped to water his horse and fill his canteen at Pitamakin Lake. He lifted the canteen to his lips and drank slowly, scanning the trail ahead as it climbed to the pass. A hawk, or was it a golden eagle, was soaring in widening circles high above him.

An hour later, he reached a narrow spine of rock that stretched between McClintock Peak and Mount Morgan—the Continental Divide, in Blackfeet legend, the Backbone of the World. Gazing out at the panorama of peaks, ridges, and valleys that stretched out as far as he could see in all directions, he understood why. He pulled up at a level slab of rock that was wide enough to dismount and rest his horse. He lifted a stirrup and hung it over the saddle horn, loosened the latigo, and let the horse blow. Squinting in the high elevation glare, to the northeast he could see the curvature of the earth and just make out the three peaks of the Sweetgrass Hills near the Canadian border. Far below to the west he could see turkey vultures gliding on thermals above some prize. He guessed probably a mountain goat or bighorn that had run out of luck on the cliffs. Up ahead, he observed a slab of wet rock that sloped across the trail at a dangerous angle and dropped off to a series of cliffs below. He hesitated, looking for some way around it, and decided there wasn't any. He cinched up the latigo and remounted. As he drew to its edge, he could see a tiny stream of water trickling down from above and splashing into a thin, slippery sheen that covered most of its smooth surface.

Easy does it, Poia, he said under his breath, stroking the horse's muzzle after he dismounted to examine the slab for the best footing. Something caught his eye. Skid marks. Then he saw a horseshoe bent and wedged in a crack. He looked out again at the vultures circling below, and then down at the area beneath them. Could it be the sorrel?

* * * * *

Keno was three ledges above the carcass before he could tell for sure that his hunch was right. The remains were scattered along a ledge. Vultures and other scavengers had been on it. As he moved closer, he could see there wasn't much left but the skull, rib cage, and the hooves, one of them, he knew, shoeless. Even the pungent odor of decaying flesh that drew the scavengers to the site was stale and beginning to fade. When he got down to the ledge, he stopped. Then with a reassuring word for his horse, he dropped the reins and, crouching low for balance, began to inch his way across the ledge for a closer look. Large black ravens that were vying with the vultures for what little cartilage remained on the bones began to squawk and flap their wings, but he knew it was all bluster. Still he moved slowly, not only for fear of falling, he didn't want to be the target of a vulture's projectile vomit. But they cleared out as he approached, settling on nearby ledges to wait for him to leave, just as they had for a big grizzly days before.

He could tell from the way the large leg bones had been splintered and vertebrae chewed that a bear or bears, maybe a wolverine, something with powerful jaws, had been on the carcass. He stepped over and around abundant scat, most of it dry. Only a few flies left, bunched up low out of the wind. Days old, he decided, as he leaned down to examine the scat. He whistled softly. He had never seen anything like it. It was a huge grizzly. He looked for sign of it on the trail that snaked below him, but saw nothing. He decided that the bear had probably moved on days before. Toward the valley, he guessed, the same way he was.

He squatted down to get a closer look at the badly damaged saddle, the leather split open, exposing its bent metal shank. The saddlebags had torn open but were still attached. It was an eerie sight, the latigo still looped loosely under the rib cage. He moved slowly around the carcass, bending low, using one arm for balance, to get a closer look at the clothing he could see scattered around and below the torn saddlebags.

A yellow L.L. Bean windbreaker, a wool hiking sock, both on the small side, were near the bags, and a little farther off a sports bra and a pair of pastel-colored panties were tangled together. Gary must have the girl. How that had happened, or why, he couldn't be sure. Why else would he have all her clothing? But was she on the horse when it fell? He scanned the area above and below. No body in sight, only what appeared to be clothing scattered here and there on the talus slopes and ledges. He guessed that Gary probably had her. If she was still alive.

As Keno led the paint down toward the valley floor, Nyack Creek was a thin ribbon of brightness here and there among the trees and shadows of afternoon sunlight. Up high on the slopes, he could see swaths of aspens were shimmering gold in the afternoon light and, lower down, the birches were turning fast from the spent green of late summer. On the open slopes, he scanned wide, bright crimson patches of huckleberry bushes scorched by recent frosts, looking for grizzlies he knew were around. Abundant bear sign was all along the trail—scat, over turned rocks, and trenches dug in the search for ground squirrels and marmots. He guessed the bear, or bears, he was now following was moving into the valley to gorge on what remained of the berry crop and whatever nourishment could be found at lower elevations before the big snows.

But a chance encounter with a big grizzly was a secondary consideration for him now. As he adjusted the sling on the rifle he carried across his shoulders, his thoughts never strayed far from Gary and, now, the hostage he was convinced that he probably had with him.

* * * * *

It was late afternoon when Keno remounted the paint where the trail leveled out, leaving the last of the talus behind, and followed it slowly as it meandered through meadows of marshland grasses, patches of alder and willow, and stands of pine, fir and spruce that thickened and merged, becoming the dense forest of the Nyack Creek Valley.

He saw a thicket of serviceberries and stopped to rest his horse. He dismounted, dropped the reins, and loosened the latigo to let the paint blow. The patch had been ransacked by bears, or *the* bear. As he absentmindedly munched the few berries left—late season, dried out, woody taste—he knew he had to be on the alert. Farther along, he noticed a rotting cottonwood stump that had been shredded by a bear foraging on insects, then a thicket of cow parsnip that had been ripped and uprooted. He was leading his horse through a thicket of alder and willow when he spotted an open area at creek's edge and a clear pool for his thirsty horse.

That's when he noticed the campfire ring. He walked over to it, picked up a stick, and gently stirred the blackened ashes. A couple of partially burned candy bar wrappers. A short distance away, the grass was flattened where someone had probably spread out a sleeping bag. He walked over and pushed the grass aside with his boot. He stooped down for a closer look. An unused tampon removed all doubt. Gary had the girl.

Leaden clouds were piling up and darkness was closing in as he made camp. He knew Glacier Park is a moody place that changes from bright and friendly to dark and angry in a shift of the wind; bright sunshine to blizzard in twenty minutes. Except for the rippling sounds of the creek and the muffled sounds of the unsaddled paint, hobbled, grazing in the grass, it was still. Too still, he was thinking watching a line of darkness rise from the valley floor to the rimrock of Cut Bank Pass. He spread out the poncho, arranged the saddle for a headrest, and rolled out his blankets. Too edgy to eat, he picked up the Winchester, levered a round into the chamber, and propped it against a log next to him, his thoughts on Gary, but with the approaching darkness, also grizzlies on the prowl.

Less than a half-mile away, low on the south slope of Razoredge Mountain, a grizzly with two yearling cubs rose on her hind legs, Keno's scent on the breeze.

———◆◆◆———

30

Saturday morning, September 29. A cold drizzle was beading up on the hood of Harry Dawkin's Silverado as he stowed Beth's backpack in the back beside his. He wasn't about to let a little rain deter them from doing an interesting three-day backcountry hike he had been talking up for a couple of weeks. Summer and good hiking weather were running out, so come rain or shine, this was the weekend to do it. A big change in the weather was predicted within a few days with a cold front moving in. Their destination was a deep gorge with a series of waterfalls, and an old, abandoned ranger cabin he had visited as a teenager in the remote Nyack Creek Valley. The cabin's not on the new park maps, he told Beth, but I'm sure I can find it unless it's burned or been torn down.

It sounds like a great adventure, she said without much enthusiasm, looking at the low hanging clouds, thinking she wasn't sure about starting a hike in the rain. Harry opened the pickup door for her and she was about to step in when they heard a muffled ring. Wait, I think that's my phone, she said. Sorry, but if I hear it, I have to see who it is. She hurried back into the townhouse, wondering if it was the call from the sheriff's office she had been hoping for.

Hello, Beth Blanchard? Louie Moore.

Beth caught her breath. Yes, detective. I was hoping to hear from you. This must be important. What's up?

Well, your theory was right on the money. Our background check revealed a prime suspect: wrangler, white male, thirty-nine years old, worked in the park for Sundown Outfitters. Was working at Grand Canyon when the two Navajo women were murdered and he's been living in West Glacier since May. That means he could have killed the two victims here.

Wow, that's exciting. What …

Hold on, there's more. A background check in Oregon, where his mother lives, revealed a sexual assault charge in Portland that was dismissed. Involved a prostitute. No DNA. That was, let me see here, yeah, about eight years ago. But, more interesting, his Oregon record revealed he had served time as a juvenile in Arkansas for murder. Twelve-year-old girl. He was fourteen. Name's Gary Ray Kemp.

So have you made an arrest?

No, that's the bad news. Kemp quit his job nearly a month ago, August 31st, Friday before Labor Day. Told his boss his mother was dyin' and he had to go to Portland to be with her. But Portland police located his mother, name's Loretta Jean Kemp. She's not dyin'. Says the last she heard from him was a note sayin' he was changin' jobs and that he'd get back to her. She said that was about a month ago and she hasn't heard from him since. So we doubt he headed for Portland, but we got plate numbers and we're optimistic about runnin' him down.

When Beth put down the phone, her heart was pounding. She rushed outside where Harry was standing by the truck. Harry, that detective, Louie Moore, just called. This is exciting. They have a suspect and *I* think he's the killer, a cowboy who worked for the trail rides concessionaire in the park. And, here's the clincher: he was working at Grand Canyon when the two Indian women were murdered in Arizona three years ago. His name's Gary Ray Kemp. She went on to recount the conversation.

Beth, you nailed it. You had it figured all along. He gave her a high five and put his arm around her and kissed her forehead.

She nodded. But the bad news is he quit his job a month ago and may be headed for Portland. At least that's what he told his employer. But they're doubting the story. But who knows? If he doesn't know he's a suspect, he might've been telling the truth. Anyway, they got plate numbers and they're looking for him in Oregon and all the neighboring states.

Then she punched him softly on the shoulder. Harry, remember that guy in the pickup you had the run-in with at the post office over the dog? Then we saw him in Freda's eyeing that poor girl who was killed? He nodded. Well, I noticed he had one of those employee stickers on his windshield. You know, the kind employees in the park get for going in and out to their jobs.

Yeah, so did I. So you're thinking ...

Well, maybe it's past experience, or female intuition, but if I were going to pick the first park employee to investigate on this, it would be him. And I bet it *is* him. There was just something about that guy. Believe me, that guy's got a past. Reminds me of the creeps I've dealt with in trials.

Yeah, it makes sense all right, Harry said rubbing his chin. Workin' at the stables, dresses cowboy, bale of hay in the back of his pickup with a trailer hitch and, most importantly, Oregon plates. Damn, I bet you're right it's him. Funny, I don't think I told you, but I was talkin' with that young guy who works at the Conoco station in West Glacier about that couple the bears killed at Morning Star Lake. He told me that he'd noticed some weird dude who works in the park eyeing that couple, like you saw him doin', especially the girl, for weeks at Freda's. I bet it's the same guy. Beth, I mean it, you're a real Sherlock Holmes.

Let's hope, Harry. Yeah, but I don't know about that angle, you know, his connection to what happened to that young couple at the lake. That's quite a reach. I don't see how anyone could've been involved in that bear attack. But who knows?

By the time they had turned off Highway 2 at Red Eagle, the windshield wipers were slapping back and forth in a soft rain. They followed a gravel road a short distance to the railroad tracks and parked next to a stock loading ramp with a Nyack Creek trailhead sign standing nearby.

Well, here we are. Are you up for a little foul weather? Harry asked as he lifted their backpacks out of the truck.

Beth looked up at the threatening clouds. The steady rain seemed to have slackened, the moisture turning bright yellow cottonwood leaves a deep gold. I don't know, Harry. We've got rain gear, but look at those dark clouds.

Yeah, I know, but I'm guessing it's gonna blow over and we'll have sunshine by noon. At this time of year, the weather's so changeable, a lot of days start out like this then it clears up. If you don't take a chance on these kind of days, before you know it there's a big winter storm, the hiking season's over, and you've missed out on some great hikes. This might be our last chance to get into the backcountry this season. At my age, I don't like to put things off. You never know.

Yeah, Harry, I know, live every day like it's your last and all that, but starting a hike in the rain? And what about that winter storm that's supposed to be on its way? What was really on her mind was not the weather, but a desire to stay by the phone for more news on the investigation.

Ah, that's not supposed to arrive until next week. We'll be back before that and we can watch the first big snowfall sittin' in front of my fireplace.

Now that's my idea of a great backcountry experience, Harry. Sipping hot chocolate, curled up on a couch in front of a crackling fireplace, watching the snowfall—with *you*. Come to think of it, how about doing that and watching the rain?

He shook his head smiling and gave her shoulder a gentle punch. Come on, Beth, where's your sense of adventure.

Donning rain parkas, they shouldered their backpacks and made their way across the brushy flood plain to the river. When Beth said she could make it across on her own, he said, Yeah, if you were a little taller and thirty pounds heavier, I'd agree. But it's better not to take any chances. You don't want to be startin' a hike soakin' wet. Or worse, he thought, not mentioning the danger of being swept downstream into rapids and snags. Beth left her backpack on shore and as Harry guided her across through the swift current, she was glad to have him by her side. When they reached the far bank, he dropped his own backpack and made a return trip to retrieve Beth's.

They bushwhacked north in the wet pants and running shoes they wore to ford the river through cottonwood and birch riparian flats into a forest of larch and spruce that extended all the way to the banks of Nyack Creek. They forded the knee-deep creek and with another push through a tangle of thick brush, they found the Nyack Creek trail. It was densely timbered country with an understory of tangled brush offering only occasional views of the high snowcapped peaks that surrounded it. As they sat on a log to change into dry cargo pants and boots they had tied to their backpacks, Harry told her it was the brushy trail and the need to ford a swift, cold, potentially treacherous river to get to it that accounted for why few people ventured into this most primitive area of Glacier National Park. After stashing their wet shoes and pants in the bushes for the return trip, they pushed ahead on the overgrown trail.

A few minutes later, Harry said, Hey, look here. Someone's been back in here with horses. He pointed his hiking stick to hoof prints and manure. But not in a while. Probably the Park Service closin' out the patrol cabins for the season. Like I said, not many people come back this way. Not like the old days, when this was the main trail the Indians used to get back and forth across the mountains to hunt buffalo on the plains.

By mid-morning, the rain had turned to drizzle then stopped. They looked up as a long blade of sunlight pierced through the forest canopy. Sunshine, Harry, look, just like you predicted. Let's take a break, Beth said, pointing to a log beside a large glacial rock, where lichens grew rusty-brown shading into yellow-green. I'm getting hungry and there's a nice log with a backrest over there to sit on.

They shrugged off their backpacks and leaned them against a tree. Ah, that feels better. My shoulders and neck are aching, Beth said as she stretched her arms over her head. Then with her back to him, she spread her legs and bent over, touching the ground with the palms of her hands. Harry was about to stretch as well, but stopped to watch. She caught him and smiled. It made him blush.

Beth took a couple of apples out of her backpack, handed one to Harry, and sat down on the log, resting her back against the rock. They didn't speak for a while as they munched their apples, then she said, You know I keep thinking about that young couple who were killed by the bears. Such nice, good-looking young kids. Everything to live for. What a shame. Is that place, Morning Star Lake, far from here?

Yeah, pretty far for us, probably about fifteen/twenty miles, across the Divide, but not for bears if, in fact, those bears actually killed them, he said as he sat down next to her.

What do you mean, *if*? Isn't that what the Park Service concluded? If not the bears … What's your point, Harry? Oh yeah, you're still thinking that they might have been murdered by the weirdo who'd been eyeing them— who may be Gary Ray Kemp. She tossed her apple core. I don't think, Harry. I have a gut feeling that the post office guy is probably Gary Ray Kemp, and he killed those Indian women. But that couple? So we know he had his eye on that girl that night, but how many other young girls does a guy like that eye? I just don't see how it would be possible for him or anyone else to arrange the way things apparently happened at that lake with the bears.

Yeah, you're right. Seems impossible that anyone else could have been involved in somethin' like that. I'm just not convinced they got the right bears or bear.

Well, I'm just hoping that the police find Kemp. Like I said, there's a western states alert out on him, so we'll see when we get back. I'll be back in a minute, she said, as she stood up and brushed off the back of her pants and walked off into the bushes to relieve herself. A few minutes later, she returned. Lead on, Harry, but please steer clear of bears.

An hour later, they slowed their pace as the trail crossed a marshy area.

We're gettin' close. Harry said. That old patrol cabin can't be far from here, as I recall. If it's still standin' after all these years. You know, there's been a lot of horse crap on this trail. Have you noticed? Like all this along here. He pointed to clumps of manure that spread out along the trail. Looks like more activity than I imagined back in here this summer. Wonder who … He stopped and pointed. Beth, look over there. See them, he said in a whisper. See back there in the shadows, a moose cow and her calf.

————◆◆◆————

31

———◆———

Saturday afternoon, September 29. They could hear the roar of white water before they saw it. Then as the trees thinned out near the rim of the Nyack Creek gorge, they could see clouds of mist floating up from below.

Wow! This is as spectacular as you said it was, Harry, Beth said as she knelt down to look over the edge at the roaring chasm below. She could see three waterfalls separated by large boulders and roiling white water. Beautiful. Is there any way to get down there? Not that I would want to.

You can rappel down, Harry said over the roar. There's also a climber's route down, but I don't advise it. See over there, he pointed, that narrow chimney that cuts down through the rock below those alder bushes just to the left of the falls?

She shook her head.

See right there on the left of the first falls, he said, taking hold of her arm and turning her slightly as he pointed with the other.

Oh yeah, okay, now I see.

Old timers called that the 'maiden's crack,' for reasons you might guess—the bushes, the slit below …

Yes, Harry, I think I get it, she said, rolling her eyes.

When it's dry, with a little rock climbin' experience, it's possible to shimmy down that chimney. If heights don't bother you. But if you slip, you're in a world of trouble. See those big rocks thirty-forty feet below. Most of the time, the walls of that chimney are too wet and slick to give you the traction you need to get down safely. And gettin' back out that route in those conditions is a technical challenge. You wouldn't want to try it without ropes and knowhow. Even then, it'd be pretty risky. See how the rock is rotten, I mean real soft and crumbly, breaks off under pressure. Rotten rock is a killer if you're climbing. Anyway, I wouldn't want to try it.

Beth nodded. Me either, needless to say.

Okay, now see the second falls over there downstream from the first? he said pointing. That's called 'Maiden's Leap Falls.' It's the only one of the three with its own name. Not a formal name. You won't see it on any maps, but that's what it's called by people who know the story.

So what's the story?

Back in the early 1900s or so, before the park was established, I'm not sure exactly when, doesn't matter, after the Great Northern built the railroad, a young teenage girl, the daughter of homesteaders on the Nyack Flats, near where my place is now, disappeared. Just vanished. They thought she might have drowned in the river, or maybe a grizzly or a cougar got her, but no trace. It was a mystery.

What supposedly happened was this: A railroad crew was working near their homestead on tracks that washed out when the Middle Fork flooded. One of the gandy dancers who hired on the track crew that summer ran a trapline up Nyack Creek in the winter. He had a cabin somewhere not far from these falls. Now it may be the same cabin that Joe Cosley might've built, that I hope we can find the ruins of, but that's another story.

Who's Joe Cosley, again?

Legendary trapper, ranger in the park when it was first established, turned outlaw—accused of poachin' in the park. But the guy did some incredible things, like hikin' over Ahern Pass in the dead of winter.

Okay, go on.

Well, anyway, this guy, the gandy dancer, had his eye on this girl and eventually kidnapped her, got her across the river, and back in here to his cabin. Not long after, the story goes, the girl escapes and gets as far as the falls here with her abductor in hot pursuit. But her escape is blocked by the gorge, and backtrackin' to the trail means she'd run right into him. So she risks her life by starting down that chimney, hoping she makes it, and he doesn't see her. Well somehow she makes it to the creek, but he spots her down there. He follows the same route, slips, and is killed on the rocks below.

Now she doesn't have to worry about him, but she's trapped in the gorge because she can't get back up that slippery chimney. So she makes her way downstream, climbin' over and around those big boulders you see down there to the top of the second falls—see over there to your right—lookin' for a way out.

Beth nodded, engrossed in the story.

Those falls drop about thirty feet into a deep pool. See, you can just see part of it below. Now there's no way she could've known how deep that pool is, or whether there are boulders just beneath the surface. But she's desperate, so she jumps, probably from that ledge, see there on the left, hits the water safely, stays out of the current, and makes it to the bank. That pool's at least ten feet deep, even during the dry season. Years ago, when I was a kid growing up, we used to fish it for bull trout. If she hadn't gotten out quick, she would've been swept over the third falls. That would have been curtains for her because—you can't see it from here—there's nothing but jagged rocks and white water beneath it.

He took hold of her hand. Now if you lean over a bit—be careful now I don't want to be hikin' out of here with you over my shoulders—you can see it's a fairly easy climb out from the second falls on those rocks that slab up to the rim. That's the route we took to get in and out to fish there. And that's how she got out.

So that's why the second falls got its name, 'Maiden's Leap.' Fascinating story, Beth said still looking at the falls. Is it a true?

Who knows? It's supposed to be, but maybe it's just a good story. You don't see the falls named on park maps, but old timers, at least when I was growin' up, claimed it's a true story. Anyway, the girl makes it back home and lives happily ever after.

Hmm, well I'm glad her abductor supposedly got what he deserved. I've tried a lot of cases involving rapists. Three of them who killed their victims are on death row I'm pleased to say. There should be four. Disgusting people.

Yeah, that case you told me about involving that creep, Atwood, was that his name? who abducted and killed that little girl in Tucson. People like that, that's why I'm for the death penalty.

She nodded. Certainly for sex offenders who molest, rape, and kill innocent victims, especially children. Losing a child at any age is the worst tragedy I can imagine. Crimes like that demand retribution. That's why I did what I did on that Gowan case.

Yeah, and you did the right thing. He nodded and patted her on the back. Ready to go? Let's walk back to the trail and check out that old cabin. It can't be much farther, as I recall, no more than a quarter mile, or so. When I was a teenager, we'd stay in it when we hiked back in here to fish in the gorge. We figured out if we pulled down on the old padlock they had on the door, it would pop open. He smiled at the thought. Yeah, lots of memories back in this wilderness. I was lucky to have kind of a Huckleberry Finn/Tom Sawyer boyhood. The Park Service built a new patrol cabin farther east but, as far as I know, they never tore down the old one. But they might've. As I said, it's not on the park maps anymore. You'll see it's kinda interesting, if it's still standin'. We'll set up our camp somewhere near there. Then we'll have plenty of time to come back here and explore the area over the next day or so. Maybe even climb down to the second falls.

Beth gave him a look. I don't think so, Harry. I'm no climber. You know me and heights, especially after you took me on that terrifying goat trail across the north face of that mountain. If you don't mind, I'll just enjoy the views from up here on the rim.

Yeah, but you did it, Beth, and if you ever do something like that again, now you'll have confidence that you can do it, Harry said, thinking she's right, I probably shouldn't have taken her on that route.

Kind of like boot camp, huh, Harry?

Harry laughed. Yeah, the same idea now that you mention it. Anyway, if you're feeling peppy tomorrow, we could keep goin' toward Surprise

Pass. According to the map, that new patrol cabin is near there. Pretty scenery. Opens up more. Great views of Pumpelly Glacier and Mount Stimson, but that's a pretty good hike for the time we have. And we'll have to keep an eye on the weather. Maybe a little too far, I'm thinkin', for this trip. We'll see how we feel tomorrow.

Yeah, I don't know, sounds like it might be a lot of hiking. Let's just keep it simple and enjoy ourselves. I like it here. This is beautiful, the gorge and falls and all. Nice place to sit and read a book. I don't want to go too far and maybe get caught in bad weather. I'm not in the mood for an endurance contest. We don't have anything to prove, do we?

Not a thing, Beth. We're here just to enjoy ourselves, see real back-country, and do exactly what we feel like. Which is what we're doin', right?

You bet, Harry, she said as she put her arm around his waist and pulled him close. I just like being with you, no matter what we're doing.

He put his arm around her shoulder and leaned down kissing her softly on the lips. I feel the same way, he said after clearing the unexpected frog in his throat. It wasn't what either one of them had planned, but they both knew falling in love isn't a matter of choice, it just happens, and they knew it had happened to them.

Time out, my turn. Damn prostate of mine, Harry said, breaking the spell. Be back in a minute. He stepped off the trail and pushed through the brush, heading for a tall spruce tree. Go on ahead, if you want, I'll catch up.

No way, Harry. Not in this country. I'll wait right here.

Moments later, he called, Hey, Beth, come here I want to show you something.

No thanks, Harry, she said with a laugh. I'm quite familiar with the endangered one-eyed worm.

Worm? Come on now. You really know how to hurt a guy. Seriously, come look at this tree.

What about it? she said as she pushed through the brush toward the tree, its roots radiating out over the rocky ground like veins on an old man's hands. The lower branches of the big spruce tree were broken off, exposing a trunk of rough bark that seemed to glow in the sunlight.

It's a scratchin' tree. I bet you've never seen one. This is something. A good-size bear's come through here. Look at how high that hair's stickin' on the bark. Got to be at least eight-ten feet high, he said stretching to reach as high as he could. She could see coarse, dark hair with bronze and silver highlights and swarming fleas, backlit by a shaft of sunlight that made the tree trunk glow. He pulled some hair from the bark and handed it to her. She hesitantly held out her palm. Sometimes these scratchin' trees can fool you because of snow depth. If a bear's standin' on four feet of snow when he's scratchin' … well, you get the picture. Maybe not twelve feet tall, but still a very big bear. Yeah, look here. He was leaning over looking at the ground. Look at the size of this paw print! This bear didn't need a snowdrift to reach that high. Just look at that! This is one heck of a big bear. That paw print must be a foot-and-a-half long and half that wide. Beth knelt down beside him for a closer look, placing her hand inside the print.

My God, she whispered.

Yeah, that's a big bear all right, a grizzly for sure, he said. This is a right front paw. You can tell by the length of the claws. Gotta be a good four-five inches beyond the pad. With claws like that, a griz can peel a person's face off with one swipe.

Beth, grimacing, looked at Harry and down at the paw print, shaking her head. Harry, do you think we should be wandering around here with an animal like that in the area?

Harry was frowning. The sign was recent. He turned to Beth. You know, you're right. I'm thinkin' we better change our plans. I don't like the looks of this. I'm guessing that bear's come through here pretty recently, maybe today. Did you notice the fleas buzzing around the hair on that scratchin' tree? That means it was pretty recent. This has got to be a big boar. Much too large for a sow.

Yes, let's turn around. I was hoping maybe we'd see a grizzly at a distance, like we did on that hike to Granite Park, but not up close and personal, as they say. She slipped a canister of bear spray from the holster on her backpack. Don't laugh, she said. Harry didn't, his concerns deepening.

As they ventured back through thick timber to reach the trail, they noticed more bear sign. A rotting, ant-infested log had been shredded. Large swaths of chest-high cow parsnip and devils claw that pressed in on the trail had been flattened. Farther along, in a small clearing, the soil looked as if it had been plowed, as probably the same animal dug for roots.

Up ahead the sun shone brightly on the trail through a break in the clouds. Whoa, look at this. That's one big pile of bear scat. Look at the size of the bore, Harry said, as he held his thumbs and forefingers together to form a circle. This stuff is fresh, very fresh, can't be more than a couple of hours old, if that.

How can you tell?

Look at all the flies and the way it glistens. It's still wet. That means it's fresh. Flies don't swarm like this on old scat. If you touch it, it's probably still warm.

And it smells. No thanks, Harry. I'll take your word for it, she said, holding her nose. Let's get out of here.

Yeah, lots of bear sign. Not good, he said almost to himself. Beth could see worry in his eyes. Then he shouted, Hey bear! Hey bear!

His shouts startled her and she grabbed his arm. It's okay, he said without taking his eyes off the forest. I'm just lettin' him know we're here. Never want to surprise a grizzly. We're headin' back. Don't want to take any chances. That bear's nearby. He looked over and took her hand in his. Remember, now, let's stay alert. We gotta be careful. The only predictable thing about grizzlies is they're unpredictable.

Then something in the scat caught her attention.

Harry, what's that shining, there in the middle of it. See it? Looks like something silver. Is that a buckle? My God, it looks like a watchband.

Hmm, I'm not sure. Let's take a closer look, Harry said as he broke a stick from a dead branch to retrieve the object. Sweet Jesus, you're right, it's what's left of a watchband. Either this bear has raided someone's campsite recently or …

At the same moment, they both noticed remnants of what appeared to be a piece of plaid flannel cloth in the putrid mound of excrement.

Oh my God, it's killed and eaten someone, she said, like those bears at Morning Star Lake. Harry, I'm scared. Let's get out of here.

Okay, okay, let's stay calm. We're on our way, he said laying his hand on her shoulder. Then something caught his eye. Wait a minute. Oh Christ, wait, look way over there, to the left of that small clearing, see beneath the roots of that big fallen tree, he said, pointing. See, right there at its base where the roots are heaved out of the ground.

Beth raised her fingers to her lips. Oh good Lord! Harry, is that a boot sticking out?

Yeah, I think so, and it ain't empty. This isn't good. That's a bear cache, Beth. They don't bury empty boots. This is trouble. We gotta get away from here quick. That bear has cached a kill there, and that means he's going to make damn sure nothin' gets near it.

Harry, what if it's a person, still alive, needs help? What can we do?

What do you mean *if* it's a person? It's a person and whoever it is is beyond help, he said as he craned his neck for a better look. The ground around the base of the uprooted tree looked as though it had been trenched and plowed by a machine. It's a person all right, he said as he approached the spot cautiously. He walked back quickly and reached for her hand. Come on, let's haul ass, head back to the river. Just hope that bear stays away for a while, because sure as hell he'll be back here. Be real quiet. Noise won't work now. We don't want him knowin' we're near his cache.

As they moved quickly down the trail, Harry stopped and pointed. Look, the old cabin back there hidden in the trees. We missed it. They must have rerouted this trail. Still standin'. Looks in pretty good shape, too. Maybe we could …

They were startled by a woman's voice. Help, help me, please, please help me.

Before they could respond, Harry pointed and whispered, Holy Christ! Look, there's the bear.

Where?

Comin' this way out of the trees just behind the cabin.

Oh my God, Harry, what should we do?

The huge animal, less than fifty yards away, hesitated and reared on his hind legs as the woman's shouts became more frantic. Look out, look out, a bear, a bear …

Seemingly confused by the cries, odors, and new circumstances that surrounded him, the grizzly remained upright on his dark hind legs, nose in the air, turning back and forth, his massive back and shoulders a lighter, bronze color.

Harry, what'll we do? Beth whispered again, her breath coming in short gasps.

Harry, motionless, took a deep breath and didn't speak as he considered their options. Then he whispered, Be cool. Too late for the cabin. Can't make it. He's in the way, headin' back here to his cache. Whoever it is, the woman, she's safe in the cabin. He can't get her inside. What the hell's she doin' there? We'll figure that out later. We gotta backtrack away from that cache.

Whatever you say, she whispered.

They moved quickly, crouched low and crab stepping sideways to keep the bear in sight but avoiding eye contact, both breathing hard.

Okay, seems like he's focused on the cabin. Let's pick it up, head for the gorge away from the cache, Harry said. The hysterical screams from the cabin continued to pierce the air and, again, they looked back to see the big animal hesitate, turning back toward the cabin. The delay gave them a few precious moments.

Harry grabbed Beth's hand and pulled her along behind him until they reached the edge of the gorge. They stopped to catch their breath. The bear was now out of sight.

We'll follow the creek west along the rim of the gorge to get out of here as fast and as far away from that cache as we can, he said. It's more open along the rim and we can make better time until we're far enough away to cut back and pick up the trail and head back to the Middle Fork.

Moments later there was a crashing sound and a snarl from the brush to their right as the great bear charged. Beth raised the pepper spray canister and squeezed. Stunning impact. Falling. Then darkness.

* * * * *

When Beth regained consciousness, she was lying on her back surrounded by roaring, cascading water, staring up into a halo of dim light in the mist above the gorge. Confused and in pain, a pounding headache and burning pain radiated from her left wrist and shoulder. She had no memory of the bear striking them, or falling, but she knew this was no dream. She reached up and touched her face, trying to clear her head, and felt the soreness and crusty moisture of blood drying on a ragged cut on her forehead. Her shoulders were bare, her windbreaker ripped down the middle of her back, exposing welts and parallel linear wounds left by raking claws. *Where's Harry?* Harry, Harry, she called out, Where are you? Are you all right?

As she struggled to roll on her side, she recoiled in horror. Harry was lying beneath her, a leg bent at a sickening angle behind him, his head tilted too far to the side, resting against his shoulder. She let out a faint cry and rolled away, then reached back, rolling to her knees and leaning over to cradle his head with one arm. There was a deep gash in his forehead and the blood that ran from his nose and mouth and puddled in his ears was dry.

Harry, Harry! Oh my God, Harry, speak to me … Please dear God, she whispered as she leaned down close to his face. His eyes were closed, as she searched for a pulse in his neck. Oh God, no, please no, please no. Harry, oh my dearest Harry. She pulled his backpack away from his body.

Feeling a faint pulse, she knelt over him and, with her one good arm, began CPR. Some time later, at the point of exhaustion, she saw his lips part in shallow and irregular breathing. Oh, dear God, please, please don't let him … she whispered as she laid her hand gently on his forehead. It was cold. Then she saw her backpack and Harry's sleeping bag, knocked loose in the fall, in the rocks a short distance away. She made her way over to them, got Harry's sleeping bag and crawled back. She opened it out and wrapped it around him. Darkness was closing in when she crawled beneath it, holding him close, her cheek pressed against his.

32

S *unday, September 30.* Harry Dawkins died in her arms during the night. There was nothing she could do but hold him close until the terrible blackness in the gorge receded into a gray dawn. The outside of the sleeping bag was wet from mist and a shower during the night, but the inside had remained dry. Overwhelmed with grief and fear, she sat up and knelt beside him, struggling to comprehend a man so strong, so confident, so alive, now dead. After a long cry, she forced herself to consider the situation—alone, trapped in the depths of a deep gorge from which there seemed no escape, a rogue grizzly prowling the rim if she did somehow manage to get out. She let her eyes rest on Harry's face, then turned away, trying to imagine it was all a bad dream. Choking back sobs, she embraced him and stroked the silver hair now caked with dried blood. After a moment of whispered words, she gently kissed his cheek. Then, looking into his face, she kissed her fingertips and pressed them against his lips.

She crawled to his backpack, a short distance away, removed the remaining bungee cord, pulled the poncho loose, and crawled back to Harry's body, dragging the poncho behind her. She was about to pull the sleeping bag and poncho over him when she hesitated, then turned away and crawled back to her backpack where its contents were scattered on the ground. She picked up a bright yellow inflatable pillow he had kidded her about bringing and made her way back to the body. After inflating it, she lifted his head gently and placed the pillow under it. So kind, so funny, such good times, like I've never known before. I love you so much, so much, Harry, she whispered as she knelt beside him and stroked his face. After covering him with the sleeping bag and poncho, she rocked back on her heels and looked up into the mist, a feeling of awful desolation. *Why?* she felt like screaming. Then, one by one, she placed rocks around the edges of the poncho to weigh it down against the wind.

She sat back against a large boulder, took a deep breath, and swallowed hard, trying to come to terms with the thought that this was the end, that Harry was gone, that she was going to die here. She could tell from the throbbing pain in her wrist and shoulder that bones were broken. She tried to press her palms against the sides of her aching head, but it was too painful to raise her left arm. She reached for her backpack. When she opened the flap, pieces of glass and plastic from her broken binoculars spilled out. A roll of film dangled loosely from the cracked case of the camera. Turning the pack upside down, she dumped its contents on the ground and picked up an orange nylon tote bag. She struggled to untie the knot in the drawstrings with fingers that were now numb. She was about to scream in frustration when, holding one end in her teeth, she finally pulled it loose. She opened it and fumbled through an assortment of standard first aid materials—ace wrap, moleskin, gauze, bandages, adhesive tape, clean wipes, waterproof matches, until she found a square plastic container. Prying off the lid with her teeth, she removed three vials of pills—aspirin, her thyroid medicine, and the Percodan she was looking for.

It was an old habit. Saving prescription painkillers for when she *really* needed them. Until now, she never had, and so had endured some bothersome, but tolerable, discomfort after dental and medical procedures only to flush the unused pills at their expiration dates. This time was different. Pulling a Nalgene container of water, that somehow didn't break in the fall, from its sheath on the side of her backpack, she washed down a couple Percodans.

She looked around then gazed up to the rim of the gorge. A sinking feeling. A chilling breeze off the cascading water blew steadily through the gorge, stirring the mist that floated up to the rim. Above the rim, she could see the morning sun moving in and out of foreboding clouds. She swallowed hard against the sour taste that rose in her throat. The utter indifference of nature was a daunting reality she had never imagined.

She thought about Harry's story of the girl who managed to get out of the gorge. The thought of leaping from a waterfall was a terrifying prospect, especially with a broken wrist and shoulder. But it was the only way out. Still she wasn't sure she could do it. She reached back and touched the sore, fresh claw marks that ridged her neck and shoulders. She bit her lip and squeezed her eyes shut to blot out the images that were flashing through her mind.

She forced herself to recall outdoor challenges that she had over-come. *Suck it up. Think positive.* She remembered how frightened she was on the traverse across the north face of a mountain whose name she couldn't recall, on a climb they shouldn't have attempted. She was following Harry on a faint goat trail across a sloping ledge that was no wider than her hips, jagged peaks and razor-thin ridges blading up thousands of feet everywhere she looked. She'd pressed against a cold wall of wet rock that rose through the mist to the top of high cliffs that she had to lean back to see. If she dared. Deadly exposure. Down hundreds of feet below, a talus slope angling steeply to the top of another cliff. Then thin air. *Eternity waiting.* She was terrified and afraid to move. Harry gripped her wrist gently, the wind blowing his words away, *It's okay, take a deep breath, be strong, and don't look down.* The exhilarating sense of accomplishment she experienced afterward was like nothing she had ever felt.

As they were driving back home that night discussing what could have happened, she remembered him saying that whenever *it* happens—when the fat lady sings, he joked—he hoped it would be somewhere *out there* and not wired up in a hospital room with tubes in his nose. He said Vietnam made him a fatalist. She asked him if that's why he wouldn't wear a seat belt. Like I said, she could still hear him saying, when it's your time to go, you go. But, Harry, dearest Harry, she whispered now, this was too soon.

She closed her eyes and breathed a quick prayer. Be strong, she whispered. No appetite, but she knew she had to eat something to gain the energy and strength to survive challenges that seemed overwhelming. Rummaging through both backpacks, she pulled out the expensive, ultra-lite stove she had bought especially for this trip. It was bent, broken, useless. She tossed it aside and looked at the dried food packages beneath it. Also useless without a stove to heat water. She looked around seeing lots of wood, but all of it too wet to burn. Opening a package of trail mix, she forced herself to chew a handful. The raisins, nuts, and dried fruit tasted like wood chips. Only the chocolate chips had any flavor. She forced down another handful and was about to reach for a candy bar when she threw up.

The sky darkened and the rain foretold by gathering storm clouds began to fall, forming rivulets of water that drained off the boulders, pooled in their concave surfaces, and soaked into the gravel and soggy sand. Heavy raindrops splattered on the poncho that covered Harry's body, puddled in its folds and creases, and broke her heart.

33

---

*B*eth waited until the rain let up and occasional rays of sunlight broke through the mist and early morning *fog*. But the weather hardly mattered. The situation seemed hopeless. Percodan took the edge off the pain, but her left shoulder and arm were useless. The form under the poncho brought tears to her eyes. She turned away and looked toward her objective, the maiden's leap, as she stood up and tried to bend and stretch the stiffness out of her legs. The brink of the second falls was only a stone's throw away, but she would have to climb over and around fallen trees and chest-high stacks of tangled driftwood wedged between large boulders. It would be tough going dragging a backpack with only one good arm. She sat down to fashion a sling for her injured wrist and arm with a roll of Ace wrap and a bandanna. When she finished, she looked up toward the rim, searching for any sign of the bear. All she could see through the lifting mist were ragged layers of ledges and fissures of rock clogged with brush.

Kneeling down beside her backpack, she began to sort through its contents for only the bare essentials she would need if she was lucky enough to survive the plunge over the falls and able to climb out of the gorge. Her main objective after that, she decided, would be to get back to the woman she and Harry had heard calling from the old cabin.

The call for help wasn't reassuring, but what choice did she have? The chances of making her way back seven miles to the truck—injured and alone over difficult terrain and across a treacherous river—were not good. She tried to put thoughts of the grizzly, and other predators with an instinct for injured prey, out of her mind.

She discarded extra clothing, the useless dried food packets, the damaged binoculars, camera, and stove. She took only the essentials— a parka, another fleece top, extra socks, and silk underwear. She struggled to stuff everything into the pack. Dammit, I can't get this shit in with only one hand, she cried as she dropped her good arm to her side and rocked back on her haunches in frustration. Finally she did. The four remaining candy bars, two packages of M&Ms, water bottles, and her medications, she zipped into side pouches. She rolled her sleeping bag into the tent rain fly and pressed it down on top. Then, using her teeth and one hand, she pulled the flap over and secured the drawstring.

She tested the weight, lifting the backpack and slinging it awkwardly over her good shoulder. Pain radiated across her shoulders and neck, even with the Percodan. Lowering it back to the ground, she checked the straps and zippers, hoping it would withstand the impact when she threw it over the falls, wondering if she would fare as well. She looked down at her watchband that was cutting into her swollen wrist, leaving no doubt that it was broken. She was about to discard it when she noticed the time, *2:33, when the watch stopped.* She hesitated, then zipped it into the side pocket of her backpack. Why, she wasn't sure.

Dragging the backpack behind her, she crawled over and around boulders, fallen trees, and tangled thickets of driftwood toward the second waterfall. Winded and damp with perspiration by the time she got to the top of the falls, she released the backpack and made her way to the edge for the dreaded look below. It was as terrifying as she knew it would be. Thirty feet below she could see her blurred reflection and the sky above in the smooth, dark surface of a pool. It seemed bottomless, and the reflection made it seem as if she was at the center of the universe. Oddly, the thought occurred to her that Thoreau had written about the same feeling sitting in his tiny rowboat on Walden Pond. I'll trade places with you, Henry, she whispered.

Downstream from the pool, a roiling cascade of white water spilled out through jagged rocks over the third waterfall. She closed her eyes, attempting to banish the thought that her body probably would be found below the third falls. If at all. She hesitated, eyes fixed on the rocks below, the sound of roaring water flooding her senses. No way, she said aloud and turned away and covered her eyes. She thought of the remaining Percodan and considered returning to Harry's body. Call for help? Fruitless, she decided. It would be drowned out by the roar of the falls. Just do it, she said aloud.

Taking a deep breath, she wiped tears from her eyes and scanned the area below, looking for a spot to throw her backpack. A small, smooth stretch of gravel near the water's edge caught her eye. Afraid to stand for fear she would slip, she crawled to her right to a spot directly above it. She was about to drop the backpack when she realized that it made no sense to jump with her clothes on. Wet clothes meant hypothermia in this weather.

She thought for a moment, then sat down and removed her hiking boots and socks, stuffing the socks inside the boots and using the laces to tie them to leather loops on the sides of the backpack. Then she began to undress. With only one good hand to use, it took time. Opening the backpack, she pressed the clothes she removed inside. She had stripped down and was about to remove her silk panties and bra when she hesitated. No, I don't want to be found naked, she said to herself. One last check and she moved carefully to the edge of the precipice, pushing the backpack ahead of her. She paused to estimate the distance. Then mustering all her strength, she stretched to lift the backpack as high as she could with one arm and heaved it out, holding her breath as she watched it arc toward the tiny strip of gravel below. A sigh of relief as she watched it land, bounce, and roll, intact and dry against a pile of driftwood.

No choice now. This is it, she whispered. Jump, or perish here on top of this waterfall in your sexy silk underwear. She almost smiled at the thought. Making her way back to a spot directly above the pool, she stopped to adjust the sling on her swollen wrist and forearm. Nerves stretched like piano wire, shivering with fear and the chill of the cold mist rising from the falls, she stared at the abyss below. Dear God, please help me, she whispered, unable to bring herself to say what she was thinking, *Holy Mary, Mother of God, pray for us sinners now and at the hour of our death.* Biting her lower lip, she crossed herself, something she hadn't done in a long time, took a deep breath, then with eyes squeezed shut, jaw set, and injured arm held tight against her chest, she leaped out as far from the ledge as she could.

It seemed forever before the surface of the water stung the soles of her bare feet, slamming her knees up hard against her chest. Her injured arm, which she tried to hold close to her chest, smashed upward into her face as pain, frigid water and darkness enveloped her. Panic. Seconds later, an exhilarating sense of relief and euphoria swept over her as she broke the surface, and gulped in a breath of air. After catching her breath, she swam sidestroke, paddling with her good arm, the short distance to shore. I did it … I did it … I'm okay, she gasped aloud as she crawled up on a large flat rock at the pool's edge.

Even the cold, hard surface of solid rock felt good as she rolled over on her back and blinked at a bright spot in the overcast sky. In the adrenaline rush, the pain of her injuries was momentarily blotted out and she tried to stand. Too soon. Lightheaded, she slipped on the wet rock, falling hard, pain radiating up from her hips. She waited for it to subside, then crawled on her hands and knees to the backpack. Teeth chattering with the chill and excitement, she struggled and eventually got the backpack open. She pulled out a fleece top and dried herself clumsily with it. Then she changed into dry underwear and pulled on her clothes, wearing as many layers as she could to lighten the weight of the backpack.

She surveyed the sides of the gorge then sat down to put on her boots. She could see, just as Harry had told her, that irregular slabs of rock angled upward from the banks of the creek, forming a steep, but climbable incline to the top. The backpack was a problem. She considered leaving it behind for fear that it might throw her off balance on the climb. Just in case, she removed her medications and a candy bar and put them in a Velcro-sealed pocket in her parka. Then, pushing the backpack ahead of her, she began her ascent, slowly gaining handholds with her one good hand and using her feet and knees for leverage, she inched her way up the slick, cold layers of rock toward the ridgeline and treetops she could see above it.

Near the top, a rock overhang blocked her route. No problem, she thought, if only I had two hands. She stopped, wedging the toe of her boot into a crack in the rock, and looked for an alternate route. She decided to make her way across a thirty-degree slope of slick, mossy rock to the far edge of the ledge and climb up a narrow chute to the top. Half way across, the backpack slipped from her grip and tumbled into the gorge. She closed her eyes and didn't look down.

She had almost reached the chute when she slipped. She grabbed a small pine sapling that grew out of a crack in the rock and held tight as she felt its roots pulling loose. Biting her lip, afraid to take a breath or move, she waited. But the sapling held. Using it for leverage, she regained a toehold and slowly inched her way to the bottom of the chute. From there, it was an easy climb out.

Except for the clothes she wore, her medications, and the candy bar in her pocket, the rest of her belongings were in the backpack at the bottom of the gorge. There was no time to dwell on that. She had to find the cabin while avoiding a dangerous bear that was aggressively guarding a cache somewhere nearby that contained a human body but, disoriented, she wasn't sure *where*.

Fallen trees like tangled matchsticks and thick brush meant a direct route was impossible. She crawled over and under the deadfall, branches, and brush tearing at her clothes and scraping abrasions on her face and hands. It was tough going, absorbing her concentration, leaving little time to worry about the bear. Then just as she felt she was lost, exhausted, and could not continue any further, she came across the trail. Wet with perspiration, and breathing hard, she slumped to the ground to rest.

She looked up at the sky. From the angle of the sunlight breaking through the overcast, she guessed it was probably early afternoon and the cabin couldn't be far away. The weather was still unsettled, dark clouds, a brief shower, then blue skies and bright sunlight before it would cloud up again.

As she made her way along the trail, she looked for landmarks that she and Harry had seen the day before. She hadn't walked far when she recognized tread marks of their boots in soft, wet spots on the trail and knew she was headed in the right direction. Then she saw it. Up ahead, a clearing and at its far edge, the cabin, a thin wisp of smoke drifting from the stovepipe on its roof. Hesitant to approach, she stopped and waited, looking, listening for signs of life. And the bear. *Nothing.* After a while, she called out, Hello, hello, is someone there? She waited. There was no response. Another call. Then she saw movement in a window.

She called out again, this time pleading in desperation. Please, I need help. I'm hurt.

An arm appeared out the window, someone waving, then a woman's voice, restrained, difficult to hear. Beth was just able to make out, Don't call, *he'll* hear you. Come closer. I can't get out. I'm chained to the floor.

Chained to the floor? Until those last words, Beth assumed the faceless woman was talking about the bear. She waved her good arm back and forth over her head. Can you see me? she called. I'm at the far end of the clearing, directly in front of you. I'm hurt. I can't move very well.

Yes, I can see you now. Please don't call out any more. He'll hear you. Just hurry before he comes back.

Beth closed her eyes and took a deep breath. Can you open the door? she called, despite the warning not to.

No, no, I can't reach it. Come to the window.

Is the window open? she asked to be sure.

Yes, it's open. You can pull yourself in. I can't reach beyond the window. Please hurry.

Beth scanned the clearing, looking for the bear and not knowing what else. She took a deep breath, crossed herself, and began to run, it seemed as though on a treadmill, the distance seeming to expand, the bear closing in behind her, as in a bad dream. Tall grass and brush pulled at her clothes and tangled in the laces of her boots. Her breath was coming in short gasps as she neared the cabin and saw the figure in the shadowy interior beyond the window.

Hurry, hurry, please hurry, the woman called.

Beth was staggering, exhausted and reaching for the wall of the cabin when she looked up to see the haggard face of a woman framed in the window. *That face...where ...* flickered through her mind and was gone. She was still beyond reach of the window, adrenaline now masking the pain in her wrist and shoulder. Drawing on the last remnants of her strength, she stumbled to the window and reached for the sill. But numb and weakened fingers slipped. Clawing at the logs with the fingers of her good hand, she was able to pull herself to her feet and took hold of the outer edge of the windowsill. She took a deep breath and, calling on all her remaining strength, she reached across the sill and locked her fingers over its inner edge. As she strained to lift herself through, the woman inside grabbed hold of her parka and pulled her inside. Beth fell to the floor and lay there, eyes closed, pain radiating from collarbone to wrist, breath coming in gasps. Neither of them spoke.

When Beth opened her eyes, she found herself looking into the bruised, swollen face of a young woman with matted auburn hair. They looked at one another in disbelief, each wondering about the bizarre circumstances that brought them together at a God-forsaken cabin deep in the backcountry. Beth still thinking she looked familiar, but *who? Where?*

Winded and dry mouthed, Beth swallowed and spoke, her voice a hoarse whisper. Thank you ... can't believe this ..., and her voice trailed off as she shook her head. Thought I ... like a bad dream. It wasn't clear whether she was talking to herself or to the young woman. She reached out and placed her hand gently on the woman's arm. Am I imagining this? Are you ... she whispered.

The young woman almost smiled, eyes brimming with tears. I'm so glad you found me, she whispered.

Beth looked closely at her, thin and pale, the left side of her face was swollen, a discolored crescent extended from her eyebrow across her nose down to her swollen lips. *My God, can this be the girl that we ... Morning Star ...* recycling through her mind. Are you ... she started to ask again then noticed the chain that was attached to her ankle. She sat up and struggled unsteadily to her feet.

My God, what's happened to you? she asked, reaching out again to touch the woman's arm. Who did this to you? Did we meet once? Are you …?

The only sound was the sigh of the wind under the eaves of the cabin. Beth reached for her hand. When she did, the young woman leaned forward and pressed her forehead against Beth's shoulder. After a moment, she lifted her head and whispered, I'm Vicki Hathaway. I'm supposed to be dead.

——◆◆◆——

34

---◆---

Sunday afternoon, September 30. By the time Beth met Vicki Hathaway at the cabin, Gary Ray Kemp was several miles away in the valley below Mount Thompson, sitting on a log inside a blind he had built out of logs and brush. The place looked perfect for moose, a lush bog that spread out at the confluence of three small streams that flowed down off the mountain. Except for the occasional snorts and stirring of his horse grazing in a grassy area behind the blind, and the twittering and ticking of juncos and pine siskins, it was quiet. He looked out over several acres of shallow water and marsh grass broken by patches of horsetails and small islands of dead trees.

At the far end, he could see a loon diving for fish. He hadn't seen it at first, but then it gave its call, that lonely, melancholy sound heard only in the wild. It reminded him of the scene in *The Godfather* where Michael Corleone has his henchman shoot his brother in the back of the head as they sit together at dusk in a rowboat on Lake Tahoe. Gary found that scene particularly satisfying, a justification for what he believed— that losers were meant to go. Darwin's rules. *Yeah, and you don't fucking betray people who are good to you.* Fredo knew he had it coming.

His thoughts returned to the present. Ideal habitat, but so far no moose, although there was plenty of scat and tracks. A nice fat cow was what he was hoping for. Tender, better tasting than bulls. Better yet, a moose calf. He thought about the outcry from bleeding-heart environmentalists. Hey motherfuckers, you eat lamb chops?

He was angry, frustrated, depression settling in like a wintry fog. It had been for days, and the loon didn't help. It was a lot of things, but most of all the betrayal. He had recurring doubts about her denial and couldn't get them out of his mind. He gave little thought to the hiker he had murdered, no more than he would have to the wild game he killed. He wondered about that, the wild game that is. It had been scarce recently and he couldn't figure it out. Elk were in the rut. He could hear the bulls bugling back and forth, that strange eerie, sound—something between groaning and screeching—reverberating off the slopes and across the valley, especially in the evenings. But only one shot, and he missed.

When they first moved into the cabin, deer seemed to be everywhere. Every morning and evening he would see three or four, sometimes more, in the clearing. Deer were so stupid. They would just stand there and look at him, curious, with those big brown eyes—especially the mule deer, like that goddamn doe with the fawn *she* was bawling her eyes out over, they were the dumbest—until he shot them. She still didn't get it, probably never would.

He had lost track of how many deer he had killed. Without refrigeration and no other way to preserve meat, he had to hunt every day or two. Sure, it's a lot of killing, he told her, but Lewis and Clark did the same. Every day of that fucking expedition, they were shooting and eating anything that moved, even dogs and horses.

Most of his kills he gutted and butchered where they fell, taking the best cuts of meat and leaving the rest. He knew the gut piles and carcasses he was leaving behind would attract bears and other scavengers, but there was little to be done about it. For a while he tried to bury gut piles and drag carcasses away from the cabin, but it got to be too much and the accumulation of dead flesh continued. He had already shot a cougar and a black bear that were feeding on deer carcasses. And he knew others would follow, but he didn't mind killing them so long as he didn't use up too much ammunition. He knew some people ate bear and said it was pretty good, but he wanted no part of eating carnivores. There was something about eating animals that ate flesh that didn't appeal to him. He laughed when he tried to joke with Vicki that he might be a serial killer, but he was no goddamn Hannibal Lecter. She smiled that smile of hers, but he could tell she wasn't really.

A lot of what was going on made him depressed. Things weren't working out the way he planned. Part of it was the monotonous diet. He was getting tired of eating stringy, tough venison stew every day. Deer were browsing on pine needles now that the grass and summer plants were giving out, and the meat tasted and smelled like turpentine. The dried packaged stuff was gone, but he was sick of it anyway. Beef stroganoff, spaghetti and meatballs, chicken chow mein, it all tasted the same, like salted sawdust. The canned food was better, the beef stew, corn beef hash, beans and wieners, but now that was almost gone. He yearned for a good chicken-fried steak, gravy, and mashed potatoes at the Spruce Park Cafe, or a big bacon-cheeseburger and fries at the Glacier Highland.

The scarcity of good grass was showing on his horse. He'd thought about hay when he was stocking the cabin, but there was no time and no way to haul it in. He had taken off its bridle, attached a hobble to let it graze on the shin-deep grass that remained in the meadow behind the blind, but nightly frosts had turned it brown and drained the nutrients. Bright summer wildflowers had been transformed into colorless dry husks scratching in the wind. He watched the buckskin hungrily chewing the dying grass, its ribs, and hipbones poking out like they might break through the skin. He hated to think about shooting him, but knew that was in the cards before winter. No way would he let old Buck die a slow death, starving and freezing. He had to admit that Darwin's rules were hard to accept sometimes. He was closer to that horse than he had ever been to any person.

He thought that might change with her. But it didn't. *The betrayal. Why?* He couldn't shake it. He couldn't understand why she didn't appreciate all he had done for her. Saving her fucking life. Twice. Sometimes when he'd been gone for a long time, she seemed glad when he returned. But most of the time she was like some goddamned zombie, staring off into space. When she wasn't doing that, she was crying, probably over the fucking boyfriend. At least she had stopped asking him to let her go, take her back to her family, but he couldn't escape the gloom of her unhappiness. The cabin reeked of despair. It was dragging him down, the one person, next to his mother and grandmother, he had tried to love, but only his grandmother, in her fashion, returned it, and she was long gone. Heart attack. Matches in hand, an unlit cigarette between her fingers. At least it was quick. Not a mattress fire like that old hag two trailers away.

So now he wasn't sure what to do with her. She ate little and it was showing. When he watched her bathe, something he never missed, he could see that she was getting skinny, ribs and hip bones sticking out like the Holocaust victims he remembered seeing in a documentary film at the detention center. Then he read a book about it and found out that all that was just a lot of goddamn propaganda put out by New York Jews. She said the steady diet of wild meat was making her sick and she'd lost her appetite. He wasn't sure whether she was telling the truth or whether she was trying to starve herself to death. Her small breasts seemed to have shrunk, those thimble-sized pink nipples, were now tiny and dark like raisins, and the gap between her thighs had widened.

His fantasies about her had changed. Sometimes in troubling dreams, she appeared dark-skinned and ugly and his mother would be laughing and pointing. He wanted to have sex with her in the worst way, the way he had fantasized about all summer, and did for a while, but now he couldn't. He could only get up for the oral sex. But that made him angry and depressed because he didn't want her to become like all the others, the disgusting pigs who went down on him for money before he strangled them. And it always brought back childhood memories of his mother he wanted to forget, like the time he was placed in child protective custody when she was arrested for prostitution. He remembered the bedwetting and the embarrassment when he'd admitted to a caseworker that his mother insisted on bathing him when it happened. When the caseworker asked how he felt about that, he'd felt his face redden at the thought of the warm, soapy water, the fondling, and looked away not wanting to answer before blurting out that she only did it to be sure he was clean. He could tell the caseworker didn't believe him. She asked if his mother was still doing that. He refused to answer. He was in the fifth grade.

His thoughts returned to Vicki. His feelings about her now were ambivalent, confusing. Why, if it disgusted *him*, would she do it? Didn't she understand that's why he hit her? Didn't she fucking understand that's why he killed the others? He was having trouble sleeping because he realized he was beginning to feel about her the way he did about the others, and he knew where that would end. That wasn't what he wanted, and he wished it didn't have to be, but it looked like that was well what? *Darwinian?* He just knew there was no way he would ever let her go. She was his.

Something caught his eye at the edge of the bog, where clumps of sedge grass met a stand of aspen. I'll be damned, he whispered to himself, there they are. He watched a moose cow and her yearling calf as they emerged out of the timber and began to browse, stripping the bark from aspen saplings along the edge of the bog, the calf following behind. Occasionally they would look up, stand very still, lift their noses in the air for scents that might signal danger, then return to browsing. He watched as they moved slowly toward him, lowering their heads into the water to feed on what was left of the summer's pondweed and lily pads. He was downwind and out of sight in the blind. He turned to see the buckskin, nervous, moving closer. Don't whinny, he whispered to himself. He was excited, perspiration prickling his armpits, as he slowly raised the Marlin, the barrel making a faint scraping sound, sliding across the log in front of him.

The big moose had just raised her head from the water, pond lilies dripping from her mouth, when he held his breath, steadied the rifle, and squeezed off a shot. She stumbled, rear legs buckling, falling back on her haunches, and splashed sideways into the water. She struggled briefly, trying to get up, then took his second shot and fell back on her side, only the dark curve of her belly visible above the water. If he had wanted her for meat, shooting her in the water would have been a mistake. He knew a moose that size would've been way too heavy to move, and it would've been difficult to butcher the best cuts of meat in two or three feet of water. He just wanted her out of the way so she wouldn't interfere, as he knew she would, trying to protect her calf when he shot it.

He watched for a moment as the perplexed calf, which had bolted away, returned, pawing, pushing its nose against her. He could see the cow struggling to keep her head above the water when he squeezed off a head shot, this time dropping the calf in a cloud of pink mist into the water beside her. He rose from his crouched position, levered another bullet into the chamber, and turned to smile at the buckskin, as if expecting his approval.

A kill made him feel good, and a double kill doubled the satisfaction, made him feel powerful, in control, and he liked that feeling. It didn't matter whether it was an animal or some fucking whore. But even that feeling was beginning to fade as his depression deepened. He began to walk slowly toward the moose, carrying the Marlin at the ready, just in case she had any life left in her. He knew a wounded moose was dangerous. As he got closer, he could see the cow's head was submerged, blood spreading out like a crimson oil slick over the surface of the pond. Suddenly the big moose raised her head and looked directly at him. He jumped back, stumbling backwards, nearly falling into the water before he regained his balance, took aim, and was about to squeeze off another shot. Then he saw the light go slowly out of her eyes and her head splashed back under the water. He waited until the bubbles stopped and then walked over to the calf.

The morning had begun in gloom and despair and then the low clouds and fog burned off, leaving an hour or two of Indian summer in the afternoon that helped elevate his spirits a little bit. Now the light was thinning and the shadows were lengthening as the sun was tilting toward evening. A chill breeze washed down off the mountain as he lifted the hind legs of the calf out of the water and dragged it to dry ground. He looked up at the darkening sky. He decided to gut and butcher it later. It was getting late and cold. It would keep. Time to head back, he said to himself, as he secured the carcass behind the saddle, tying the front and rear hooves together with rope looped under the horse. As he turned the buckskin east toward the cabin, he again thought about the grass, withered and turning brown, and shook his head. No hay for winter. When the snows come, then what?

In the distance, he could see dark clouds gathering over Mount Stimson as they usually did this time of year. Moments later, a fork of lightning and the rumble of thunder. Thunderstorm in October, that usually meant snow in the high country, rain and sleet in the valley, maybe snow by morning. He couldn't be sure because the goddamn batteries on the radio had given out, so he hadn't heard a weather report lately. He zipped his parka up closer to his neck and pulled his Stetson lower on his forehead as the wind licked around his throat. Moments later the sun was lost in the forest canopy. He looked at his watch. It was a little after four, and the days were getting shorter, dark by five thirty. It would take an hour, or so, to get back on the trail and cover the distance to the cabin. Then what? Why did she have to do it, become like *her*, and ruin everything?

35

For Beth, too much had happened too fast. Harry's death, the ordeal in the gorge, and now meeting a young woman, supposedly dead, who was, instead, being held hostage. The chain on Vicki's ankle and the welts and bruises on her face and arms left no doubt in Beth's mind that she was caught in a nightmarish ordeal worthy of David Lynch's best films. For minutes, neither of them spoke. Then Beth reached out to hold her hand and whispered, Who did this to you?

In a barely audible, childlike voice, Vicki said, He hits me when I make him angry. She told Beth in halting language about her experience in the cabin. When Beth asked her about Morning Star Lake, she lowered her head and shut her eyes and didn't answer. Then with tears rolling down her cheeks, she shook her head, I can't ... I ... Gary brought me here ... you can't stay... He'll be back and he'll kill you like he did that poor hiker.

His name's Gary? This is incredible. Is this man Gary Ray Kemp?

Surprise in Vicki's expression. You know about him?

White, about five-ten, sandy hair, bad teeth?

Vicki nodded.

It's got to be him. He's killed two Indian women.

He's killed lots of women. He showed me photos.

Beth shook her head in amazement, thinking Harry was right, that Gary Ray Kemp, the guy at the post office, was somehow connected to the mauling at Morning Star Lake.

Beth wanted to *how*, but there was no time to waste. She recognized the symptoms of post-traumatic stress. Vicki would tell her story when she was able. But how to deal with the immediate situation? Beth needed help and this traumatized young woman was her only hope. How could they both get out of here before this killer returned?

Beth tried using a paring knife to cut the leather and steel ring around Vicki's ankle, but it was useless. And there was nothing else to use to cut or break the chain. Gary had thought through all that. Beth realized their only hope was for her to leave and somehow find help. But first she needed to dress her wounds. Using gauze pads Vicki took from a first aid kit that Gary kept under his bunk, Vicki helped clean the crusted blood from Beth's forehead and the back of her neck. They were adjusting the Ace wrap sling for Beth's injured wrist and shoulder when they heard a horse whinny in the distance.

What was that? Is that him? Beth asked, her voice rising with alarm.

Oh no, God no. Yes, yes, that's his horse, that's him, that's Gary, Vicki said, eyes wide, a panicked look on her face, wired, her voice no longer a whisper. He's coming back. He'll be here soon. You've got to get out of here *now*. If he finds you here, he'll kill you.

Where should I go? What direction? Which way is he coming?

I don't know what to tell you because I don't know where I am. The sun sets in that direction, she said pointing toward the door, but I've never been away from the cabin. You have to get out of here and hide, anywhere, it doesn't matter where, before he comes back.

I know, I know, Beth interrupted. But where is he *now*, dammit? She pointed toward the door. The sound, the horse, sounded like it came from that direction, didn't it?

Vicki hesitated, biting down on the knuckle of her index finger. Beth could see the fear in her eyes and trembling hands. She took hold of Vicki's arm and shook it gently. Vicki, Vicki, look at me. Don't fade out on me now.

Vicki blinked and shook her head. I, I … I'm not sure … Her voice trailed off.

Well, I can't wait till we see him and *then* leave, Beth said with more sarcasm than she intended. I'll just have to take a chance that he's coming that way, she said, motioning to the door. Let's hope and pray I'm right.

What will you do then? Vicki asked, voiced strained, lips trembling, wringing her hands.

Beth knew it was up to her to save them both. Her mind was racing. Could they surprise him, maybe stab him with the paring knife, or hit him over the head with something when he walked in? She looked at Vicki, pale, emaciated, an ankle chained to the floor, her with a useless arm, and decided it wouldn't work. He'd kill us both. I'm not sure, she said. It'll be dark soon. I'll just have to hide somewhere in the forest and wait for daylight.

But what about that bear? It'll …you'll be … Vicki said, unable to express the thought.   No time to worry about the bear now, Beth said, an image of Gary at the post office in her mind. She had to get away quick and find someplace to hide in the forest. She was pulling on her parka and stuffing a refilled Nalgene container back into her pocket when Vicki glanced out the window.

Oh, God, here he comes. There, see him, she said pointing. He's right there at the edge of the clearing. Hurry, go out the back window. Hide, I'll try to keep him occupied here. Hurry, hurry, get out the back window.

Beth wanted to get a closer look—can it really be *him?*—but there was no time. As she slipped out the window, Vicki watched Gary stop and dismount at the edge of the clearing. He was adjusting the ropes that held an animal carcass he had tied behind the saddle. She turned back to the window and saw Beth crouched low, running into the thick timber behind the cabin.

She turned back in Gary's direction, terrified, but thinking clearly. Gary, Gary, she called out. I'm so glad you're back. I was worried about you.

He looked up, but didn't return her wave, thinking, *Glad? Worried?* What the hell's this all about? Vicki watched as he quickened his pace, leading his horse across the clearing and tying the reins in a quick knot to the hitching rail. Another glance out the back window revealed that Beth was out of sight.

As Gary entered the cabin, panic followed as her eyes immediately traced his to a bloodstained gauze pad on the floor beneath the table. What's this? he said, kicking the gauze toward her. You cut yourself? He grabbed her arm and spun her around. Where's the cut, bitch?

A pleading, helpless look on her face, too frightened to speak.

You lyin' sneaky, no-good bitch. I thought somethin' was up, yeah, you're so glad to see me. Someone was here, goddammit. Who was it? Where'd they go? He slapped her hard across the face, knocking her to the floor, then grabbed her arm and jerked her back to her feet. Who was it? Where's *he* hidin'? Was he lookin' for that other sonofabitch? What'd you tell 'em? His voice was rising to a shriek as he hit her again and again until she slipped from his grip and collapsed on the floor.

Dazed from the blows, room spinning, she struggled to break through the pain to think of some way to conceal the truth, to protect Beth, to save her own life.

It … it was a lost hiker, Gary … honest, like … like the other one, she blurted out. Please don't hit me anymore … please. *He* just came by like the other one … I didn't know … He was hurt … I helped bandage a cut on his head. That's all. I didn't tell him anything. Then he left.

Which way did he go? he screamed, his fist raised above her head.

He went that way, she lied, pointing toward the door.

Oh sure and I passed him on the trail, right? Don't lie to me, bitch. He slapped her again. Why didn't you tell me? What're you tryin' to hide, bitch? This is the second time you fuckin' betrayed me … all I've done for you … the second fuckin' time. He was trembling, tears in his eyes, when he hit her with a closed fist. She flew backward, her head striking the woodstove, the sickening sound of bone on metal. He blinked several times, looked down at his trembling hands, then toward the motionless body on the floor, and began to sob. He dropped to his knees and gathered her in his arms. Vicki, Vicki …

36

―――◆―――

Movement was difficult as Beth made her way east through the trackless forest, struggling to put distance between herself and the cabin through thick, tangled brush and fallen trees that crisscrossed in front of her. She wasn't sure how much time had passed before she cut back to the south and reached the Nyack Creek trail where she stopped, her breath coming in ragged gasps, hoping she was a safe distance from the cabin. The adrenaline rush was spent. The brief surge of confidence and determination she felt at the cabin was ebbing, exhaustion and the pain in her shoulder and wrist draining her strength. All that remained was fear and the faint hope that somehow she would be able to make it back to Red Eagle and summon help.

Far enough, she whispered, her voice sounding strange to her. Got to rest, conserve my strength. Ahead was an arduous backtrack around the cabin—without being detected—to get back onto the main trail to the river. No way to complete that journey in the dark. The immediate challenge was how to get through the night, avoid a rogue grizzly prowling the area and, now, a savage human killer. She remembered Harry telling her that a predator can make a thousand mistakes, the prey, only one. She thought about how she was pushing her luck, convinced another encounter with that monster bear would seal her fate. And now, Gary Ray Kemp, a human predator probably more dangerous than the grizzly.

Sitting down, her back against a fallen tree she was too tired to climb across, she took out her pills and her Nalgene container. As she looked at her surroundings, the recurring thought—*the utter indifference of nature.* It seemed surreal, the stillness, the cold settling in on the darkening forest, the smell of rain, maybe snow, fallen leaves, and, she imagined, death. Was this really happening? Was she, Elizabeth Blanchard, Tucson attorney, adjunct law professor, Racquet Club member, really here, entirely alone in this immense wilderness, or was this a terrible dream? She washed down another Percodan.

She considered gathering up leaves and twigs to get a fire started. She took out a book of matches and was about to strike one. What's the use? she whispered, the sound of her own voice deepening the feeling of isolation in the enveloping silence of the forest. Too tired, too wet, won't burn, she said as she put the matches back into her pocket.

She zipped her fleece top tight around her neck, pulled her hooded Gore-Tex parka over her head and curled up as best she could within it. She hoped the silk underwear would help as she stared up at a cold darkening night sky through the branches of a large spruce tree. She could see galaxies of bright stars beginning to appear through breaks in the cloud cover. It reminded her of *The Lawrence Tree,* the Georgia O'Keefe print she had hanging in the bedroom of her Tucson condo. *Why would I think of that now*? She pressed a palm against her cheek. *What I wouldn't give to be back there.* Then she felt something in the inside pocket of the parka. She pulled out what looked like a rectangular fold of aluminum foil in cellophane. It was the space blanket she thought she would never use. A feeling of relief as she opened it out and wrapped herself in it. At least I won't freeze, she whispered. One last furtive glance into the malevolent darkness before she closed her eyes. The wind had died down and a hush had fallen over the forest that was heavy and impenetrable, like the lid of a casket closing.

A cold, mean drizzle and a restless night of morbid dreams followed the painkillers, half-dreaming, half-thinking about death—Harry, her sister, the victims of killers she had prosecuted, and, oddly, the heaving chest and last death house gasps of a particularly vicious killer whose execution she had witnessed. Visions of dark forms emerging from the trees made her lurch upright, and when they vanished in a blink, she waited, shivering in fear and cold, not trusting her senses, afraid to fall back asleep. When she dozed off night sounds of a primeval wilderness wakened her—the frenzied, high-pitched barking of coyotes on a kill, the hoot of an owl and the terrifying flap of its wings as it flew low beneath the forest canopy above her, the shrill cry of a cougar that sounded like a child in distress. And the pain. The eastern sky was just beginning to brighten when she took another Percodan and fell exhausted in a deep dreamless sleep.

37

—◆—

Monday morning, October 1. When Beth awakened, puffy white clouds were scudding beneath a hazy sun high in the sky. Confused, then surprised, she guessed it was mid-day, thinking exhaustion and painkillers, *I must've passed out.* It was cold. Her wrist and shoulder were throbbing. She reached into her pocket for the Percodan and shook one out of the vial, but when she lifted the water container to her lips, it was frozen. For the first time since the fall into the gorge, she felt hungry, very hungry. She folded up the space blanket, stuffed it in her parka, and unwrapped a candy bar. As she savored the dark chocolate, she rubbed the sleep from her eyes and stood up to stretch the cold and hours on hard ground from her muscles.

When she squatted to pee, she heard something stirring. Holding her breath to listen, she quickly pulled up her pants. It was moving toward her. *Gary? the grizzly?* She craned her neck and squinted into the forest shadows, but she could see nothing except thick brush and the trunks and branches of trees. A freshening breeze brought with it a strong pungent animal scent and the rattle of dying leaves. Moments later, a snorting sound and branches breaking. *The grizzly.* Fear like a current of electricity went through her as she hid behind the big spruce she had slept under. With her back to the tree, she looked up through the branches and crossed herself. She held her breath and waited, heart pulsating in her temples and throat. Then a strange numbness and feeling of resignation settled over her. *This is it. I'm going to die.*

* * * * *

It was mid-day when Keno heard a noise, a rustling sound, something in the brush off the trail ahead. He had been tracking Gary since dawn when he left his campsite at the headwaters of Nyack Creek.

Gary? he whispered under his breath, thinking, Or could it be that big griz I've been following? He raised a leg over the paint's neck and slid off. Crouching low, Winchester at the ready, he strained to see through the thick brush. Movement. A human figure disappeared behind a tree. He quickly took cover behind a large lichen-covered boulder.

Beth remained behind the tree, thinking it was the bear before a quick look revealed a human figure partially hidden behind a large boulder, the thin sunlight glinting off the dark barrel of a rifle aimed in her direction. *It's Gary. I'm trapped.* Then she heard a voice, calm, matter-of-fact. Okay, Gary, I know it's you. I know you're behind that tree. I've got you in my sights. Drop your weapon and step out, or I'll put a bullet through your goddamn head. A pause. You got that, Gary? Right through your goddamn head.

Silence. Keno waited. Then a woman's voice, No, no, no, please don't shoot. I'm not Gary. Keno eased the rifle away from his shoulder for a better look. Hey, Gary, don't try to fuck with me. I know you've got that girl. I know you're makin' her talk. Throw down your weapon and step out or I'll blow your goddamn head off.

No, no. I'm not Gary. Please don't shoot, Beth called out again, anxious, uncertain, but relieved it wasn't Gary. No one else is here.

Keno watched as a woman emerged tentatively from behind the tree. He could see her clothes were soiled and tattered, her arm in a makeshift sling. As she approached, he noticed the bandage on her forehead and scratches on her face. The hesitant movements told of pain, and there was no mistaking the fear in her eyes. He remained to the side the boulder, the Winchester still aimed in her direction, still expecting Gary to appear. Where's Gary? he said. Are you the woman from Morning Star?

No, no. That's someone else. The Gary you're looking for is holding her at a cabin. It's back that way, she said turning and pointing behind her to the west. He's a killer… shot and killed a hiker. He's holding her there. Oh, thank God. I thought you were Gary.

Keno hesitated, still unsure, then said, Okay, keep comin' toward me. I'm not gonna shoot you. She took a few steps in his direction. Hold it right there. You sure you're alone? Because if you're lyin' to me … He didn't finish. Slowly, rifle shouldered, ready to fire, he stepped away from the boulder. Then, satisfied that she was telling the truth, he lowered the rifle and moved toward her, taking her hand and helping her step over the branches of a fallen tree, an older woman, maybe his age, not the young woman who disappeared at Morning Star Lake. Who are you? What're you doin' here? he asked again.

My God, first I thought you were the bear, then Gary, she replied, relief in her voice. It's a long story and hard to explain, but I'll try. Just give me a minute. She sat down on a flat rock. I feel lightheaded, need to take a breath.

After a moment of silence, she took a deep breath and began to relate the story, the words tumbling out so fast Keno found it difficult to follow, so he let most of his questions go and focused on the immediate situation.

This girl, she's the one missin' from Morning Star Lake, right? You sure?

Yes, yes. Her name's Vicki Hathaway. She said that he, this Gary person brought her here after the bear attack. Not sure how that happened, but he's a serial killer, a real psycho. The police are looking for him. Showed her photos of women he's killed. She couldn't remember much—or maybe just couldn't talk about what happened at the lake, horrific, the boyfriend being killed and all, probably repressed memory, but she said this Gary brought her here to the cabin. He's raped and beaten her and chains her to the floor when he leaves the cabin. They're almost out of food. She says he hunts and they've been living mainly on wild meat. She's in bad shape.

But, so as far as you know, he doesn't know that you were there at the cabin, right?

I hope not. Like I said, I don't think he knows, or he would've come after me, but maybe he's looking for me now. I just don't know.

Keno didn't say anything for a while, his eyes fixed on the trail ahead. So that means maybe he's not expectin' anything, unless … He didn't finish the thought, talking more to himself than her. So we got two problems to think about. Gary and that big grizzly that attacked you and your friend. That griz has probably staked out the area because of all the food he's been leavin' layin' around—gut piles, carcasses, and you say, this hiker's body. This time a year, food isn't the main thing grizzlies care about, it's the *only* thing. They can smell food for miles. That bear's protectin' his cache, and he's not gonna let anyone or anything near it. We gotta try to stir clear of that. Stumblin' into that cache's big trouble.

He looked around at the forest and then back at her. I'm concerned about runnin' into that bear, but I'm not lookin' for him. I'm *huntin'* for Gary. That's why I'm here. He took a deep breath and then said softly, He killed my daughter.

Oh no, oh my God, I'm so sorry, she said lifting her fingers to her lips. The woman they found in the riv . . .—? She didn't finish.

Keno nodded. He didn't say anything for a while as he stared into the forest, taping his fingers on the stock of the Winchester, considering the situation. Beth looked at his weathered face—copper-tones, high cheek bones, the red bandanna and dark braided hair that framed it—a face from the past, a face like those she'd seen on the Winold Reiss prints on the walls of the Belton Chalet that evening with Harry. *Harry.* She squeezed her eyes shut and swallowed.

Keno looked back when he felt her eyes. Have you had anything to eat? Are you hungry? I don't have much left, some jerky, maybe a hard-boiled egg. I think there's one left.

The question brought her back. Yes, a little, but I'm very thirsty. My water's still frozen from last night.

Yeah, so was mine, but I got fresh from the crick, he said as he handed her his canteen. She took a long drink as he pulled the jerky and an egg from a saddlebag.

What about your injuries? he said, as he watched her eating. Is there anything I can do? Your arm?

No, I'm okay, she said through a mouthful of jerky, except I think my wrist and shoulder are broken. Sure feels like it. But I still have some painkillers left and that helps.

How 'bout if I rewrap that sling for you. Your arm needs to be wrapped close to your body so it doesn't move. That should help with the pain. Here let me show you.

Keno propped the Winchester against a tree and undid the elastic wrap. Then he re-positioned her injured arm below her breasts and wrapped the elastic across it and around her back and waist. There, he said when he finished, that should feel better if it's not flopping back and forth like before.

Beth heaved a sigh, Oh yes, that's better, that helps. Thank you.

He stepped back and rubbed the back of his neck. Beth could tell he was pondering their next move and she wasn't sure what that would be.

Okay, then, here's the plan, he said finally. We can ride double on the paint if we take it slow. He's a strong horse, but we can't afford to wear him out. You sit behind the saddle. We'll have better visibility up on the horse than we would on foot, but we'll also be easier targets if Gary's out prowlin' around. He's got the horse there, so one thing we gotta worry about is Poia here, he nodded toward the paint, gettin' the scent of his horse, and whinnyin'. That'd tip 'em off that someone's around. Surprise is important. We gotta get the drop on him or, sure as hell, he'll hurt the girl, or use her as a hostage.

Yes, yes. That's important. We can't let him harm her, Beth said as she got to her feet and adjusted the sling on her arm. She said that he told her that he'll never be taken alive.

Figures, Keno nodded as he placed his left foot into the stirrup and swung up on the paint. He leaned down and put his arm around her. Hold on to my arm and swing your leg over behind me when I lift. Beth grimaced in pain as she settled behind the saddle and blanket roll, adjusting her legs between it and the saddlebags. All set?

I think so.

Okay, so let's get movin', he said over his shoulder.

As they moved out down the trail, Keno carried the Winchester across his lap. Beth held on to the back of the saddle, feeling unsteady, afraid of slipping off, but resisting the impulse to put her good arm around his waist.

He turned his head to the side, What's your name? They call me Keno.

Beth, she said and took a deep breath, letting it out with, I'm so glad you found me.

As they made their way through tangles of trees and brush on the overgrown trail, Keno gripped the reins in his left hand, resting the Winchester upright against his right shoulder with the other, scanning the forest for the danger he knew was ahead. Like VC in the jungle, Gary could be anywhere.

——◆◆◆——

38

---◆◆◆---

Monday afternoon, October 1. There's it is, Keno said in a whisper, pointing to the cabin just visible through the trees. It was almost dusk. They could see a thin, windblown, column of smoke twisting out of the stovepipe on the roof, but there was no sign of other activity. Keno eased Beth off the horse, then dismounted. We're going to leave Poia back here hidden in the trees and hope he doesn't start whinnyin' to the other horse. But if he does, we want to be somewhere else, so attention's on him and not us. I don't see Gary's horse. Must be on the other side of the cabin, he said as he tied the paint to a branch of a fallen tree.

Maybe, Beth said. I remember there was a hitching rail there. Or, maybe we're in luck and he's not here.

We'll see. Okay, easy now. Just follow me, Keno said as they made their way around the edge of the clearing, crouching low, moving from tree to tree, using the thick brush and timber for cover, keeping a safe distance, but an easy shot, away from the cabin. As they reached the far side of the clearing, they could see Gary's saddled buckskin tied to the hitching rail. There was no sign of either Gary or the girl. Keno motioned for Beth to stop.

That's when they heard a door open and close. What if he found out I was there? Beth whispered. If he did, he'll kill her like the others.

Keno didn't say anything, his mind clicking through possible rescue scenarios. It was quiet except for the sound of their own breathing.

Do you think he's …?

Keno shrugged, eyes on the cabin, jaw set, the thought and proximity of Gary igniting searing thoughts of what he had done to Dinah. He swallowed hard, his mouth and throat dry. They waited for what seemed like a long time, when they heard a door close again.

There he is, Keno whispered. See him, he's comin' around the side of the cabin. They watched as Gary stopped and peed. Then he walked back around the cabin out of sight.

Wait here, Keno said. Then he crept back to the paint and led him deeper into the brush and tied him to a tree. When he returned, he said under his breath, Quick, stay low and follow me around to the other side of the clearing. He motioned with his rifle. We can take up a position over there in the trees where we can see the front of the cabin and wait for him to come out. As they drew closer to the spot, he hesitated, pressing his arm back against Beth.

They could see Gary walking toward a crossbeam that was suspended between two trees. The moose calf he had killed the day before was hanging by its hind legs from it. He was carrying a rifle and a large metal pot. When he got to the crossbeam, he set the pot on the ground, leaned his rifle against one of the trees, and removed a knife from a sheath on his belt.

That's him. My God, that's him, Beth whispered, excitement in her voice. That's the same guy Harry had the run-in with at the post office. That's Gary Ray Kemp.

Keno glanced at her, not sure what she was referring to, and didn't ask.

What's he doing? Beth whispered.

Keno held a figure to his lips, not taking his eyes off Gary.

Steadying the carcass with one hand, Gary plunged the blade into the underbelly and slit down to where the ribs joined, the entrails spilling out in a stinking pile of slime on the ground. The sight and stench that drifted toward them made Beth retch.

Keno could tell Gary was experienced with the knife as he watched him make deft cuts, removing meat from bone, tossing bloody chunks into the pot. It was an easy shot, and he deserved no better, but shooting Gary in the back from ambush was not what he wanted to do. He wanted to be up close, wanted Gary to know what was happening and, more importantly, *why*. Those thoughts were running through his mind when, for whatever reason, the strong odor of the gut pile, or the scent of another horse, the paint whinnied. Gary whirled around, looking away from Keno and Beth toward the trees and the sound, as he dropped the knife and reached for his rifle.

Beth held her breath when Keno raised the Winchester to his shoulder and took aim. Gary craned his neck, squinting, looking for movement in the brush, thinking it was Vicki's visitor of the day before. They watched as he began moving back and forth, craning his neck for a better view, holding the rifle at the ready prepared to fire. Keno could hear Beth's rapid breathing crouched behind him, and turned to her, raising a finger to his lips. She nodded, eyes fixed on Gary, thinking, *Yes, the man at the post office, the weirdo eyeing the girl at Freda's. Incredible.*

Another shrill whinny as the paint reared into view, bucking, throwing his head from side to side, trying to pull loose from the tree Keno had tied him to. Gary stopped. He could see the rearing horse partially concealed in the brush. He stopped and raised the rifle to his shoulder.

Keno quickly shouldered the Winchester and took aim, his sights on Gary's chest. No way was Gary going to shoot that horse. Then behind Gary, out of his line of vision, Keno spotted the reason for the paint's distress. A large grizzly was approaching from the far side of the clearing. He nudged Beth with an elbow, nodding in that direction. The bear was moving at a quick pace, its large body rocking back and forth as it moved toward the carcass, the gut pile beside it, and Gary. Keno could see its broad back and the mound of muscle rippling over its shoulders as it moved in the shadowy light. It was a massive animal, the biggest he had ever seen. He guessed it was the trophy grizzly people had been talking about the past couple of years, the bear whose tracks he had been following from Cut Bank Pass.

Beth reached for Keno and gripped the back of his belt. That's the same bear that …, she whispered, her breath giving out.

Unaware of the approaching bear, Gary was focused on the commotion as the paint reared and bucked in panic. Then, sensing something behind him, he whirled around and saw it. But too late. The bear charged. They watched as he tried to raise his rifle. The shot went wild as the bear hit him, knocking him over backward, his jacket flaring out like a cape as he spun in the air.

Then the snarling grizzly was on top of Gary, knocking the rifle out of his hands as he tried to get to his feet, spinning him sideways, arms flailing as he hit the ground, its huge claws raking and tearing at the body now beneath it. They could hear Gary's muffled cries and groans. In the background they could hear screams coming from the cabin. The grizzly settled back on its haunches with Gary's right thigh in its mouth, his arms hanging limp. Then it turned and dropped the body. There was no other sound from Gary.

Beth couldn't take her eyes off the bear and Gary, the savagery, shuddering at the thought of how close she had come to the same fate. Strangely, Keno's thoughts flashed back to something his grandfather had told him long ago. He remembered the old man recounting the legend of a mythic grizzly that roamed the Cut Bank Valley—the *Medicine Grizzly*—a sacred creature, a friend of the Blackfeet, an avenger that saved a wounded warrior's life. *Was this meant to be? Dinah's avenger?* He took a deep breath and let it out slowly, eyes fixed on the bear. Beth glanced over at him when she heard him whisper words she didn't understand.

It was quiet except for the grizzly's soft woofing sounds as it began to nose Gary, lying face down, motionless. She could see the blood on his arms and legs. The bear continued sniffing, nudging the body, as if to determine what? Beth wondered. Whether life remained? Whether to begin …? Oh God, no. She shut her eyes, reliving that moment of terror when the great bear charged her and Harry. She looked up again, then covered her eyes. Oh no, he's going to … no, no, dear God, don't let him …, Keno heard her whisper. Then the grizzly hesitated and reared up on its hind legs, turning its head from side to side as it sniffed the air.

Keno guessed the bear stood eight feet tall on its hind legs, with a wide, bronze-colored head that reached almost to the crossbeam where the moose carcass was hanging.

He's picked up our scent, Keno whispered to Beth. She put her fingers to her lips, fear in her eyes. Keno took a deep breath, held it, and slowly raised the rifle to his shoulder, his finger on the trigger, ready to squeeze off a head shot. But the big grizzly turned away, knocked over the pot, and wolfed down the meat Gary had put in it. Then with one swipe of its huge paw, pulled the moose carcass down and began feasting on bloody chunks of red meat it ripped loose with powerful jaws.

Keno and Beth watched, hidden in the brush only a stone's throw away. The bear seemed indifferent to their presence. But why? Keno was wondering. Was it because they were downwind of the animal? But, no, the wind had shifted. *That grizzly had to know. The Medicine Grizzly?*

Is there anything we can do? Beth whispered. Should you shoot it? Maybe he's still alive and we can save him. Keno held a finger to his lips, eyes fixed on the bear, and shook his head. *Why?* he thought to himself, but didn't say it.

They watched as the grizzly stood on its hind legs and looked around, then dropping back to the ground, it picked up the remains of the moose carcass in its jaws and retraced its approach back across the clearing, dragging the carcass beneath its belly. Moments later it disappeared in the darkening forest. The body left behind remained motionless.

He's draggin' it back to his cache, Keno said under his breath. Beth nodded, then closed her eyes, thinking about the foot in the boot.

It was quiet, not a sound but their breathing and the wind in the trees. Keno stood up and extended his hand to Beth and helped her to her feet.

Predators rule, but not *that* predator, not any more, he said, looking toward Gary's bloody body.

Should we do something, see if we can ... Beth started to ask.

Keno shook his head. First we get Poia, then check on the girl. Gary's not goin' anywhere.

A brief questioning look played across Beth's face as she looked toward the body then back to Keno, but she said nothing.

When Beth and Keno, leading the paint, reached the other side of the cabin, they could see that Gary's horse had broken loose from the hitching rail and was nowhere in sight. I hope we can find that horse, Keno said as he tied the paint to the rail. We could use another horse to get outta here. Maybe I can find him later. Before the bear.

The cabin door was ajar. Beth pushed it open and paused to let her eyes adjust to the darkened room. Keno held back, standing in the doorway. Vicki, Vicki, where are … Then they saw her. She was sitting on the floor in the far corner of the cabin, arms clutched tightly around knees drawn up to her chest. She was clothed, but her feet were bare. They could see the chain and the leather collar around her ankle. Pale, trembling, eyes wide and unblinking, she didn't move as Beth rushed over to her.

Vicki, Vicki, are you all right, are you okay? Then softly, It's over, Vicki, as she knelt down beside her and ran her hand gently up and down her back. Everything's going to be okay now. Vicki shook her head and tightened the grip on her legs when Beth tried to embrace her. Still she said nothing. When Vicki turned her head slightly, Beth's eyes had adjusted to the dim interior of the cabin, and she could see her face was freshly bruised and swollen.

Vicki, Vicki, it's going to be okay now, Beth whispered again as she gently embraced her. Did he know I was here? Keno stood back watching. She lifted Vicki's hair for a closer look at the bruises.

Vicki nodded briefly to Beth, then looked off into space. He came back, saw the gauze … Nothing I could say … He hit me … She closed her eyes and lowered her head. Giving Keno a worried look, Beth took a vial out of her pocket and shook out a Percodan into her palm. After a moment, Vicki whispered, *But he said he was sorry* … and started to cry. *That bear … Matt …* She covered her face with her hands. *Now Gary.*

A brief look of surprise, as Beth poured water from a container she found next to the stove into a cup and held it and the Percodan out to her. Here take this, it'll help, she said, giving Keno another concerned look. When Vicki handed the empty cup back, Beth took both Vicki's hands in hers. Vicki's fingers were ice cold. It was the first time Vicki had mentioned Matt, but it was tears for Gary that got Beth's attention. *Stockholm syndrome* crossed her mind. She put an arm around Vicki's shoulders and kissed her on the forehead. Vicki, it's over, she repeated softly as Keno looked on. It's going to be all right. Then she lowered her head close and whispered more reassuring words in her ear. Nodding toward Keno, who was still standing by the door, she said, This is Keno. He's going to help us. We're going to take you home, Vicki. Gary's not going to hurt you anymore. The nightmare's over.

Vicki didn't speak as Beth and Keno helped her to her feet and walked her over to one of the bunks where she lay down and closed her eyes. Keno stepped back, not sure what to say. Beth turned to him and began to mouth words that he couldn't hear. He raised his hand and cupped his ear, shaking his head. Beth nodded and they walked to the edge of the room with their backs to her.

She's seen a lot. Think about it. Two fatal bear attacks—let alone seeing people you care about being killed—could do it, Beth said. I've seen it before in trauma victims—*Post Traumatic Stress.*

Keno nodded that he understood, even had a touch of it himself, he had to admit, when he returned from Vietnam. A doctor at the VA Hospital in Helena had written PTSD on a medical report he wasn't supposed to see. It went on to say that it had something to do with the onset of his alcoholism. He remembered asking someone what the letters stood for.

Yeah, probably, he said as he looked over at Vicki who hadn't moved, her eyes closed. I saw it plenty in Nam and ... His voice trailed off as he laid a hand gently on Beth's shoulder. Just keep reassurin' her that it's over, he said. We need to get that chain off her ankle. Maybe I can find somethin' to break it with without hurtin' her.

There's a key. She said he kept it hanging on a nail over there on the wall, Beth said, pointing, but it's gone. She said he takes it with him when he leaves.

Keno thought a minute, then he said. I'll go take a look. There's not much else we can do except get her outta here as soon as we can. Maybe something hot to drink, coffee or tea would help if you can find any. He turned toward the door. When I come back, I'll rekindle the stove. But first, I'm gonna check out the other situation, see if that key's on him. It was almost dark.

———•••———

39

A full moon was breaking in and out of dark clouds as Keno approached the spot where he had last seen Gary's body. He walked slowly, carrying the Winchester at the ready, wary that the body was now almost certain to become part of the big grizzly's cache. Moments later, he licked his lips and sucked in a soft whistle. The body was gone. He scanned the surrounding timber, alert for any sign of the big animal, but it was too dark to see beyond the edge of the forest. Dragged him off already, he was thinking. Then he saw Gary. I'll be damned, he said to himself, the sonofabitch is still alive. Still dazed from the attack, Gary was sitting against a tree at the edge of the clearing some thirty feet away, facing away from Keno, probably watching for the grizzly's return. Keno could see that he had retrieved his rifle and had it laying across his lap.

Keno hesitated to take stock of the situation then reached down and picked up a fist-sized rock. Crouching low, rock in one hand, rifle in the other, he silently circled in the brush at the edge of the clearing, making his way slowly toward Gary. A small branch snapped under his foot. Gary jerked around toward the sound, rifle raised, straining to see into the darkness. Holding his breath, Keno crouched motionless in the bushes and waited, now only a short distance away. It seemed like a long time before Gary lowered the rifle and reached down to his injured leg. At that moment, Keno threw the rock into the darkness on the opposite side of the clearing. Gary jerked the rifle awkwardly to his shoulder, this time firing a shot toward the sound, the bullet snapping through the underbrush. Keno seized the opportunity. Before Gary could lever another round into the chamber, Keno was on him, twisting the rifle out of his hands and throwing it out of reach.

What the hell you doin' ... who ... who're you? Gary stammered as Keno stood looking down at him. Hey, man, gimme that rifle back. There's a grizzly ... I'm hurt, bear attacked me ...

Gary didn't recognize Keno in the darkness and assumed he was the injured hiker who, Vicki claimed, had stopped by the cabin the day before. But he also realized there was no way to deal with that now. He needed help. His voice was strained, his face streaked with blood. His torn shirt was bloody and one pant leg had been ripped off. Keno could see deep puncture wounds in his thigh, but not the holstered .38 on Gary's belt hidden beneath his jacket and elbow.

From the cabin, Keno heard Beth call out, Are you okay?

It's all right, Keno called back over his shoulder, never taking his eyes off the man sitting in the darkness at his feet. Looks like you're a little banged up, Keno said, speaking in a pleasant, conversational tone, holding the Winchester at waist level, aimed at Gary's chest. He stooped over and waved his hand across Gary's face. There, that's better. Got rid of them pesterin' fleas. Think they'd be gone this time a year, but warm blood attracts 'em, even seen 'em out during a chinook in the dead of winter. Where they come from? Damn grizzlies, full of fleas. Don't you hate 'em, *Gary*, the fleas, I mean?

At the mention of his name, Gary stiffened and glanced briefly at Keno, still without recognition, still thinking he's the *visitor* and Vicki must have told him his name. Then he said, Hey, man, can't you see I'm hurt? Gimme a break. I need help ... leg's broke ... there's a first aid kit in the cabin.

Keno took a deep breath and sighed as though he were commenting on the weather or some other mundane topic. Yeah, grizzlies can be so goddamn mean sometimes. You're lucky though, Gary. You're not as banged up as I thought. I guess that playin' dead tactic really works, just layin' there so still, makin' 'em think you're dead and no threat. Yeah, I thought you were a goner, but you should be fine in time. Nothin' fatal, leg'll mend, some nasty puncture wounds, a few rips and tears here and there but, what the hell, you didn't bleed out, and he didn't drag you off to his cache where he's got that hiker stashed, you know, *the one you shot.*

Gary looked up, a surprised look on his face, hesitated, then said, I don't know what you're talkin' about. I didn't shoot nobody.

Keno ignored the denial. All in all you're pretty lucky, Gary. No serious bleedin'. Yeah, you'll be limpin' around for a while with a busted leg, but, hell, you'll be able to get back to doin' what you been doin' a lot quicker than I thought when I saw that big griz workin' you over. Hell, you don't look no worse than that girl you got chained in the cabin.

Look, I know what you're thinkin' and you're wrong, Gary said, eyes blinking the lie. I saved that girl's life over at Morning Star. That bear was goin' for her. So give me a break. Help me get over to the cabin. You can't just leave me here. That bear'll be comin' back … my leg's broke.

Hmm, yeah could be … hmm … yeah, come to think of it, I bet you're right about that big griz comin' back. What a shame. But *help?* You know who you're talkin' to, Gary? Look at me. Remember me? I helped you once. Boarded your horses. Took good care of 'em for you. Remember that?

Gary dropped his eyes, considered the pistol, the awkward reach for it, then used both hands to push himself up straighter against the tree for better leverage.

Yeah, I guess you thought I believed all that bullshit about you collectin' grizzly hair for DNA research. He coughed a laugh. Well, by the looks of things, Gary, I'm guessin' you got all the grizzly hair you'll need for a while. But back to the girl. She's pretty banged up, looks like you been workin' her over pretty good. I'm gonna need the key to get that lock off, you know, the one you have around her ankle so she doesn't run off.

Gary looked away and didn't answer, plotting his move.

Keno squatted down beside him, laying the Winchester across his lap. Hands clasped, forearms resting on his knees, he looked directly at

Gary as Gary reached into his shirt pocket and took out the key. As Keno took the key, Gary looked away, shifting his weight to elevate the holster concealed at his side.

Too bad about that little sorrel of yours, Keno said. Maybe you shoulda' fixed that loose shoe like I told you. Then he paused, turning away to look into the darkness for any sign of the bear. But, you know, things have a way of workin' out sometimes, right? If you'd got that shoe fixed, maybe I wouldn't 've been able to track you down. A short dry laugh as he looked back at Gary. Yeah, but you know somethin', Gary? I would've never stopped lookin'. Keno paused, leaning toward Gary's face, close enough that they could smell one another's breath. *Never.*

Gary turned his eyes briefly toward Keno, then looked away, twisting slightly, feeling the weight of the .38 at his side. So I lied about the DNA study. What's that got to do with helpin' me now? That bear's comin' back. Remember I saved that girl's life. Gary, confused, thinking—*Why's this fucking Indian tracking me? What's his game? I paid the sonofabitch—* still wondering whether Keno was Vicki's visitor the day before.

Keno looked briefly at the key he held in his palm, shaking his head, then slipped it into his shirt pocket.

Come on, I asked you a question, Gary, or whatever the fuck your name is. Do you remember me? Keno, last name, Spotted Wolf? You must remember. Let me repeat, you know, the dumb fuckin' Indian who you thought believed all your bullshit about doin' research on grizzly bears, the one that took care of your horses?

Keno could see the confusion, anxiety, deepening in Gary's shifting eyes when he spoke. Yeah, I remember you. So what're you gettin' at? I paid you. You got my truck and trailer. I need help. That bear …

Keno got to his feet, standing motionless, holding the rifle in one hand, looking down at Gary, now in his moon shadow when he said, Let me ask you this, Gary. You remember a nice young woman you met sometime, not sure where, last May? Name's Dinah. Gary turned his head away. Keno gently put his hand along Gary's cheek and pulled it back. Come on, Gary, look at me when I'm talkin' to you. Any memory of her, Gary? Come on now; think real hard.

Gary looked at Keno, then lowered his eyes.

I asked you a question, Gary. Do you remember a nice young Blackfeet woman—well, I guess a *prairie nigger* to you—named Dinah?

Prairie nigger made Gary catch his breath. Keno waited for an answer that didn't come as Gary, suddenly recalling that cold, rainy night in May, turned away, raising one hand to his forehead, the other now slowly edging the pistol out of the holster beneath his jacket.

He remembered her reaching for the door handle, opening the door when he grabbed her hair and slapped her hard across the face. He remembered the sharp crack when her head smashed against the rear window, then grabbing her by the neck, unzipping his fly with his other hand, and pushing her face down into his lap. He remembered her resisting, pushing against his legs, then grabbing his scrotum and squeezing. The pain, screaming, then frantically reaching for the screwdriver on the dashboard, jamming it into the back of her neck, pressing it in, feeling her stiffen and go limp.

Sure you remember, don't you? Look at me, Gary. I'm talkin' to you, Keno said as he reached down, placing his hand under Gary's chin and turning his head back. Come on, you must remember Dinah, Gary. I found her necklace in your pickup. He paused, waiting for a reaction. There was none. That's right. Can you believe it? Keno shook his head and coughed, hands trembling with rage.

He remembered the agony, clutching his genitals, screaming in pain, stomping and kicking her head and shoulders as she slumped to the floor.

Keno cleared his throat, his voice calm, the tone flat. Gary, listen to me. There it was that beautiful necklace that she loved right there in the mud and shit back behind the seat. Guess you missed it there under the jumper cables and dirty rags. Inlaid silver feather with turquoise. Hopi. Very pretty. Had her name engraved on the back. I gave it to her, Gary, a long time ago. She always wore it, almost like a crucifix. Now you remember her?

He remembered staggering to the passenger side of the truck, opening the door, taking hold of her ankles, jerking, pulling, and cursing as one of her lifeless arms became caught around the stick shift, then the arm flopping loose and her body sliding like a rag doll to the ground.

Come on, look at me, Gary. Why won't you look at me? I want you to look at me when I'm talkin' to you. Keno stepped closer, placing his hand again gently under Gary's chin, easing it back again so they were facing one another. There, that's better, Gary. Now let me try this again. Do you remember a woman, a woman named Dinah? About five foot four, pretty little Blackfeet woman. Think hard, Gary.

He remembered squatting down beside the body and, with both hands, ripping open the flannel shirt she wore, pulling her bra up away from her breasts, reaching back and taking the Buck knife out of the leather sheath, opening the blade, slicing an X into the flesh above her left breast, dragging the body through the brush and across gravel and rock to the water's edge, feeling a raw blast of windblown rain pelting down in sheets and hearing the sound of rushing water, lifting the body and heaving it out into the dark current, watching as it rolled and twisted around rocks and disappeared in the black water closing over it.

I … I … I don't know what you're talkin' about, the stutter in Gary's voice betraying his anxiety. He turned his head, avoiding Keno's stare, but watching him out of the corner of his eye, as he eased his hand slowly toward the trigger guard at his fingertips.

Keno took a deep breath and let it out with, See, Gary, she was my daughter, my first born, and I loved her very much … the words catching in his throat … more than life.

Gary could see Keno was distracted. His chance. He groaned, turned his head away, but the eyes that seemed to be closed weren't, thinking, *One shot's all I get.*

Keno swallowed the grief and cleared his throat. Hey, Gary, look at me, he said as he laid his rifle aside and removed the bone-handled knife from the sheath on his belt. He pulled Gary's head back to face him, this time with a jerk. Don't look away, Gary. I want you to see what I'm gonna do. Scared, Gary? Yeah, real goddamn scared, right? You know, like Dinah was when you … his words thickening with rage.

Gary's eyes, wide, snapping back and forth, followed Keno's every move, the moon's silvery glint on the knife blade. Keno hesitated, straightening, looking down on Gary, rolling the knife over slowly in the palm of his right hand with his thumb. Thinking. Waiting. Savoring the *fear*. Seconds that seemed like minutes passed in silence in which it seemed neither man breathed before Keno took a deep breath and let it out with, This is for Dinah, Gary. It's an old prairie nigger custom.

Suddenly he reached down and grabbed the forelock of Gary's hair with his left hand, jerking his head back. Gary grasped the pistol and tried to raise it, but the hammer caught on his shirt. When it did, he let go, throwing his hands up to protect his throat, screaming, No, wait, I didn't do it. Still unaware of the pistol, Keno knocked his hands away and was about to draw the blade across Gary's throat when he hesitated. Blood seeped down the side Gary's neck below his ear where the blade was pressed lightly against the skin. Gary's eyes, wide unblinking, shifting from side to side, panting, Keno thinking like the cornered animal he was.

After a long moment, eyes boring into Gary's, Keno shook his head, released his grip, and stepped back, wondering why he couldn't do it. When he did, Gary dropped his hands. A rustling sound in the darkness. Then a sharp crack. A branch breaking. *The grizzly*. Keno turned toward the sound. When he did, Gary reached beneath his jacket, raised the pistol, and fired.

40

---◆◆◆---

When Beth heard the first shot Gary fired into the darkness, she guessed Keno had encountered the bear. Keno's call back was a relief, but the big grizzly was still on her mind when minutes later she and Vicki heard the second shot. Beth ran to the door and pulled it open, eyes straining to see. Keno, Keno, are you all right? she called into the darkness. No response. She turned to Vicki. My God, the bear must have come back. Keno's not answering. Something's happened to him. Another call. Still no answer. She called again. Silence. She turned to Vicki. We can't just leave Keno out there if he's hurt … She bit her lip, weighing her options. Then, I'm going out. Is there a gun, a flashlight?

But, you can't … the bear … Vicki said, wringing her hands.

I know, but there's no choice. Got to take a chance. If Keno's hurt, we've got to try to help him. We can't just do nothing. Without him to help us, we'll all die in this God-forsaken place.

Vicki shook her head and pointed to the shelf. He always takes the guns. There's only the flashlight, but it's …

Beth took the flashlight and flicked it on. The batteries were weak, but it would have to do. She turned to look around the room for something, she didn't know what, to protect herself. She considered the lantern. Animals are afraid of fire. I could throw it at him. She shook her head. Not with this useless shoulder and wrist.

When she stepped outside and closed the cabin door, the bright full moon was ducking in and out of dark scudding clouds. It was still, the only sound the wind stirring the tree tops high above her at the edge of the clearing. She hesitated to let her eyes adjust to the darkness before she turned on the flashlight, swinging its beam side to side, and began to make her way slowly across the clearing to the spot where she had last seen Gary's body.

Keno, can you hear me? she called out, heart pounding, casting the beam of light slowly around the edge of the clearing. She called again, Where are you? Say something. Help me if you can.

Then, in the dim beam of light, she saw the body twenty feet away, face down. *Gary.*

Keno where are you? she hesitated, breathing hard, hands trembling, terrified that there was no answer, thinking, where is he? the grizzly's got him? run for the cabin? Panic closing in. Oh, my God, what can I do?

Gary grabbed her from behind, knocking the flashlight from her grasp, a forearm locked across her throat, the barrel of the .38 pressed against her cheek. That's him on the ground, bitch, but he ain't talkin'.

Stunned, breathless, blinding pain radiating from the shoulder he was leaning on, her first words were, Stop, damn you, you're hurting me. My shoulder… it's broke. Let go.

As the moon reappeared, she could recognize Keno sprawled on the ground, braided hair and torn bandana glistening with blood that ran down the side of his face into his shirt. Fear, anger, frustration welling up inside. *He's dead. We're all dead.*

Let go? No way, bitch. I don't give a damn about your fuckin' shoulder. You're gonna help me get back to the cabin with this busted leg. He was breathing hard, in pain, his voice a thin rasp of foul breath, his clothes reeking the pungent odor of blood, urine, and the big grizzly.

You cold-blooded bastard, you've killed him, she said, anger trumping fear.

Yeah, I killed him. It was me or him, so that fuckin' Indian's dead, gone to the Happy Hunting Ground with the rest of his fuckin' prairie nigger kin, right where he fuckin' belongs. He caught his breath and coughed. Now you're gonna help me get to the cabin to see what I can do about this leg 'fore that bear comes back. He stumbled, squeezing against her neck and shoulder. Beth groaned in pain, nearly falling under his weight before Gary, cursing, regained his balance. He paused, short of breath, leaning hard on her shoulder, before he spoke.

That motherfuckin' grizzly came back for *me*. I heard him. Shot must've scared him off, but he'll be back, but it'll be that fuckin' Indian's carcass he drags off, not mine. He took another deep breath, letting it out with, You're gonna help me get to the cabin. The pain's killin' me. Then you're gonna tell me who the fuck you are and what you're doin' here, because you … you smart-mouthed bitch, made a huge goddamn mistake.

* * * * *

Vicki looked up when the door swung open and Gary, arm locked around Beth's neck, hobbled in, dragging the broken leg. Beth was pale, grimacing in pain from the weight on her shoulder.

Well, bitch, surprised to see me aren't you? he rasped through tight lips. Thought I was dead and glad of it, right? You lying, double-dealin' whore, after all I done for you. He had one arm around Beth's shoulder as he dragged himself to a chair. After easing himself into it, he pushed Beth away with one hand, the pistol gripped in the other resting on the table.

Now get a fire goin' in that stove to heat water to clean up these wounds. Get that first aid kit, bitch, he said to Vicki, and that fifth of whiskey over there on the shelf. Pain's killin' me. Fuckin' leg's broke, goddammit.

Vicki nodded and whispered, I'm sorry.

Wha'd you say, bitch?

I said I'm sorry, Gary. Honest, I am. He still could barely hear her.

Yeah, you're sorry all right, sorry I'm alive. Now get that goddamn stove goin' and bring me that whiskey. And you, he said, motioning to Beth with the pistol, get me that axe handle over there in the corner for a splint. And don't try nothin'.

Gary groaned, swore, and sipped Jim Beam from the bottle as Beth and Vicki cleaned and bandaged his wounds and rigged up a splint for his broken leg. By the time they finished, he was slumped back into the chair, nodding, blinking away the glaze that was gathering in his eyes, injured leg extended with the axe-handle splint, the pistol, now loosely gripped, resting on the table. Beth's eyes never left him, gaging how much whiskey he was draining from the bottle, thinking when he dozes off, she would try to get the gun.

Vicki looked at her and whispered, Keno?

Gary's head snapped up. I heard that. He's fuckin' dead, bitch. I shot him. He was glassy-eyed, slurring words, a thin line of spit leaking from the corner of his mouth.

Beth's expression didn't change. Staring into space, empty eyes concealing her anger and determination. Waiting. Minutes that seemed like hours passed. She was about to make her move when Gary shook his head, blinked and looked over at her, and, waving the pistol in her direction, said, Whad'ya lookin' at, bitch? With one hand, he rubbed his eyes. Don't even think about it, but himself thinking, *It really doesn't matter anymore.* He shifted his weight to ease the pain. He knew there was no way could he make it out of there on a broken leg, no way to hunt for food, cut firewood, and survive the winter if he remained. He looked up into the rafters, the cobwebs ghost-like in the lamplight, thinking he would take care of Vicki and this other bitch, whoever she is, then he would figure out what to do with himself and Buck. He lifted the pistol, turned it toward himself, and stared into its barrel, into that black hole, then closed his eyes, a brief sad smile played across his face. Then he looked up, hiccupped, and took another swallow of whiskey, almost spilling the near-empty bottle as he set it back on the table.

Vicki had moved back to her bunk when Beth caught her attention and shifted her eyes to Gary. He was beginning to nod, breathing deeper through parted lips, chin angling down to his chest. Vicki leaned forward, a questioning look on her face. Beth pointed to herself then to Gary, squeezing her thumb and forefinger together mimicking a gun, mouthing, *Help me.* Vicki nodded, her expression changing, for the first time a resolute look on her face. Beth took a deep breath, determination fueling her courage, but wondering whether she had the strength and dexterity with just one arm. *There's no choice.* He's desperate, knows he's finished, he'll kill us both, then himself. She thought about Harry, the incident at the post office, the kind of person he was. Please, dear God, help me. *I owe him a good ending.*

When Gary began to snore, Beth made her move, slowly at first, creeping toward the table. Then she lunged, grabbing the pistol with her good hand. Like a cat, Gary was awake, jerking the pistol and Beth with it across the table, chair and table toppling, Beth falling on top of him to the floor, the pistol skidding across the floor toward Vicki. Gary rolled, now on top of Beth, kneeling on one leg over her, the splint extending the broken leg to the side at an odd angle. Cursing, he punched her in the face then locked his hands around her throat, thumbs pressing down hard.

Vicki picked up the pistol and, holding it with trembling hands, took aim. Stop, Gary. Let her go. Now, Gary, now. Now goddamn you, she screamed in a voice he had never heard before.

Fuck you, go ahead and shoot, Vicki Hathaway, he shouted, not looking at her, elbows locked, pressing down on Beth's throat, her face crimson, gasping for air, eyes wide, looking at Vicki, pleading.

Both bullets struck him in the chest. He toppled over sideways, rolled on his back, and lay motionless. Then he lifted his head slowly, blood soaking through his shirt, smiled at Vicki, and fell back dead.

Moments later, the door slammed open against the wall. Keno, face bloody, shirt bloodstained to his waist, stepped inside, the Winchester at his shoulder, sweeping the room. Where is he? the shots ... Then he saw the body behind the overturned table. His eyes remained fixed on it to be sure before he took a deep breath, lowered the rifle, and turned to Beth. The coppery smell of fresh blood filled the room.

Beth was sitting on the bunk, Vicki beside her, head pressed against Beth's chest. Vicki was sobbing.

Are you okay? Is she hurt? he said.

Beth nodded as she caressed Vicki's head. Swollen red thumb prints on her throat, she could barely get the words out. She had to shoot, she whispered. There was no choice. It was him or us. He got what he deserved—and *wanted.*

* * * * *

After the chain had been removed from Vicki's ankle, she and Beth cleaned and wrapped gauze around Keno's head wound. He explained how the bullet had grazed his temple, knocking him unconscious. A fraction of an inch and it would've been all over for me, he said. Gary must've seen all the blood and figured I was dead. Lucky for me. He thought a minute not sure whether to continue, then, When I came to, I looked up and there's that big grizzly staring down at me, just lookin' at me, so close I could feel and smell his hot breath on my face. I shut my eyes, expectin' the worst. Then after a while, seemed like a helluva long time to me, he made this soft woofing sound, and when I opened my eyes, he was gone. Keno was going to say that it was almost as if the bear wanted to be sure he was okay before he left. But he didn't, thinking they wouldn't understand, and not sure that he did.

When they finished bandaging his head, Keno lifted Gary by the armpits and dragged his body outside to the clearing. When he returned, he soaked up the blood on the floor with towels. It was almost midnight with a big day ahead.

— ◦◦◦ —

41

---◆---

Tuesday, October 2. Dawn broke cold and foggy. Keno felt as though he hadn't slept. The head wound ached, and the hard, splintery boards beneath him made it worse. His mind had been replaying those final minutes with Gary, wondering why he had hesitated, wishing he had been there for the kill. He reached up, tracing the wound that ran upward along his ear, now covered with a gauze wraparound bandage, thinking how close he had come.

Each time he awoke during the night, he rolled out of his blankets, checked the stove, added wood to the fire. It was still, eerie, except for the murmurings of the two sleeping women and the occasional hoot of an owl out there somewhere in the darkness. When a cold draft leaked across the floor, he pulled a flannel shirt from a nail on the wall and stuffed it into a crack beneath the door. *Gary's shirt.*

He heard Beth stir and wondered if she was awake, but didn't speak. He got up, pulled on his boots and jacket, eased the door open, and stepped outside. The paint whinnied as he walked toward it through a thick fog that felt and smelled like snow. He stood for a moment to pee, staring down at the steam rising from the frost-covered ground, still replaying the night before, thinking that sonofabitch will never hurt anyone again. He zipped his fly and walked over and rubbed the horse's soft nose as he looked out toward the edge of the clearing where he had dragged the body. *Did the grizzly return?* But the fog was too thick to see.

Back at the cabin, he quietly pushed the door open and picked up the Winchester that was leaning against the door jam. He closed the door softly and levered a bullet into the chamber. Holding the rifle at the ready, wary of the bear, he walked slowly, cautiously through thick fog to the edge of the clearing. The body was gone. He could see where it had been dragged off into the timber. Only one of Gary's boots and the bloody towels remained. His rifle lay on the ground not far away. Keno walked over and picked it up, turning it over in his hands. After a moment, he propped it against a tree, then a second thought, and took it with him as he walked back to his horse.

The tops of the tall larch trees were shrouded in a cold mist, and a thin sheet of ice coated the branches and brush from rain that had fallen during the night. A film of ice coated the surface of the bucket he had set out for his horse and glistened on the saddle blanket he had draped and tied over its back. He lifted the blanket off the horse and shook it before rubbing him down and draping the blanket again over his back. He walked to the hitching rail and reached into the saddlebags hanging over it and took out a couple packets of sugar cubes, a smile as the paint eagerly chewed the sugar from his palm. Then he went back to the cabin and propped Gary's rifle against the wall inside the door.

The sound of Keno adding wood to the smoking embers in the wood-stove awakened Beth from a restless night of bad dreams of Gary's hands around her throat, thumbs pressing hard into her windpipe, the crazed look in his eye, the panic, thinking she was going to die, the two shots ringing in her ears. And Harry, always Harry, alive in her dreams. What time is it? she asked, her voice hoarse. She swallowed hard against the pain in her throat and tried again, fingers touching the swollen bruises on her neck. Through the window, faint gray light.

It's almost eight, Keno said, looking at his watch as he lit a kerosene lamp. He was speaking softly, nodding toward the sleeping girl. Heat and light radiated out into the room when he opened the stove to add a log to the flames. Better wake her. We gotta get movin'. Big day ahead. He closed the stove and poured water from a plastic jug into a pan and set it on the stovetop to heat.

Beth watched him standing next to the stove rubbing his hands together over the rising heat. How do you feel? she asked. The side of your face is really swollen. It must hurt. I have a Percodan you can …

No, it's okay. Save 'em for yourself and her. Bleedin's stopped, probably looks worse than it is. A little headache, he said, understating the discomfort, but I'm fine. What about you, those bruises on your neck, that swollen cheek? Can you swallow all right?

I'm okay. Glad to be alive. Just anxious to get the hell out of here.

As the water began to steam for what little remained of the instant coffee, Keno opened the last two cans of pork and beans, dumped them into a pot, and set it on the stovetop. By that time, Vicki was awake and Beth poured the water for coffee into enameled tin cups. Keno couldn't help noticing how thin and vulnerable Vicki looked, holding the cup in both hands, looking like a small child as she took tentative sips. He was struck by her natural beauty, evident in spite of the swelling and bruises. He noticed how her eyes would sometimes glaze and thought about the headache. Probably a concussion. Gary. The sonofabitch died too easy. I should have cut his throat.

As they shared the pork and beans, no one spoke, eyes lowered, avoiding the bloodstain on the floor. Only the occasional sound of spoons scraping metal bowls broke the silence, the unspoken night before on everyone's mind. Finally Beth said, Let's get going. I just want to get out of here, as far away from this place as soon as we can.

Keno nodded and set his empty bowl down. I'm gonna look around for that other horse. Another horse'll make the trip a lot quicker and easier. But I'm not gonna waste a lot of time lookin' if he's not close by. He picked up his rifle and walked to the door. We gotta get movin', if we wanna get outta here before nightfall. After saddling the paint, he swung up on the saddle. Okay, Poia, let's see if we can find that spooked buckskin.

* * * * *

It wasn't long before Beth heard a horse whinny and rushed to the door. Keno was on the paint coming across the clearing, Gary's buckskin on a lead rope following behind. Keno tied the horses to the hitching rail and walked back to the creek behind the cabin to refill the water bucket. When he returned, he watched the buckskin drink, still wearing the saddle Gary had put on him. Keno thought about that when he removed the saddle and rubbed the emaciated horse down with the saddle blanket, its backbone and ribs pressing through a thin layer of skin. He removed the sack of oats from his saddlebag and divided what was left between the two horses. It wasn't much. Neither horse was going to hold up much longer without nourishing food. A day or two at most was all he could get out of the paint, less than that, he guessed, from the buckskin.

When Beth opened the door, with Vicki behind her, she looked around for Gary's body and back to Keno. Where? she mouthed with an inquisitive look. The area was still shrouded in fog. Gone, he mouthed and nodded toward the trees at the edge of the clearing. She closed her eyes and nodded.

Okay, we're gonna travel as light as possible, he said, so don't take anything that you can't wear. Even the sleeping bags, leave 'em here, they're too bulky. But dress warm. A winter storm's blowin' in and it's gonna get cold. We gotta take it slow, but we should be able to cover the distance to the river in about three hours if we don't run into problems.

It was a big *if*. The problem uppermost in his mind as he walked over to the hitching rail and untied the buckskin was the big grizzly that had cached Gary's body during the night, the same grizzly, he didn't need to remind himself, that had stood over him as he lay helpless on the ground, then walked away.

You two are gonna ride double on the buckskin here, Keno said as he tied the lead rope to a ring on the cantle of his horse's saddle. I'll lead the way on Poia. We gotta be on the lookout for that grizzly. He's still in the area, no doubt about that. Bears don't leave a cache, and we know he's somewhere nearby, so we gotta be especially alert, gotta try to avoid gettin' anywhere near that cache wherever it is. Don't want to provoke him.

But if he shows up, I got the rifle, thinking the last thing he wanted to do was shoot the grizzly that had worked over Gary and spared his own life.

Here, I'll help you up, he said after saddling the buckskin. He moved to the horse's side and lowered his clasped hands for Beth to step into. It was awkward as he boosted her up on the saddle, her one arm immobilized in the sling beneath her parka. Then he lifted Vicki up behind her where she could hold on with her arms around Beth's waist. When he lifted Vicki, she was feather light, skin and bones. Keno guessed she weighed less than a hundred pounds.

Okay, are we ready? he said. Any questions, before we move out?

Beth looked at him, a sad expression swept over her face and tears welled in her eyes. No, but, well … She hesitated and looked down. There's only … but it's okay … I know there's nothing we can do.

What's that? Keno asked as he was about to sling the Winchester across his shoulders.

It's my friend … Harry … I … The words caught in her throat. I just wish we didn't have to leave him in this God-forsaken place. She sniffed and wiped a tear that ran down her cheek with the back of her hand. But I know there's no way to …

Keno was standing beside them holding the buckskin's bridle. I'm sorry, he said. I wish we could, but there's no time. We gotta move fast to get outta here. Front's movin' in, temperature's droppin'. He looked up at the sky. Could snow. Days are short, not much daylight. Can't take a chance. He looked back at Beth. Plus, we're out of food and you both need medical attention. He looked away and shook his head. I mean, I'm really sorry. It's too bad, I know how you feel, but Search and Rescue'll be able to get back in here with equipment and get him out later, maybe tomorrow, *if* we can make it out today.

Oh, I know, I know, she said, looking down, shaking her head slowly, fingers to her lips. It's okay. There's nothing to be done.

Keno was moved, but without words. He shook his head in an empty gesture that bothered him, and turned to adjust the stirrups on the buckskin. He felt compelled to say something. I'm sorry, he said. Who was he? What was his name? What stupid questions he thought as soon as he uttered the words. What's his name, for Chrissakes, as if that mattered. He was embarrassed.

Harry, Harry Dawkins, she said softly.

Keno looked up from the stirrup, surprise on his face. Harry Dawkins? Marines? Vietnam?

Beth nodded. Did you know him?

Harry Dawkins? Lieutenant Harry Dawkins? Yeah, I knew him. I was in Lieutenant Dawkins's platoon in Vietnam. Before that we were in the same company for advanced combat training at Camp Pendleton.

Oh my God, you were? Beth said.

A flashback to 1968. Keno recalling a wounded Lieutenant Harry Dawkins's bravery as he led their platoon during an ambush and a savage firefight near Khe Sanh. He thought about the following year when he had stood shoulder to shoulder with then-Captain Dawkins at Camp Pendleton as the Commandant of the Marine Corps pinned Silver Stars on them both. He remembered the last time he had seen Harry Dawkins, by then a retired lieutenant colonel, at a Marine Corps birthday celebration in Whitefish. How long ago was that? They talked about old times, that battle, lost buddies on The Wall in Washington, and Harry said some nice things that he would never forget. They were going to get together again, but never did. Keno knew part of the reason was his alcoholism but, also, because Vietnam was something they both wanted to forget.

He turned and nodded to Beth, Yeah, I knew Lieutenant Dawkins. Can you show me where he is?

—— ••• ——

42

---◆---

Keno led the way on foot with the two horses trailing behind, the women riding double on the buckskin, as they pushed through the brush and downfall the short distance to the edge of the gorge. Beth pointed to the spot below where the body lay. Boulders and driftwood obscured the view, but Keno could see the edge of the poncho. He knew he had to work fast. After helping the women dismount, he dropped the paint's reins and tied the buckskin to a tree. He guessed it was about a forty-foot drop to the boulders at the bottom. He wondered if he had enough rope and decided a length of rope that he'd found in the cabin tied to his own coil of rope should be enough. After tying the two ropes together, he tied one end around the thick trunk of a larch tree that stood near the edge of the ravine. Vicki and Beth watched as he unbuckled the flap on the saddlebag and removed a pair of leather calf-roping gloves.

Okay, he said, as he pulled the gloves on and coiled the rope. He took the other end and secured a climber's loop around his waist. Then he looked up at Beth and said, I'm gonna rappel down and see what we can do. The fog was lifting and the rising mist from the falls was cold on their faces as the two women watched Keno make his way slowly down the side of the gorge, deftly maneuvering around rock outcroppings and brush. Beth could tell he had done this before, probably in the Marines. When he reached the bottom, they could see him in the mist as he made his way through the boulders and piles of tangled deadwood to Harry's body.

Below, at stream's edge, Keno knelt down beside the poncho on wet, ice-crusted gravel to remove the rocks that Beth had used to hold it in place. He paused, his mind again awash in memories. He had done this too many times in Vietnam. He took a deep breath and exhaled as he lifted the poncho and saw the form of Harry's body enclosed in the sleeping bag. He unzipped the bag just far enough to lift a corner. The thick, dark hair Keno remembered in Vietnam, now silver and thinner, the once ruddy complexion, now colorless with the familiar sheen of death he had seen on the faces of other brave men he knew.

He took another deep breath and let it out as he gently pulled the sleeping bag back over Harry's face and zipped it closed. Then, squatting, he placed his arms under the mid-section and, with great effort, stood, lifting the body and cradling it in his arms. *Rigor mortis* had faded. The body was limp. He steadied himself then made his way slowly to the base of the ravine where he laid it down gently near the end of the rope he'd used to rappel down.

Keno wrapped and knotted the extra length of rope and wrapped it around the body, forming a sling so that it would remain in a horizontal position as it was being pulled up. Then he stepped back and called to Beth, Everything up there look okay? When Beth checked the knot at the tree and called back that it was, he took hold of the rope and, using his feet for leverage, began to climb hand-over-hand up the side of the gorge. Vicki reached out to help him over the edge when he reached the top, then both women stood back out of the way and watched as he took off his gloves and removed the rope he had tied around the tree and re-tied it to the saddle of the paint. He checked the saddle again, cinching it tight beneath the horse's belly. Satisfied that it was secure, he stepped back and looked around until he spotted a smooth log. He walked over and picked it up and carried it to the edge of the gorge, positioning it so the rope could slide over it smoothly without snagging or fraying. Then he anchored the log with large rocks he gathered and piled at the ends of either side.

Okay, I think we're ready, he said as he stood back and pulled his gloves back on. I'm gonna haul him up slow. You two watch and yell if that sleeping bag gets caught on anything. I won't be able to see.

Keno mounted the paint and nudged it forward slowly until the rope tightened. As Beth looked back into the gorge, she could see the sleeping bag with Harry's body begin to rise, twisting slowly around back and forth. She grimaced and blinked back tears, averting her eyes, fingers pressed to her lips, as it brushed and scraped against the side of the ravine.

How's it comin'? Keno called over his shoulder.

It's okay, just don't go any faster, she called back, twisting her body and grimacing, wanting to lessen the impact as Harry's body bumped and slid over ledges and through brush that grew out of the side of the ravine.

Wait, wait, both women called out. It's caught below a ledge. Keno dismounted and walked back to the edge, the paint holding the rope taut as it had been trained to do for calf roping. Keno could see the sleeping bag was snagged below a brushy overhang some ten feet below the rim. He tried to maneuver the rope to dislodge it, but couldn't for fear of loosening the sling and having the body drop. Rubbing his chin, he walked back and forth along the rim of the gorge, angling for a better look.

Here's what we gotta do, he said, thinking aloud, when he returned, I'm gonna climb down and get it loose. You stand by the paint. Be sure he holds steady. He should be okay. The women looked on, standing back out of the way as Keno began a hand-over-hand descent down the rope. Then rocks gave way and he was dangling in space. Vicki grabbed Beth's arm and turned her head away, both certain he was going to fall. Helpless to do anything, they watched as he scrambled to regain his footing above the overhang. Beth let out the breath she was holding when they saw him find a foothold. Then with the added leverage, Keno was able to swing the body free and ease it up over the jagged rocks.

Okay, it's loose, he called up to them, breathing hard, face glistening with perspiration, before he used the rope to climb back up over the edge. Everyone knew it was a close call, an act of courage and, Beth knew, something more. They watched him remount the paint and urge it forward slowly, looking back over his shoulder to watch the rope as it slid slowly over the log until the body reached the top. Beth and Vicki knelt down and took hold of the ends of the sleeping bag and tried to pull it over the edge but didn't have the strength. The dead weight was too much.

Damn it, damn it, we can't do it, Beth called out.

Hold on. It's okay, it's okay, Keno, now some thirty feet away, called to her as he dismounted. Wait, I'll get it. As the paint stood fast against the weight, he walked back and eased the body up over the edge. Beth bit a knuckle held to her lips as she and Vicki watched silently as Keno removed the rope and carried Harry's body back to the paint.

How to transport the body back? Keno thought as he squatted down and eased the body to the ground. A *travois* crossed his mind. Plenty of downed lodgepole to construct one, but he decided it wouldn't work. The trail was too overgrown and rough and then there was the river. No way. The strong current would catch a *travois* and roll it and the horse dragging it.

He turned to Beth and in a soft, almost apologetic way, he said, Look, I'm gonna have to drape him over the saddle and I'll walk. It'll be slower, but it's the only way we can get him out. Otherwise, we'd have to leave him here … night … whatever animals come along … He shook his head. Not gonna do it.

No, no, we can't do that, Beth agreed, shaking her head.

Keno studied the situation, playing with the coil of rope he held in his hands before he lifted the body and gently positioned it face-down across the saddle. Then he secured the ends of the sleeping bag with rope beneath the horse's belly. Okay, I guess that should hold, he said as he patted the paint's neck and stepped back, looked up at a slate-gray sky, then his watch. It was almost noon and dark clouds were piling up to the west, the direction they were headed. An ominous north wind had started to blow, stripping leaves from aspens and making the forest groan and squeak as trees swayed and bowed to its force. Then a loud clap of thunder, a blast of wind, and a cold rain began to fall. Within minutes, it turned to sleet and time was fast running out.

Keno knew he could make it out by himself, but wasn't sure about making it with two spent horses loaded down with two injured women and Harry Dawkins's body. For a moment, he thought about leaving the women and the body behind at the cabin while he went for help alone, but decided against it. Too risky. No food, an aggressive grizzly prowling the area, and a winter storm blowing in. What if they got snowed in and couldn't keep the stove going? He knew that the temperature could drop fifty degrees in no time in Glacier. That would mean well below zero. He thought about fording the river at night. He knew all it would take was a horse stumbling, getting crazy, someone slipping off into that icy current in the dark. He shook his head to clear the what ifs. There was no choice. They had to make it out before nightfall. A big chance, but they had to take it.

After securing the buckskin's lead rope with a roper's knot to the ring behind the paint's saddle, Keno boosted the women up on the buckskin. He picked up the Winchester and was about to sling it across his shoulders, then reconsidered as he stood watching the paint's ears flicking in the sleet. He levered a round into the chamber and, holding the rifle in his right hand, gripped the reins with his left. Okay, he said over his shoulder, we're on our way.

43

---◆---

Keno walked ahead, leading the paint, scanning the forest ahead in a wide arc and keeping an eye to the rear on the body across the saddle rocking slowly back and forth. Everything okay? he called over his shoulder every so often to the two women on the buckskin following behind as they headed west on the trail toward the ford at Red Eagle. Keno was nervous, alert, scanning the forest, waiting for the big grizzly he knew was in the area to make its move, hoping it wouldn't. He gripped the stock of the Winchester just below the trigger guard with his right hand, the barrel resting on his shoulder, holding the reins with his left. He knew that the cache had to be close by, and he guessed, the big grizzly probably was on it.

A short time later, a shrill whinny as the paint balked and reared. Keno struggled to get a grip on the bridle. The startled buckskin pulled back and reared, its hooves raking the hindquarters of the paint, barely missing the sleeping bag with Harry's body. Beth lost her single-handed grip on the saddle horn and began to fall backward into Vicki. Vicki dropped her hands from Beth's waist and reached around her to grab the pommel. The move prevented them both from being thrown.

In one fluid movement, Keno dropped his rifle and, holding the bridle of the paint with one hand, quickly jerked the lead rope of the buckskin loose with the other. Then pulling the horses' heads low to prevent them from rearing, he completed a quick wrap of the lead rope and reins around separate trees as the two frightened women held tight to the saddle. With the horses under control, he lifted them both down from the buckskin, pointing to a spot a safe distance away from the menacing hooves. A quick glance and tug on the rope sling revealed the sleeping bag hadn't slipped loose on the paint's back. He retrieved the Winchester, a clicking sound as he eased the lever back just far enough to be doubly sure he had a round in the chamber.

Okay, listen carefully, he said, trying to catch his breath. That grizzly's close by. The horses, they picked up the scent. I want you both to stay here with the horses, but keep clear of 'em so you don't get kicked. I'm going to see what I can see before we move any farther down the trail. I won't go far, so call out if you see the bear, or anything happens.

Beth nodded as she held Vicki's hand, struggling to remain calm as memories of the sight, smell, and terror of the two grizzly attacks flooded her mind. When she glanced at Vicki, she could see wide-eyed fear. She wanted to say something reassuring, but what could she say to someone who had seen a bear, maybe this one, kill someone she loved, and attack and badly injure another, about whom Beth could sense Vicki's ambivalence still remained. Gary was dead. Now the huge grizzly was everyone's worst fear.

Out of their sight and scanning the forest with every step, Keno moved slowly down the trail, turning frequently, rifle at the ready, wary of an ambush in the dense forest, as he'd been on reconnaissance patrols in the jungles of Vietnam. Movement to his right caught his attention. He stopped, taking cover behind a large tree, squinting to sharpen his view into a thick growth of alder. Then he saw it, a large dark shape that looked at first like one of the countless glacial boulders that were scattered through the valley. Then it moved, and he could make out its head, no more than fifty paces away, a distance he knew the big grizzly could cover in seconds. Keno waited, motionless, breathing shallow, watching as it approached in slow deliberate movements, head low, moving effortlessly over a large fallen tree. Then he could see its eyes glistening above jaws powerful enough to crush the backbone of a moose.

Except for an occasional wind gust, it was silent, even the sleet had let up. He could hear the sound of branches snapping and deadfall splintering beneath the big animal's weight as it moved toward him. Then it stopped as their eyes locked. Never make eye contact with a grizzly was meaningless now. There was no way not to make eye contact with an animal this size, this close. Heart pounding, he took a deep breath and held it, easing the rifle to his shoulder and resting the barrel against the tree trunk. As he took aim, the grizzly raised his head. He could see and hear his jaws snapping, ears flattened above the dished face. It was an easy head shot, no more than twenty yards, and probably the only way to kill a grizzly this size quickly, even with a .44-.40 caliber rifle. Neither man nor beast moved as they contemplated the other's next move. Feeling and hearing his heart thumping, Keno let his breath out and swallowed before he took another, the almost forgotten but still familiar adrenaline rush of combat flowing fresh in his veins. A soft metallic click broke the stillness as he eased the hammer back and lined up the front sight in the V of the rear sight, settling on the spot between the grizzly's eyes, his finger resting on the trigger, his close call the night before and the Medicine Grizzly legend resonating in his mind. *Don't make me do it. Please don't make me do it.*

Time seemed to stand still. Keno, mouth dry, eyes fixed on the bear, afraid even to blink. Then he slowly lowered his rifle, holding it at the ready across his chest. He took a deep breath and held it. When he did, the grizzly hesitated and shook himself, the huge humped mass of shoulder muscle rippling above his head, the ears now erect. Then the bear reared up on its hind legs, hesitated, looking at him—the same look as the night before?—an immense animal, one he would never forget. Then the great bear turned away. Keno was letting his breath leak out slowly when, suddenly, the big grizzly turned back toward him, again locking its eyes with his. Keno caught his breath and waited, a white-knuckled grip on the Winchester, but resisting the impulse to raise it to his shoulder. A standoff, each taking the other's measure, each waiting for the other to blink, or was it something else. Keno knew what he wanted to believe, but couldn't take a chance, couldn't be sure. Then the big grizzly dropped to the ground, shook himself again, as if to break the spell and, with a parting woof, lumbered off into the thick timber. Keno blinked away the stress that was stinging the corners of his eyes as he eased the hammer down, the tension slipping slowly away, knowing that if he had raised his rifle and broken the *bond,* that bear would have charged.

Did you see the bear? Is it gone? Beth whispered when he returned, fear stitched into both her and Vicki's tightened facial muscles.

Yeah, I saw him and he saw me. He shook his head. Then he wandered off. He didn't speak for a while, staring at the ground slowly shaking his head. Then he looked up and said, *That's twice.* Another pause before he said, Legend has it that grizzlies are protectors, don't attack Blackfeet. Still shaking his head, he looked down at his feet, thinking the *Medicine Grizzly.* After a moment, he looked up with kind of a smile, I'll tell you about it later. For reasons he knew his grandfather would have understood, Keno felt at peace.

———◆◆◆———

44

———◆———

Tuesday evening, October 2. By the time Keno reined in the horses at the Middle Fork, daylight was fading fast. The steady downpour of rain and sleet had turned to snow that was falling fast in flakes the size of quarters. For a brief moment, the ridges and peaks of Penrose and Great Bear Mountains on the far side of the river were bathed in rose-colored alpenglow before fading into darkness and driving snow.

Shh, listen, Keno said, turning back toward Beth and Vickie, holding a finger to his lips. Hear it? In the distance they could hear distant rumbling that sounded at first like thunder. Then they heard the approaching whistle and recognized the groan of diesel engines and the screeching sound of steel rolling on steel. Burlington Northern, he said, a smile on his face and snow sticking to eyebrows beneath the wrap-around gauze bandage that had replaced his torn and bloodstained bandana. We're almost there. We're gonna make it.

Beth reached for Vicki's hands locked around her waist and squeezed them. Listen to that whistle, Vicki, she said through chattering teeth. Civilization. I don't think I've ever heard a more beautiful sound. Vicki nodded a wan smile and whispered, I'm glad.

At water's edge, Keno helped the women dismount. They stretched their legs while the thirsty horses drank. Keno checked the saddles and adjusted the ropes that held the sleeping bag with Harry's body.

Everything was okay. The river was running gray and fast, but wide at the ford and, he hoped, no higher than the horses' bellies. Squinting into thick, swirling snow, he guessed visibility on the river at no more than seventy-five yards. He watched a piece of driftwood dancing crazily in a swirling eddy. Had to be careful. Anyone falling in would be out of sight in no time.

Okay, here's the way we're gonna do it, he said, looking out at the river then turning to the women. I'm gonna lead Poia over with Colonel Dawkins, then I'll come back and do the same with you both on the buckskin. He thought for a minute, rubbing the back of his neck. Is the buckskin up to it with both riders? he wondered. Probably. No time. Additional trips would mean additional risk. He checked the rigging on the sleeping bag again and slung the Winchester over his shoulders before he waded into the river, reins held high, with the paint following. He could feel the cold as water filled his boots and then the force of the current as it pushed against his legs and rose into his crotch. The water at its deepest reached the ends of the sleeping bag. Moving slowly and carefully, planting each foot before taking the next step, he made it across without stumbling. When he waded out on the far bank, he waved okay to the women, tied the paint to a silvery stump of driftwood, and made his return using a stick of driftwood to brace himself against the current.

There was the squeak of wet leather as Keno boosted the women back on the buckskin and took hold of the lead rope. When he waded back into the river, he moved slowly, cautiously tugging the snorting and whickering buckskin into the current, but easing back to give the weakened horse time to adjust to the smooth rocks and swift current. In midstream where the current was strongest, the horse stumbled, making a shrill sound. Keno thought they were going over. Hold tight, he shouted over the rush of water as he pulled the buckskin's head up, wedging his body against its shoulder to keep it from falling sideways as it lurched and twisted, struggling to regain its footing. With his other arm, he pushed against Beth who had lost her grip on the saddle and was slipping sideways off the saddle with Vicki clinging to her waist with one hand and holding on to the saddle with the other. After a few frantic moments, the buckskin regained its footing and neither Beth nor Vicki were thrown off into the river.

When they reached the other bank, Keno took a deep breath and let it out with, Close call, but the hard part's over. It won't be long now, he said, as much to himself as to the two shaken women, forcing what could have been out of his thoughts, knowing that if anyone had slipped off into that cold, swift current, there would've been nothing he could do. They would've been swept away and drowned.

With Keno leading the paint, they followed a trail away from the river through the riparian brush of the flood plain, the horses' hooves making a soft clopping sound in the deepening snow. When they reached a steep embankment below the railroad tracks, Keno helped the women down off the buckskin, then led the paint, one hand gripping the sleeping bag, slowly up over embankment. Beth and Vicki followed leading the buckskin. In the distance, they heard the blast of a truck's horn on the highway.

We'll see if we can get help at that house, Keno said, pointing toward a break in the trees where they could see a ranch house in a stand of tall cottonwoods between the railroad tracks and the highway, its windows brightly lit against the gathering darkness. Smoke from the chimney was swirling in the wind, rising toward the faint honking of migrating geese lost in the overcast.

A thin woman, gray hair pulled back in a ponytail, dressed in jeans, western boots, and flannel shirt came out on the porch as they approached. Keno dismounted and explained what had happened. When he finished, she nodded, snuffed out an unfiltered cigarette on the heel of her boot, and helped get the two women inside to the warmth of a woodstove. The woman was calm, as if she was accustomed to emergencies and knew how to deal with them. After calling 911, she got blankets for the women and heated water for hot cocoa. While Beth and Vicki, wrapped in the warm blankets she'd brought out, sipped steaming mugs of hot cocoa and warmed themselves by the woodstove, Keno, his wet jeans crusted with snow and ice crystals, walked back outside to the corral fence where he had tied the horses. He removed the ropes holding the sleeping bag with Harry's body, now covered with wet snow, and lifted it from the paint, easing it gently to the ground. Then he walked back to the house and asked the woman if she had some hay to spare and whether he could put the two horses in the corral by the slab-board barn that stood next to it.

They're both about ready to give out, he said. I'm worried about 'em, especially with the temperature droppin' like it is. Neither of 'em have any slack left, especially that buckskin. He's skin and bones.

No problem, the woman replied when he said that he sure would really appreciate it. There's plenty of hay in the barn and you're welcome to it. There's good shelter under that overhang and some blankets out there on a sawhorse you can use. There's a mare and her colt in the barn, but our other horses are in the far pasture.

A short time later, after he had taken care of the horses, Keno heard the rhythmic thump of an approaching helicopter. It circled and hovered above before setting down in an open area between the house and the corral. Not long afterward, he could hear the sound of approaching sirens on Highway 2. Moments later, an ambulance and three Flathead County Sheriff patrol cars turned through the trees, dome lights flashing, mud splashing up through the beams of headlights as they pulled to a stop near the helicopter, wipers splattering snowflakes across windshields.

Keno told the two paramedics who came in on the chopper that the bloodstained bandage around his head was nothing. Just a scratch, he said. There's a couple of injured women inside, and pointed toward the house. A paramedic insisted on taking a look. As he dressed the wound and applied a fresh bandage, allowing that Keno was damn lucky, and that he'd better get out of the wet clothes before he got hypothermia. Keno nodded that he was okay as he watched paramedics carry collapsible gurneys to the porch and go inside. Freshly bandaged, Keno walked over to the two sheriff's deputies who were standing by the sleeping bag and explained what had happened. Shielding the sight as best they could from anyone looking out from the house, they opened the sleeping bag and lifted Harry's body out and eased it into a rubberized body bag that Keno helped carry to the ambulance. He turned to see paramedics wheeling someone on a gurney toward the chopper. It was Vicki, wrapped in a thermal blanket.

Moments later, he watched as two other paramedics wheeled Beth out on the second gurney. She looked up when she saw him, forced a weary smile when he approached. Keno guessed from the calm, dreamy look on her face that they had given her an injection for the pain. The fresh splint on her wrist was just visible at the edge of the thermal blanket that covered her.

Keno, thanks … thank you, she whispered as she reached for his hand. We couldn't have made it without you.

A nod and a quick smile. No, no, we did it together.

She squeezed his hand. Vicki really came through, didn't she? Saved my life. Poor girl … been through so much.

You both have, he said, still holding her hand, a lot of thoughts running though his mind as his eyes held hers. All that pain and she never complained. Tough. No pissing and moaning from her. Broken wrist and collarbone and risks her life to get that gun away from Gary. Like diving on a grenade to save lives. If not for her and the girl and, yes, that grizzly, that sonofabitch might've killed us all. He lifted his eyes and looked out toward the Nyack Creek Valley. As much to himself as to her, he said, A cold-blooded killer got exactly what he deserved. Predators rule in the backcountry, but not that predator, and not ever again.

Beth nodded, thinking about what he'd said. Gary Ray Kemp had died angry, unloved, and unforgiven, her conception of Hell. She looked up at Keno. *Vengeance*, she whispered as she reached for his hand. I understand that feeling. He nodded and squeezed her hand. Good-bye, Keno. I hope we'll meet again.

As she was being carried to the helicopter, Beth could hear a voice crackling over the radio in one of the patrol cars, … Harry Dawkins, Elizabeth Blanchard, Vicki Hathaway, Kenneth Spotted Wolf … She closed her eyes. Incredible. *Spotted Wolf.* She looked back at Keno, snow crusting on his shoulders and braided hair. Predators and prey. Was it simply irony, she wondered, that a vulnerable, traumatized young woman would finally bring down a heartless human predator who had preyed upon so many women? And was there something—yes something Darwinian—about his end being hastened by an encounter with a grizzly bear and a man whose name, she had just learned, was Spotted Wolf?

A young paramedic in a blue jumpsuit, a military haircut bristling beneath a layer of snow, came over to Keno. I'm glad you guys made it. Lucky. Just in time. Everyone's gonna be okay. Yeah, this storm's supposed to dump a lot of snow. Maybe two-three feet. Would not want to be in the backcountry tonight. He stepped back and motioned to the pilot, Okay, time to go.

Before she was lifted into the chopper, Beth turned back for a last look at the high peaks that framed the Nyack Creek Valley, now barely visible through snow falling through the last light of a day. *That* is wilderness, she thought, recalling the loneliness, vulnerability, and terror she felt in that beautiful and serenely indifferent natural world. The pilot began to rev the chopper engine in preparation for takeoff. The noise was deafening.

* * * * *

A sheriff's deputy, the flaps of a winter cap pulled down over his ears and a clipboard in hand, was watching as they lifted Beth into the chopper. A faint wave as the door closed. He looked over at Keno who stood close by. Hope you can help me answer a few more questions, he said. We need to have some more details about what exactly happened back there in the park. It's pretty confusing. You say there are two bodies still back there?

Before Keno could respond, they both turned to watch as the helicopter, the accelerating thumping sound of its blades drowning out their conversation, forcing them to lower their heads and shield their eyes from a swirling blast of propwash as it lifted into the air and rotated around. For Keno, the sensation brought back memories of a war he wished he could forget. He wondered if those sounds now would trigger the same kind of bad memories for Beth and Vicki. Probably, he guessed, as the noise receded and he watched the blinking lights of the chopper disappear in the falling snow and advancing darkness. They made it, he thought of Beth and Vicki, but you can't run from sadness, the loss of someone you love, it'll always track you down. Time would help a little, but sad things remain forever sad. No one knew that better than he did.

Keno turned back to the deputy, shivering, the cold, wet Wranglers stiffening around his legs. He tried to answer the questions he was asked, but the questions missed the point. It's a complicated story, he told the deputy, of bear attacks, a fatal fall, a brave, desperate woman, a slain hiker, and a young woman, thought to be dead but wasn't, who killed a serial killer in self-defense. He wasn't sure the young deputy understood completely as he tried to summarize, as best he could, the convergence of so many seemingly unrelated events and people. Yes, he told the deputy, there were two bodies back in there, probably not far from the Nyack Creek gorge. He was going to mention the big grizzly that claimed them, but decided not to.

Some story, the deputy said, shaking his head, when he finished. We can fill in the details tomorrow.

Yeah, Keno said. It'll take some more explainin' later. But right now, I'm hopin' maybe you guys can help me out. The wind had picked up and was blowing snow, now stinging icy crystals, coming in sideways, as he tucked his head and turned up the collar on his jacket. His jeans were crusted with ice. I'm gonna need to get a motel room somewhere for tonight, get out of these wet clothes, get a hot shower. Maybe the Highland in West Glacier?

The deputy took a close look at Keno and shook his head. Maybe later. Right now, I'm thinking hypothermia, pardner. We're gettin' you in a warm car for a ride to the ER in Kalispell to thaw out and get that head wound checked out. After that, we'll take care of the other stuff.

You sure? I'm okay. Just a scratch. West Glacier's close. I'll be fine if I get outta these wet clothes and into a hot shower.

Sorry, pardner. Like I said, you're goin' to Kalispell first. Hypothermia sneaks up on you, messes with your mind. Before you know it, you start thinking you're all nice and warm, then you're dead.

Okay, I get it. But then tomorrow, when you're through with me, I'm gonna need a ride back to my place on the eastside to get my pickup and a trailer so I can come back and haul a couple of horses back to the ranch. He paused, thinking *Gary's* trailer and horse, then let it go. Yeah, I been gone a few days and I got four dogs over there, missin' me, gettin' hungry, and wonderin' where the hell I been.

—◆◆◆—

Epilogue

For months Keno grieved for his daughter. There was no relief for his deepening depression. It was dawn on a frosty autumn morning when he stepped out of his trailer after another sleepless night. The aspen and cottonwood were ablaze in fall colors below a clear blue sky. To the north, *Ninah Stako,* Chief Mountain, its cliffs peach-colored in the rays of the rising sun, a monolith dominating the northern horizon and the prairie to the east. He sat down on his stoop, eyes fixed on the mountain, thinking about its significance in Blackfeet legend. A medicine man had told him once of a vision quest to the peak, and how he had united with the spirit world, and the communion he felt with those who had passed from this earth before him. As a young man, Keno had doubts. Now, well, maybe.

He went inside and wrote a letter to Emma, explaining that he was going away for a few days. He didn't say where. He filled a canteen with water and stuck a few strips of buffalo jerky in the pocket of his fleece jacket. Enough to get to the top. On the way out to the highway, he stopped at a neighbor's place and asked if he would look after his dogs and horses for a few days and mail the letter to Emma.

He parked the pickup in a pullout, got out, and stood for a few minutes gazing up at the mountain. It took him the rest of the day to climb the steep, rock strewn, southwest route. The sun was setting behind dark clouds when he reached the top in a gusting wind. A storm front had moved in. The temperature was dropping fast and it had begun to snow as he sat down on a smooth rock, turned up his collar, and closed his eyes. For how long, he wasn't sure. When he opened them again, the wind had let up and snowflakes were falling through alpenglow that bathed the peak in soft-pink light. A voice. Someone calling from the saddle to his left. He turned to see a young woman in a hooded, fur-lined parka pulled low over her face, beckoning to him. In the distance behind her, he could see the flames of a campfire and other human figures. Come this way, she called. We're over here.

* * * * *

On a cool, crisp late September day, a year after the tragedy at Morning Star Lake, bright sunlight glistened on fresh snow that dusted the rimrock that stretches out below the horn of Flinsch Peak as two hikers made their way west along the Dry Fork trail. They were enthralled. The valley was an extravaganza of autumn color. Against a dark evergreen forest, splashes of scarlet and crimson marked patches of ash, scrub maple, and alder on the slopes of Rising Wolf Mountain. An understory of brush in shades blending pink and peach and gold was visible above a thickening russet carpet of fallen leaves and needles on the forest floor. Corridors of birch and cottonwood, bright yellow in the sunshine, traced the banks of streams that flowed through the valley. Higher on the slopes, groves of aspen and larch were revealed in swaths of orange and burnished amber like paint on an artist's palette. To the northwest, they could see Pitamakin Pass, a crystalline snow-crusted ridgeline against a clear blue sky. The colors were glorious, a scene for a Sierra Club calendar, a photographer's delight.

Below the pass, the hikers spotted a large grizzly bear far above on an avalanche chute that cut a wide swath down from Rising Wolf's high cliffs. As his companion fumbled excitedly in her backpack for a telephoto lens, the young man, with binoculars, could see its bronze head, humped shoulders, and broad back glowing in the late morning sunshine. With terrible claws and awesome shoulder strength, the huge beast churned the earth like some primordial machine, overturning and pushing aside and rolling heavy boulders like beach balls, in pursuit of some unseen quarry. The giant grizzly, with a copper-jacketed bullet embedded in its shoulder, was utterly indifferent to the young couple on the trail below.

Acknowledgments

As this story evolved, a number of people offered comments and suggestions for which I am grateful. In no particular order, they are: my editor, Hilary Hinzmann, Ken Mayers, Michael McGarrity, Patricia Burke, Tom Zoellner, Michael Keith, Eric Kildahl, Ryan Thomas, Steve Nienaber, Sevek Finkel, Pancho Medina, Amanda Robinson, James Mitchell, Robert Dahl, Gail Jokerst, Brian Shott, Robert Glennon, and Beth Hodder. Over more than two decades I have enjoyed, and sometimes endured, many memorable experiences in the backcountry of Glacier National Park, often with my family – Julie, Courtney, Michael and Ludmila – and friends, Roger and Sue Sherman, and Kyle Topham. My wife, Jeanne, provided advice and encouragement from beginning to end.

23962771R00185